ELDER

S.G. PRINCE

ELDER Copyright © 2020 by Summerhold Publishing

All rights reserved. Printed in the United States of America. No part of this book may be used or reproduced in any manner without written permission except in the case of brief quotations embodied in critical articles or reviews.

This book is a work of fiction. Names, characters, businesses, organizations, places, events and incidents either are the product of the author's imagination or are used fictitiously. Any resemblance to actual persons, living or dead, events, or locales is entirely coincidental.

ISBN: 9781658062176

First Edition

Cover design by Damonza

To Monster, for making my world safe and happy and warm and bright,

so that there's space enough left to dream.

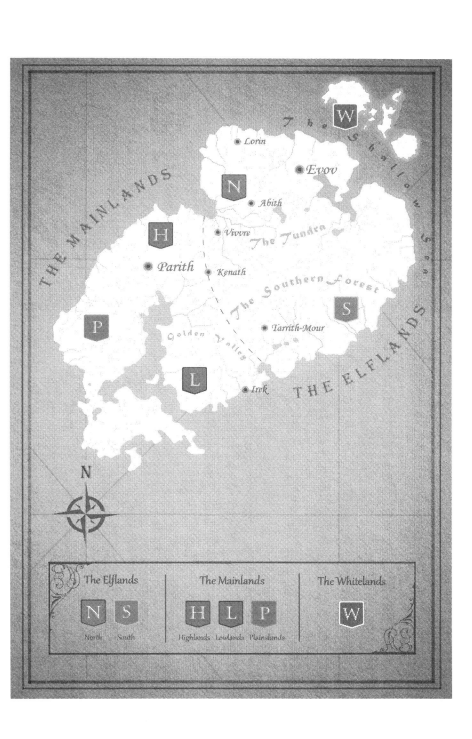

ONE

This was a bad idea.

Venick adjusted his hood and tried to ignore the roil in his gut, the dread and irritation and *hell*. Evov's streets were crowded, elves packed shoulder to shoulder. Barely enough room to breathe. Certainly not enough room to draw a weapon, and reeking gods, he wanted to.

But that would do Venick no good. Not here, not when he was supposed to be avoiding attention. His hood felt like a meager defense against this crowd of hundreds. All it would take was one elf getting curious, one elf looking too closely. If any of these elves discovered a human in their midst—not to mention this human—there would be trouble. And then he really would have to draw his weapon.

Not much good it'll do you.

There was a time when Venick could have fought his way out of Evov alive. He'd done it once already. But that was before the southern elves had succeeded in overthrowing the queen and occupying this city. Venick caught glimpses of those elves—tall, cloaked, shadowed—in the windows above, the alleys, even out here in the open. It didn't matter that Venick could have escaped Evov before. If the southerners noticed him now, he didn't stand a chance.

So don't be noticed.

Right. Even though he was broader than most elves. Even though he moved like a human, smelled like a human, spoke like a human. His only hope was that the crowd would be too large, the elves too preoccupied to give him a second glance.

Which they were. The city of Evov was a layered maze. Its streets and buildings had been carved into the side of a mountain, and most walkways were tight and winding. The elves moved around him with a fluidity Venick would never possess, streaming through the streets like water through a channel, each distracted by their own tasks, their own problems. They didn't look at Venick.

But he looked at them. He noted their pearly skin, their long limbs. He marked the weapons on all of them, swords and daggers mostly, the occasional crossbow. And their faces. Those high brows and angled cheekbones. Beautiful, yes, all elves were, but utterly blank. That was typical; elves rarely allowed their emotions to show in their expressions.

And yet, this wasn't to say their emotions were hidden. Dampened, yes, disguised, but still discernible if you knew what to look for. Venick did. He'd spent time around elves, more time than most humans, and so he'd grown accustomed to their subtleties. As Venick scanned the elves around him, he noticed their too-flat mouths, their sideways glances. He saw the way their hands fluttered over their weapons and thought he could sense it just under the surface: something pulsing. Brimming.

Tension. That was the feeling that claimed this city. No guessing why.

It wasn't every day that a new elven queen took the throne.

Killed for the throne, you mean.

Venick's stomach soured at the thought. He'd been there in the palace stateroom to witness Farah's betrayal, how she and Raffan allied with the southerners and plotted to overthrow the queen. How they'd spread the rumor of Queen Rishiana's ill-ability to rule, her *merciful* removal. Had it only been eight days since Farah had stabbed Rishiana on the stateroom floor? Since the southerners had infiltrated this supposedly hidden city and slaughtered legionnaires and most of the royal court? And Ellina…

"Conjuror on your left." Dourin's voice came in close at Venick's ear. Venick aimed a glance back at his elven companion, who pulled his hood up a little higher, then jerked his chin to the side. "Two in that window overhead."

"You don't have to do that," Venick muttered.

"Another in that alley."

"I can spot them for myself."

"And one more—"

"*Dourin.*"

Dourin gave Venick a long look—half exasperated, half reproachful—then shrugged. The gesture was classically human. Wrong, to see it on an elf, and dangerous, should anyone notice. Dourin seemed to realize his mistake. He tugged again at the edges of his hood, glancing to their left and right to see if he'd been observed.

He hadn't. Thank the gods.

"What you can tell me," Venick murmured as they moved off the main thoroughfare and into a crowded market, "is what you plan to do if we're stopped on the palace bridge."

"We will not be stopped."

"Really."

"No."

But Dourin's confidence was absurd. Venick had seen the royal palace, had spent the better part of a month locked behind its high stone walls. He'd seen its bridge too, wide and ancient and black. That bridge was the only path in or out of the palace, unless you wanted to risk a swim across the bay far below, and elves didn't swim. Though the palace bridge hadn't been heavily guarded when Venick had seen it last, surely it would be now. Farah wasn't stupid. Her claim to the throne was new and therefore vulnerable. Bet she'd positioned a whole host of guards on that bridge to keep watch. Bet she'd positioned conjurors there too, to protect their new queen.

"So what then?" Venick asked, dodging a horse-drawn cart and moving under a display of colorful lanterns. "You think Farah's conjurors will just let us in?"

"No." Dourin's reply came easily. "But it will not matter. We are not going to the palace."

Venick halted so abruptly that Dourin nearly collided into him. He spun around. "What do you mean we aren't going to the palace?"

"Lower your voice."

"That's the whole reason we're here."

"We are here to find Ellina," the elf countered, "in whatever way is least likely to get us killed. Perhaps *you* would like to battle conjurors to get across the bridge—"

"I never said—"

"—which fits, seeing as you like to bludgeon your way through every problem—"

"I do not *bludgeon*—"

"—but I would like to accomplish this mission with some finesse—"

"Oh for gods' sake, Dourin." Venick's anger spiked. His hands clenched to fists. He was aware that they'd stopped in the center of the market, that this argument was likely to draw attention, but instead of dropping his voice and moving on, his volume only grew. "Where do you expect to find her, if not at the palace? We can't search the whole city."

"We can, if that is what it takes."

"You're not serious."

"We owe it to her," Dourin insisted. "We both do."

Venick crossed his arms. He didn't owe Ellina anything. He had half a mind to call it quits, and damn Dourin anyway. Safer to stay put and let the elf risk his own neck. Better yet, safer to turn around and abandon this rescue mission altogether. They'd barely managed to escape Evov the first time. Insane, the both of them, for coming back to this place without a real strategy, other than *find Ellina.*

In the days since the stateroom coup and the queen's death, only a handful of palace elves had managed to escape the city. Those elves—most of whom had witnessed Queen Rishiana's murder and now feared the consequences—had been hiding out in the foothills around Evov for the last eight days, trying to agree on a plan and generally fighting amongst themselves. Dourin and Venick had been at the center of those fights. Dourin believed that since Ellina had not escaped with the rest of them, she must have been caught in the stateroom battle and was now being held prisoner in the city. Venick, who no longer trusted anything he once thought he knew about Ellina, suggested that maybe she didn't want to escape. Maybe she had chosen to join her traitorous sister instead.

Neither of them mentioned the third option.

Venick's frustration gathered. It condensed, palpable, in the air between them. He'd made it clear that he didn't want to return to this city. Had spent the last handful of nights trying to convince Dourin out of it, convince him that they had better things to worry about. The southerners had succeeded in overthrowing Queen Rishiana and conquering Evov. According to the rumors, those southerners—under Farah's command and with the support of her soldiers—were swiftly spreading their power, taking the elflands into their control one city at a time. And they wouldn't stop there. Once they had conquered the north, they would continue west, bringing war to the mainlands—Venick's home. If the northern resistance stood a chance, they needed to rally their allies, and they needed to do it quickly. But instead here they were, risking their necks to chase a traitor.

You don't know that she is.

Venick drew his eyes skyward. It was true. He couldn't be sure Ellina had betrayed them. And if he was being honest with himself, maybe he would admit that betrayal didn't make sense. Ellina cared deeply for her country. She'd been a legionnaire, sworn to protect and defend it. And Ellina and Farah, despite being sisters, had never been allies. Ellina and her bondmate Raffan certainly hadn't. Wasn't it possible, then, that Ellina truly had been captured in the fighting? Wasn't it possible that she was now being held prisoner here against her will?

Maybe. Yet it was easier to think of Ellina as the enemy. Easier for Venick to justify his sudden, terrible repulsion of her. If Ellina was a traitor to the north, Venick could think of how she had forgone her values and her oaths. He could focus on the ways she had wronged Dourin and the legion. He could think of anything, how she had betrayed her country, how she had turned her back on her very self…anything other than how she had betrayed *him*, and cast him out, and wished him dead.

"If she is being held prisoner, they would not keep her in the palace anyway," Dourin said now. "She would be in the dungeons, which are in the city."

"So that's where we're going? The dungeons?"

"No."

Infuriating. The elf was infuriating. "Dourin. This is ridiculous."

"I have a plan."

"Then maybe it's time you *share it*." Venick's voice snapped through the market, louder than he'd intended. He saw his error at once. And he should have known better, should have realized they'd been standing there too long, that they'd already gained the attention of nearby traders and shoppers. But Venick had been thoughtless. He'd been angry.

There was a sudden bubble of silence. The flash of golden eyes turning their way. Venick grimaced, trying to undo the damage by ducking his head, but too late. More heads were turning now, eyes slimming as the crowd's attention jumped from Dourin to Venick, noticing the strange size of him, the strange way he moved. Not an elf. Not one of them.

Human.

"Well," Dourin said dryly as two conjurors materialized into view. "That did not take very long."

The mood of the market quickly darkened. The citizens backed away from Venick and Dourin as the conjurors approached, the anonymity of the crowd shedding off them like water. More than ample room now to draw a weapon, with space enough to swing it.

Just like you wanted.

Huh. Teach him to be careful what he wished for.

Venick moved to Dourin's side. His hand went to the green glass sword at his hip, readying for the draw, and never mind that they were woefully outmatched. Venick had battled conjurors before. He'd seen the way they used their power to bend the world around them, the tricks they employed to gain the upper hand. Unnatural tricks, like shadow-weaving and storm-summoning and blindness. Hell. If one of the approaching conjurors decided to blind Venick now, his sword wouldn't do a damn thing.

So. To Dourin: "Think of a way to finesse us out of this, will you?"

"Oh, you are a funny one."

Venick scanned the elves around them, the narrow streets, colorful merchant stalls on every side. Outnumbered, well and truly, with no easy escape. "It wasn't a joke."

"No? Then listen. We use a diversion."

"A diversion?"

"There is a brazier behind you."

Venick glanced. It was a bowl of fire contained within a metal grate, the kind merchants used to illuminate their wares and ward off the worst of the mountain chill. Venick could have laughed. Knocking it over would buy them a few seconds at best. It would backfire at worst. He imagined the city up in flames. "That's your plan?"

"On my count."

"Gods, it really is."

"One."

Venick shifted onto the balls of his feet. There were bodies on all sides. A bustling market gone still. Any of these elves could draw their weapons, but aside from the two conjurors quickly closing in, none of the citizens made any move to attack.

"Two."

Venick wondered how many of these northern elves knew the truth about Farah's rise to power. How many opposed her new regime. Farah had built an army of southern soldiers and conjurors, then used a loophole in Evov's protective magic to march that army into this city. Her execution had been swift, fierce—perfect. Venick could admit that it was perfect. Could admit, too, that its perfection worried him. He wasn't even sure that humans, who were bred for war, could have pulled off such a takeover.

"*Three.*"

The conjurors descended at the same time Venick kicked over the brazier, sending sparks and coals flying. And then he and Dourin were off, bolting blindly through the market and back into winding city streets. For one wild moment Venick thought it had worked, that their diversion had been enough to shake their pursuers. He thought—

Please.

—that they'd gotten lucky, that they might actually make it out of this alive.

You won't.

No, they wouldn't, because a moment later Venick heard the distinct sound of cloaks flapping in the wind behind them. The *thap thap thap* of leather-soled boots on the road. He risked a glance back and saw them then, two black-haired elves quickly gaining ground.

Venick put on a burst of speed. He followed Dourin closely as the elf took a hard right, then another. Narrow streets gave way to even narrower alleys, sunless paths that looped up and around and back on themselves. Venick quickly lost track of their location. *High*, he thought, and then *lost*, because he could no longer tell where they were headed. No landmarks. No clear view of the city. Just tall buildings set into the rock and a network of back alleys and two conjurors following close behind.

Until they weren't. Suddenly, inexplicably, the sounds of their pursuers vanished. Venick threw another look behind him to discover the street was empty. The conjurors had disappeared.

Venick skidded to a halt.

A trick. A trap. It had to be.

He drew his sword.

Dourin stopped too. "Put that away." Venick ignored him. He scanned nearby windows and rooftops, then looked higher, up into a suspended web of footpaths and archways. They were in a quieter part of the city now. A neighborhood, Venick realized, though the buildings here only vaguely resembled homes. They were cruder than the shops back near Evov's center, more roughly carved, as if they'd been molded with child's clay.

"I said put it away," Dourin snapped. "Do you want the whole street to see you?"

"The conjurors—"

"We lost them."

But that didn't make sense. Those elves had been right on their heels. Venick turned to tell Dourin so, but paused when he realized Dourin had moved into the doorway of one of the houses. The elf pushed inside without knocking. "What—?"

"You asked where we were going," Dourin said. He gestured into the home's dark entryway. "Well, you have your answer. We are here."

TWO

Venick's attention wasn't where it should have been.

It was back with the conjurors in the street. It was listening to the sound of their cloaks in the wind, the light patter of their feet on loose gravel, there one instant and then just…gone. Like they'd given up the chase. Like their robes had turned to wings and borne them away.

Venick's mind was absorbed by the puzzle of this. It was consumed, trapped between the *why* and *how* of it, which was why—when Dourin led him into the mysterious house and pulled the door closed behind them—Venick didn't notice the elf inside, or the dagger in that elf's hand.

At least, not until that dagger was set to Venick's neck.

Venick froze. His eyes dropped to the blade, then slid up the arm of the elf who held it. Fine white hairs, corded muscle, blue veins. Fingers easy on the dagger's hilt, the wrist tilted just so, like this stranger knew exactly how to hold a weapon, and where to stick it.

He's an elf, Venick. What'd you expect?

Hell. An ally? A peaceable citizen? A little mercy from the gods, maybe, just this once.

"Traegar." Dourin's voice came from Venick's left. Coolly, and without any urgency. "Put the weapon down."

The elf, Traegar, didn't take his eyes off Venick. "What are you doing in my house?"

Dourin answered. "We encountered a bit of trouble."

"And you came here."

"Do not make me ask again." Dourin sounded impatient. Venick might have cautioned him on the wisdom of goading an enemy, had he not been otherwise preoccupied. "Put the weapon down."

This time—to Venick's surprise—Traegar listened. He took a swift step back and lowered the dagger, folding his arms smoothly into the loose sleeves of his robes. Weapon sheathed and out of sight just like that, as if he hadn't been about to spill human blood. As if he hadn't looked eager to do it. Venick mimicked the motion, stepping back, folding his arms. He glanced around the room—a darkly-lit foyer, simply furnished, one shuttered window—and wished *he* had a dagger to hide up his sleeve. Something he could draw quickly if this elf happened to change his mind.

Or if the conjurors return. Think of that.

Traegar's eyes cut to Dourin. "That door was locked."

"It is good to see you too."

"You still have a key."

"I kept one, for just such an occasion." Dourin was smiling. "Now, are you going to offer us a drink? A place to sit? Come, Traegar. Is this any way to greet an old friend?"

Traegar was handsome, even by elven standards. He was taller than most elves, artistically built, with a long face and full mouth. Striking, certainly, but also…different. Unlike many elves whose skin was pale, Traegar was deeply tanned. His hair, too, was unusual: shoulder-length and wavy, rather than sleek and straight. Yet his eyes were the same bright golden of all elves. And—Venick's neck twinged to remind him—he knew how to wield a weapon.

"You should not be here," Traegar said.

Dourin's smile twisted. "I see your manners have not improved with age."

"The Dark Queen has been looking for you."

"Is that what they call Farah now? The Dark Queen?"

"It is not a joke."

"I am not laughing." Yet Dourin did not seem all that concerned either, for someone who had just escaped two of the queen's conjurors. He leaned a shoulder against the nearest wall, crossed his arms and ankles. It was an easy posture. Relaxed. Opposite how Venick was standing, or how Traegar was: with guarded uncertainty. "Farah's conjurors spotted us. We need a place to stay until our trail runs cold. And we need information. I was hoping you could provide both."

Traegar appeared unmoved. "And what do I get in return for the trouble?"

"Is that how you want it to be between us? Favors exchanged for favors?"

"I want it to be like nothing between us."

Dourin shrugged, but there was something off about the movement, something stiff, and it was only then that Venick realized he'd been wrong. Dourin wasn't relaxed—he was *troubled*, and doing his best to hide it.

"In that case," Dourin replied, "do it to assist a worthy cause. You know who this is, don't you?" He jerked his chin in Venick's direction.

Traegar's voice went low. "Everyone knows who he is."

"Then you must also know why Farah and her conjurors are after us."

"I...have heard rumors."

"Good." As if that settled things, Dourin pushed off the wall and disappeared down the hall. Into a kitchen, Venick presumed, from the sudden sound of cabinets opening and closing. Traegar let him go but made no move to follow and Venick—reluctant to turn his back on this new elf—didn't either.

There was a tense moment of silence as they appraised each other.

"You surprised me," Traegar finally admitted. It wasn't an apology, but something close. Venick relaxed a little. He made the elvish hand motion for *no harm*, which earned him two lifted brows. "They said you spoke elvish. I was not sure whether to believe it. It is unusual for humans to speak our language." For the first time, Traegar switched to elvish. *"They say humans can lie in elvish."*

"No one can lie in elvish," Venick replied in that same tongue. The words came easily and without pain: proof of their authenticity.

"No," Traegar agreed, switching back to mainlander. "I suppose not." He looked down the hall where Dourin could still be heard rummaging. "He has always been cocky. I forgot that about him."

The comment—the familiarity of it—surprised Venick. "And arrogant."

"He drives me insane."

"That makes two of us."

Traegar skimmed another look in Venick's direction. His eyes still held that gilded keenness, but there was something else there now, too.

Curiosity. Amusement.

Without comment, they started down the hall together.

Venick had never seen the inside of a northerner's home. He'd seen their city certainly, and the queen's palace, and he supposed if he'd thought anything, the elves' homes would be like that: grand, cold. But Traegar's home was neither grand nor cold. The shallow hallway gave way to a low-ceilinged kitchen that reminded Venick, vividly, of Irek. There was a furnace burning brightly in one corner, a row of pans arranged in order of size, a pot of sweet-smelling stew simmering on the stovetop. The table was made of unpolished wood, its chairs heaped in warm furs. The whole scene was…quaint. Cozy.

"No tea," Dourin announced as they entered. "But I see you still keep a supply of *rezahe*." He held up a tumbler filled with two fingerwidths of golden-brown liquid. "I took the liberty."

"Of course you did."

Dourin motioned towards the kitchen window with that same hand, sloshing some of the tumbler's contents. "You have been redecorating. Those curtains are new." And drawn, Venick saw, though it was only midday.

"A precaution," Traegar replied.

"Against the sun?"

"Against the southerners." Traegar sank into a seat at the table. He didn't slouch as a human might, didn't lean back in his chair. His movements were poised. Precise. Still, he looked tired. "It has been madness. Southern elves here, in Evov. Our city has protected us from outsiders for a thousand-thousand years, but now…" He trailed off. Dourin moved to claim the chair opposite him, Venick opting to lean against the wall. Traegar continued. "Did you know that Farah has ordered us to open our homes to her army? We are meant to house and clothe and feed them. The barracks simply cannot supply them all. But the southerners are barbarians."

Venick thought he understood. Unlike northern elves, southerners were a wild breed, brutal and prone to violence. Before Farah united them under the red and black flag, they'd been living in isolated clans in the southern forests. No leader, no real rule of law. They'd been unruly before, and they would be now, no matter how their station had changed. Perhaps they would be *worse* now, given the fact that they were armed, with the queen on their side.

Some of Dourin's false cheer leaked away. "Have they been violent?"

"Only when they are not getting what they want."

"Have they hurt you?"

Traegar did not immediately answer that. In the way of someone who'd done it many times before, the elf angled his gaze to peer out the kitchen window, then blinked as if remembering that view was now blocked. He shook his head. "No, they have not hurt me. But things here are not as they once were. The city is not safe, not with southerners prowling every street corner, hunting Farah's opposers and looking for fights." Traegar pointed his gaze at Venick, clear-eyed and solemn. "You tried to warn us."

Hell, yes, he'd *tried*. Venick had been the first one to discover the southern army and had raced here to alert the northerners. But they hadn't believed him. "Little good it did."

"We were fools," Traegar said bluntly. "And now Queen Rishiana is dead."

"Murdered," Dourin corrected, "by her own daughter."

"So those rumors are true too? I cannot say I am surprised. Farah marched an army of southern soldiers into this city. We all know what she really is. What I want to know now is why *you* are here."

Dourin studied the glass in his hand. For all his earlier bravado, he seemed suddenly hesitant. "We came for Ellina."

"The princess?"

Dourin glanced up. "Is she alive?"

"Oh, she lives."

Venick sank back against the wall. The news dropped deep. He'd never truly allowed himself to consider this possibility, to think that Ellina might be dead. Now that he knew she wasn't, he felt…odd. Strangely lightheaded.

Just say it Venick: relieved.

Dourin looked relieved too. He deflated, thumping back in his chair. His eyes crossed the room, and Venick read the thoughts behind them. *I told you. See? She is here. She needs us.*

Dourin asked, "Where are they holding her?"

Traegar gave Dourin a strange look. "Holding her?"

"As a prisoner. Is she in the dungeons? Or in the palace?"

"Neither."

"But you just said—"

"I said she is alive, and she is. Alive and free."

"That…" Dourin frowned. "That cannot be."

"I assure you it is true." Traegar paused. He seemed to see the gap in understanding. Venick saw it too. He knew what Traegar would say next. He'd known from the start.

What he hadn't known was how it would feel: a flash of resentment, sharp like winter rain.

What he hadn't known was that it would surprise him.

He'd run through it a hundred ways, but had come again and again to the same conclusion. Ellina was twofaced. She was a box with a false bottom. She must be, because what else could explain how she'd turned so callous, how she'd kissed him and then called for his death within the span of an hour? Ellina wasn't who he believed her to be. She was capable of these treacheries and worse. And yet, despite this supposed certainty, Venick found that he wasn't ready to hear his suspicions confirmed.

He tried not to. He tried to be far away from himself when the news came. Traegar spoke the words gently. "Perhaps you have not heard? Well, you have been gone. Ellina was named Farah's right hand. Her advisor. She has pledged her loyalty to Farah's cause. The north is calling her a traitor."

THREE

Ellina counted how many ways there were to kill an elf.

A dagger through the eye, the gut, the throat. Poison. A snapped neck. Arrows in the lungs, the heart. Both at once, maybe, if the shooter was good enough.

She was. Raffan had made her learn. Ellina remembered those hard lessons, the relentless training. She remembered his eyes on her, the way he would nod when she succeeded. As a young legionnaire, she had craved those nods. She had been so eager to please him. The memory wormed a hole inside her.

But Ellina was not thinking about memories. She was not thinking about the present, either. Not the cool, elegant dining hall where she currently sat. Not the table before her, piled high with delicacies from the north and east. Not Raffan in the chair by her side, or Farah at the table's head, or the conjurors prowling the room's perimeter.

Ellina was counting.

It was as good a strategy as any to keep her face clear. And she must keep her face clear, her expression empty of emotion, because a guard had just appeared in this dining hall, and he had come with a message. *The human has returned to the city.*

The elf had spoken the words to Farah, but it was as if the message was meant for Ellina alone. She felt those words catch somewhere between her ribs and her heart. *The human.* The guard had not mentioned a name. There was no need. They all knew who he meant.

Farah set her utensils down. Her finger hovered over her knife, tracing a slow line up its edge. "Where was this?"

"On the east end of the city, near Gold's Row," the guard replied. "They were spotted in the market."

"They?"

"The human was not alone. He had a companion."

"Another human?"

The guard hesitated. "We...do not think so."

Farah's expression was inscrutable. Like most elves, she was an expert at concealing her emotions. Still, Ellina thought she could sense her sister's displeasure. It showed itself in small ways: the finger on her knife. The heavy press of silence. And finally, an answer too long in coming. "You do not *think*?"

"They were wearing cloaks," the guard explained. "Hoods. We could not see their faces. One was clearly human. The other...could have been too."

Dourin. It had to be. Ellina recalled how Dourin had begun to pick up certain human traits, becoming more expressive not just with his face, but with his hands and body, too. That was what happened to elves who spent too much time around humans. They lost their ability to hide themselves.

As Ellina had.

As she could no longer afford to have. She turned her attention inward, sensing how she had tensed, how her surprise must be written into the lines of her frame. A dangerous lapse. She exhaled a slow breath, willing her shoulders down, her palms open. She let them rest against the cotton of her trousers, which she had recently persuaded Farah to allow her to wear in place of silken robes. The trousers were not armor. They were not the hard legion-issued leather Ellina craved. But they were a step.

"What *can* you tell me?" Farah asked the guard.

"The pair was last seen heading north towards the mines."

"And you did not confront them?"

"No." The guard became uncomfortable. "You ordered us not to. Youvan and Balid went after them, but we called them off."

Because of the bargain Farah and Ellina had struck the night of the coup. After the queen's murder, when Ellina had been beaten and bound and at Farah's mercy, she had thought Farah would kill her. In a logical, detached sort of way, Ellina could see the sense in it. Ellina was one of the few surviving elves who knew the truth of Farah's plots: how Farah yearned for the throne, how she feared their mother would never crown her. How she allied with the southerners and corrupted the city's guard in order to kill the queen and stage her takeover. Ellina had witnessed it all, making her a loose end. A liability. If Farah was smart, she would have killed Ellina too.

Yet instead of killing her, Farah had surprised Ellina with a bargain: Venick's life and the safety of his home-city Irek, for Ellina's cooperation.

Farah seemed to understand that her claim to the throne was tenuous. Though some elves might believe the rumors she was spreading—

that Queen Rishiana had succumbed to the same disease that killed her sister Ara, that the sickness drove her to madness, that her death was both an accident and a mercy—not all elves were so easily fooled. Many had known the city was in danger. Many expected this invasion. If Farah wanted to tighten her hold on the throne, she needed to snuff out any resistance...and she could use Ellina's influence as a once-beloved legionnaire to do it.

"Sister," Farah addressed Ellina. "You spent time with the human. You know him best. What do you think he is doing here?"

The question was a coiled snake. It lifted its bony head, flicked out a forked tongue. Ellina knew better than to answer such a question head on. She replied carefully, at an angle. "The human often worries over his homeland. He is likely wondering how your new position as queen will affect his people. He could have returned to gather information."

"To spy, you mean."

"Yes." Any other answer would have seemed false.

"Is that all?"

It was not just the question that was serpentine, but Farah herself. Ellina saw her sister's gaze and thought of plated scales. She thought of venomous fangs. She thought of Dourin in the city, and how his reappearance presented a chance that was both unexpected and invaluable.

"Well?" Farah prompted.

"It is also possible that the human came to recruit northern elves who are...unhappy about your alliance with the southerners," Ellina said. "He might hope to lead a rebellion against you."

"My soldiers outnumber native citizens. They will stop him if he tries. But come, sister." Farah tilted her head. "Can you think of no other reason why the human might have returned? We already established that he is not working alone. Why not send a companion back to the city in his stead? Why risk himself, when he is so easily spotted as an outsider?"

To anyone else, it might seem as though this insistent questioning stemmed from a real desire to discover the human's motives. Venick was a known threat. He too was a loose end. His return to Evov raised many questions; Farah *should* seek to uncover his purpose. Yet Ellina knew her sister, and so she knew the truth: Farah was testing her.

It had been like this ever since their bargain. Farah constantly aimed to challenge her sister's loyalty, to push at the underworking of Ellina's thoughts to see if they would push back. Farah had always suspected that there was something romantic between Venick and Ellina. She suspected, too, that Ellina was not being wholly truthful when she had agreed to their deal. It did not matter that Ellina had both refuted her feelings for Venick and pledged her loyalty to Farah in elvish, or that lying in elvish was supposed to be impossible. Farah's suspicions remained.

Ellina was careful not to drop her sister's gaze. She met Farah's stare coolly, observing her sharp cheekbones, her haughty mouth, the slim line of golden earrings that signified her new rank as queen.

Ellina was grateful for Farah's distrust. She was grateful for the way that distrust had become like a tool in Ellina's palm: a mirror that could be angled into the light to blind Farah. Because if Farah was busy worrying over Ellina's secrets, Ellina could make a move that looked nothing like a move.

"You are right," Ellina said lightly. "There is another possibility. It is possible that Venick returned to Evov for me."

It was the answer Farah had been waiting for. Her eyes flashed with triumph. With glee, even, as if she had just exposed some dark secret. "And why would he do that?"

Because he was reckless. Because he tended to follow his gut. Because he knew when Ellina was lying, had always been able to see right through her, and she had hurt him, and he would never just let that go. Not without demanding an explanation.

"Venick thinks he owes me something," Ellina said. A half-truth. "It is the way human life prices work. He might not know that I have pledged my loyalty to you. We were...separated in the stateroom fighting. He would come back for me if he thought I was a prisoner here."

Farah's eyes danced. "And are you a prisoner here, dear sister?"

"Of course not."

"Then you will have to tell him so."

Ellina's heart lurched. Her hands fisted under the table.

In truth, Farah had good reason to suspect Ellina, because Ellina *had* lied when she swore fealty to Farah. She lied when she pledged to help unite the legion under Farah's rule. Even now she was lying. She had manipulated this conversation to get exactly what she wanted: a chance to escape the palace and speak not with Venick, but with Dourin.

"You will go into the city," Farah ordered. "Find the human and his mysterious companion. Make it clear that they are to leave Evov immediately, or face the consequences. And while you are at it, you can clear up any—*misapprehensions* about your position here. I will send a conjuror to escort you," Farah continued airily. "For your safety, of course."

Ellina's heart was beating hard now. She strove to keep her voice even. "If that is what you wish."

In the days since Farah's takeover, Ellina had been stripped of her weapons, ordered out of her armor. She was permitted to roam the palace and its grounds but had been barred from crossing the palace's bridge into the city. And she was being watched. Not only by Farah and Raffan, but also by the servants, the guards, the newly appointed senators. Farah doled out freedoms in small measures—the pants, access to pen and parchment, permission to walk the palace gardens—but these liberties were two-sided. They were meant to tempt Ellina into showing her hand, to catch her fumbling in some suspected deceit. And Ellina, who was anxious to put her own plans into motion, had been trapped. It did not even matter that she had secretly learned to lie in elvish, a language that until now had always forced the speaker to tell the truth. That power must be used carefully, or else risk discovery. Thus far it had been of little advantage.

The frustration of it all made her want to scream.

But now, this chance. An opportunity to escape the palace, if only for a short time. If Ellina could find Dourin, could speak to him privately…she felt the weight of this opportunity, and what it would mean for the north if she succeeded.

And Venick…

Ellina's chest tightened. Her pulse continued to pound, differently now. She had not seen Venick since his trial when she had announced to a court full of elves that he meant nothing to her, that she would not even mind him dead. She had told those lies in elvish and Venick, unaware of Ellina's newfound ability, had believed her.

It was the last time she had seen him.

And the last time she *would* see him, at least for now, if Ellina could help it. Venick could not be allowed to know the truth about her position here, or her plots, or her lies. If he knew how she risked herself—let alone that *he* was part of her bargain—he would never allow it. He would come for her, and in doing so reveal her as a spy. He would get himself killed in the process. And then everything would be ruined.

No. Ellina could venture into the city under the pretense of finding Venick, but it would be safer if she avoided him altogether.

But she should not think of that now. Ellina was aware of all eyes on her, and how vital it was that she not allow her thoughts to show in this moment.

The ways to kill an elf. Count them.

A sword through the neck.

She ignored the double rhythm of her heart.

Drowned in a river.

She pushed away any thought of the task ahead.

An axe in the back.

She counted, and allowed the counting to soothe her.

There had been a time when Ellina had refused to kill elves, refused even to consider its possibility. This was old law, sacred to their race even during times of war, and Ellina would not break it. But that was before, and this was now, and Ellina knew that now she would kill elves. She would kill as many as it took to protect her city, to defeat Farah, and to win her country back.

FOUR

"I do not believe it."

Dourin's chair scraped back hard against the kitchen floor as he stood, eyes bright with anger. "Ellina and Farah hate each other. Ellina would never pledge herself to her sister. Not after what happened in the stateroom."

"I am sorry," Traegar replied, and he seemed to mean it. That was real sorrow in his eyes. Real remorse. For all he'd insisted he didn't want anything to do with Dourin, Traegar's eyes were full of care. "I know she was your friend. She was mine as well, but—"

"No." Dourin cut him off with a hand. "I am saying it *cannot be*."

Venick turned away from the elves. He took two steps and ran out of space, so he stopped and scowled at nothing and did not, by any measure, turn back around. Venick didn't want to see Dourin's stricken face. Didn't want to think of how it must mirror his own. There was no reason for the ugly drop in Venick's gut at the news of Ellina's betrayal, the steely lurch of anger that followed. No reason at all for the shock or disbelief, because Venick had expected this, hadn't he? All along, he'd predicted Ellina's treachery. Hell, he'd insisted on it.

"I know it is hard to believe," Venick heard Traegar say. "But Ellina gave her oaths publicly, in elvish. She attends every stateroom assembly, every court function. And she has been meeting with legionnaires in the palace, championing Farah's cause."

"That proves nothing," Dourin argued.

"It proves *everything*," Venick cut in, whipping back around. "She pledged herself to Farah in elvish. What more evidence do you need?"

"I want to speak with her."

"That's not going to happen."

Dourin's eyes went dark. "Really. And you are going to stop me?"

"Yes." Through teeth. "If it keeps you from getting yourself killed. You can thank me when you come back to your senses."

"You think I am the one without sense?"

"Ellina switched sides. Why is that so hard to believe?"

"Because this is not like her."

"She could have changed."

"Not like this."

"*Yes* like this." Venick's chest heaved. His jaw clenched. He fought a flash of memory: Ellina standing before a court of elves, calmly calling for his death. "All the evidence is there. You'd realize it if you stopped letting your feelings get in the way of your judgment."

"Says the human who's still in love with her."

Like a slap to the face. Dourin's words landed sharply, cold at first, then stinging, burning.

Shame, hot and thick, poured into Venick.

"I didn't—" Dourin looked appalled by his own words. "You know I did not mean that."

Venick turned away. "Forget it."

"Venick…"

"We've wasted enough time here." Venick was suddenly desperate to be gone. He needed to get out of this house, out of this city, to leave this final, stupid mistake far behind. "We came for answers, and now you have them. We should get back to camp. Let the others know what we've learned."

"No," Traegar cut in. "It is not safe for you to leave yet. You will wait until nightfall."

"We've fought the conjurors before." Venick wanted to stab something.

"It is as you said." Traegar's voice gentled, and Venick didn't like that. He didn't want Traegar's pity, or to know there was something in his own expression that must have prompted that pity. "There is no need to be foolish."

Venick might have laughed. Hell and damn, but he was a fool. He hadn't thought he still harbored any hope for Ellina. Or if he did, it was the kind of hope that knows itself for what it is. The kind that reaches for the bottle even when the liquor has run dry. Venick's hope was like Traegar glancing at the curtained window: an old habit he'd been meaning to quit.

He was an idiot for his hope. Not just now, but always. When he and Ellina had traveled together, fought together, grown to know each other. When he'd started to…feel things. For her. Venick had allowed his hope to deceive him. He'd been ensnared by it. He'd fallen deep into its watery depths.

Now it felt like he was breaking the surface. Venick wiped the water from his eyes. He saw his hope as if for the first time, and he understood it in a way he hadn't before. Venick could see that he'd always had a blind spot for Ellina. Or a soft spot. Something vulnerable, anyway.

It hardened. That soft place inside him became as solid as stone.

Traegar said something, but Venick wasn't listening. He was remembering the day he and Ellina had first met. He could feel again the searing pain of the bear trap clamped around his foot as he bargained for his life in the forest last summer. Venick had crossed illegally from the mainlands into the elflands in search of food, but he'd been caught, and he should have been killed for it. Yet instead of killing him, Ellina had shattered the bear trap and set him free.

He remembered her eyes in that moment. Her anger, like chiseled stone.

And how it had been after. When she'd stitched his wound and dragged him to a cave and worked to keep him alive. Ellina had saved Venick at a time when he'd most needed saving, and in return he'd put his trust in her. He'd believed in her. He'd needed that: something to believe in.

"Well?" Traegar asked again. "Will you stay?"

Venick blinked up to find both elves watching him. He hesitated, knowing his answer, knowing it was the only *right* answer, yet hating it anyway. "We'll stay until nightfall, but no later than that. No, Dourin." Venick cut the elf off before he could object. "There's nothing left for us here. You know it as well as I do."

Dourin wanted to argue. Venick saw that clearly in the elf's eyes, in his still-open mouth. He knew it, because that was habit between them.

And he knew that Dourin must have heard some truth in his words, when instead of arguing the elf shut his mouth again. His shoulders slumped. He looked at the floor and was silent.

Just like you wanted.

Hell, that was twice now Venick had gotten what he'd wished for. Teach him to stop *wishing*. It hurt, seeing Dourin like that. Venick almost preferred the arguing. But he'd meant it when he said they'd wasted enough time there. Venick was anxious to get back to camp. He worried about the resistance in their absence. It had become clear that those elves weren't safe hiding out so close to the city. They needed to move, soon. And they had a war to plan.

As they settled in to wait for nightfall, Venick found himself thinking of his father, who'd been a military general, and had passed much of his knowledge to his son. Venick remembered his mother declaring proudly that Venick had been born during wartime. An honor for their people.

He remembered the day he'd murdered his father. How easy it had been to destroy that honor.

Venick had been blind when it came to Ellina. That was true. He'd been too soft, too unthinking, too quick to trust. He'd wanted to fit her into the story of his bandaged foot, or the way her eyes had burned right before he'd kissed her. Venick had let his heart get in the way of his head, and he'd paid for it. Was paying for it still. But he had survived worse. And he'd learned from his mistakes.

He wouldn't make them again.

FIVE

Ellina kept a steady pace over the palace bridge. Kept a steady eye, too, on the guards barricading the bridge's far end. There were fifteen, maybe twenty elves total. Too many to count at a glance. Too many to fight alone, unarmed and unarmored as she was.

Yet Ellina was not here to fight these guards. She was exiting the palace with Farah's permission, on her orders. In her fist was a white envelope stamped with the queen's seal, and inside that envelope was a letter written in Farah's slanted hand, explaining as much. If the guards doubted the integrity of that letter, they could always ask Ellina in elvish whether the message was true. She would answer, and they would believe her, despite having been warned not to trust the princess. They did not know Ellina could lie in elvish.

Of course, if the guards did suspect some sleight of hand, there was yet still a third option—they could confer with the conjuror who had been sent as Ellina's escort and now followed in her shadow. *For your safety*, Farah had said, though they both knew what the conjuror really was.

The guards watched Ellina approach. They took the offered letter, then exchanged quick words with the conjuror, whose name was Youvan. The midday sun sharpened their profiles. Their voices were white with cold.

Ellina moved to the bridge's railing. She did not want to listen to them discussing her, evaluating her worth like a sheep up for market. Ellina could not tell if these elves were northerners-turned-traitor, or southerners. They all looked the same in their red and black livery, their metal armor. They all looked at *her* the same, too: with obvious distaste.

Finally, the guards nodded and allowed them to pass.

"Wait." Youvan spoke from behind. "Before we go."

He lifted his hands. Like most conjurors, Youvan was tall—gangly, even—with unusually long arms and fingers. He sunk those fingers into the air now, drawing them down with a flex of his thin shoulders before pausing, hands outstretched, as if waiting for something to happen.

Nothing did. Ellina shifted. Her hand went to the place at her hip where a sword usually hung. She pinched the fabric there. Let it fall. And when still nothing happened, she decided it was best to simply ignore the conjuror. She started to move away.

Except, at that moment Ellina noticed it. Youvan's shadow seemed to quiver. It twitched. It crawled away from his body and stretched towards Ellina in a long, slanted line.

"No," Ellina managed. "Wait."

Youvan did not wait. He watched with something like satisfaction as his shadow slipped across the bridge and pooled at Ellina's feet, sinking into her own shadow, taking its place. Ellina's stomach dipped with dread. Though she had never seen the conjuring performed firsthand, she knew what this was. Shadow-binding.

"Was that necessary?" Ellina asked, voice rising. Though her shadow looked much the same as it had before, now that she was shadow-bound Youvan would always know her location. Until the conjuring was released, he would be able to follow her anywhere.

Her task had just become more complicated.

Youvan settled back onto his heels. "Do you object?"

"I am not a dog for you to leash."

"The queen seems to think otherwise."

Ellina's eyes flashed up. "And *you*, doing her bidding. Are you any better?"

"We have allied with the queen."

"She controls you."

"No." But his voice betrayed him. It constricted in anger.

Ellina reined in her own anger. She knew better than to argue with a conjuror, especially here, with Farah's guards watching. She took a breath, forced her fisted hands to open. They hung empty and useless at her sides.

In that moment, Ellina hated her hands.

She hated that she could not use them as she had been trained to use them.

And she hated Youvan's hands too, because he *could*.

"I think we should move on," Ellina said tightly.

Once off the bridge, it was a short walk from the palace to the city. The path was lightly trafficked, the day clear and bright. Ellina led the way, Youvan following close behind. She listened to the brush of his feet across the dusty footpath, the cadence and gait. She counted its rhythm. Committed it to memory.

As they neared Evov's entrance, the path widened into a true road, a glossy white-grey street that funneled horses and foot traffic up into the mountain. The street was more crowded here, the city's congestion clogging at the gates. Ellina pushed through the throng, dipping and dodging. Soon, a gap appeared between her and Youvan. He did not hurry to close it. Ellina was shadow-bound, and he was unconcerned.

Ellina glanced again at that shadow-binding. Maybe her shadow was a little wider than before. Maybe it was a little darker. It was hard to be sure. Here under the midday sun, everyone's shadows looked wide and dark. Still, something seemed different. As Ellina watched her silhouette race across the road, it appeared split between worlds, a bridge between here and…somewhere else.

The thought gave her pause. She blinked, and it felt suddenly as if *she* was the one who was split, as if *she* hovered between worlds. Her heart thudded, pulsing like it did when Ellina was on the verge of some new idea, which made her realize that, actually, she was.

She changed course. She followed the road until it forked, taking a quick right into an open square, which put her briefly out of Youvan's sight. In two swift movements Ellina stepped out of her slippers, leaving them there on the street behind her, then unwound the sash from her waist and tossed it into a convenient fire grate. Both the shoes and the sash were impractical, silken, useless. Made for courtiers concerned with easy palace living. They would slow her down, where she was going.

She moved on. High in the distance she could see Gold's Row, which was the wealthiest area of the city, and also the largest. At the Row's southernmost end was a river fed by snowmelt from farther up the mountain, and over that river was a set of planks—wooden, uneven—that had been nailed together to create a makeshift bridge.

Ellina knew this river. It was elven-made, built to provide the city's lower tiers with fresh water for drinking and bathing. And she knew this plank-bridge. It was rarely used by citizens, who preferred the longer, safer route through the eastern streets, but it was a popular shortcut for merchants who needed to cut a quick path from the working district to their stalls and storefronts in Gold's Row. At present, a clothier was urging her horse and the two-wheeled cart it hauled over the planks. The elf had her horse's reins in one hand, the bribe of an apple in the other. She was muttering in elvish, soothing the horse with soft words.

Ellina risked another glance behind her. Youvan was just now turning into the square. The distance between them had grown wider still.

She felt calmer now. Though Ellina would always wish for the comforting weight of her sword and bow in hand, these were not her only weapons. Perhaps they were not even her best weapons. Opportunity was. Her eye for an opening was.

She started for the bridge.

The river was startlingly clear. And it looked cold. As Ellina came upon the swift water, her hands went numb, as if she had dipped her fingers into that current, had felt its frigid bite.

The clothier continued to coax her horse. She did not notice Ellina approach.

Ellina stepped onto the bridge and imagined what Youvan would see. The horse, starting and stopping in short bursts, uneasy on the planks, which warped and shifted under the cart's weight. The clothier, struggling to pull the animal along. And Ellina, who moved too quickly, and stepped at the wrong moment, and startled the horse from behind. The horse reared and bucked. The cart clattered on its wheels. And Ellina—at risk of being trampled—reeled out of the way.

It would seem like an accident, that she stepped too far. A misstep, that that her foot slipped into air.

Her arms went wide. The world heaved.

She tumbled over the bridge's edge into the water below.

. . .

The cold was a blow to the gut. It drove the air from Ellina's lungs. That was bad, Ellina knew that it was, yet before she could do anything to correct it the river wrapped icy fingers around her waist and *pulled*, sucking her under. She was quickly swept away.

And it was nothing like she remembered. Ellina had done this before, she could recall it: hands at her waist, the push into the sky. Then, blackness. Her lungs screaming for air. Kicking to the water's surface, her sword in one fist, her free hand groping, catching something, holding on. A terrible strength. During this first, earlier time in Kenath, Ellina had responded to the river on instinct. There was no time for thought, no chance to prepare. The pain and the cold and the fear would come later, but in that moment Ellina had simply acted.

It was not like that now. Ellina had planned this escape into the river, she had known what was coming, and so there was no kick of instinct. No gut reaction to guide her. As the river pulled Ellina under, she was wholly conscious of her body, which had become a ragdoll in the current's grip. She could do nothing but flail.

Which she did, with vigor. Even as her vision spotted and her lungs begged for air, Ellina twisted and thrashed, fighting for the surface, which appeared and vanished and appeared again in dizzying flashes of blue and white. Her eyes—open under the water—burned. Her chest convulsed. She fought the urge to inhale.

And fought her mounting dread. Ellina was sick with the sudden certainty that she had made a terrible mistake, that she had grossly miscalculated. What had she been thinking, when she stood on those planks and stared calmly into the water below, as if it held all her answers? Ellina could not swim. No elves could—their fear of water prevented them from ever learning. She had thought, before…but of course one distracted swimming lesson in a calm everpool could not have prepared her for *this*.

Panic punched into her. It felt suddenly as if her heart, and not her eyes, was burning. Ellina saw her future clearly, as stark and cold as this water. Blue and black and white. The colors of her death.

No, said a small voice inside her. Firm. Not her own.

You must remember.

Ellina continued to struggle. Her mind was closing over. Her ears roared, and that too sounded like death.

No, said that voice again, stronger now. *This is important, Ellina.*

Whatever you do.

You must remember not to panic.

Ellina recognized that voice at the same time the memory broke open, revealing itself more fully. Calm water. A wide sky, winter eyes. And those words, the steady instructions. *That's first, Ellina. No matter what else happens, it's important to stay calm.*

Venick. It was Venick's voice in her mind, his words in her memory. He had said that to her in the everpool when he had tried to teach her how to swim.

Ellina might have laughed, had she the air for it. The memory did nothing to help her now. As the river pulled her along, she silently raged at herself and at him. How could he tell her to stay calm, when her chest felt like daggers and her hands were huge and fumbling and her mind was begging her to *do something*.

But: *Don't panic.*

But: *This is important, Ellina.*

Whatever you do. Don't just swim with your arms. Use your legs. Kick hard.

Ellina did: a single, desperate kick.

Her feet met the river's bottom. There was a quick surge of movement, darkness, then bright light. And it was enough, it was somehow just enough, as if the moment had been planned, as if guided by the hands of gods she did not believe in.

She broke the surface with a gasp.

A flood of color and sound. Elves were shouting. They had spotted her, they were running along the riverbank. For a half-moment Ellina could hear their dismay. Then her head went under again.

She was smarter this time. She spun once, righted herself, and kicked again. Her feet met the river's steep bank. She was propelled sideways. She crashed into something soft and yielding. It tangled her limbs, pinning her arms to her body, and for a terrifying moment Ellina was trapped. Then her head broke the surface once more. One arm came free. She reached for that soft something and realized what she held: a black and red banner. It had been tossed into the water by the elves on the riverbank. Ellina gripped hard, using the banner as an anchor. She pulled herself to the river's edge as hands came down to haul her out.

She was immediately sick all over the rocky riverbank. She heaved water. The elves who had saved her backed out of range. They were silent as it continued.

Ellina spat, wiped her mouth, and looked up.

It was unclear if the elves knew, before, who they had been pulling from the river. But they knew now. Their faces showed varying degrees of shock.

"*Cessena?*" Princess?

Ellina coughed again, a wet, hacking sound. Every breath was a knife to her ribs. She brought a palm to her lips and drew it away, expecting blood.

"Did you fall?"

"Were you pushed?"

"What happened?"

Once the questions started they did not stop. Elves pushed forward, offering their hands, crowding her with queries and concerns. But Ellina's time was ticking now. The river would slow Youvan down, but it would not stop him for good. He would know where she had gone. And he would be coming.

She shoved herself up and broke into a run.

She was unsteady at first, clumsy on her feet, which were bare and frozen. Every step spiked pain up her heels, the gravelly road like needles in her flesh. She pushed past the pain, forced herself to focus as she mentally tallied all the many places Dourin might have gone. The green glass mines, she thought first, then the legion barracks. Yet the guard said they were spotted east of Gold's Row…

Ellina changed course. She climbed. She was up on the roofs now. From this vantage point the houses all looked the same: shapeless, pocketed by shadows. Smoke winnowed out of skinny chimneys, and Ellina imagined families sitting by warm fires below. Elves unaware, safe inside, surrounded by loved ones.

She paused on that imagining. She thought again of Dourin.

She knew where to go.

SIX

Venick settled into the kitchen chair. He crossed his arms, tipped back his head. Dourin and Traegar had moved into an adjacent room—a bedroom, Venick presumed, or a study—and were now speaking in low tones. The wall muted their voices so that Venick couldn't quite make out the words. Couldn't hear what they were discussing. But he could guess. He remembered Dourin's false calm in the foyer. Traegar's guarded eyes. Those two had old arguments between them. And now, a chance to work them out.

Venick set his hands against the table. He thumbed the wooden edge, then pushed, tipping onto the chair's back legs. He balanced there, thinking of old wounds. Of wrongs made right. He thought of his mother and imagined speaking to her as Traegar spoke to Dourin now. Would their voices be soft, or raised? Would his mother point and accuse, or agree to listen?

Sometimes Venick could still see the boy he'd once been. He envisioned the way he would dig his fists into his mother's skirt, bury his face in the fabric. He felt the warm weight of her hand on his head. He used to do this all the time. Child-Venick would make a mistake, would come to his mother tearfully and hide his face in her dress and apologize into the cloth. His voice would come out muffled. Woolen. He knew now that his mother wouldn't have been able to understand him, but the words themselves had never really mattered. It was the act of his apology that counted in her eyes.

If only things were still so simple.

Venick tipped the chair back farther still, testing its limits. He had long dreamed of a chance to return home. Soon, he would have it. Venick had been banished from the lowlands for murdering his father, but as a former soldier, he was allowed a chance at redemption—a single opportunity to undo his crimes and reverse his exile. Tradition dictated that he must first make a sacrifice, and that those he had wronged would decide if that sacrifice was enough to absolve him. Venick thought that allying with the northern elves and fighting to protect his homeland might be enough to earn forgiveness from his mother, but now…he wasn't so sure. If *he* were his mother, he didn't think he could ever forgive himself for what he'd done. Him? Excused for the murder of his own father? Never.

In an instant Venick would have avoided if he could have, his mind jumped to Ellina. He remembered again how she'd been in the stateroom. The way her mouth had moved as she uttered the words that would break him. *He is human. Kill him, if it matters that much to you. What do I care?* Venick saw the way her fingers gripped her sword's pommel. Her face had closed along well-worn lines.

Yes, Venick thought. Some wrongs could never be forgiven.

Except, his heart seemed to stumble on the thought. It pulled like fabric caught on a nail, unraveled and said *wait*. Venick frowned. He again pictured Ellina's face as it had been that afternoon: the empty eyes, that tight mouth. Cold. She had seemed so foreign to him in that moment. Yet also, oddly, familiar.

Venick dug into the memory. He raked his fingers through the earth of it, pulling up roots. He'd always been able to read Ellina. Even before she'd lost her ability to hide her emotions, it was her decided *lack* of emotion that gave her away, the concentrated absence of any tells. During their time together, Venick had seen Ellina do this many times. She would empty her expression, smoothing her features until they were as calm and still as glass.

A thought. A slow idea. Because there was only one reason Ellina ever shut down like that. And he realized that it *had* been familiar. It was an expression he'd come to know, because she'd used it both on him and for him. That was how Ellina looked when she was lying.

Venick let the chair fall forward. Its legs slammed down.

He was furious with himself.

He shouldn't do this. It was painful, the way his mind reached for some alternate explanation for what had happened that day in the stateroom. When Ellina said she didn't care about him, that he was merely a tool at her disposal, she hadn't been lying. Gods, she'd spoken those words in *elvish*. Ellina might be a skilled deceiver, but no one could lie like that in elvish.

Dourin reentered the kitchen. "What did you break?"

"Nothing."

"I heard a crash."

"It was just the chair."

Dourin pursed his lips, and Venick had the sense of being scrutinized. He knew what his face must show: a strange mix of hurt and frustration and anger.

"I think—" Dourin started, but a sudden shuffle upstairs interrupted him. It was a light patter, as if something had alighted on the roof. A small creature.

Or a conjuror.

Venick and Dourin exchanged a look.

"Is there anyone else in this house besides us?" Venick asked.

"No." Dourin's hand was at his sword. Venick started to stand, but Dourin waved him back. He still had that look on his face, the one that told Venick he knew exactly why the chair had slammed down, even if it was impossible for him to know it. "You stay. I will check."

"You shouldn't go alone," Venick said.

"This calls for a bit of stealth."

"I can be stealthy."

Dourin gave Venick a look that said, loudly, exactly how stealthy he thought Venick could be. "It is probably nothing," Dourin assured him. "Do not worry yourself. I will only be a minute." He disappeared down the hall.

Instinct told Venick that he shouldn't let Dourin go without him. At the very least, they should call for Traegar. Let *him* go with Dourin. Except, Venick was still angry. He wasn't thinking clearly. Ellina's face swam in his vision, and she smirked at him. In his mind, this pretend-Ellina looked at him as Dourin just had: like she knew too much.

Venick stayed where he was.

• • •

Ellina's stomach was in knots. Her heart was made of lead. She set a hand flat against the door that opened off the balcony into Traegar's upstairs bedroom, exhaling a slow breath.

She had been to this house only once, years ago, yet she remembered it clearly. Not the bedroom. Ellina had never seen Traegar's bedroom. But his kitchen. His study. She remembered thinking that Traegar seemed too grand for his own home, having qualities she found both regal and intimidating. Traegar, like Ellina and Dourin, had been recruited into the legion, and the three of them had trained together early on, though Traegar had resigned before taking his oaths.

But now: his balcony. The rough wood of his bedroom door. Ellina touched that door with a light finger, tracing the grain.

She was stalling. She knew that she was, yet could not quite force herself to continue. Coming here had been a gamble. She had no proof that Dourin was hiding in Traegar's house. It was possible that he had gone somewhere else entirely…

Ellina shook herself. Enough. She had laid her bets. Her time was up. There was nothing left to do now but flip her cards and see if she had won, or lost.

She dropped to her knees and pulled out her lockpicks.

Her plan was simple. She would pick the lock and enter quietly through Traegar's upstairs bedroom. If she was lucky enough to find Dourin first, alone, she would explain everything: her plans, her reasons. If she found Dourin and Venick together, she would pass along Farah's message, then conspire to speak to Dourin after. And if she found *Venick* alone…

Another steadying breath. Another grinding of her will. Ellina leaned in, working her picks, feeling around inside the lock's guts. The doorknob was ornate, the backplate inlaid with thin golden whorls. She stared at the design as if it were a message she could decode, which made her realize she was trying to decode whether or not she wished to find Venick alone.

Insanity. It was utter insanity that she might even consider wanting to see the one person who was most likely to undo all her plans. Ellina put the thought away. She buried any consideration of it. She refocused, maneuvering her lockpicks, listening to the faint click and tap of the lock's pins. The afternoon sun glinted against the door's metal. The knob looked hot to the touch.

And suddenly it was turning. Ellina startled. Someone was opening the door from the inside. It swung inward and Ellina came swiftly to her feet, clutching her lockpicks like a weapon, then loosening when she saw who stood on the other side.

Dourin.

...

Venick found Traegar in a nearby sitting room. The elf stood before the hearth, one hand braced against the mantle, his expression drawn. Before, Venick had assumed that Traegar must be around Dourin's age. Now though, the elf seemed older.

Venick was about to tell Traegar about the noise upstairs when the elf spoke. "I have something for you."

It was a book. Small, bound in deerskin, the title etched roughly into the hard leather. *Jouvl-aian Rauam*, the cover read. It was not a phrase Venick knew.

He flipped the book open. Inside, the yellowed pages showed handwritten writing, some in elvish, some in mainlander, all of it done in messy, lopsided lines. The crammed script appeared to describe recipes, their measurements and ingredients outlined in detail.

No, Venick thought. Not recipes. *Potions*.

"You are *eondghi*," Venick said, using the elven word for it. "A healer."

"I was."

Venick searched the elf's face.

"The potions in that book are of my own invention," Traegar explained. "I wore the healer's ring for a few years," he tapped his ear, "and I might have served in the legion, but the academy revoked my rights after they discovered my…experiments." He clasped his hands behind his back, and the movement made Venick wonder if this was difficult for the elf, and if it was, which part was difficult? Remembering his dismissal from the healer's academy, or admitting it to a human? "The academy has rules about such things. And some of my methods can be used to harm as well as to heal. They destroyed my records, but they missed one."

Venick's eyes dropped back to the book. He was no healer himself, but he could appreciate the value of such a volume, especially during wartime. He could appreciate the significance of the gesture, too, both the gift and its giving.

Traegar said, "I knew Queen Rishiana rather well." He caught Venick's surprised glance and gave a slight smile. "She had an interest in healing. It was an interest we shared. Her duties did not allow her much time to explore the craft, but still, I admired her for it. She had a sharp mind, even if there were times…" He stopped himself. "She was a strong leader. And she loved this country. She did not deserve to die as she did, no matter what mistakes she might have made."

"The queen's death was not her own fault," Venick argued. "No one could have predicted what Farah planned."

"You are right."

Yet Traegar had hesitated, and Venick had the sense that the elf, rather than push a point, had decided to let some unspoken matter drop.

· · ·

Dourin's eyes went wide at the sight of Ellina. His face shone with quick emotion. "*You.*"

Ellina stepped back as Dourin slid onto the balcony, pulling the door closed behind him. He took in her missing weapons, her damp hair, the black and red attire. Farah's colors. "So it is true." His expression closed. "Traegar told us everything. I did not believe it. I did not want to believe it. Ellina." Dourin's eyes lifted to hers. "What are you *doing?*"

"Spying for the resistance," Ellina replied simply. Dourin blinked. His anger evaporated.

"No."

"Yes."

"I did not think..." He pressed both palms to his eyes. "I should have known."

"It is better that you did not. I need to appear loyal."

"I doubted you." Dourin spoke from behind his hands. "I should not have. Forgive me."

Ellina gripped Dourin's wrists, pulling his hands free. "There is nothing to forgive."

He did not believe her, she could see that he did not. His regret hung like a shield between them. But Ellina could spend no time on it. She had none left to waste.

She asked the question she dreaded. "Where is Venick?"

"Downstairs, with Traegar. He will never *believe...*"

"Wait." Ellina shot a nervous look behind her, half-expecting to see Youvan there already. She moved into the shadow of the balcony, pulling Dourin after her. "We must speak quickly. I need you to trust me.

And I need your help."

She told him everything, starting with the secrets she had learned from the wilding chieftain in the forest and ending with her choices in the stateroom. She explained how her dark hair—unusual for an elf, and even more so for a northerner—marked her as a conjuror, and how northern conjurors had one specific skill: they could learn to lie in elvish.

"Impossible," Dourin whispered. "No one can lie—"

"Yes they can. *I* can." Ellina switched to elvish. "*I can lie in this language. I am a northern conjuror, and I have been learning to tell lies in elvish.*"

"That..." Dourin's eyes were round. "That is..." She saw the moment he understood, the way his disbelief morphed into something like horrified fascination. "The stateroom. Everything you said about Venick. And Farah. You swore loyalty to her..."

"I lied."

Ellina described the physical agony of her first lies. How they weakened her, made it easy for Raffan to subdue her. The blood rose to Ellina's cheeks, stinging, as she explained how Raffan had dragged her away, then bound and locked her in her own suite. He and Farah had debated what to do with her.

"They wanted to use me," Ellina said. "They wanted me to pledge my allegiance to them. They threatened my life, and when that did not work, they threatened Venick's life. His home. Farah and I..." She hesitated. "We made a bargain."

Dourin's voice went low. "What bargain?"

"Farah is moving swiftly," Ellina continued. "She intends to conquer the elflands as quickly as possible before anyone can rise against her. She must suspect that you are gathering a resistance, but she does nothing for now because she does not need to. Your army is not strong enough to pose any real threat to her…yet."

"Ellina."

"We can make it stronger."

Ellina did another scan of the streets below. She was growing more anxious. She had yet to explain the most important part of her plan. "My position in the palace is valuable. I might overhear something. The everpools…"

"I know how they work," Dourin interrupted, "and my answer is no."

"I can uncover Farah's plans. I can use the everpools to pass that information to you."

"It is not safe. What you are suggesting…Farah's guards will catch you."

"No."

"They will kill you."

"They won't."

Dourin was shaking his head, firm denial, but Ellina was not finished. "There is one more thing." It surprised her, how heavy these words felt on her tongue. She heaved them out. "You must keep my position as a spy here a secret. No one can know."

"Venick…"

"Especially not Venick."

Dourin drew back a little. "He deserves to know."

"It is not so simple as deserving."

"But why?"

Ellina quieted. "Do you know the reason Venick was outlawed from his homeland?" Dourin shook his head. "He once loved an elf. Years ago, in Irek. His father discovered their relationship and alerted the southerners, who came to kill her. Venick murdered his father for betraying their secret."

"I—" Dourin's mouth parted. "I never knew."

"But do you understand? Venick knew that he would be banished, yet killed his father anyway. It is his honor. He is bound by it. He will do what he believes is right, even if he ruins himself to do it. If he knew the truth…" Ellina did not have to finish. If Venick knew the truth about her bargain with Farah, he would never accept it. If he knew what she planned, he would fight it.

They will catch you, he would say, just as Dourin had.

They will kill you.

I can't let you do it Ellina. Not like this. Not for me. There must be another way.

Venick would beg Ellina to change her mind. And then? Without Ellina in the palace to gather intelligence, they would lose what was quite possibly their best hope for victory. Farah would retaliate, and Irek would be the first to fall to her wrath. The conjurors would rise uncontested, the resistance would fail, and Venick would die anyway.

"Please," Ellina said to Dourin. "Promise me."

Dourin was unhappy. "Venick thinks you betrayed us. He has been… different since that day." Ellina's heart pinched, because she knew how Venick had been. Hurt. Conflicted. Like her. "Are you certain this is what you want?"

"I am certain."

"Then I promise. I will keep your secret."

"Promise me—" *in elvish*, Ellina almost said. Dourin was not a conjuror. He was still bound by the rules of their language. If Dourin made that promise in elvish, he would be forever bound to his oath. And yet, Ellina knew too well the hidden dangers of such promises. She changed her mind at the last moment. "Promise me…on your life," she said instead.

"I promise you on my life."

Ellina should have felt relieved. She had done what she had come here to do. Yet as she stared into the face of her friend, her chest ached. She felt suddenly a fledgling again, green and uncertain, as she had been in the days when she was struggling to find her place in the world, and her mother had not understood her, and she had not understood herself. Ellina had never fit in at court, so she joined the legion against her mother's wishes, determined to carve her own path. Dourin had been there when the queen stormed into the legion barracks, furious that her daughter had disobeyed her, and more furious because Ellina had already sworn her oaths to the legion and there was nothing Rishiana could do to reverse them. After their fight, Dourin had not tried to soothe Ellina with words, but knew how to cheer her best—by taking her to the training ground with sparring swords, and beating her, and then showing her how to beat him back.

Ellina wanted to say all of this. She wanted to explain what it meant to have someone to trust in a world where trust was rare. She wanted to take Dourin's hand and squeeze it, even though such sentiments were typically scorned by elves, who saw physical affection as a human affliction. But Dourin would not scorn Ellina. This she knew: he would squeeze her hand back.

Before Ellina could do or say any of this, however, a shuffle from behind caught her attention. It was faint, the subtle scrape of cloth on stone. She turned...

To see Youvan climbing onto the balcony.

• • •

Venick was tucking Traegar's book into his pocket when the elf asked, "Where is Dourin?"

The question startled Venick. He'd been distracted, he'd forgotten. How long had Dourin been upstairs?

Too long.

Venick regretted allowing his friend to investigate alone. He quickly told Traegar what had happened. Together, they went up the stairs.

. . .

"Ellina." Youvan swept forward. His face looked bleached, almost skeletal beneath the sun's harsh rays. He did not look at Dourin. His eyes were for her only. "I thought I had—*lost* you back there."

"Lucky that you did not." Ellina's voice could not possibly be her own. It was cool and calm and perfectly imperious. "Farah would have been unhappy."

"I am not concerned with Farah's unhappiness. I am concerned with—"

"Interrupting my assignment? Yes, clearly."

Youvan made no effort to conceal his anger. He let it flare in his golden eyes, let it flash through his fingers as he snapped his wrist, summoning his shadow back to himself. The shadow shivered—in echo of its master's fury or in fear of it, Ellina did not know—before racing over the balcony back to Youvan's feet. Ellina should have been glad to be rid of that shadow binding, and she would have been, had she not also worried that Youvan only called his shadow back so that he could use it in some other, worse way.

Youvan said, "You ran."

"I fell."

"On purpose."

"Elves cannot swim. Why would I fall into a river on purpose?"

"So that you could escape."

"But I did not escape. I came here to deliver Farah's message, as instructed."

"Say it in elvish."

Simply. As if there was no risk in asking, no insult. Most elves would never dare insist the princess prove her truths in elvish. That language was meant to be offered, not taken. Demanding that another speak in elvish was the highest offense. And it was dangerous. Socially, politically. To make such a demand—and to have your assumptions proven wrong—had consequences for the asker, too.

Youvan seemed to care about none of it. He waited, shoulders back, arrogance now mixed in with the anger. He wanted Ellina's answers, and he would have them, even if he must take them by force.

Well. There would be no need.

"*It was an accident,*" Ellina lied in elvish. The words met only slight resistance, as skin might resist a knife. She pushed a little harder and felt the membrane of the lie split. Then the words flowed free as blood. "*A horse startled as I crossed the planks. I tried to move out of its way and slipped, as I think you saw. It was unexpected. I did not run.*"

"*Then why not wait for me once you reached the shore?*" Youvan demanded.

"*And miss my opportunity to deliver Farah's message? I think not.*"

Youvan eyed her. Like the guards, he had been warned not to trust Ellina, to be wary of her ability to twist words in elvish. That particular skill of hers was no secret; practically everyone knew Ellina could be slippery, and that was without her newfound ability. Raffan had grown used to Ellina's ways and knew how to read her. Queen Rishiana had warned that if Ellina was ever caught lying to *her*, she would be punished. As for everyone else, they were left to do what Youvan was doing now—studying Ellina, picking her apart, looking for the half-truths hidden in her words.

Youvan found none. Of course he did not. Ellina had spoken plainly.

"*I did not think you so...eager,*" he said.

"*I believe I have made my allegiance to my sister clear.*"

Youvan paused a half-beat. He looked at Dourin.

"*Leave him alone,*" Ellina cut in.

"*Maybe I have questions for your friend as well.*"

Ellina's confidence vanished. She felt that old familiar pulse of fear. She could lie in elvish, but Dourin could not.

Youvan asked, "*Who are you?*"

"*A member of this household,*" Dourin answered smoothly in elvish.

"*What did the princess say to you?*"

The question was poorly worded. Youvan was no expert interrogator if he would ask such an open-ended inquiry and expect an honest answer. To corner answers in elvish, one must be specific. *What did the princess say to you?* Ellina saw the question's soft spots, the places Dourin could bend and mold.

Dourin saw them too. His answer was glib. "*She came to deliver a message.*"

"*What was the message?*"

"*That she has a new role in Farah's court. That she wishes to remain here in the city.*"

True, and true. Ellina smothered a triumphant smile. She steadied her expression as Youvan peered between them, seeming to struggle. He clipped out the words. "My...apologies."

The apology itself was no great victory—there was a reason Youvan had switched back to mainlander for its delivery—but it served Ellina's purposes. The sooner she got off this balcony and got Youvan away from Dourin, the better.

"Good," Ellina said. "If that is all…"

"Ellina?"

That voice. This time, there was no gap in recollection. Ellina knew it immediately. She turned, and still she was stunned, because she had not heard the balcony door open behind her, had not heard him appear.

Venick.

SEVEN

She was not prepared.

Ellina thought she had planned for this. She had rehearsed—silently, in the most private recesses of her mind—what she would say to Venick if she saw him again. In her imagination, it was easy. She would lie as she had in the stateroom. She would make her words to be careless, offhanded. Venick would have his suspicions, surely, but she would deny them. She would say whatever she must to make him believe that she was his enemy, and then to make him leave.

That was how it went in her head.

But this was reality: Venick standing before her, his eyes blown wide with shock.

Ellina's unsteady heart, cracking open at the sight of him.

The sharp, sudden certainty that she could not hurt him again.

And the understanding—equally sharp, equally certain—that she *must*.

Traegar appeared a moment later, and it was he who broke the silence. "Ellina?" His eyes jumped from her to Youvan and back again. "What are you doing here?"

Ellina struggled to speak.

"Yes, Ellina," Venick repeated. "What *are* you doing here?"

His voice was low. His eyes: guarded. Shaken, and trying to hide it. Conflicted, too. Ellina saw each of Venick's emotions like beads on a string, bits of colored glass clicking together. They rattled her. She was rattled, to see him here, looking at her as he was. She had forgotten that he could be like this, that it could feel like this. As Venick's eyes met hers, she felt as if she had forgotten everything.

"Ellina."

He spoke her name like a curse. It brought her back to herself a little. Ellina focused her attention, assuming a legion stance, legs shoulder-width apart, hands behind her back. It did not matter that the sight of Venick—so raw, so vivid, so *human*—had Ellina wishing she could take back every lie she had ever told him. They were not alone on this balcony. Youvan loomed in her periphery, a solid, silent reminder that whatever Ellina said would be witnessed and reported. She could not afford to slip, not here, not now.

"I came to deliver a message," Ellina said. She cooled her voice, her expression. She imagined herself a clear winter sky, the vision of indifference. "From Farah. You are not welcome in this city."

Venick stared. "Really."

"Of course," Ellina continued airily, "this is not news to you. You never *were* welcome here. But Farah is gracious. She is offering you a chance. You may exit Evov unharmed, on the condition that you leave immediately and never return."

"Why allow me to leave at all?"

"What?"

"Why not just kill me?" Then, almost as if Venick could sense how the question had unbalanced her, and aimed to topple her fully: "That's what you're good at, isn't it? Killing humans?"

Ellina flinched. She tried to hide that she had flinched, but Venick saw it anyway.

And it changed him. His eyes narrowed, his face transforming into a map of the very feelings Ellina feared she would see in him: doubt, suspicion.

"Is that what you wish?" Ellina asked. "For me to kill you?"

"I asked you a question."

"It is not wise to ask questions. Not when the queen has extended such a generous offer."

"But *why* has she extended the offer?" Venick moved closer. His sudden proximity disarmed her. She knew better than to take a step back, knew from years of training that it would be foolish to show that kind of weakness, not when she needed to remain collected, not when Venick's nearness was not supposed to matter to her one way or the other. Yet she did step back, and felt with that step how the battle began to slip, sliding through her fingers like silk from a spool. She felt the moment it all started to unravel.

"Farah wants me dead," Venick said, the words low now, meant only for them. "She has always wanted me dead. So why the sudden change of heart?"

"Truly, Venick." Ellina's voice sounded like it was swallowing itself. "I have no idea."

"Really?"

"No."

He did not believe her. His disbelief was as clear to Ellina as her lie must be to him. Venick's eyes roved her face, and Ellina felt the way a diamond must feel when it catches the light, all its inner facets illuminated.

He said, "I think you do."

Dourin, who had been watching the scene unfold, and sensed the danger, stepped in. "Venick." He gripped Venick by the shoulder. "I think we have heard enough."

"You said it yourself. You wanted to speak to her."

"I have. There is nothing more to say."

"Maybe *I* have more to say."

"*Venick.*"

But Venick was shrugging out of Dourin's grasp, he was stepping closer still. Ellina's pulse rode high in her throat. Her hands ached for something to grip: a bow, a knife, the hilt of her sword—anything to ground her. But Ellina was weaponless. Defenseless. Stripped bare, as she always had been, standing before him.

"Dourin was right," Venick said. "This," he waved a hand vaguely over her black and red outfit, "doesn't make sense. Farah killed your mother. She sided—" he glanced at Youvan "—with the southerners. The same southerners who killed Lorana. The southerners who tried to kill *you*. And I just…" He took a breath. Emotions danced across his features, anger and doubt and regret and suspicion, there and back and gone again in such quick flashes that it made Ellina dizzy. Then his expression hardened, and his mouth set in a way that frightened her. "Farah wants the mainlands, Ellina. She's going to come after my home. She'll kill every human she can to get it, and plenty of elves besides, and I…how could you side with someone like that? It isn't right. This isn't you."

It took all of Ellina's strength not to look at Youvan then, to try and guess what he made of Venick's accusations. Already, Ellina feared the conjuror had seen too much, that he could sense her treachery…or soon would. Her heart felt dipped in oil. Venick's glance was a spark. She was going to catch fire from within, and Venick would see all her truths burning, and Youvan would too.

This was a disaster.

Venick gave a frustrated sigh. "Ellina."

She could not look at him.

"Answer me."

She studied the open collar of his shirt. It was elven-made. The stitching had begun to fray.

"You owe me an explanation," he insisted. "Don't you think you owe me an explanation?"

A desperate laugh bubbled in her throat. No, she could say. I do not owe you anything.

Venick must have read the thought on her face. He pulled away. "You were not always so heartless."

Was there a moment when everything changes? When you make the choice that sets your fate into stone? Ellina was cold with that question, as cold as she had been before ever meeting Venick, before the forest and the stateroom and his promises and hers. Elves did not believe in the divine, yet Ellina had the sense that she was gambling with destiny. This was her path, set like the moon into the sky.

Youvan shifted in her periphery. He, too, waited to hear what she would say.

She would lie this final time. She would lie hard enough that the lie erased her truths. She would do this, because she knew what would happen if she did not. She gathered the words first in her mind, then in her mouth. "You doubt me."

Venick made a breathless noise. "Yes, I doubt you."

"Why?"

He ran a hand through his hair. "Because I know you. Say what you want about me. Say that you don't care and never did. Fine. But I know *you*. And I know that you've always been loyal to your country."

"This *is* my country."

Venick wavered. He had no good answer for that.

"Farah is my sister," Ellina continued, swallowing the words whole. Trying not to taste them. "She is family. We have had our disagreements, certainly, but we have put them behind us. As for her aspirations…we share a vision."

"Which is?"

"Prosperity for elvenkind. The expansion of our lands and race. Honestly, Venick. Is that really so difficult to understand? Farah will be queen of all the known world one day. She is the most powerful ruler of our era, and I have an opportunity to stand by her side."

"You shouldn't *want* to stand by her side."

"Why? Because she has blood on her hands? You said it yourself. I do, too. As for how much I care about humans…" Ellina gave a shrug. "Well. You and I have misunderstood each other on that point before. But I thought I made my feelings clear. On that last day."

Youvan would think Ellina was talking about Venick's trial, but Ellina knew that Venick understood her true meaning. In the everpool, he had kissed her, and she pulled away. He admitted his feelings for her, and she gave him nothing back.

Color bled into Venick's cheeks. "I see."

"Do you? It seems to me that you have been confused."

"Yes," he said slowly. "Maybe I have been."

"It is my fault for not being clear enough, then. Perhaps it is time that I spoke plainly." This lie did not come easily. It seemed to burn on the way out. But Ellina spoke the words clearly, deliberately, in elvish. "*I am loyal to Farah, and I am here to enforce her will. If you do not leave now, I will kill you myself.*"

It was as if a spell had been cast, or broken. Venick's expression changed as a sky does, in shades and shadows, and Ellina saw it: the moment he believed her.

He did not speak again. He did not even look back as he disappeared through the balcony door. Gone.

EIGHT

Venick cursed.

He'd been going too fast, he hadn't been watching his footing. In his haste to put as much distance between himself and Evov as he could he'd stumbled over an obvious rock and slipped, catching his weight with one arm. Pain spiked up his wrist. He slid a few feet down the mountain before coming to a shaky stop.

Dourin light-footed to his side, brows lifted.

"Don't say it," Venick grumbled, pushing back to his feet.

"Do not say what?"

"Whatever you're about to say."

It seemed that for once the elf would listen. Dourin studied Venick in silence as Venick rolled his wrist, testing the joint. He couldn't afford a sprain. Couldn't believe he had even *risked* a sprain, and in such a stupid way. A fall. Going too fast, letting his head get in the way of his feet. Venick flexed his fingers, working feeling back into the hand and doing his best to ignore Dourin, who was looking like he'd decided to say something after all. The elf pursed his lips. "I do not think we should tell the others about Ellina."

Venick blinked up. That wasn't what he'd expected Dourin to say. "They deserve to know."

"Morale among our troops is low enough as it is. Our numbers are pitiful, and our soldiers know it."

"Which is why we're going to gather more soldiers."

"If we can."

"We will."

"We will try, of course," Dourin replied, "but we must face facts. Farah is moving quickly. Her army has already invaded many northern cities. Cities *we* had planned to visit."

"Then we'll head for the mainlands first," Venick countered, and wondered how he'd even landed himself on this side of the argument. It was usually *him* doing the doubting. "We'll recruit humans to our side before Farah can march on the border."

Dourin wrung out a dry smile. "Another gamble."

"Yes, but—hell, Dourin. I thought you were the optimist here."

"My point is that our soldiers are worried. They are confused. For a hundred years they lived safely in the knowledge that elves did not kill other elves, and yet many of them have now witnessed the murder of their queen by her own daughter. They witnessed the death of their friends. It has them concerned. Disturbed, even."

"It should have them *motivated*."

"Regardless, I do not think they can handle Ellina's betrayal, too."

Venick folded his arms. His anger—which hung so close to the surface these days—flared. It wasn't his duty to coddle their soldiers. Ellina had betrayed them. Lying about it wouldn't change the truth.

Yet there was a part of him that could admit, grudgingly, that Dourin had a point. Since the stateroom coup, he and Dourin had managed to rally only a small force of elves, about sixty soldiers total. It wasn't an army. Not even close. And it was true, Farah would be quick to invade northern cities, just like she'd invaded Evov and Kenath. She had the larger army. She had the stronger fighters. Reeking gods, she had a horde of southern conjurors, ready to do her bidding.

"The others will find out about Ellina anyway," Venick hedged.

"Eventually, but not yet."

"What do you propose we tell them, if not the truth?"

"That we searched for Ellina but never found her," Dourin supplied. "That we do not know what happened to her."

"They'll think she's dead."

"Better dead than a traitor."

Venick peered up into the sky. Clouds gathered overhead; a storm was coming. The wind picked up and it muted Dourin's voice, carrying it away.

Not far enough. Those words rang clearly in his ears. *Better dead than a traitor.* The thought swept Venick with a fierce, merciless kind of desire. He would have never believed it possible to feel this way, not about someone he'd once cared for. Yet as he envisioned Ellina, his heart filled with venom. It pulsed through his veins.

"You're right," Venick replied. "It *would* be better if she was dead."

Dourin's expression changed. "Venick..."

But Venick was already turning away. "Let's just get off this mountain."

They started back down the trail. Venick focused on his footing. On the day and the clouds and the sound of the wind in his ears. He concentrated on these things rather than his anger, which had crawled up his spine and made its den somewhere in his neck. Venick rolled his shoulders and tried to relax, to breathe deeply, to tell himself that it didn't matter, he didn't care.

Venick's anger, however, wasn't interested in platitudes. It revolted, hatching a life of its own, and soon Venick found himself replaying all his many injustices. How Ellina had used him. Tricked him. Allowed him to believe she cared about him when all she really cared about was honoring her dead sister's memory, then learning war tactics from a battle-born human.

She would use those tactics against them now. Everything he'd taught her, all the many hours they'd spent together discussing war, thinking they were on the same side…

"Venick." Dourin called out from behind, but Venick wasn't listening. He was thinking about how Ellina had been on the balcony. How cold she had seemed, how empty, how different. It was difficult to hold this new Ellina beside the memory of the one he'd come to know, the one who'd saved his life, who fought beside him, who stirred within him feelings that were warm and deep and rich…

"Venick." Dourin's voice came again. "Are you hearing me?"

"What?" Venick turned, halting at the sight of Dourin's expression. He saw it then over the elf's shoulder: a lone figure on the ridge ahead, stalking through the shadows.

"We are being followed."

...

They detoured west at a snail's pace, slow enough that their unnamed visitor could have easily closed the distance between them if he'd wanted-ed. Which he didn't. The elf—and it was an elf, Venick could see that clearly now—kept a healthy stretch of mountain between them, stopping when they stopped, moving when they moved, routing himself through the shadows in an attempt to follow unseen.

It was a poor attempt. A laughable one. Clearly, this elf was no trained assassin. No great expert in stealth, either, if his current performance was any measure. He was too obvious, too slow to duck whenever Venick glanced back. And he was *loud*, upturning gravel and muttering, the echoes of which were carried down plainly by the wind.

An assassin would've known that would happen. An Evov-born citizen might not. But a citizen would have had no reason to stay hidden, slinking behind boulders like a thief. Ask who this visitor was, then. Ask what business he had creeping along in their wake.

Or don't. It would be easy for Venick and Dourin to add a little speed and lose this elf for good. Venick had half a mind to do just that. Instead, he turned around and crossed his arms and faced their follower squarely. It took two full breaths for the elf to notice. Another two before he got his legs moving, bolting back for the shadows.

"Don't do that," Dourin muttered.

"This is taking too long. And he's an idiot."

"It could be a trap."

"Could be," Venick agreed, watching the elf peek out from behind a rock before ducking away again. "So let's ask him."

"We will. Soon."

They angled south. Overhead the storm was blowing over, pulling weak sunlight back in behind it. Venick was grateful for the late daylight, even if it did little to warm him. It was colder here than it had been these past weeks, cold enough for Venick's breath to fog the air. It rolled out of him like smoke from a chimney.

And cut off, abruptly, as they reached a sharp drop. Venick held his breath and looked down the cliff, judging the distance to the nearest jutted rock. He aimed another glance back at their follower. The elf had lost ground on them. Venick could just make out his dark outline in the distance.

They jumped the ledge. The drop to the outcrop wasn't far, but the landing was steep, and he and Dourin skidded on knees and palms before catching their balance. Together, they moved up against the ledge's crumbling wall, pressing against it to wait.

The minutes ticked by. Venick strained to hear. The wind had died down a little, which was good. It made it easier to hear—yes, *that*. The soft sound of breathing. Muted footfalls. A fresh crackle of rock tumbling loose overhead.

The elf didn't see them. He jumped the ledge right over their heads, landing just as they had, sliding on dusty earth and scrambling to keep his footing. His hands were occupied, his body exposed.

Easy prey.

In one swift movement Venick stepped forward, swinging his leg to trip the intruder while Dourin came up on his opposite side, drawing his sword and moving it to the elf's pale neck. In an instant, they had the stranger on his back, hands up in surrender.

"Who are you?" Dourin demanded.

"Please," the elf squeaked. He wore commoner's clothing—silk, finely made—and appeared unarmed. That might have been a comfort, if not for the fact that *unarmed* rarely meant *harmless*, where elves were concerned.

"Who *are* you?" Dourin asked again, touching his blade to the elf's delicate skin.

"Rahven," the elf replied quickly. "My name is Rahven. I saw you leaving the city. I know who you are, and I wish to join you."

"By following silently behind us? Why not announce yourself?"

"I was afraid."

"Afraid of what?"

"Of this!" Rahven pleaded. "Of you. I have...heard stories." His eyes darted in Venick's direction.

Venick stiffened. "Let's make this quick." He switched to elvish. "*Are you a southerner?*"

"*No.*" Rahven answered earnestly in that same language.

"*Do you have any ties to Farah or the southern army?*"

"*The Dark Queen is no friend of mine.*"

"That," Dourin said, "is not an answer."

Rahven's elven mask—already brittle—crumbled. His eyes darted fearfully between them. "Please. I am a scholar. I served *Queen Rishiana on her council before...*" He swallowed. "*I was loyal to her. Farah knows it. Her conjurors came for me. They said they would have me killed if I did not join Farah. They gave me a choice...*"

"*What choice?*"

"*Join their new regime, or die.*"

"*And so you wish to avoid death by joining us?*"

"*Yes,*" the elf answered on a breathless exhale, pressing away from Dourin's sword. "I am not a fighter," he added quickly in mainlander, "but I have other skills."

Dourin and Venick exchanged a look. Rahven wouldn't be the first non-soldier to join their group. Plenty of stateroom evacuees were former senators or scholars, too. The refugees were a burden on their army's speed and supplies, but Venick and Dourin couldn't exactly turn them away, not when saving northerners was the whole *point*.

Dourin seemed to share Venick's thoughts, because he withdrew his sword and held out a hand to help the elf up. "A scholar, did you say?"

Dourin asked.

"A chronicler, actually." Rahven brushed the dust from his trousers.

"A chronicler," Dourin repeated, making up for the rough treatment with a voice gone soft. "Well. We could use a distraction. Maybe tonight you can tell us some stories."

· · ·

Venick was careful the rest of the way down the mountain. He didn't trip again. Still, the incline was steep, the path dusted over with fragmented rock. It made for treacherous footing. When they came into view of the campsite where the rest of their party was hiding near the base of the mountain, he felt a wash of relief.

Dourin took charge of the report. *We could not find Ellina*, he explained in mainlander. *We do not know where she is. We can only hope that she escaped...* If the other elves noticed the way Dourin's mouth turned down slightly as he spoke, or how he folded and unfolded his hands at every pause, it was not mentioned. Only Rahven, who had recently come from the palace itself, might have been able to correct Dourin's claims, but after Dourin was finished he pulled the chronicler aside to speak privately, and in the end Rahven said nothing either.

Night came. The elves were ordered to light no fires. The air was bitterly cold, but Venick found that he wasn't bothered. He didn't huddle into himself, didn't grit his teeth against the wind's chill. He was glad for the cold, the discomfort. It was a distraction. It kept him from thinking of other things.

But the cold could not distract him for long, because though it was a distraction, it was a reminder, too.

It was a reminder of the mountains where Venick had been exiled.

He remembered it: the shuddering grief, the bitter days, the way his lips would crack and bleed. At night, the endless shivering, the certainty that he would never again be warm.

It was a reminder of the tundra where Venick had promised himself to Ellina. He'd wandered that barren land alone, lost, half starved. He had been so determined to reach Evov that he'd hardly noticed his wrecked body, his terrible weakness, the way his mind had become like a sunken hole.

It was a reminder of the forest where Ellina had saved his life. Where he'd pulled her into his arms and dug his fingers into her hair and kissed her. She'd kissed him back, and Venick had felt a savage sort of hope.

He'd known there could be nothing between them.

He'd clung to the idea that there could be something between them.

Venick rubbed a hand over his face and peered around their small camp. Even in the dark, he was aware of how the elves watched him. They stole glances as they gathered water or brushed their horses or hunched under cloaks. These elves didn't trust Venick, not entirely. And yet, each time he caught them looking, there seemed to be this silent expectation. They knew who he was. They knew what he had done. Humans weren't allowed inside the elflands, but here Venick was, fighting for them, befriending them. Their gazes lingered, and Venick had the sense that they were waiting for something more.

He put some distance between himself and the camp. He climbed higher into the foothills. Here, the shrubs were gnarled by the wind. The rock looked chalky and white.

The cold was a reminder of how Ellina had been cold, and how she had warmed for him.

He saw her bend to pick a flower. They were rare in the forest, but these had bloomed in a swath of dappled sunlight. Their petals were a shock of purple. Star-shaped. He remembered the way she glanced up at him. She held out the little green stem.

Venick had taken that flower from her fingers. He hesitated, shy, not yet understanding what was changing in her, what was changing between them. He'd brought the flower to his nose and inhaled. Her mouth fanned a smile.

He could see again that smile, and all the ones that came after.

Her trust in him. How strange trust was for her.

Fire in her gaze. Secrets whispered and revealed. Her willpower, utterly unbreakable.

Venick closed his eyes and remembered how it had been in the palace, teaching her the human art of war. He would move to her side, brush his shoulder against hers, just to see if she'd pull away.

He thought again of the stateroom and the balcony. Ellina's confessions in elvish. All her lies revealed.

Venick wondered if there was a part of him that was drawn to lies. He felt like a moth beating himself dizzy against a lantern's glass. Even now, he could not fully wrap his mind around what Ellina had done. It went against everything he knew about her…or thought he knew.

Venick came upon a ridge. A dark valley spanned beneath him. The night was thick—he could not see the valley's bottom. There could be an entire ocean down there. A forest. An army. There could be a whole other world and he wouldn't know it.

The truth, Venick decided, was that he hadn't really known Ellina. She was like this valley. He'd imagined the shape of her. He'd filled in the blanks with ridges and slopes. But really, those details were all in his head.

A fantasy.

NINE

Venick saw the horses trotting down the mountain path early the next morning, a whole crooked line of them. Riderless, no saddles or bags. They could have been wild, except wild horses didn't roam this far north. Even if they did, it wasn't right, the way they all filed along like that in neat order, heading straight for their camp. Which could only mean—

"You summoned homing horses?" Venick asked Dourin. Venick knew that elves could summon homing horses with their minds, even from great distances. Not all elves had the same level of skill, and not every horse responded to every elf. Only horses who were bonded to their riders would answer the call.

So. Call Dourin busy then, if this many horses answered to him.

Busy? You mean gifted, Venick.

Gifted. Hell. *Stupid*, to think he could summon a whole herd of horses and not draw unwanted attention. It wasn't the first time Dourin had made that mistake either. Venick remembered standing outside the border-city Kenath, watching two homing horses glide across the dark valley. Their bodies had been lean. Elegant. They'd parted the tall grass like ships parting waves.

Ellina had shot them dead. She had worried then what Venick worried now: that the horses could be recognized, shadow-bound, followed. They could be used to guide an enemy straight to their waiting camp. Ellina had killed Dourin's horses with a cold brutality that Venick had overlooked, because it had been convenient to overlook. *Fierce*, he'd thought of her, when what he really should have been thinking was *heartless*.

"They're not exactly inconspicuous," Venick told Dourin now.

Dourin fought a smile. "Neither are we."

"They might have been tracked."

"Would you rather *walk* across the tundra?"

Venick shot the elf a look.

"If you must know," Dourin said wryly, "I did not summon these horses from the city. They have been roaming wild. I let them loose soon after you appeared in Evov with your warning." The elf crossed his arms, settling into the posture. Pleased. "You may congratulate me on my forward thinking."

"You believed me all along." When Venick had come to Evov to warn the elves about the southern army, Dourin had always acted as if Venick was a liar. Or a lunatic.

"Perhaps."

"I sometimes really don't like you."

Dourin smirked. "Come. I have chosen one especially for you."

She was a tall buckskin mare, sleek, beautiful. Venick approached slowly, admiring her long underline, the refined neck, all well-proportioned. When he came around to her head, however, he paused. "She's blind." The horse's eyes were milky white.

Dourin said, "You *are* astute."

"How am I supposed to ride a blind horse?"

"As you would ride any horse. On her back."

"This isn't funny."

"Mildly amusing, though."

"I can't ride a blind horse."

"You are welcome to choose another." Dourin motioned around them with an easy hand.

Too easy. Venick eyed the elf, sensing a trap, though he couldn't fathom its shape or size. Dourin's face became a mask of polite interest. He clapped his fingers together, bounced them once against his hips and said, "Well?"

The scene was drawing eyes. Elves watched as Venick—apprehensive, a little uneasy—approached a sighted horse...who immediately shied away from him. Venick threw another glance in Dourin's direction, but the elf's bland smile made his message clear. He would be no help.

Frowning, Venick moved towards another sighted homing horse, but just as before, the horse shied away. She was anxious. Clearly agitated. Almost as if...

"They're afraid of me." The realization burrowed between Venick's ribs, wedged and stuck. "Because I'm human."

"Because you move like a human," Dourin corrected. "You are too aggressive."

"I don't even know what that means."

"You throw your weight around. If I were a horse, I would not want you riding me either." Dourin's expression softened. He came forward, set a hand to Venick's shoulder. "If you want to ride a sighted homing horse, you will need to learn to move like an elf. To gain control of yourself. Become more fluid."

"And if I can't learn?"

Dourin nudged him towards the buckskin. "Then you must be grateful for what you can get."

. . .

Their party moved slowly, first south, then southwest. The land below Evov was barren, the earth scattered with clumps of dry grass that looked grey and withered, that not even the horses wanted to eat. Often the trail would narrow, wedging elves together, sometimes even forcing them to move single file.

Venick never liked that. He avoided it whenever possible, riding ahead in search of alternatives. When none could be found, Venick would go first, then turn and wait as the elves came—slowly, so slowly—along behind him, squeezing between boulders or over natural river bridges one at a time. Venick would watch, and scan the surrounding lands, and try not to think about how vulnerable they looked all spread out like that. How easy it would be for an enemy to ambush them. They'd be picked off like target practice, one by one.

It's what he would have done. If Venick was in Farah's position, he would have ordered a battalion to ambush their budding army now, while they were untrained and unprepared and exposed. Farah must know that a resistance was gathering against her, which meant she must also know that *this* was her best opportunity to end that resistance. As the days wore on, Venick found himself scanning the horizon, watching for the attack he was sure to come. He could almost see it: southern elves emerging from behind rocks. Southern elves rising over the top of the hillside. The glint of their green glass arrows, bows cresting in their hands. He imagined Ellina among them, and Venick could see this, too: her slender shadow, her wind-tossed braid, the sharp outline of her silhouette. She would shoot them down as she had shot Dourin's horses down. As she had almost shot Venick down, once.

But Ellina never came. The southerners didn't. The land remained still.

Venick's horse was named Eywen, and she was a problem. Oh certainly, she was *rideable*, but only in the loosest sense of the word—she tolerated Venick on her back, but little else. And indeed, her blindness, rather than tempering her spirit, seemed to fuel it. Venick imagined the mare's delight as he urged her one way and she went the other, as he pulled back and she charged ahead. He felt his will grinding against hers, like teeth.

"You're going to get me killed," he muttered to the horse after a spectacularly bad run, gripping her mane in frustration—but not pulling. Just squeezing tight. "I swear to gods you're going to kill us both."

"I would too, if you hissed at me like that all the time," said an elf named Lin Lill. She was a former legion ranger and the benefactor of Venick's horse tack, which she'd agreed to lend him in exchange for a price yet to be named. Lin Lill rode bareback now without the use of halter or reins, leaving her hands free to pin Venick with an accusing finger. "Do you think Eywen cannot sense your frustration?"

Venick blinked.

He loosened his hold.

After that, they started to learn better. Venick stopped jerking the reins and began speaking softly in elvish, which Eywen seemed to prefer over mainlander. Eywen learned to listen to Venick's clicks and murmurs and to trust in his guidance. Slowly, they settled into each other.

Then she was unfailing.

The mountains shrank behind them. Soon, they were nothing but a hazy smear.

They neared Abith. Venick and Dourin had carefully weighed the risks of visiting a city so close to Evov, eventually deciding that Abith was a better option than Lorin or Vivvre because of its size and location. The city was small—meaning there was a chance that it had escaped Farah's notice—but still large enough to have everything a growing army might need: weapons, armor, dry goods, and the potential to recruit more soldiers.

In the evenings, Venick worked with the elves on battle formations, teaching them how to move as a single unit, how to regroup quickly in case of a surprise attack. They ran drills, Venick hollering himself hoarse as he coached the elves through a dozen possible battle scenarios. He showed them what to do if an enemy split their ranks, how to react if they lost their commander mid-fight, how to recover if an explosion rendered them deaf.

It had happened to him once. Venick had been nineteen. That year, like most years, they'd gone to war with the highlanders after those men attempted to invade the Golden Valley. The highland leader—a man they called the Elder—wanted the land because it was fertile and lush, good for growing crops. Also good for collecting wildflowers, which were used to make potions and perfumes and other, less savory materials. The lowlanders had defended that valley for centuries, and as Venick's regiment set out to war early one summer morning, they promised each other they'd defend it again.

They hadn't. The Elder, it seemed, had grown his army. There had long been rumors of the man's ever-expanding wealth and resources, but the lowlanders weren't prepared for the sheer *scale* of it, the seemingly endless supply of arrows and cannonballs and bodies. When highland troops were lost, they were quickly replaced. When food ran low, more was sent in. The Elder's army was no mere army. It was a living, breathing machine.

A month into the fighting, Venick's men were desperate. What they'd done was later praised as a stroke of brilliance, but at the time Venick had seen it for what it was: a last resort.

They called a retreat. The highlanders—believing themselves triumphant—flooded into the valley. For three nights they celebrated on that stolen land. Their victory songs rang throughout the basin.

On the fourth night, Venick and six other men loaded their supply wagons with as much black powder as they could manage. They drove the wagons into the valley where the highlanders slept. Venick remembered fields of hip-high golden wheat. Corn sprouting from its stalks. Moonlight flowed into the valley like a river of light.

A trail of black powder was poured in a straight line from the wagons to their group of seven waiting fifty paces away.

Venick hadn't lit the match, but he'd seen the man who had.

It sparked. The flame ran down the line.

They ran, and seconds later an explosion shook the world. It rendered Venick temporarily deaf. Though his vision remained unharmed, loss of hearing made the world look strange. He'd watched smoke cover the moon.

That year, the valley and all of its crops had burned. But so had their enemy.

• • •

"You are still favoring your right side," Lin Lill said, twirling the tip of her sword in Venick's face. "And you could be quicker."

"I'll never be as quick as an elf."

"Not with that attitude you won't be."

Venick pushed Lin Lill's blade away, then used his shirt to wipe the sweat from his face. They'd spent the past hour like this, sparring and bickering in turns. After four days of "freeloading my horse tack," as Lin Lill put it, she had finally named the price of the trade. Venick was to be her new sparring partner.

Venick had been quick to agree to this condition. He understood that while he had things to teach the elves about battle, they had things to teach him about swordplay. And who better to learn from than Lin Lill? As a former legionnaire and an elite ranger, she was one of their best fighters.

She was also, he learned, utterly merciless.

"Also, your draw is pathetic," Lin Lill went on. She was around his height, with a square jaw and a straight-nosed profile. Her skin was porcelain-smooth, except for a thick silver scar cutting through her left cheek. *From a knife fight with a southerner*, she'd told Venick the first time she'd caught him staring. He might have believed that, had he not later heard her tell someone else that she'd gotten the scar from a wanewolf. "Who taught you to draw your sword across your body like that?"

"That's how everyone does it."

"That is not how I do it."

The first time they'd sparred, Lin Lill had used her green glass sword to reflect the sun into Venick's eyes, then slashed open the buckles of his breastplate. He'd stood in stunned silence, not sure whether to be angry at the dirty tactic and ruined gear, or impressed.

"That is the problem with humans," she had said, clicking her teeth in irritation. "You are so *polite*."

Venick hadn't understood what she'd meant until they sparred again, and Lin Lill had executed a ruthless combination of feints that ended with Venick in a chokehold, their swords forgotten in the dirt. That time he had gotten angry, but Lin Lill remained unfazed. "I won. *How* does not matter." She spread three fingers, an elven motion meant to emphasize a point. "When your life is on the line, there are no rules."

"Tomorrow, we will practice with spears," Lin Lill said now, sheathing her sword. "In the meantime, you should work on your footwork. You are as clumsy as a—"

"Alright, Lin." Venick pressed two fingers to his temple, grinning in a way that felt more like a grimace. "I get it. I need work."

"At least you know how to take criticism."

"Almost as well as you know how to give it."

She might have chuckled at that had she been anyone else, but Lin Lill was classic granite-hard elf, blunt, humorless. Venick doubted she'd spent much time around humans. Doubted she'd ever even spoken to a human, before him. Lin Lill reminded Venick of how Ellina had been when they'd first…

He shut down that thought.

"Well," Lin Lill said, making a different hand motion now, one Venick didn't recognize. "Until tomorrow."

The sun dipped behind the horizon. Around Venick, the rest of the camp was settling in for the night, unloading horse packs and polishing armor and counting their meager stores of food and supplies. The elves worked smoothly, none in each other's way, like petals floating down a river. It was nothing like the hive of human wartime preparation, everyone crawling over everyone else, elbows and fists used if needed. This way, Venick knew, was better. Still, as he moved back towards his own tent, he found himself missing the fervor of home.

A few fires down, Rahven could be heard telling a story to a group of soldiers. True to his word, the elf spent most nights regaling tales by fireside. Sometimes, Venick stopped to listen.

He did now. Rahven was a practiced storyteller. It was his voice, Venick thought: the dips, the drawn-out pauses. Though Rahven's expression remained composed, his tone moved freely, weaving meaning into the words. His voice brought his stories to life.

"The currigon hawk has eight tailfeathers," Rahven was saying. "It is said that every feather bestowed the currigon a unique virtue. One for strength, one for cunning, for bravery, wisdom, loyalty, honesty, grace and hope. Long before elves roamed these lands, the currigon hawk was the king of beasts. He possessed these most prized qualities, and was revered.

"But the currigon had a weakness. For his feathers, though virtuous, did not prevent certain evils: arrogance, for instance, and vanity. One day, the currigon hawk came upon a young creature unlike any he had seen before. It was Vilguard, the first elf. *What beautiful feathers you have*, Vilguard said. *I would love to borrow one, just for the day. I wish to know what it is to be as wise as you.*

"The hawk, knowing better than to lend away his wisdom, refused. Yet young Vilguard was persistent. *Please, hawk. I promise to return the feather to you. Surely you could be without your wisdom for only a day? You have so many other virtues. Grace and honesty and loyalty. You are the envy of all others.* Pleased by the elf's praise, the hawk agreed, and handed over his feather of wisdom.

"Vilguard returned the next day, as promised. *Hawk! Your feather of wisdom is brilliant. I have never felt so clear of mind. Please, I must know how it feels to be brave as well. May I borrow your feather of bravery?* And the hawk, who was no longer wise enough to sense the trap, agreed.

"And so it went, the elf returning each day, asking for the next feather and then the next: strength, cunning, loyalty, honesty and grace. Vilguard took these feathers for himself, leaving the hawk only with the feather of hope, which the elf could see no value in. *What need have I for hope*, Vilguard thought, *when I have all the other virtues?* He kept these qualities for himself, and passed them to his offspring, and so on, into the generations of today.

"The hawk, without his feathers, was no longer brave enough or strong enough to take back what had been stolen. He did, however, keep the virtue of hope. That is why to this day we use currigon feathers in our fletching, in the hope that the wind will calm and our arrows will fly true. And when we see a currigon hawk in the sky, we know it as a symbol of hope."

Soon after Rahven's story was finished, the elves dispersed. Venick, however, lingered. Overhead, the night sky was clear and cloudless. The stars seemed to dance.

"She suffers."

Venick dropped his eyes. He hadn't heard Rahven approach.

"Ellina," the elf clarified, though Venick had known whom he'd meant. "She suffers."

Venick shouldn't ask. He shouldn't care what the chronicler meant by that, or why he felt the need to share it now. Ellina's suffering wasn't Venick's concern. Not anymore.

And yet...Ellina was tied to Farah, who was tied to the war and the future of his homeland. If Rahven had information about Ellina and her conditions at court, how could that *not* concern him?

It was for this reason, Venick told himself, that instead of walking away he asked, "What do you mean, she suffers?"

"As a servant of the queen, I lived in the palace. I saw Ellina a few times in the days before my escape. Something happened to her. She was hurt."

Venick ignored the way his stomach flipped at those words. He ignored the way his mind offered up a slew of images, all the many things that could have been done to Ellina since he'd seen her last. Because Venick *had* seen her, on Traegar's balcony, and she hadn't seemed injured then. Oddly wet, now that he thought about it. Shoeless. But not injured.

Then again, she'd been wearing long sleeves. A high collar. If she was hurt, would he have noticed?

"She fought in the stateroom battle," Venick replied, trying to organize the mess of his thoughts. "Many elves were hurt."

"Yes but…it was her wrists. They were bruised. And there is something else. She was not allowed to leave the palace. All the servants knew the rule. We were supposed to report to Farah if she attempted to escape."

"But Ellina did leave the palace. She came to find me in the city."

"I know, I just—I am only telling you what I witnessed." A pause. "You cared for her."

Whatever interest Venick had in this conversation died with those words. He made a noise—of disgust, of contempt, he didn't even know—and began to stalk away. Venick hated this, how his feelings for Ellina were so widely known. How they marked him.

"She was always good to us," Rahven called after him. "To those beneath her. Servants and subjects like myself. We respected her for it. Ellina was not like Miria, who tended not to notice us, or like Farah, who was cruel to us. Ellina—she was not kind, exactly. But she was good."

Venick must have halted, because he found himself facing Rahven once more. "She used to be good."

"She still is, I think."

Venick eyed the elf. "Do you know something else that I don't?"

"No."

"Really? Because it sounds like you've got more to say."

Rahven's expression was careful. His words were, too, when he finally replied. "I am sorry to have upset you. I only meant to pass on my information."

Venick returned to his own fireside. He pitched his tent in the shadowy dark, going mostly by feel, trying to distract himself with the work. He let out a hard breath.

He'd never sleep now.

He crouched by the fire, feeding pine needles into the flames, watching them shrink and curl. He thought about Ellina, imagined her in the palace, imagined that she suffered. A part of him—the newer, darker side—smiled a grim little smile. She deserved to suffer.

But another part of him—the older, quieter side—frowned. It turned its eyes back towards Evov. It filled him with questions he couldn't answer, the edge of an idea he didn't trust. Like a trick of light in the corner of his eye, it was gone before he could turn his head.

TEN

Ellina avoided her reading room.

She avoided the archives. The everpool, the stateroom, the north tower. All the places that reminded her of him.

It did not work. Ellina had known that it would not, because even if she did not visit the places that most reminded her of him, she still had to be with herself, and she could not escape her own mind.

The memories were a problem. They were always there, tugging at her attention, threatening to invade…and to show on her face. They came unbidden, bringing with them the most dangerous of feelings: doubt, regret. Ellina could not help but replay again and again the things she had said to Venick on the balcony, the words she had used to make him leave. It had pained her to speak them, a poison to eat away at her tongue. But they had worked. Venick had flinched away from them… and from her.

Seeing him like that had been like stepping onto a thin sheet of ice. The ominous creaking. The feathered veins. The certainty that she would step wrong, that the ice would crack and break and plunge her world into blackness. All it had taken was one devastated look from Venick and she had been ready to tell him everything. Her secrets. Her reasons.

Ellina moved from her writing desk to the bedroom window. Outside, the sky was a muted grey. She gazed up at the clouds and thought of snow: that white nothingness, the simple unknowing. She felt a stab of jealousy.

Ridiculous, for her to be jealous of the clouds. And misguided. Ellina did not truly wish for that kind of numbness. She needed this pain, because it was a reminder of everything that had been taken from her, and everything that might be taken still.

She stepped away from the window. A small washbasin of warm water had been set by her bedside. It was refilled twice a day by a servant Ellina never saw. Though her hands were not dirty, she dipped her fingers into the steaming water. Mist swirled around her wrists.

Maybe Venick hated her. Maybe it hurt to think of his hatred. But he was alive, was he not? He was free. And for now at least, he was out of Farah's reach. These things Ellina could be grateful for. As for Venick's hatred...Ellina still clung to the idea that if the resistance won, she would have a chance to explain everything. *I am sorry*, she would tell him. *I never wanted to hurt you*, she would tell him. The imagining gave her hope, and yet...

It could be years before the war was won. Even if Ellina was given the chance to explain herself to Venick, would he listen?

By the time he learned the truth, would it be too late?

. . .

There were other memories. Little moments, random conversations between them. Ellina remembered the way Venick spoke her language: fluently, with only the hint of an accent. She remembered the way his mouth tended to lift at the corners. His winter eyes, always on her. Ellina did not mean to allow these memories to rule her, but they were all she had.

Until the night she had her first dream.

Elves did not dream, not like humans did. Yet as Ellina dipped to sleep one night, she *saw* things. Not a memory. Not a recollection. This was nothing that had ever happened before.

She saw herself curled in Venick's arms. They lay on a grassy slope overlooking a deep valley. The sky was wide open, the weather warm and dry. Springtime, or maybe summer. Ellina could smell the soap Venick had used to bathe. His scruff tickled her cheek as he leaned down to whisper in her ear. *I am yours*, he said, *as long as you'll have me.*

She turned in his arms. She wanted to see his face. His lips parted under her gaze.

Well, Ellina? Will you have me?

She startled awake in her bed. The room was dark. She was breathing too heavily. Afraid.

And then, more afraid when the dream slid from her mind. Was it normal for dreams to disappear so quickly? She tried to hold onto the vision. She clung to its wispy threads, but too late. Already, the dream was gone.

• • •

The palace's main dining hall was full of elves when Ellina arrived the following morning. Farah had sent word with a servant that they would take their breakfast there today rather than in the queen's private chambers. The letter had simply instructed that Ellina arrive at the appointed time. It had not stated a reason.

The atmosphere in the hall was lazy that morning as soldiers and servants slowly waked, lounging in cushioned chairs at any one of the hall's three long tables, cupping their tea and talking of small things. Ellina scanned the room, noting the elves she knew: a few senators, several guards. And one legionnaire.

Kaji watched Ellina from his seat across the room. Aside from Raffan, Kaji was the last of her troopmates to remain in the city. The elder elf met her eye, then looked pointedly down the table.

To where Raffan was sitting. He too watched Ellina. His face remained carefully impassive as she came to claim the chair across from him, rather than the one to his right—the one meant for his bondmate. Raffan had watched Ellina do this many times now, but said nothing. Their bondmating had been ordered by Queen Rishiana, and Rishiana was gone. Though this did not absolve Ellina and Raffan of their duty, the only elf who could enforce their bonding now was Farah, and Farah had shown little interest in doing so.

"You are late," Raffan muttered. "Farah is unhappy."

Ellina unfolded a cloth napkin from the table and set it in her lap. She smoothed the fabric over her thighs, searching the room for her sister, but Farah was nowhere. "That is an interesting trick," Ellina commented, "for my sister to know that I am late, and feel unhappy over it, when she herself is not even here."

"That is not what I meant."

There was a pause. Raffan was waiting for Ellina to ask, *Then why is Farah unhappy?* so that he could drag out his answer, and watch Ellina twist under the knife of whatever information he had that she did not. It was a move she had seen Raffan use on others. One that put him in a position of power.

"Well," Ellina said instead, "whatever the reason, *you* should be able to assuage her."

Raffan threw her a sharp look. After the stateroom battle, Ellina had accused Farah of loving Raffan. Though she was no longer sure if it was true—she had seen no more affection between them since that day—her words seemed to touch a nerve. Raffan's mood soured. "Youvan reports that things did not go according to plan in the city."

"Farah and I have already spoken about that." Ellina had given her sister the same story she had given Youvan, and Youvan—apparently unwilling to make a fool of himself twice—had confirmed it.

"You spoke with another elf," Raffan said.

"As Farah instructed."

"No. She ordered you to speak with the human. Yet Youvan reports that when he arrived, you were talking to an elf. The human only arrived after." Raffan leaned forward. "Who was that other elf?"

Ellina did not like this. She did not like how Raffan was probing into a topic Farah had not, or how each of his words struck like a hammer on a wedge, widening the cracks in her plot. "Youvan did not say?"

"He did not know."

Was that possible? The northern legion was divided into several dozen troops just like Ellina's, but Ellina's regiment had been well known, in part because of her. It was unusual for highborns to serve in the legion, and Ellina was not only that, but also the queen's daughter. Her status had always drawn attention, both to herself and to her troop.

And yet, Youvan was from the south. He would have had no reason to learn the identities of Ellina's troopmates. Even if Youvan did know

Dourin, it was possible that he knew him by name only. But Ellina had not used Dourin's name in Youvan's presence...had she?

A palace servant appeared then, bearing a platter of fruit and cheese. She fussed around the table, poring broth, offering watered wine. Ellina watched her in silence.

She could lie. She could tell Raffan that the other elf was no one. She could say it in elvish.

But what if Raffan already knew the elf was Dourin? What if this was some sort of test?

"I do not see why it matters," Ellina said after the servant had bustled away. "I passed along Farah's message as instructed. That other elf was no one important."

Raffan switched to elvish. "*But you did know him.*"

Ellina had no choice now but to follow Raffan into that language. She took a risk. "*No. He was no one I had ever met.*"

Raffan did not immediately react, except to lean back in his seat. Ellina waited. She could not read his thoughts, and as the silence continued she felt how it peeled her open, digging fingers under her nerves, plucking at them like strings.

Raffan said, "You think you are safe, but you are not."

He knew. Ellina's stomach bottomed even as she opened her mouth to explain, to find some way to twist her way out of this. Raffan spoke again. "Farah had planned for Youvan to kill your human."

Ellina shut her mouth. Her thoughts spun. "She *what?*"

"Did you think Farah truly cared to pass him a message?" Raffan's laugh was dark. "It was a ploy, Ellina. You were supposed to lead Youvan to the human. Youvan was going to start a fight that ended in his death. That was the plan."

Ellina felt as if she had plunged into the river all over again. She could not catch her breath. "But Youvan did not kill him. What changed Farah's mind?"

"I did."

"You—?"

"You and Farah had a deal. You would give Farah your support, and Irek—including all of its citizens—would remain unharmed. I convinced Farah that if the human died, you would retaliate, and then Youvan would have to kill *you*." Raffan would not look at Ellina. He adjusted his sleeves, pulling them down over his wrists. "I could not let that happen."

But this made no sense. Ellina and Raffan were not allies. They were not even friends…not anymore. Not since their bondmating had ruined things between them. Half the time, Ellina thought Raffan might want to kill her himself.

"Raffan." Her voice drew his eyes back to her. "I do not understand."

He did not elaborate. Instead, he pushed away from the table. "You should know that Farah has arranged for you to visit the servants' quarters with Youvan. One of the servants was caught breaking their new curfew. Farah suspects that he was somewhere he should not have been, and she wants to know why."

So *that* was why Farah was unhappy. "I was never trained in interrogation."

"You will not be doing the interrogating. You are simply there to observe." And with that, he quit the table.

Ellina slouched in her seat. She rubbed a thumb over one hand, feeling suddenly exhausted. It was the confusion, she thought. The dizzying turns this conversation had taken. Who was the servant Farah wanted her to see?

And more importantly, why?

. . .

The servants stood stiff and still at attention. They crowded together in one corner of the kitchen, their shoulders touching. The palace kitchens were large enough that the servants could have laid flat with their arms and legs outstretched and still plenty of room to spare, but these elves were afraid. They huddled like cornered mice under Youvan's cold gaze.

Youvan had come to collect Ellina shortly after breakfast, then marched them down to the working quarters in silence. The path to the kitchens was dark, the interlocking passages dank and narrow. Here, there were no jeweled sconces or merry fireplaces, no windows ablaze with morning sunlight. Instead, a single, smoking torch had been affixed to the wall at the tunnel's entrance. Ellina had taken up that torch, intending to light the way, but Youvan had sneered. "Do you think you are to be trusted with such a weapon?"

"You take it then," Ellina replied, and thrust the torch toward him.

He jerked away. "No."

"Then how will we see?"

"Conjurors do not need fire to see in the dark."

That information was new to Ellina, but she said only, "I am not a conjuror."

"That is none of my concern."

He wanted to be difficult. He wanted to punish Ellina for the way things had gone in the city, or to make her angry enough that she would say something she would regret. Ellina stared at the torch in her hand. She envisioned doing with it what Youvan worried she would do with it.

Carefully, she set the torch back in its frame. "Let's go."

Now, they stood in the low light of the kitchens. Youvan had turned up his nose at the closed, stifling heat, ordering that the oven fires be doused. Then he commanded that every kitchen servant—maybe thirty elves total—come to stand before him. The elves, wide-eyed and wordless, did as he said.

Youvan spoke. "Which one of you broke curfew last night?"

The servants stared. Their faces hung like pale moons in the dim light. No one replied.

"Let us not make this difficult." Youvan paced down the line. "It has come to my attention that one of you was out after hours. Perhaps, because you have never before had a curfew, you presume this new rule does not apply to you. Or is it simply that you do not care to follow Queen Farah's orders?"

More silence.

"I need an answer." Youvan halted. Some color had returned to his cheeks now that he again wore his own shadow, though it did little to soften him. "I will question each of you one by one if I must, and you will not like my methods."

Still no reply.

"Very well." Youvan drew a green glass dagger from within his robes. Ellina had never seen Youvan with a weapon. Most conjurors did not carry them. "If that is how you wish it to be…"

"Wait." An elf pushed forward from the back of the group. He was younger than the others, his shoulders stooped, muscles undefined. He tried to meet Youvan's gaze and failed. "It was me."

Youvan tipped his head. "What is your name?"

"Ermese."

"Ermese. Your cooperation will be rewarded. Any defiance will be punished. Do you understand?" Ermese gave a nod. "What were you doing snooping around the palace after dark?"

The servant's eyes flicked up. "I was not snooping."

"Now." Youvan fingered the dagger. It occurred to Ellina that he had brought that weapon merely so that he could use it as he was using it now: as a means of intimidation. "What did I say about rewarding your cooperation?"

"It is true," Ermese insisted. "I was…visiting the crypts. To pay my respects to the dead."

"Really."

"Yes."

"Say it in elvish."

The servants stiffened. Ellina did, too. She watched the young servant lick his lips, his head bobbing on a too-skinny neck, the soft skin of his throat exposed. "*I went to the crypts,*" Ermese began in elvish, "*so that I could—*"

The words caught in his chest. He doubled over, gagging.

Youvan gave the dagger an idle twirl. "Try again."

"*I went…*" Ermese wheezed, hands braced against his knees. "*I went to the crypts because…*"

"Because you were spying," Youvan interjected. "What did you see, down in the crypts?"

"N-nothing."

"In *elvish.*"

But this, Ermese could not do. He strained, his tongue working uselessly as he fought against the power of their language. It did not matter what he would have said. He was no conjuror, northern or otherwise, and his attempts at a lie were obvious.

The servant knew his own doom. He glanced at Ellina: a helpless plea.

"Look at *me*," Youvan snapped. "We do not pay respects to our dead. We do not believe in an afterlife, or in the gods. We do not think there is anything down there to pay respects *to*. No one goes to the crypts, except to bury bodies."

"That...that is not true."

"You went to the crypts because you were snooping. You were looking for information to be used against Queen Farah."

"No, I swear—"

"Who are you passing your information to?"

"No one."

"Do you know," Youvan warned, "what I will do if you continue to lie to me?" In a motion too quick for Ellina to follow, Youvan hurled his dagger into the cluster of onlooking servants. The blade missed hitting anyone—barely—but the servants reacted with predictable panic, some crying out, others ducking to flee. Ellina cried out, too. "What are you *doing*?" She gripped Youvan by the sleeve.

He shook her off. "Do not interfere." He bore down on a petrified Ermese. "Do you take me for a fool? Do you think we do not know that the resistance has spies among us? Or perhaps you did not consider that we might have our own spies, like the ones in Abith, waiting to attack your friends as soon as they step foot within those city walls. Our messenger-raven reports movement from your ranks—"

"I swear, I am not—"

"We are *everywhere*, and your attempts at espionage are pitiful. This is your last chance. I need a name. I want to know who is leading you, or the next time I throw my knife, I will not miss."

"Please," Ermese begged. "I am not a spy."

"*Say it in elvish.*"

Ellina's heart was pounding hard. Youvan's dagger lay on the floor at the back of the kitchen. She could grab it. Or perhaps she could find another weapon. A knife, or a heavy pot. The kitchen was full of them.

And if Youvan realized what she intended? He would stop her, and there would be consequences.

But if she did nothing? This servant would suffer. He would suffer as surely as she would.

Ellina was scanning the counters for a nearby weapon when Youvan lifted his hands.

"Wait," Ellina said, but her plea was drowned out by the sound of Ermese's scream. He folded at the waist, clutching his face with both hands as Youvan seemed to dig in, bearing down, grinding the air with his fingers. Ellina watched in frozen horror as Ermese clawed at his eyes, his scream devolving into choked cries. He whimpered, gulping air.

Youvan relaxed his grip. The servant went silent. When he pulled his shaking hands away, Ellina flinched. The elf's eyes were white. Blank and blurred over. Youvan had conjured him blind.

ELEVEN

Ellina's knock was loud on Kaji's door.

The legionnaire's room—just a single room, not a suite—was located in the palace's lowest guest chambers. Though these halls were a step above mountain-underground, the air here was chilly, the corridors heavily patrolled by guards. When Kaji answered, his brows rose in surprise. Ellina cut him off before he could speak. "I brought you something."

The elder elf glanced at what she held. "A book?"

"May I come in?"

He stepped aside to allow her through.

Ellina waited until he had closed the door behind them before tossing the book onto a divan, then striding to the window to peer out across the palace grounds. The sky was bruised with the coming dusk, the night's first stars blinking to life. In the distance, Ellina could just see the stone gardens.

Kaji's voice changed. "A diversion." He noted the book's cover. "Still, an interesting choice."

Ellina spun around. "Have there always been so many guards stationed outside your door?"

"They suspect me. Probably more so now that the princess is visiting me in my private chamber, delivering books."

Ellina shot him a flat look, then told him what had happened in the kitchens. By the time she finished, Kaji had sobered. "His eyesight?"

"Gone," Ellina said.

"But why *was* the servant down in the crypts? He is not truly one of our spies." Kaji rubbed a palm over his chin. "This is cause for concern."

"I agree. If Farah is hiding something…"

"That is not what I meant. It is concerning that conjurors are using their power against servants. It always starts with the lowest ranking among us, but who will be next? You need to be careful, Ellina, and I think—" He broke off. "Do I want to know what you are doing?"

Ellina had opened Kaji's wardrobe and was rummaging through its contents. "I need your legion uniform." When Kaji did not reply, she glanced over her shoulder. "We are about the same size."

"Yes, but why—?"

"I need to get to the everpool without being seen. And this—" she pulled at her own clothing, the loose silk, billowing trousers practically *made* for tripping "—is all wrong."

Kaji's disapproval was clear. "It will be dark soon. Did you, or did you not, just witness a conjuror blind a servant for breaking curfew?"

"Farah's curfew does not apply to me."

"You are a fool if you believe that."

"I will not be caught."

"Double the fool."

Ellina held up a black shirt, then discarded it in the growing pile at her feet. "I learned something else in the kitchens. Farah has soldiers stationed in Abith. They will ambush the resistance when they pass through that city. Dourin cannot go that way."

"If Dourin has not reached Abith already, one more night will make no difference. You could wait until morning to send your message."

"This cannot wait."

"Honestly Ellina, you should not be going at all."

At last, Ellina found what she had been looking for. She pulled Kaji's legion uniform from the back of his wardrobe and began undressing. Kaji turned dutifully away. "I thought we agreed," he said with his back to her. "We will gather information as it comes to us, nudge events as we can, but we should not take unnecessary risks."

"This risk is necessary."

"If your mother was here—"

"If my mother was here, none of this would be happening," Ellina interrupted. "But she is not here. She is gone."

"And missed," Kaji said gently.

Ellina slowed her buttoning. Her chest expanded: a breath full of words she did not know how to speak.

Ellina and her mother had never been close. They were too different. They even looked different. Rishiana was tall, regal, with moon-white hair and a proud, sharp face, while Ellina was small and lean, dark-haired, wiry. Ellina looked more like her eldest sister Miria, whose hair was also black. It was Farah who most closely resembled the queen.

And so it had surprised Ellina, how deeply the knife of her mother's death seemed to reach. Ellina felt as if *she* was the one who had been stabbed, as if it was her blood pouring out onto the floor. Worse, she felt guilty that her grief was so unexpected. She and Rishiana might not have been close, but her mother was still her mother.

Ellina had mourned Rishiana, albeit in silence. This was very elven. Elves grieved by staying quiet, by not speaking of the dead. To discuss those lost was to tarnish the memory of their lives, it was said. To show outward grief was dishonorable. For an elf to mourn properly, she should think of death, and remember life, and move on.

How convenient for Farah, Ellina thought bitterly, that she did not have to feign her grief. How ironic, that the daughter who most closely resembled the mother had been the one to take her life.

Ellina paused on that thought. Something—some half-formed idea—nudged her mind.

"There was a reason my mother did not want Farah to be queen," Ellina said slowly.

"Yes," Kaji agreed. "Farah has shown her true self."

Ellina was not sure that was what she meant, but she quickly finished dressing and said only, "You can turn around now." Kaji did. He appraised her, then glanced at the book on his divan. "Keep it," Ellina told him. "If you need to reach me, you can pretend you are returning it."

"Yes, but could you not have chosen something more…subtle?"

Elves and War was the title of the volume Ellina had chosen to bring. It was the same book she had given Venick a month earlier when he was bedridden from a knife wound to the hip and insistent on teaching her battle strategy. Ellina remembered Venick's surprise when he realized what she had brought. *Elves have books about war?* he had asked.

History books, mostly, Ellina replied.

Books about the purge, you mean.

It was a bloody mark on their history. Centuries ago, conjurors had not been elven, but human. Human conjurors possessed many of the same powers elven conjurors did today, using their magic to shape stone and summon shadows and weave storms. Elves—concerned with what humans might do with that kind of power—decided to put it to an end. They rounded up human conjurors, beheaded them and burned the bodies.

Necessary, Ellina's mother said when she first told her daughters the story. *We did it to protect ourselves. Humans are undisciplined. They cannot be trusted with such power.*

Messy, others said later, when Ellina had grown older. *Do you know how much blood a human body contains? Do you know what they smell like when they burn?*

She had not, at least not then. But she had learned. In the legion, Ellina had killed more humans than she cared to count. Occasionally they burned the bodies. The smell was acrid, sometimes even sweet. It would cling to Ellina's clothes for days.

"I think the book is fitting," Ellina said.

Kaji twirled the single golden ring he wore on his smallest finger, then dropped his hand to his dagger, unbelting it. "If you must go, take this."

"Kaji, no. If I am caught, they will trace it back to you."

"I thought you said you will not be caught."

"In which case I will not need a dagger anyway."

The elf's brow creased. He looked as if he might again try to council Ellina on the perils of making reckless choices, but in the end he merely sighed and said, "Be careful."

Ellina offered a small smile. Then she climbed out his window.

• • •

She knew her route. She had planned it carefully, running through it so many times that it seemed burned behind her eyes. Ellina leapt from Kaji's window onto an awning, then down into a windy courtyard. It was fully night now, and Ellina listened as deer listen, for the faintest sound, a footstep, a breath. She darted quickly through the shadows, concealed in the dark in Kaji's uniform. She was not seen.

The everpool glowed in the moonlight. It looked exactly as it always did: pearled, calm. Despite the wind whipping through the stony garden square, the water remained still.

Ellina stepped to the pool's edge. It was impossible not to remember the last time she had come here. She had asked Venick to accompany her, gripped by a wanting she could no longer deny…and an uncharacteristic daring whose danger she should have recognized.

It is an everpool, she had explained. All elves knew about the power of the everpools, but most humans did not. *You step inside and ask it your questions. Sometimes, it gives you answers.*

Ellina slipped out of her shoes and rolled up the hem of Kaji's pants. She stepped into the pool on the far side where the water was most shallow, no more than ankle deep, and pulled a letter from her pocket. The message she had scrawled was simple. *There are soldiers waiting for you in Abith. They will attack as soon as you arrive. You must not go that way.*

Quietly, Ellina whispered to the water in elvish. "*I come bearing a message for Dourin. Show it to him and him alone, should he ask for it.*" She set the parchment into the pool.

As soon as paper met water, the everpool began to ripple, not from the point of contact but from its center—the everpool's core. The water glowed faintly, shining with a light from within. The message vanished, and the water stilled once more.

Ellina exhaled. It was done, she could go. Yet she stared at that water a moment longer, envisioning the network of everpools that would carry her message into Dourin's waiting hands. She thought of her letter traversing leagues in an instant, zipping along its way.

She imagined that she had gone with it.

TWELVE

Venick was up early. His sleep had been fitful, marked by strange dreams. He'd woken long before the sky began to turn, staring at the vaulting ceiling of his tent, counting the minutes until dawn.

Eventually, he gave up. Morning would come when it did, but hell if he'd keep waiting. Venick rolled to his knees, shrugged on a borrowed jacket. He began his preparations in the dark: bundling belongings, breaking down his tent, carefully stowing Traegar's book. In his pocket he secured the silver necklace that he still carried, but never wore. He tried to work slowly, to draw out the tasks until morning, but by the time he'd finished the sky remained stubbornly black.

He went to Dourin's tent. Knowing it would annoy the sleeping elf—and maybe doing it in part for that reason—Venick called to him. When Dourin didn't answer, Venick stuck his face through the tent's flap. There was a rumpled bedroll, a burnt-out lantern, the scattered remains of today's breakfast rations…and no Dourin.

Venick let the flap fall closed. Around the camp, a few other early risers were stirring. The morning was murky, the air thick with fog. Venick walked between tents and bedrolls, asking if anyone had seen Dourin. *No*, the elves replied, and *no* and *no*.

Venick busied himself with more chores, undoing things he had done already to do them again. He was brushing Eywen sometime after dawn when Dourin reappeared.

"Where've you been?" Venick asked. He heard the accusing note in his voice and smoothed it out. "I went to your tent this morning, but you—"

"I think we should head to the lowlands first," Dourin interrupted.

Venick lifted the brush off Eywen's back, surprised. "I thought we already agreed." An old feeling rose up within him, as if in greeting. It clung to his throat, changed his voice. "We agreed that we'd recruit our elven allies first. And Abith—it's less than a day's ride away. You want to reroute us *now*?"

"I had thought that best, too. To head to Abith, then work our way north. But I do not think that plan is wise anymore." Dourin went to retrieve his map, returning to unroll it against Eywen's broad side. "Abith is not as safe as we assumed. Farah has soldiers stationed there. They will be waiting to ambush us as soon as we arrive. We are not strong enough to stand against them, not as we are now. We should veer south instead."

"How do you know they're waiting to ambush us?"

"It is obvious."

Venick peered at the elf.

"We thought Farah might have overlooked Abith," Dourin continued. "But we did not consider that Abith is the only city between Evov and Vivvre. Farah's army will have to pass through it. When they do, she will leave a contingent behind."

"Leaving a contingent behind is not the same thing as planning an ambush."

"Let's assume that it is."

"We can't afford to change course now. We need supplies. We need to recruit more soldiers to our side before Farah recruits them to hers."

"And we will. In Ulla and Esota."

But Venick was still skeptical. "Those are farming villages. Small."

"And more likely to have escaped Farah's notice." Dourin rolled up the map and tucked it under his arm. "We will reroute through those villages before heading for the lowlands."

"I still don't understand. If we sent a scout ahead to Abith—"

"It was *your* idea to travel to the mainlands first."

"Yes, but—"

"You are afraid."

Venick froze. "What?"

"To go home. You have not been back to the lowlands in almost four years. You are afraid."

Venick began brushing Eywen again, slowly. He watched her coat twitch and jump under the bristles. "I was banished." Venick had only ever told the story of his banishment once before. He wasn't sure he wanted to tell it again. But he made himself say, "I killed my father."

After Venick had fled into exile, he'd tried to understand how it had happened. He'd spent four years trying to understand it. He would sit, head in hands, thumbing through the memories—not just of the murder, but all the days and weeks leading up to it. He pulled at their strings in an attempt to untangle it all, but in the end he only ever made a tighter knot.

Venick regretted killing his father...and he didn't. If given the chance, he wasn't sure he would take it back. Wasn't sure he *could*.

But his mother. Venick realized that he'd stopped brushing Eywen, that he was staring blankly at her thick side. His mother had been a gentle woman. Kind, softhearted. Young, when Venick had been born. Young when he left. She didn't deserve what had been done to her. What *he* had done.

Venick met Dourin's eye. "The law says I get my chance at redemption, but my father wasn't just anyone. He was a military general. High-ranking, well-respected, all of it. And he served on the council. Irek took his death as a personal offence. They won't welcome me back."

"We do not need their welcome," Dourin replied. "We just need them to listen."

"You say that like it's simple."

"It will be." The elf patted the map under his arm, and though Venick had not actually agreed to anything, Dourin nodded as if he had. "I will tell the others."

. . .

Their party altered course. The land changed as they traveled, rocky paths giving way to barren tundra and later, soft grasslands. The weather warmed a little as they moved south, bringing with it the smell of soil and rain. Insects hummed, their *ticks* and *burrs* a constant symphony.

As discussed, they passed through Ulla and Esota and any other elven village they happened upon, always with the same message. *The queen is dead by Farah's hand. We gather a resistance against her. Will you join us?* The elven villagers were not trained warriors, but living out here in the most remote regions of the elflands had taught them a few things about survival, and survival was, ultimately, all war *was*. The village elves knew how to mix salves and set bones, how to slide unseen through tall grass and send coded signals using birdsong. Better than that, they were eager. Most of these elves knew about the stateroom coup. Some had even witnessed the southern army trekking north. Like an apparition, one elf described. Like the shadow under a storm. The Dark Army, as elves had begun to call it, was like nothing they had ever seen before. The villagers understood the danger and wanted to fight.

It was in this way that their group grew from sixty to eighty to many hundreds of elves and more.

In the evenings, Venick continued drilling their new soldiers, then used whatever sunlight remained to spar with Lin Lill. Sometimes Dourin would join the sparring too, which inspired his old troopmates Artis and Branton to join, which inspired the other legionnaires, and Rahven, and everyone else, until the whole camp was finishing their afternoon drills with more drills. At the end of one of their sessions, Branton gave Venick the same elven hand motion Lin Lill had made once before, the one Venick didn't recognize. The elf spread his fingers, then clutched them in a fist over his chest.

Venick asked Dourin what the motion meant.

"Oh, that," Dourin replied, his eyes cutting sideways. "It is how we show respect for our commanders."

Venick's reply was automatic. "I'm not the elven commander."

"No? Then who is?" When Venick didn't answer, Dourin gave a wide-eyed laugh. "You thought it would be *me*? Oh, little human. You are as blind as your horse."

Except, Venick had seen this. He saw it in the way the elves looked at him with their shining eyes, in the way he gave an order and it was obeyed. He saw it when they ran drills or divvied rations or organized their tents at night in spirals rather than in rows, just as Venick had instructed.

It was in the way the elves had begun to smile at him. Their hesitant lips pulling up at the corners, uncertain, trying it out. Emulating him, as children do.

"You cannot be surprised," Dourin went on in a voice that might have either been serious, or mock serious. "Who better to lead us than the mighty, battle-born warrior?"

"I just…" Venick sought to name his doubt. "I'm human."

"So?"

"The elves wouldn't choose a human to lead them."

Dourin dropped his teasing tone. "Venick." For once, his smile was true. "They already have."

. . .

They left autumn behind. The days grew longer as they moved deeper into southern elflands and then—unceremoniously, but with a meaningful look exchanged amongst them—over the border into the mainlands.

Venick had been thinking a lot. He tried to think less. He focused on the land, the sky. At night, he browsed Traegar's book by lamplight. What started as simple interest became habit, then necessity. Venick wasn't sleeping well, but the book was an easy distraction. It lulled him into a kind of non-thinking, helped set him closer to sleep. He would prop the volume up on one knee and read about plants and potions until his lids grew heavy, until he began to see ingredient lists dancing behind his eyes. Then he would drop—thankfully, mercifully—into dreams.

Except that sometimes he didn't. Sometimes, no amount of reading could lull him. On those nights, Venick would lie awake, gazing up at the dark canvas of his tent. He liked to pretend that his sleeplessness was born of anxiety over his homecoming. That it was due to thoughts of seeing his mother and the anticipation of his redemption. He told himself that his restless mind had everything to do with his future and not his past. Yet Venick had come to learn the shape a lie might take, especially in the dark, especially with himself.

He would think of Ellina. Sometimes it was a memory, sometimes simple fantasy. Her face would float in his mind, as vivid as if she was lying there next to him, and his anger would stun him all over again. Then Venick would grimace, and stand from his tent, and rove the dark camp. The night would envelop him. The world would be still, except for the occasional soldier, and Rahven, who seemed haunted by his own demons and slept even less than Venick did.

Venick left the campfires behind. He sought the glittering stars, the call of bullfrogs, and the way that on moonless nights it became so dark that he couldn't see his own hands. He would hold them blindly in front of his face and feel as if he didn't exist at all.

...

Irek appeared like a ship over the horizon: the mast, then the sail, then all the rest.

Venick thought he had remembered. If anyone had asked, he would have answered easily. Of course he remembered this place. He'd been born in Irek, he'd grown up there. And anyway, four years away was not so long a time. Four years couldn't erase what he'd spent a lifetime knowing. Irek was his home. *Of course* he remembered it.

But he hadn't. Not really.

Now though, as he watched the city emerge in the distance, it all came rushing back. Those buildings, those roads, the ocean. There would be bugs in the dirt, lizards in the trees. Venick knew how the afternoon market would swell with sound, the way it would smell. He knew how it felt to stand on the shore, to close his eyes and stretch out his arms and turn his face to the sun. The memories washed over him like an ocean wave, leaving him drenched, shaking, salt-stung. They caught his breath, and he hadn't even set foot inside Irek's boundaries yet. He hadn't been home in years.

Home.

The word was a cold blast of air. It dried the salt of memories to his skin.

Home.

That feeling—the one he'd been nursing ever since Dourin first suggested this change of course—ballooned. It pushed up between his ribs, shallowed his breath.

Home.

He thought of his mother. He thought of his father.

He slowed Eywen to a stop.

"Well, human?" Dourin rode to his side. The elf's long white hair danced in the breeze. It matched his white horse, who was slender and fierce and named—Dourin had told him this with a grin—Grey. "What say you?"

Venick was quiet. Then he said, "I think I've explained that my people won't—*rejoice* at my return?"

Dourin's tone was arch. "You may have mentioned it."

"As in, it's possible that I'll be attacked as soon as I set foot inside the city."

"Lucky you."

"I need to find my mother first. And I need to do it before anyone recognizes me."

Dourin made an impatient gesture. "So pull up your hood and walk fast."

"It's not that simple. I'm not even sure where she lives anymore." Venick doubted Lira would have chosen to stay in the house where she'd watched her son murder her husband. It wasn't easy, scrubbing bloodstains out of wood. It couldn't be easy scrubbing that kind of memory out, either. Even with a good scrubbing, there had been a lot of blood. Venick had a hard time imagining his mother walking over that spot every day. Washing linens, cooking, hosting company on her husband's remains.

"So what are you saying?" Dourin asked.

"I'm saying that we don't just walk in."

The elf made a show of looking him over. "You haven't exactly sprouted wings."

"No," Venick replied. "But I do have an idea."

THIRTEEN

There was a saying in Irek. *She stands strong on weathered legs.* It was meant to be inspirational, an ode to their people. Irek was a secluded city, built at the ocean on the edge of the world. Her people were grizzled, older, mostly women. That wasn't surprising, not when you considered that all the young men born in Irek went to battle, and most young men died there.

But the saying was true in the literal sense as well. With an ocean to the south and marshlands to the north, Irek's buildings were at the mercy of tides and shifting sands and summer storms. Flooding wasn't uncommon. Neither was erosion. To combat these elements, many of Irek's homes had been built on wooden stilts. They dotted the land like tall, spindly-legged water bugs.

She stands strong. Of course, the saying had its ironies. The buildings didn't always stand strong. Once or twice a year, a home would collapse into the marsh, sometimes with its inhabitants still inside. Wood rot would do that. So would the wind storms. To help prevent this kind of downfall, an intricate network of ropes had been rigged between buildings, tethering them together, neighbors holding neighbors strong.

Not the best system, if you thought about it—which Venick had often as a boy. The most obvious issue was that if a house did collapse, it might drag several others down with it. A childhood friend of Venick's had died that way, crushed under his own home after it was pulled down by another. When Venick tried voicing this concern to his father, however, he was quickly silenced.

We do it this way because we've always done it this way, his father had replied in a tone that brooked no argument. *It is custom.*

Call it yet another hallmark of their people, this stubbornness for tradition, the unwillingness to change. You rigged your house to your neighbor's even if you knew it was stupid, even if theirs looked ready to fall, because that's how things had always been done. Because they'd do it for you. Solidarity won out over common sense, every time.

Venick found himself smiling vaguely at the memory. He realized how he must look and wiped the smile from his face. Not that there was anyone to see him, hidden here in the river reeds at the city's edge, but still…what did he have to smile about? The tragic passing of a friend? His father's inflexibility? It was inflexibility that led to his father's death, in the end.

To his murder, you mean.

Venick put the thought away. He refocused on what he was doing, which was examining a network of such ropes and riggings, and the two watchtowers they tethered together.

He readjusted the axe in his hand.

There were no walls around Irek. The city's leaders often argued over the merits of building a wall, something huge and fortified like the battlements containing the highland capitol of Parith where the Elder lived, but whenever the issue was raised it was invariably shut down. Walls were for cowards, the lowlanders said. If a man wanted to protect his home, he did it with steel and muscle and his own two fists. The citizens of Irek were not rabbits to hide in their warrens.

This was—Venick thought with another almost-smile—somewhat disingenuous, since the marshlands made it difficult for an enemy to invade Irek by land, and thereby acted as a *natural* wall. But no one ever mentioned that.

Venick stood knee-deep in those marshy waters now, staring up at the two watchtowers that marked the city's entrance. The towers hadn't just been built on stilts—they were *mostly* stilts. Thin, crisscrossed wooden bars led to a small box perched at the top of each where the watchman would sit. An eagle's nest in a tree.

For the dozenth time, Venick checked his surroundings, and for the dozenth time, he found himself alone. There wasn't anyone in sight—not his army, which was hidden in the nearby northern woods, or even Dourin, who waited in the reeds on the watchtower's opposite side. It was early afternoon, meaning the city would be awake and alive, but the watchtowers were set away from the main streets, too far for anyone to simply wander this way, unless they had business.

Please, that no one did today. Please, that the road leading into the city stayed empty of travelers as Venick lifted the axe over his head and brought it down again with a heavy-handed swing.

The *whack* of the weapon through the rigging. The *zizz* of the rope splitting under the blade, buckling up into the air. One of the watchtowers gave a shudder as its support fell away, but remained standing. That was good. Venick didn't want it to collapse.

Not yet, anyway.

He left his axe in the river and sloshed out of the brown water. Luckily, it wasn't that uncommon to see townspeople in various stages of *muddy* and *wet*, since many families had to climb through the muck to reach their own front doors. True, some houses had canoes, slender river rafts designed to sweep women and children from their doorsteps to dry land and back again, but such vessels were a luxury. It was a symbol of status in Irek to be able to move in and out of your own home without soiling your skirts.

Some luxury.

But wasn't this what Venick had missed about his city? Wasn't it *this?* The gritty earth, the sticky air, the muddy roads and dirty horses and wayward people? Even now, Venick could hear the occasional burst of laughter from distant streets, and the low beat of drums, which were often played and shared—the instruments passed around in turns—for the enjoyment of all. This was Irek: soggy boots and lively music and shared pleasures.

Venick shook off the worst of the mud before climbing the wooden ladder up the watchtower. He balanced on the skinny platform at the top and rapped the door with his fist.

The answering watchman was middle-aged, unshaven, groggy. He squinted at Venick as if he were far away. "What'd you want?"

Venick arranged his expression into his best imitation of urgency. "This watchtower. It's about to fall. You need to get down immediately."

The man rubbed his red eyes. "This some kind o' joke?" Words slurred, gaze unfocused. He looked exhausted.

Or drunk.

"It's not a joke." Venick still couldn't see Dourin. He couldn't have said exactly where the elf was now. But he did see one of the final remaining ropes that tethered this watchtower upright begin to vibrate, as if caught in a sudden wind—or under the edge of someone's saw.

"Can' leave my post," the watchman said.

"Are you hearing me?" Venick had been counting on the watchman's easy acceptance of the danger. Had not been counting on a drunken idiot. He let some real urgency enter his voice. "The tower is about to fall. If you stay here, you'll be crushed."

"I check them ropes every night, and I didn'—hey." The man's eyes seemed to focus. "I know you."

Venick glanced again at the rigging. He hadn't told Dourin *look for my signal* or *wait until we're down to safety*. Had only handed over the saw and trusted the elf to do the rest.

So. There wasn't much time before the final rope snapped. Not much time at all before this whole tower became a splintered heap of rubble, and them along with it. Venick grabbed the watchman's arm. "Come with me, *now*."

"Now wait just a—"

The final rope split. It curled into the air like a flying snake. The watchtower gave a shudder, then pitched sideways. This time, it was the watchman who hollered, "Go!"

They slid down the ladder, hands and legs wide, skimming over the rungs. Venick's feet hit the earth first, followed closely by the watchman's. They barreled out of the tower's way, turning back just in time to see it fall.

Venick had hunted large game before. He knew how it was to burst from the brush, bow lifted, prey set in his sights. To release the arrow and watch the elk or deer—running, always running—trip and crash. Big game always fell more quickly than seemed possible. Slid farther.

The tower did, too.

It dropped in an instant, careening into the earth with a thunderous *crash*. The watchman stood at Venick's side, gaping at his ruined post. "But—how did you know?"

"The rigging," Venick replied gravely. "It was frayed. One of the ropes had already snapped. The other looked ready to give."

"You saved me." The watchman's face was pale. "You saved my life." He dropped to one knee, bowing his head. "My life's price. It's yours. Anything—anything at all that you require. I am in your debt."

Venick set his eyes on his city. Overhead, a seagull whirled. Its black-tipped wings cut a line through the blue sky. "Actually," Venick said, "there *is* something you can do for me."

· · ·

The watchman's name was Jarol. And he was not happy.

He led Venick through Irek's streets, his steps uneven, his expression grim. He'd balked when Venick had first named his price, then narrowed his eyes, piecing it together. Some stranger appearing in town, mid-twenties, asking for a woman named Lira. A lowlander, and vaguely familiar. The watchman blinked when he connected two and two to get—*oh*. He'd realized then who Venick was. Realized he'd just given his life price to an outlaw and a killer. For a moment, Venick thought Jarol might revoke his price, that he might simply drop his hand to his sword and attack.

Venick had known that was a possibility. Knew it well enough to station Branton and Lin Lill in the nearby marsh, hidden like tigers in the reeds, their bows nocked and drawn. But killing the watchman hadn't been necessary, because Jarol didn't attack. To revoke one's life price was to earn dishonor among his people. Maybe even among the gods. Venick watched Jarol think this through, weighing the possible risks and consequences before firming his jaw and nodding his agreement. Venick had won Jarol's life price freely—or so he assumed—just as Jarol had given it willingly. He wouldn't take it back, not even from an outlaw.

"Alright," the watchman had said. "I'll take you to Lira."

"And?" Venick prompted.

A heavy sigh. "And I'll make sure no one stabs you in the back along the way."

They trudged together through the city streets. Venick cast his gaze around, trying to soak it all in. The smell of fish and saltwater. The tink and clatter of people and livestock. Wide ferns hanging from porches, vines creeping up walls, water pooling in cracks in the cobblestone. Venick felt his homesickness wash anew with each sight remembered, like a wave against the shore: surging high, then retreating, and again.

At first, no one recognized him. Then someone did. About halfway through the market square, a woman met Venick's eye and froze, dropping the fresh basket of laundry she'd been carrying. It toppled and muddied on the pavement.

Her shock drew attention. Heads turned as others tried to see what she saw, and did. Faces hardened. Fists closed over weapons. Venick ducked his head, shoving his hands into his pockets. He wished then that he'd chosen to seek redemption under the cover of night rather than in the bustle of midafternoon, even if one of the reasons he hadn't come at night was because he didn't want to feel like he felt now: a beaten dog slinking home.

By the time they reached the fat double doors of Irek's central tavern, it seemed like the entire city was staring.

"The council convenes soon," Jarol said gruffly.

Venick lifted his eyes. The tavern was a bloated three stories of sticky floors and wood-paneled walls and activity. Meetings were held here, weddings performed here, babies born and blessed here. The tavern was the beating heart of the city.

But: "I asked you to bring me to my mother."

Jarol nodded. "I am."

"Lira is…here?"

"Yes."

Venick still didn't understand. Was this where his mother worked now? Behind the bar, serving food to the locals? Or—the thought cracked itself open—was this where she *lived*?

"She's usually the first to arrive," Jarol continued. "Your mother, I mean. The councillors don' like to start late."

"Jarol." Venick heard something in the watchman's words that he'd missed before. "Are you saying Lira is *on* the council?"

"'Course. She's our Spokesman." He corrected himself. "Woman."

He pushed the doors wide.

Venick's stomach did a funny flip. The Spokesman was the leader of the council, the highest-ranking member among them. Eight councillors in total, one for every lowland city, and if a vote was split, it went in favor of the Spokesman.

It wasn't unheard of for women to serve on the council. And it made sense that his mother would have taken her husband's place. Councillors were voted in by sitting members. Anyone could be nominated, but preference was always given to family—the closest the lowlands would ever come to having their own sovereignty. After the death of General Atlas, the rest of the council must have offered Lira the spot. Atlas, however, had not been Spokesman. Lira would have climbed to that role on her own.

Venick looked for her among the seated row of councillors and spotted her almost immediately: her soft features, that wild brown hair, eyes the color of winter rain. She looked like Venick, or he looked like her. One glance at the two of them side by side and there was no doubting their relation.

Venick moved forward as if pulled by an invisible hand. He couldn't hear his footsteps over the din of the waiting crowd. He couldn't have said what kind of noise his boots would make. But he felt each step as if it was a gong, the thud of every footfall against the hardwood, and he thought, from the way his mother's gaze lifted, that she could hear it too.

Lira's eyes locked on his. Her face changed. She stood from her seat, one hand gripping the arm of the chair, her knuckles shining white. When she spoke, her voice was barely a whisper, yet she had the room's full attention.

"This meeting is adjourned. Everyone. Get out."

FOURTEEN

Jarol locked the tavern doors. They sealed with a dull thud. The room was nearly empty now. Only the councillors remained, seated as they had been at the back of the tavern, and Jarol, who turned away from the doors, looking vicious.

He drew his sword.

Venick's head snapped around at the sound. He blinked as the watchman came forward, weapon raised, teeth bared. For one foolish moment Venick did nothing, his thoughts slipping like boots on ice, scrambling to stay upright.

This was not part of their agreement.

"Jarol." Venick raised his hands, *hang on* and *what are you doing?* together. "I thought we had a deal."

"You asked me to take you to Lira. I've done that."

"I also asked that you not let anyone stab me in the back."

"Anyone *else*."

Venick's heart was wild. He aimed a glance at his mother. Surely she would call the watchman off. Surely she would stop this attack. But her face had gone cold, and she didn't.

"Mother."

Jarol advanced.

"Please. I only wanted—"

"We know what you want," snapped the man seated to Lira's right. Venick knew this councillor. Theledus was his name. Late thirties, hair shorn at the shoulders, his skin slightly yellowed from a jekkis habit he liked to think he kept private. Theledus was an old friend of Venick's father. "You murdered your father and fled into exile, and now you've returned, hoping your mother has forgotten all about it."

Jarol brought his sword down, a sloppy, ill-aimed blow. Venick dodged it smoothly. "I know she hasn't forgotten. But the law—"

"*Now* you care about laws."

"—says I get a chance at redemption." Jarol came again with another misaimed swing, driving his sword into a nearby chair. Venick didn't draw his own weapon. He could. He could pull out his blade and run this watchman through. Jarol was drunk, and angry, and wielding a sword that was clearly a poor match for his weight and build. But Venick doubted that killing the watchman would help his cause. He looked again at his mother, who watched the scene as if it were a bad play. "I'm only asking for a chance."

Jarol came a third time, backhanded now, his shoulder twisting. Another clean miss.

"Enough, Jarol," Lira ordered.

The watchman's cheeks were flushed. "He deserves it."

"I will decide what he deserves."

Jarol relented.

Lira was thinner than Venick remembered. Her eyes were tired holes. She didn't look much like a mother. Looked nothing at all like one, when she turned her gaze to her son and said, "I never expected to see you again. It's been four years."

"I know." Venick felt a little dizzy. "I hadn't earned my redemption before."

"And you think you've earned it now?"

"Yes."

Lira sat back in her chair. "Very well, then. You may speak."

The councillors all straightened. Venick swallowed a surge of nervousness. He started with what was easiest, because it was oldest. "War is coming."

. . .

Venick couldn't have said how long he spoke. Long enough for the afternoon sun to shift into evening, then nightfall. Long enough for the crickets and cicadas to emerge from their hovels, filling the air with their high, endless chorus. Venick spoke until he'd said it all.

When he finished, there was a long silence.

"You made allies with the elves," Theledus said.

"Yes."

"The *good* elves."

"Yes."

"Preposterous."

"It would be easy to prove to you," Venick replied. "They are waiting just outside the city."

"Waiting to *attack us*."

"Theledus," a thick-bearded councillor named Helos interjected, pinching the bridge of his nose. "That doesn't even make sense."

"It does if you're a traitor."

They continued to bicker, but Venick stopped listening. He was watching his mother. He'd watched her all throughout his story, looking for clues in her stony face, or in the formal fold of her hands in her lap. He'd been looking for *her*, too, the woman he remembered, the gentle mother who had raised him. But if that woman was still there, Lira kept her hidden.

"This Dark Army," she began, speaking over the quarreling councillors, who fell silent. "If it is as powerful as you say, it will be difficult to stop."

Not a denouncement. For one shining moment, all Venick could think was that his mother's first words after hearing his story had not been to condemn him. He inhaled around that knowledge, let it settle over his skin. Lira was willing to hear him. She was listening.

"That's true," Venick replied, "which is why we need allies."

"And you intend to build these alliances?"

"I do. The elven resistance has named me its commander. With the combined support of elves and lowlanders, I believe I can convince other humans to join our cause as well: the highlanders and the plainspeople."

There was a stunned silence. It was one thing to propose allying with elves, but this, suggesting that they forge alliances with the men and women they'd been born to kill—who had been born to kill *them*—was another matter entirely.

Theledus gave a weak laugh. "Have you been so long in exile that you've forgotten all sense? The highlanders would slit our throats in our sleep, and the plainspeople are little better."

"They won't," Venick insisted. "Not once they understand. Not now that we share a common enemy."

"*They* are our enemy, as much as these dark elves are."

"But they *shouldn't be*."

"Enough." Theledus' face was carved in deep lines. He stood, drawing up to his full height. "I will not sit here and allow you to disgrace us with your traitorous ideas. Lira, he is your son. His redemption is up to you. But let it be known that if he were my son, I would have him hanged this very night, before he can infect anyone else with these insane, insulting notions."

The room stilled. Outside, the cicadas had quieted. Even the walls seemed to hold their breath.

Lira did not immediately speak. It was as if she had become a part of the tavern, cut from the same wood, sanded by the same paper. Only her chest moved, the soft rise and fall of each breath. Again, Venick sought the mother he remembered. That woman was still there he thought, hidden around Lira's eyes. Or maybe in her shoulders, which had softened a little…hadn't they?

"You come seeking absolution for the murder of your father," Lira said. "You have explained, at length, your journey through the elflands and the dangers we face. But you have made little mention of your actual crime. Tell me, why did you kill my husband?"

"What?"

"Why did you kill Atlas?"

But Lira knew why. She had been there to witness it. "It was a mistake."

"That is not what I asked."

Her tone had hardly changed. She spoke of her dead husband as if giving a recipe for bread. It should have alerted Venick to the danger, but his mind was suddenly on that night, on the hut at the edge of the city where he'd watched Lorana die, and whether, if he went there now, the hut would still be standing. "I killed him because he told the southern elves about Lorana." Venick glimpsed those elves. Their sleek hair, their slender bodies, eyes so golden they seemed to glow. "About our relationship." An ambush in the night. Lorana backed into a corner. An arrow in her chest, followed by a sword in Venick's hand. Shining, heavy. And too late. "He's the reason they came to kill her."

It was the wrong thing to say. Venick knew that it was even before he saw his mother's eyes flash, her hands closing to fists. "No. *You* are the reason the elves came to kill her. You knew the law forbidding elven-human courtships, yet you pursued that elf anyway. And then you chose her life over your father's."

"I didn't mean—" Venick tried to backtrack. "It wasn't that simple."

"It is illegal to enter the elflands. We all know elves will kill any human who crosses into their territory. Yet they did not kill you. Why?"

"I was lucky."

"You also managed to find their hidden city. From what I understand, Evov does not simply appear for anyone. Yet it appeared for you."

"I know, I don't understand it either…"

"And now you have gathered an army of elves who, by your own admittance, follow your command."

"Please, if you just—"

"You killed your father for them, and now you've become one of them."

"No." The room seemed to tilt. "It's not like that."

"I know about the elven princess."

Venick flinched as if struck. "She's no one."

"She won your life price."

"That debt has been paid. I'm not *one of them*. I have befriended the elves, yes, but only because we need to put aside our differences to fight a common—"

"Draw your sword."

Venick snapped his mouth shut.

Lira stood from her chair. She wasn't a tall woman, but in that moment she seemed enormous. "Draw your sword."

He wanted to resist. That small, helpless part of him that couldn't stop holding onto hope begged him to stall for time, to put off the inevitable a little longer. He felt stupid and wrongheaded, like a child who didn't understand that the world had rules about who he was allowed to be, and whom he was allowed to love.

When would Venick learn? Maybe Theledus was right. Maybe he had been away too long. When Venick had journeyed through the elflands, building his army, befriending elves, he'd only been thinking about two sides of the war—the north and the south. He hadn't considered that there was a third side, and a fourth and a fifth. He had overlooked the fact that humans, too, have their grudges, and might not want to fight alongside a race who'd once burned their conjurors and exiled their ancestors. That they might consider it a betrayal that Venick did.

He drew his sword. The green glass shimmered in the dim tavern light: the weapon of elves.

"You have always been fascinated by the elves," said his mother. "Even as a boy, you begged me for stories of them. Then came your exile, and I thought you would have learned. But it seems your ties to that race have only deepened." She broke their gaze, and it was cruel, it was wrong, that the first glimpse Venick got of the old Lira was now, when she was disowning him. "Your alliances cannot be trusted."

"Let me prove myself to you."

"You cannot."

"I can." Venick's voice cracked in a way that might have shamed him had this been a different moment. Had he been a different man. But it was not, and he was not. "Everything I've done, I've done for my people. Let me prove that my loyalties have never wavered. I can fight for you—for this country." He swallowed hard. "Please."

Lira would not look at him. Her gaze settled on something, nothing, some distant memory he could not see. "You were such an easy child. You liked your books and your toys and the animals. You liked to help me, always doing as I asked. I worried over it. I thought you were too soft." Her shoulders lifted. "Then you grew and went to war. I heard men speak of your heroism and your courage. Like a well-made bow, they said. True and strong. I realized then that you were not soft. You were…" She brought her eyes back to him. "Well. You were like your father."

Venick held her gaze. He saw it again, more clearly now: that old softness. Atlas' death had changed Lira. Her son's betrayal had changed her too. But his mother was still there, she *was*, and as Venick waited for her verdict, his hope began to grow again, even as he'd promised himself that he was done hoping.

Lira fell quiet. Her silence was the silence of dreams: absolute.

When she finally spoke again, that too was like a dream.

"A probationary period," Lira announced. "You have until the new moon to prove your loyalty to our nation and our race. I will make my decision then. It is agreed."

FIFTEEN

Venick hung near the back of the tavern. He waited for the other councillors to file out, hoping for a chance to speak with his mother alone. The councillors took their time, conversing quietly, gathering their few belongings. Venick was just beginning to wonder if they were being purposely slow when he heard the singing: a low chorus of men in the distance.

"That'll be the boys," Helos said.

The boys. Their soldiers, back from battle.

Venick cast his gaze through dark tavern windows. He couldn't see the soldiers yet, but he knew what that singing meant. "They've taken prisoners."

"Yes. There will be an execution."

The way Helos said it. Venick saw this moment as these councillors must. So normal, so perfectly traditional. When soldiers returned home from war, they usually captured a few prisoners for this very purpose.

Victory on the battlefield was celebrated with a public execution of their enemy.

Venick pushed through the tavern doors just in time to watch the soldiers march into view. Forty, maybe fifty men total. His heart hitched to see that familiar armor, the steel weapons. Judging by the group's small size—and by the fact that they were on foot and not horseback—this battalion had likely come from a skirmish in the northern marshlands. Though, *where* hardly mattered. There was always some battle to be fought, some enemy to be defeated. Send enough men, the generals would say, and battle will find them.

The prisoners came next, their hands and feet bound with rope. Not many. Three men and a woman. Venick caught a glimpse of their tawny hair and knew them to be highlanders.

He returned to the tavern where the councillors had fallen back into conversation. Venick's mind felt trapped in slow motion. He knew what he was about to say, had enough time to think, *don't*.

Then he did.

"You can't execute them."

All eyes turned on him. Theledus scoffed. "Excuse me?"

"We need to start forming alliances," Venick insisted. "How can we do that if we're still cutting each other's throats?"

"We don't cut our prisoner's throats anymore," Theledus answered, still incredulous. "We throw them into a pit of fire. They burn alive. It's better, you see, because it takes longer."

Venick couldn't hide his horror. He looked at his mother. "You support this?"

"Of course she supports it," Theledus interjected, "as should you. Or did we misunderstand your promises to prove where your true loyalties lie?"

Venick ground his teeth. "When?"

"When *what*, Venick?"

"When will they be executed?"

Theledus' lips flattened into a grim smile. "As soon as the fire is hot enough."

. . .

Venick trudged back through the forest to where their army had made camp. The night was muggy, the wind mild. Beads of sweat snaked down his back.

Rahven was the first to greet him. The chronicler took one look at Venick's face and said, "Things went poorly, then?" When Venick merely shrugged, Rahven pressed, "Were you not granted redemption?"

"Not exactly."

"What do you mean, not exactly?" Rahven fell into step at Venick's side, and Venick had to fight the urge to say something sharp. He didn't want to have this conversation with Rahven right now. Didn't really want to have this conversation with anyone right now.

"I need to find Dourin," Venick said curtly. "Have you seen him?"

The elf spread his hands. No, he hadn't.

Neither had anyone else. Venick walked the camp, dodging questions about his redemption, asking after Dourin's whereabouts. The elves apologized. No one had seen Dourin in hours, they said. Not since he'd left to accompany Venick into the city. They didn't know where he'd gone.

"He was supposed to come back here with Branton and Lin Lill," Venick told a trio of soldiers he'd stopped near the camp's center. "You're telling me he never did?"

The elves exchanged glances. They shook their heads.

"And you didn't think to go looking for him?" Venick glared from face to face. "Have I not taught you *anything?* He could be hurt. He could be—"

"Right here, and *fine*." Dourin emerged from the shadows. His torso was bare, his hair loose, shirt flung over one shoulder. His mouth curled with amusement. "You worry too much. Has anyone ever told you that you worry too much?"

Venick rounded on him. "Where have you been?"

"Bathing."

"You shouldn't be wandering off alone."

Dourin cocked an impish smile. "Who says I was alone?" He surveyed Venick. "You still have all your limbs. I take that as a good sign." But when he met Venick's eye, he sobered. "You three are dismissed," Dourin told the soldiers Venick had been accosting. He waited until they'd scurried away before looking at Venick and saying, "Tell me."

So Venick did. He started at the beginning and explained it all, doing his best to describe everything that had happened since they'd parted ways. When he came to the part about his mother's accusations, however, a thick knot of anger clogged his throat.

You have always been fascinated by the elves.

"Venick?"

I know about the elven princess.

"What is it?"

"If not for Ellina—" Venick broke off, staring hard at the dark gaps between the trees. He didn't know how he'd planned on finishing that sentence. Didn't know how else his redemption could have possibly gone. He only knew that he blamed Ellina for all of it.

He still dreamed of her. Sometimes, as he rode through his army's ranks, he imagined that he saw her face. He'd spin around, heart climbing, only to realize that it wasn't Ellina at all, but someone else. Venick wondered if his mother could sense it. Maybe that's why she hadn't granted him redemption—because she could feel the way Ellina's presence still lingered, clinging to him like a scent.

Dourin looked concerned. He spoke cautiously, as if to a cornered animal. "Ellina made her choices. And she has her reasons, even if we do not understand them. I think we need to accept that."

But Dourin hadn't been there during those long hours when Venick and Ellina had stayed up late, pouring over books and maps, learning about war and each other. Dourin hadn't felt how the room would grow warm and deep and wine-rich, or seen how Ellina would linger, or lain awake long after she'd left, wondering if that soft light in her eye meant what Venick thought it meant. Dourin hadn't been haunted by the ghost of it, or been gutted to learn that none of it was real. Ellina hadn't cared for Venick. She hadn't felt anything for him at all. She was a legionnaire, trained to hunt and kill humans who entered the elflands. Her apparent affections had merely been part of her plot.

"Ellina sold herself to the highest bidder," Venick growled. A cornered animal after all. "She's worse than her sister."

Dourin inflated with argument, only to let it go in the next breath, on an exhale. "That is not the only reason you are upset."

Venick gave a tight shrug.

"What else is upsetting you?"

Venick thought again of the highland prisoners. He thought of how easily Theledus had spoken of their torture. How his mother had stood by and said nothing. He thought of the way his own skin had prickled, a mix of revulsion and anger and wrongness. Venick rubbed at his neck. "The lowland soldiers took enemy prisoners tonight. They'll be executed." At Dourin's raised brow, he added, "Burned alive, actually."

"Ah."

"I asked for them to be spared. The council said no."

"Are there no other options?" When Venick shook his head, Dourin sighed. "You can't save everyone."

Venick shrugged again. His jaw ached. His blood seemed to grasshopper inside him. He was angry, yes, but anger wasn't the whole of what he felt. He felt betrayed—by his own people's callousness, by their infuriating closed-mindedness. He was only trying to do the right thing, and they'd held it against him.

Would it always be this way? Would the differences between their races and countries always lie in such deep, rigid lines? Venick remembered the suffocating fear as he lay trapped in the bear trap last summer. The fear had clogged his throat. It darkened his vision. Venick hadn't thought that the fear could get any worse, until the elves appeared, and it had.

In his mind, Venick saw those highlanders, bound and imprisoned. He saw himself, chained to a dungeon wall. He saw southern conjurors materializing in a crowded market, and how he'd kicked over a brazier, sending coals sparking.

He saw the Golden Valley up in flames, the air reeking of black powder.

Venick saw, suddenly, an idea.

It took shape within him. It was fluid. Opaque, viscous. But growing clear.

He heard Dourin's words. *Are there no other options?*

Venick met the elf's eye. "I'm going to need your help."

SIXTEEN

Farah hosted lunch in the gardens. A gown had been sent to Ellina's rooms for the occasion, along with a servant to help. The servant seemed unnecessary—Ellina had never before needed help dressing—and she was about to send the young female away. Then she got a better look at the gown.

It was pretty, Ellina supposed, made of stiff blue fabric that bunched at the waist and spilled down in thick panels. The neckline was high, the seams done in delicate gold piping. But it was the back of the dress that made Ellina pause—it had been outfitted with a hundred tiny pearl buttons marching all the way up the spine. Ellina would never be able to get into such a dress herself...or out of it.

The servant worked quietly, starting with the buttons at the bottom and moving up. Slowly, the gown tightened around Ellina's waist. It cut into her ribs, shallowed her breathing. Ellina hated it. What had Farah been thinking, sending such an outfit? The dress was worse than a corset. She felt caged between its seams.

It occurred to Ellina that that had been the point.

The servant sensed Ellina's frustration and began working faster. Her fingers trembled, fumbling over the buttons and loops. She glanced at Ellina in the mirror once, quickly, then away. Finally, the young female stepped back. "You look beautiful," she said dutifully.

No, Ellina thought, she did not. Her eyes were stormy. Her skin looked pinched and pale. The shoulders of the dress were made of sheer gossamer, and a scar from an old whipping could be seen through the fabric.

Ellina knew how she really looked.

"Where is your partner?" Ellina asked abruptly, turning away from the mirror. "Servants usually work in pairs."

"He is...gone."

Ellina thought of the servant Youvan had blinded. She thought of the southern soldiers hunting down every last stateroom witness. She thought of her mother's blood spilling between Farah's hands.

The young elf must have seen Ellina's mind because she added, "He was sent away. By Queen Farah. He was assigned a new task elsewhere." The servant toyed with her empty hands. "He was my father."

It struck Ellina how young this servant was. She was smaller than Ellina, with wispy white-blonde hair and wide, watery eyes. Those eyes seemed unable to settle on any one object. They flitted from Ellina, to the mirror, to the gown, to the floor, back to Ellina.

"You miss him," Ellina said. The servant dropped her gaze and said nothing. It would be unwise to admit missing her father when the queen had been the one to order his leaving. To speak out against one was to speak ill of the other, and by now all the servants knew what happened to those who spoke ill of their new queen.

Ellina picked at the fabric of her dress. "I never knew my father. He died when I was young."

The servant looked up. Her restless eyes seemed to settle. "I am sorry."

Ellina shrugged. It was difficult to mourn someone she had never truly known. Her mother's bondmate had been chosen for political purposes rather than for love, as was typical. Bondmates did not hold a seat on the queen's council and were rarely qualified to enter the senate. Their sole purpose was to produce heirs, and once they had done that they were often given leave to return home. Had Ellina's father lived, it was possible that she would not have known him anyway.

"Tell me your name," Ellina said to the servant.

"It is Livila."

"Livila," Ellina repeated. "Will your father return soon?"

"I do not think it will be soon. But one day."

Ellina's smile was light. "Then you have something to look forward to."

. . .

The highlanders were pushed into the pit one by one.

Venick, alongside seven of their strongest elves, watched from the nearby woods. The lowland soldiers had prepared the pit the night before, crisscrossing thick logs at its bottom, weaving smaller fronds and dried seaweed in between to help the fire catch. Now those soldiers stood at the pit's steep edge, a torch in each of their hands, waiting for the moment when the highlanders had all been shoved down and they could throw their torches down with them. The kindling would catch. The logs would. And finally, the highlanders. *It's better, you see, because it takes longer.*

Townspeople gathered in the field outside the city to watch. The women chatted, the men grinning and knocking elbows as if this was a wedding rather than an execution. Bets were being made, Venick had heard, on which highlander would survive the longest.

The three male prisoners were thrown into the pit first. They struggled, straining against their captors, digging in their heels. The woman came next, and she struggled most of all. One of the soldiers laughed. The sound was strangely lighthearted, as if her panic was a private joke shared between them. He slapped her across the face and shoved her down with the rest.

The townspeople pushed closer. They leered over the pit's edge. They weren't worried for themselves—the hole was too deep for the highlanders to climb back out, or for fire to pose them any danger.

Usually.

Last night, Venick had asked for volunteers. Several elves had come forward, including Rahven, who seemed eager to make himself useful. "In thanks for all that you have done for me."

"You're not strong enough for what I need," Venick had told him.

"Then let me help in some other way."

Some other way had come later that same night, when Venick asked Rahven about the elves' black powder stores, only to discover that northerners didn't mine black powder. Explosives, Rahven explained, were a human weapon, and therefore shunned by the elves.

"You're telling me we don't have *any* black powder in our supplies?" Venick had asked.

"None."

So they'd stolen some.

It was a well-guarded secret that the lowlanders hid their black powder on their barges. When the generals had chosen this location, they'd smiled and clapped shoulders, pleased with their cleverness. Barges were mobile and could therefore set sail in case of a siege on the city. Their most precious weapon could be kept out of enemy hands. Better, if the city was to come under attack, the highly flammable powder would be readily accessible for firing the cannons on their warships. It was, the generals agreed, their best defensive strategy.

Convenient, that no one thought to mention that black powder, if exposed to water, was rendered useless. Convenient, that no one bothered to consider how easily a barge might be stolen or sunk. Those were more messy details to be swept away with the rest.

Sneaking onto the docks had been easy. Knocking out the single guard stationed on the pier had been slightly trickier, but Rahven managed it with surprising fluidity.

"I thought you said you couldn't fight," Venick remarked.

"This is not fighting," the chronicler replied.

When they'd taken the guard's keys from his belt, rowed a small launch out to the barge and unlocked its hull to reveal row upon row of black powder barrels, Rahven's eyes had gone wide.

"Just a little," Venick said. "We don't need much."

They'd stolen enough of the fine, sooty stuff to fill a good-sized pouch. On the way back, Venick had stooped to return the keys to the guard's belt, then dug through the man's vest until he'd found a purse of gold coins, which Venick pocketed. "Not for *me*," he'd sighed at Rahven's critical glance. "For him." When the man woke, this would all look like a case of petty thievery.

They'd returned to the execution pit—a deep, earthen hole in the ground—shortly before dawn. Venick hopped inside, pouring several thin trails of black powder from the pit's center out, towards the city.

Not far enough to pose any danger to Irek. Not large enough to hurt anyone. Just enough for what he needed.

You hope.

Rahven had helped haul him back out, and together they'd fled into the forest to wait until morning. Movement overhead had caught Venick's attention. He peered into the starry sky and spotted it: a currigon hawk. The creature looped once, twice, then winged higher. It was odd to see a wild currigon this far south. They usually ranged in the northern mountains. But Venick remembered Rahven's story about currigon hawks being a symbol of hope and was encouraged. Somehow, the hawk seemed fitting.

Now, Venick watched through the trees as the lowland soldiers threw their torches into the pit. The kindling caught. Smoke clogged the air. Venick couldn't quite see the highlanders down inside, but he could imagine how they would have moved to the pit's edges, maybe clutching each other, eyes shining with the growing flames.

Venick glanced at the elves to his left and right. Lin Lill was among them, as was Artis, an old member of Ellina's troop. The elves all watched Venick, waiting for his signal.

Not yet.

He peered back towards the pit. His heart hurt. He was, only now, seeing all the many flaws in his plan. There were a dozen things that could go wrong, a dozen ways he might accidentally kill a lowlander, or an elf, or himself.

Not the time for doubts, Venick.

He trapped his command between his teeth. Held up a fist. *Hold.*

The smoke grew thicker. It coughed and spat into the sky.

Hold.

Someone inside the pit gave a cry. The sound seemed to hang in the air for longer than possible.

Hold.

Then: a sharp crackle. A burst of light.

A whip-quick flash of fire, racing out of the pit into the crowd.

It happened fast, too fast for the eye to follow. There was a moment of hectic confusion as the grass beneath the townspeople's feet caught fire and several soldiers rushed to help stomp it out. Then a second ball of flame leapt into the crowd, and a third. They were like firecrackers, flashing and zipping, catching on the invisible trails of black powder and streaking upwards, landing on people's shoes and clothing only to be quickly smothered. In the ensuing chaos, Venick snapped his command. *Now.*

They burst from the cover of the woods, sprinting towards the pit. Venick's boots kicked up dirt. His lungs heaved. The now-solid wall of smoke loomed closer, closer, and as he approached he half expected to discover that it really *was* a wall, to slam into it head on, feel the crunch of bone.

He passed into the smoke-cloud as easily as a breath. The world was instantly thrown into a strange glowing greyness, the heat of the smoke enough to make Venick's ears ache. He ducked low, pulling his shirt up over his mouth and nose, rushing to the pit's edge with Lin Lill at his side.

He spotted the highland woman first. She was pressed flat against the crumbling dirt wall beneath him, eyes screwed closed, her face marbled with soot and sweat. The fire hadn't yet reached her, but the pit was hot enough to bring the highlanders to their knees. Around them, black powder continued to zip and crack, pushing the townspeople back, leaving those who remained distracted and frenzied. Lin Lill produced a length of rope. "Here," Venick called to the woman, throwing the rope down to her, holding tight to its other end. "*Climb.*"

The woman's eyes came open. She blinked up—a split-second moment of shock—before quickly scanning for her comrades, who were all doing as Venick had commanded: scrambling up lengths of rope held by the elves. The woman set her jaw and nodded. She began to climb.

One of the prisoners screamed.

His rope had caught fire. It seared his hands and split. He tumbled into the flames below.

A second prisoner's luck was no better. The elves began to haul him up as his rope, too, caught fire. Then Venick stopped watching, because the woman's rope began smoking under his hands. *Hang on*, Venick said, or maybe he only thought it, because then he and Lin Lill were both frantically hauling up the rope, pulling it over the pit's edge, and *please*, that the woman had the strength to hold on, *please*, that her rope didn't catch and split like the others. Overhead, smoke blotted out the sun. The fire roared like rolling thunder. Venick dug in his heels, dizzy and disoriented, lost in the smoke, unable to get enough air. His chest seized. Tears streaked his cheeks. He dug in harder, pressed back against Lin Lill as the two of them struggled, and finally, *finally*, felt the release of pressure that either meant the woman had made it over the top or had fallen to her death.

Venick blinked through the smoke. Crawled forward on hands and knees.

The highland woman lay sprawled on the grass, staring back at him. Alive.

· · ·

It was some time later, after they'd secreted the woman into the cover of the woods and the last of the fire had died away that Venick learned the rest of the story.

Irek's lowlanders were unhurt. They blamed the soldiers for stacking the logs poorly and allowing the fire to escape the pit. No one suspected black powder.

Two of the highlander men had died in the pit. The third managed to escape, but was badly burned. Venick saw him as he was being ushered away. He hardly appeared human. The skin on his face looked like an open sore, his nose a lumpen mess, both eyes missing. He'd died back at camp shortly after.

Only the woman survived. Venick went to visit her in the healer's tent. She looked to be around his age. One of her eyes was hazel, which was common among highlanders. The other probably was too, though Venick couldn't know for sure; it was bruised and blackened, swollen shut. It had happened when the soldier had slapped her.

Worse, though, were her hands. The skin was shiny and too tight. Burned. She held them stiffly away from her body.

"I'm sorry," Venick told her, and felt the uselessness of those words. "I'm sorry that this happened to you. And your friends…we tried. This shouldn't—this should never have happened." A hard sigh. "Those burns need to be treated. I'll see what we have in our supplies. Are you hurt anywhere else?"

The woman turned her face away, refusing to reply.

SEVENTEEN

Ellina arrived to the garden party late and, from the looks of it, last. If anyone asked, she planned to blame the gown's buttons for the delay, though in truth she had been standing just out of view of the gathering, mustering her resolve. Ellina knew from Farah's invitation that this lunch was to be hosted in the palace's stone gardens, but when she had seen *where* in the gardens, she had half a mind to turn back the way she had come.

Senators and courtiers gathered around the everpool. Its crystalline surface reflected the party perfectly: the earth-toned robes of the councillors, the more colorful fabric favored by youths, the slate-grey clouds looming low overhead. Guests mingled with food and drink in hand, some standing in the warm glow of braziers, others sitting on stone benches, their furred cloaks pulled up around their chins. There was the tink of china, the low din of conversation, rare and quiet laughter. Farah stood by the largest brazier on the opposite end of the everpool, surrounded by advisors.

Ellina's eyes darted back to the water. It seemed impossible that Farah had chosen this location by chance, yet when Ellina stepped out of hiding and approached her sister, Farah showed no signs of slyness, nor any indication that she was aware of the everpool at all. She beckoned Ellina with hand. "Sister. We were just discussing the problem of the western wetlands. Perhaps you can help."

The elves in Farah's circle were mostly senators, high-ranking officials whose duty it was to advise the queen on specialized matters. They were all white-haired, all golden-eyed, all bearing their weapons openly, like jewelry draped across their shoulders and hips. At Farah's invitation they shuffled aside to make room.

"The wetlands?" Ellina asked.

"Those lands are riddled with marshes and bogs. They block our path into the mainlands. Soon, the time will come to move our forces west, but it will be difficult to maneuver an army through the wetlands."

"Detour south around them," said one of the councillors, a southern elf named Awlin. "The land to the south is dry. A detour will take time, but you will have no trouble moving an army or its artillery that way."

"Leave our artillery behind," said another. "We are strong enough without the added bulk."

Leaving their artillery behind would give the resistance a better chance at victory, but it would also mean a nimbler enemy. Without their cannons and wagons to weigh them down, Farah's army would sweep quickly through the mainlands. Ellina imagined humans ambushed in the night. Doors being ripped from their hinges, children torn from their mother's arms. Those who fought back would be cut down. Their blood would soak the earth.

Farah said, "If we detour south, we lose the element of surprise. The mountains will no longer conceal our movements. And we know the humans will have *their* artillery. Leaving ours behind would put us at a disadvantage." She looked at Ellina. "Well? What do you think?"

Ellina peered up at the clouds. They donned the sky in vast waves. "Sail," she said. The elves stared.

"Sail?" Awlin repeated incredulously. "Elves do not sail. We do not even have any ships."

"Then build some."

"Sister." Farah smiled her particular smile, sharp like a little knife. "You jest."

"You speak of a surprise attack," Ellina said, "but we must assume the humans already know an attack is coming. They will be expecting an assault by land. If you were to build a fleet of ships, you could sail around the peninsula. You could land on the western shores and take the humans by surprise. And you could load your ships with as much artillery as you like. It solves all of your problems."

And it would take ages. By the time elves built their ships and learned to sail—*if* they even could—the mainlands would have had enough time to unite and prepare. Ellina, of course, would report on the construction of new ships. She would pass on information regarding the size and style of the queen's fleet, and how likely the elves were to complete the journey. By the time Farah's army set off, the resistance would be ready.

"Interesting." Farah toyed with an earring. "I like the idea of a seafaring attack. But elves are not made for water. And building an entire fleet from nothing…that is no easy feat."

"You will need to do it anyway if you intend to keep what you have won. Humans are masters of the sea. If you conquer their land, they will retaliate. And I am sure you have not forgotten that this palace sits in a bay. What will you do when humans attack you here?" Ellina laid out these arguments as if food on a table. Which would pique Farah's appetite? Which would most tempt her?

Farah was nodding, but the nod grew shallow, her thoughts moving elsewhere. Ellina knew where Farah's mind would go next. She followed the issue to its logical end, because there was another solution to the problem of human retaliation, a solution that had been utilized once before during the purge: exterminate the humans.

Ellina scrambled for something to say. She needed to redirect Farah's attention, to pull those thoughts out from under her. She cast about, as if she might find some clue hidden in the grey garden walls, or the folds and fabric of the courtiers' cloaks. There were a few conjurors in attendance that day, though not many, and none within earshot. They kept to the edges of the party, away from the commotion and the warmth of the braziers—a stark contrast to Farah, adorned in her new white armor, surrounded by councillors in the garden's center. This positioning was no accident. Farah wanted to be seen and heard: the bright core to the flame of this gathering.

Ellina saw, suddenly, a different idea.

"If you succeed at building the first elven naval fleet, you will be celebrated for it."

Farah's gaze came back to her sister. Her expression was suddenly luminous, her eyes like twin moons, and this time when she smiled, her smile was real.

・・・

Ellina sought out Kaji. "We should not keep meeting here," he told her under his breath, yet motioned that she should enter his chamber anyway.

Ellina explained what had happened in the gardens.

"This news is troubling." Kaji's expression was uncharacteristically open, and grim. "It is too soon for Farah to attack the mainlands. The resistance has not yet secured its allies. We need more time."

"Farah could be bluffing." It was becoming more and more difficult to separate Farah's truths from her lies. Her words might have been meant as another test, like the dining chamber. Like the dress, which Ellina still wore. "Farah knows how I feel about humans. She could have been trying to goad me." Then again, they had been talking about the mainlands before Ellina's arrival. And Ellina did not think Farah had faked that final smile.

"Farah wears many faces," Kaji agreed now. "Still, this bears consideration. Farah has shown little interest in the mainlands until now. She plans to conquer it one day, certainly, but she sees this war as a leisure. Why rush into the mainlands and stretch her army thin when instead she can focus her efforts here in the elflands? If Farah has changed her plans, there must be a reason." Kaji pinned Ellina with a look. "And what might that reason be?"

Ellina lifted her gaze to peer up at Kaji's ceiling. His room, like most palace rooms, had been carved straight into the mountain. The walls had no brick, no grout. They were seamless: joined as one.

Ellina said, "Farah knows about the human-elven alliance."

Kaji nodded. "I fear so."

"But how?"

"Scouts. Rumors. There are many possibilities, none of which should surprise us. Discovery has always been inevitable, especially as the resistance grows."

Inevitable perhaps, but not *immediate*. According to Dourin's reports, the resistance had only just reached the mainlands. Negotiations for an alliance had scarcely even begun. If that was true, how had Farah learned of it so quickly?

"Dourin will need to be warned," Ellina said. She would visit the everpool soon. Tonight. Already, her mind was churning with plans: the route she would take, the message she would write, Kaji's legion uniform—hidden in the back of her closet—that she would wear. Livila would be waiting in her suite to help remove Ellina's gown, but Ellina did not have the patience for a hundred buttons slowly undone. She would order Livila to fetch a knife. She would cut the dress right off her body. Ellina would enjoy hearing the fabric tear.

This thought led to another. Ellina again pictured Livila, who looked nothing like Ellina, yet reminded her very much of herself at that age. She remembered the young servant's wide, lonely eyes.

"Kaji, I want to know something. About my father."

If Kaji was surprised, he hid it well. "I never knew him."

"You served my mother in the legion before I was born. You were there for her initiation."

The elder elf moved to a nearby serving cart. He poured a glass of water from the decanter and offered it to Ellina, then poured one for himself. "Rishiana was bondmated on the eve of her initiation, as is custom. But the ceremony did not take place in Evov. I was not there to witness it."

"My father must have spent *some* time in the palace."

"Well...no." Kaji swirled the ice in his glass. "He chose to remain in his home-city Vivvre. And your mother was rarely here either. The queen is not required to rule from Evov, you know. Most queens only reside in the palace during times of war. Rishiana spent most of her early years reigning from the countryside. She often traveled between cities."

"And left my father in Vivvre."

"It was his decision to stay behind." Kaji squinted one eye at her, then let out a sigh. "I do not wish to speak ill of your father. He had a right to his choices. And you know how bondmating goes."

Ellina thought of the scars—white, crisscrossed—visible through the sheer fabric of her dress. She thought of Raffan, who had put them there.

Yes, she knew how bondmating could go.

"It caused problems between your mother and aunt," Kaji said abruptly. "Ara had her own ideas about queendom and bondmating. I think she wanted your mother to spend more time with your father. It created a rift between them that…worsened, over time."

"Their fight." It was well known that around the time of Queen Rishiana's first pregnancy, she and her sister Ara had a terrible fight that drove Ara to leave the court for good. No one seemed to know what that fight had been about…or so Ellina had thought. "Their argument was about my father?"

"I cannot say for certain," the elder elf admitted, "but I believe so. Most queens begin producing heirs immediately after their initiation, but Rishiana wanted to wait. For a decade she waited. And this was right around the time of the hundred childless years, so you must understand, things were already tense. Ara did not like the way your mother was handling the situation—not with her own heirs or with the future of our country. It was Ara who pushed Rishiana to create the border."

Ellina nearly choked on her water. "The border was *Ara's* idea?"

"The laws, the border. All of it."

The room seemed to lean. Or maybe Ellina's mind did—everything was spinning.

Elven children had always been rare. Elves did not marry as humans did, nor did they form lifetime bonds with one another. Since producing a child was *like* a marriage, elves rarely did that either. Elves and humans, however, cannot bear children together, and for a time it became more common for elves to take human partners than elven ones.

Then came the hundred childless years, and it seemed as though elves might have stopped producing offspring for good. Queen Rishiana—worried about their diminished population and the future of their race—decided to *make* elves have children. She forced bonded pairs, arranged births. She decreed new laws that prohibited elves from killing other elves even during times of war. And she drew the border, which outlawed elven-human relationships and separated their two races for good.

For a century, the laws worked. With the help of arranged bondings, their population was bolstered. Meanwhile, elves and humans grew apart. Old friendships faded, alliances crumbled. Separated by a border, fear and distrust flourished between them.

These were the laws that had, in so many ways, shaped Ellina's life. So how was it that she had never known it was her aunt, and not her mother, who had contrived them? Was this what had begun the rift that eventually estranged Queen Rishiana from her sister? Had Rishiana even *wanted* the border?

Ellina exhaled. She knew this feeling: the fish-quick dart of her thoughts, the flash of their silvery scales. The way her mind began offering up questions, locked doors to which she did not have a key.

She said to Kaji, slowly, "My mother hated humans."

There was something in the elder elf's eye, gone so fast that Ellina might have imagined it. But she did not imagine the way Kaji broke her gaze as he replied, "Of course she did."

Ellina studied the glass in her hand. She had other questions. She wanted to know why Ara—so apparently desperate for her sister to produce heirs—had chosen to leave once Rishiana was finally pregnant. She wanted to know why her mother never liked to speak of her father, not even his name, not even years later.

Ellina wanted to know if she resembled him. Did her father, too, have dark hair? Did he share her love of weapons or her skill for deception? What would her father have thought if he knew how Ellina conspired against her own sister, or that she did it in part for a human? Would he punish Ellina as easily as Raffan once had, or worse, or not at all?

In the end, though, none of this was easy to ask. She set down her glass. "I should go."

"*Irishi.*" Kaji's voice stopped her at the door. The word he used was an old one, an elven term of endearment. "Your father was robbed of the chance to know you, but had he lived to see you grown, I think he would have been proud."

These words were meant as a comfort, but Ellina was not comforted—she felt only the gap of that loss. Her father had died in the way elves fear most: by drowning. It had been an accident. A mudslide near his country home had swept him into a river. His body had washed ashore days later.

Ellina dropped her gaze, staring at the plush rug until its patterns began to swim. She glanced up to find Kaji watching her, concerned.

Her vision cleared. Ellina did not want Kaji's concern—or rather, she did not want him to believe her in need of it.

"Thank you, Kaji," she said coolly, "but the opinion of an elf I never knew hardly matters to me. If you will excuse me, I have a long night ahead."

EIGHTEEN

Ellina emerged from Kaji's room. The guards must have grown bored waiting, or else had been called to some other task. The hall was empty.

She started for the north tower. She strode through echoing halls and empty chambers, trailed her hand along grey walls that melded seamlessly into grey floors. Ellina passed a few others as she went, courtiers and servants, the occasional senator. The hem of Ellina's gown hissed against the stone, a sound that went against years of legion training: do not allow others to hear you before you hear them. She tried to take the fabric up in her hands, but the folds of the dress were many, and slipped from her fingers.

Not that it truly mattered. This was no battlefield. And anyway, most of these elves were eager to ignore her. The palace servants were afraid of Ellina, thinking that she and the queen were of a mind. The courtiers sensed that the two sisters were *not* of a mind, but this created fear of a different kind; they did not want to be seen associating with the princess in case it somehow attracted Farah's displeasure.

When Ellina was little, she found a baby bird in the grass. She remembered its ugly pink body, its bony head. She had scooped the feeble creature into her hands and tried to set it back into its nest. Farah caught her at it and laughed. *Can you not see that the bird is dead? What do you think that will fix?*

Perhaps the bird had tumbled out of the nest on its own. Perhaps it had been pushed. Ellina—so young then, a fledgling herself—had not understood. She plucked at the bird's limp body. She climbed the tree and set it back with its brothers, who peeped and cried. The next day, she found all the baby birds on the ground. This time, she knew what had happened.

You seemed so enthralled by one dead bird, Farah had told Ellina, smiling just as she had in the stone gardens. *I thought, what about six?*

Ellina understood the courtiers' fear. She knew how it felt to be set in her sister's sights. If it came to choosing sides, the palace elves would side with the queen—a choice made obvious each time they saw Ellina and found a reason to look away. Ellina could not blame them for it. This was what she told herself.

Yet the cold hall felt suddenly colder.

She quickened her pace. Late afternoon sunlight blazed through the windows, cutting hard squares into the walls and floor. Soon the sky would melt into pink and gold, then dusk. Ellina knew that Livila was likely growing anxious, wondering when her mistress would return so that she could finish her duties and retreat to her quarters before dark. Most palace elves were like this these days: nervous around dinnertime, even more so at dusk. Farah had used Ermese's blindness to make her message clear. No one, except the guards and conjurors, were to wander the halls after dark.

What Ellina had not stopped to consider, until that moment, was *why*.

She came to a stop at the top of a stairwell, ran a hand along the smooth balustrade. Ellina had assumed that Farah's curfew was a simple show of power, a way to force her subjects into submission. Better than that, it provided an opportunity to publicly punish those who disobeyed her. Farah's curfew translated into a simple command: obey.

Except, that could not be the whole of it. Because there was Raffan, in the dining hall of Ellina's mind, and Youvan, with his angry questions, and the blinded servant's lies, choked to silence.

What were you doing, Youvan had asked, *snooping around the palace after dark?*

What did you see, down in the palace crypts?

Ellina gripped the railing. She felt it again: the silvery flash of her thoughts. The way an idea seemed to shimmer—bright, cold—on the edge of her consciousness.

The sun continued its descent. Its golden rays beamed. But there was time still before dark. Time enough, Ellina thought, for a quick diversion.

• • •

The entryway to the crypts looked like most other palace entryways. There was a short, wide door fashioned from grey stone, two brass knobs, two decorative lock plates, a wall sconce set to either side. What was not like most entryways was the solitary guard stationed before those doors and the sword—unsheathed, blade down—that he held in his grasp.

Ellina continued forward even as the guard ordered, "Halt." His face was half-concealed by a helm, his chest shelled under a studded cuirass, the sigil of a raven between twin flames emblazoned onto the metal. This too was unusual. Palace guards did not often wear full battle armor, not within the city, and certainly not indoors.

"Halt, in the name of the queen," said the guard again. Ellina was close enough now that she could see his eyes narrow under the shadow of his helm. "What business do you have here?"

The tip of the guard's sword was propped on the floor, his hands folded over its pommel, his weight settled forward. It was a lazy posture. Overconfident. An enemy could easily unbalance him in a stance like that, which meant that either this guard was inexperienced and did not know it, or he did not consider Ellina an enemy.

"Well?" the guard prompted.

Ellina lifted her gaze. "I wish to visit my mother's crypt."

"I have orders. The crypts are closed."

It was no less than Ellina had expected. She feigned surprise. "But why?"

"That is none of your concern."

"I should think, as the queen's right hand, that I would be party to such knowledge."

"You would *think*."

Ellina cooled. So it would be like that, then.

The guard readjusted his grip. "Your mother is not down there anyway."

This time Ellina's surprise was real. "What do you mean?"

"Her body was taken to the city of Lorin. She will be buried beside her sister."

The news settled like a stone dropped into a river: down and down. Ellina kept her eyes clear, her expression empty, but inside she was swirling.

All differences are settled in death. It was a favorite human saying, especially as a man's last words—or so Ellina had learned from her time in the legion. The phrase was overused, she had always thought, though she could understand the strength a man might draw from it. She understood the strength *she* might. No matter what arguments had divided Rishiana and Ara during their lives, they would now rest beside each other in death. The thought filled Ellina with a measure of comfort... and disappointment. She had not known until the moment she had spoken the words that she *did* wish to visit her mother's crypt.

The guard was watching her. His pale hair gleamed orange in the light of the nearby sconce.

"You should not hold your blade like that," Ellina said.

"What?"

"It is poor form."

The guard was amused. "Green glass never loses its edge. I do not see why it matters."

"It matters if you take pride in your training."

"Perhaps you and I were trained differently."

"Perhaps you were not trained at all." The guard's amusement slid away. Ellina continued, "I wonder, what use does my sister have for an untrained soldier?"

"I am not *untrained*."

"Then you are simply lazy."

His jaw flexed. "Queen Farah chose me personally."

"To guard dead bodies? The stakes, I am sure, are very high."

"I am not just guarding dead—" He caught himself. His eyes, already narrow, became slits. "You should be careful, princess. I would hate for word of your... *curiosity* to reach the queen's ears."

"I would worry less about my curiosity, and more about what you have done to satisfy it. Why not tell me what *is* down in the crypts, and see your mistake through?"

For a moment, Ellina thought the guard would take up his sword and swing. Almost, she moved to topple him. It would be easy to throw his balance, to take his weapon for herself, even if she was wearing a dress. It was as Venick had often said: the palace guards were kittens.

But like a kitten, the guard did not take up his sword. Instead he said, "Queen Farah knows that I am devoted to her."

"Does she."

"She values my loyalty."

"How nice for you."

Ellina turned to leave. Though it tempted, there was no point in riling this guard further, not now that she had what she had come for. She reached the end of the corridor when the guard spoke again. "If the queen does not value *your* loyalty, it is because of what you are."

Ellina halted. Something about the guard's tone set her hair on end. *What do you mean?* she might have asked. *What does Farah think I am?* But no. Farah did not know that Ellina was a conjuror. No one did.

Still, Ellina's pulse was unsteady as she turned back to face the guard. She pretended to misunderstand him. "What I am. You mean, because I am a trained soldier? Because I killed guards like you on the night of the coup?" She watched the guard pale as he remembered who, exactly, he was speaking to. Elite legionnaire. Famed spy, a honed killer. Never before had a princess chosen the legion over the comforts of court, until Ellina. It had sparked stories, rumors of her prowess that were mostly overblown, but could also be used to her advantage. Like now. She slipped on her deadliest smile. "No. I do not think Farah minds at all."

· · ·

Later, Ellina apologized to a frazzled Livila.

"I did not mean to stay so long at the garden party," she said. Outside, the sky glowed pink. A chill seeped through the stones: a sign of the coming winter. "I must have lost track of time."

"It is no worry," Livila replied, dipping her head as she quickly undid the buttons of Ellina's gown. There would be no knife after all.

"But it is a worry. I would hate to be responsible for your missed curfew." A pause. "I saw what they did to Ermese."

Livila's hand flinched against Ellina's back.

Softly, Ellina asked, "Did you know him?"

"Yes. A little."

"And...what has become of him?"

"I do not know." Livila kept her eyes on her task. The buttons clicked and shuffled. "No one knows."

Ellina's brows went up. "How can that be?"

"He disappeared. He cannot be found in the kitchens, nor the servants' quarters, or even the city prisons. The rumor..." Livila glanced around, as if the walls might be listening. "The rumor is that he was banished to the whitelands."

The whitelands. That icy cluster of northern islands where elves were sent in exile. Once a year in the dead of winter, the Shallow Sea froze just enough to create an ice-bridge, which allowed new exiles to be driven into those lands. The bridge lasted only a short time—a handful of days, a fortnight at most—before melting again, trapping exiles in that bitter world.

"I see," Ellina said.

What she did not say was that winter had not yet come this year, and so Ermese could not have been sent to the whitelands.

She did not say that Queen Farah cared little about sparing elven lives, and had no reason to choose exile for a servant such as him.

Ellina did not say that Ermese was likely dead, and whatever information he possessed along with him.

NINETEEN

Venick watched the campfire with half-hooded eyes. He'd been sitting there for what might have been hours, listening to the fire eat the wood, drifting near sleep. It never got cold in the lowlands, not truly, but this night held a chill, the wind picking up the way it still did, sometimes, in his memory.

Dourin stepped into the firelight, scrutinizing Venick's slumped posture, his half-undone boots. "Long day?"

"They're all long days."

"No luck with the highlander?"

"No luck with anything."

Not his mother, not the council, not his redemption. And no, not the highland woman, who was currently holed up in a spare tent, stubbornly refusing to speak to anyone.

Dourin came to sit on the fire's opposite side. The elf looked down at his hands. Into the flames. Out into the black nothingness of the forest. He intertwined his fingers. Broke them apart.

"It's starting to hurt, watching you do that," Venick said. "Say what you have to say."

Dourin stilled. "We found a vial of poison hidden in one of the supply wagons."

"Ah."

"It is not ours, which means we have a would-be assassin in our midst. One of our new recruits, most likely. Whoever it is, they were smart enough to stash the poison where it could not be traced. We have no way of knowing who it belongs to."

"Or who it was meant for."

Dourin looked at Venick as if he was being particularly stupid. "It was meant for you."

"Don't sound so certain. Not everyone wants me dead."

"The poison was amberwood."

"And?"

"*And*, amberwood might make an elf sick, but it will kill a human."

Venick leaned back on his elbows. He wasn't surprised by the poison. Really, if there was a surprise to be had here, it was that no one had tried to kill him sooner. "I guess I'll count myself lucky then, that I have you to dispose of all evils that would end me."

"We did not dispose of it."

"No?" Venick arched a brow. "Thinking of finishing the job?"

"Must you always be so insufferable? *No*, Venick. We left the poison where we found it. I have assigned Lin Lill and Branton to survey the area. They will wait to see who returns for the vial." The elf drew up one knee, wrapped his arm around it. "Honestly. I see you with Traegar's book every night. How is it possible that you have never heard of amberwood?"

"There's a lot of material in there. Most of it goes over my head."

"Undoubtedly."

A log shifted in the fire. In the distance, Rahven could be heard telling another story.

"Who was he to you?" Venick asked. "Traegar."

Dourin gazed up at the stars. "Someone I lost." The elf's golden earrings winked in the firelight. Ash from the fire eddied along the air. "Both Traegar and I come from a long line of *geleeshi*. There is no real translation for the word, but it means roughly, *one who is gifted with horses*. You have seen my summoning. I can call homing horses to me with a thought. Perhaps you assumed it was always so easy, but it is not. Most elves must raise their homing horses from foals to create a strong enough bond for summoning. Even then, the bond does not always take. For *geleeshi*, though, we can call any homing horse, and the creature will listen.

"Traegar's family and my family were longtime friends. He and I met when we were fledglings. I think we found a kinship in each other. *Geleeshi* are highly sought after, especially in the legion. It was strange to be so young and have so much attention on us, to already have commanders knocking at our doors. But there was comfort, also, in not facing it alone.

"I did join the legion, once I was old enough to decide what I wanted. Traegar was no fighter, but after I joined he began to feel the pressure to join as well. From his family, yes, and the commanders, but also from me. I was selfish. I knew Traegar could never be happy as a fighter, but I did not care. I wanted him beside me. I could not imagine him *not* beside me." Dourin puffed out his cheeks, exhaling. "He trained as an initiate, but quit before taking his oaths. He joined the healer's academy instead. I flatter myself to think it was in spite—his healing to my killing—but in truth I think that is always what he wanted for himself."

Venick squinted at his friend. "I don't see why you had to lose him over that."

Dourin hesitated. "Traegar liked to experiment. He was good with potions and remedies—and also poisons. He met another healer who shared his interests. They became work partners and close friends. I was jealous. I told the academy about Traegar's secret research. He was removed, his titles stripped. It was vile of me, and low, and I have regretted it ever since."

They sank into silence.

Dourin said, "You knew an elf in this city, did you not? That is how you learned elvish."

Venick plucked a twig from the ground, twirled it between forefinger and thumb. "Yes."

"Tell me about them."

Venick had never told anyone about Lorana—that she was actually the lost princess Miria and Ellina's eldest sister, that her disappearance had been contrived, that she had been killed by southerners, but not in the way most elves assumed. They weren't his secrets to tell. And it shamed him, thinking about her, remembering how he'd loved her and lost her and fallen for her sister and been tricked by them both.

Venick peered up through the high trees into the black sky beyond. Coming back to Irek had been hard in dozens of ways, not the least of which was dredging up old hurts. But memories were not like clothes, to be outgrown and replaced. They were more like scars, fading over time but never truly vanishing. And if Dourin could talk about his mistakes, Venick could, too.

He sighed, and told Dourin everything.

TWENTY

Ellina went to the palace stables. Prismed light filtered in through the glass roof, scattering shadows. The animals breathed and tossed their heads.

Livila was there sweeping straw. She saw Ellina and lifted a hand, which was not the proper greeting for a servant and her mistress, but Ellina rather liked the informality. She let the gesture go unremarked.

"Would you like me to ready you a horse?" Livila asked.

"No. I was just taking a walk." Ellina had spent the morning meeting with legionnaires, advocating Farah's cause as they had agreed in their bargain. She played the role well, but the lies left her feeling drained, so she had come to see Dourin's homing horses. She thought the horses might help ease some of her loneliness. She missed her friend.

"Do you ride?" Ellina asked.

"Yes." Livila was cheerful. "I begged my father to teach me. He refused, so I bribed one of the servants to teach me instead. My father saw how inept she was and finally agreed to take on the task himself, lest I break my neck under her tutorage."

A smile pulled at Ellina's lips. "Subterfuge, Livila?" The servant succeeded in looking devious, and Ellina laughed. "And what of your mother?"

Livila leaned on her broom. "My birth was arranged. My mother served the terms of her bond, but once I was born she did not want anything to do with me."

Ellina's smile died on her lips. "Her bond."

"With my father. You know, do you not, that Queen Rishiana's servants were bondmated first? It made sense, since we were already bound to her will. We helped end the hundred childless years."

It felt as if Ellina had taken a too-large swig of wine. She swallowed the reminder of her mother's decree, then swallowed again at even needing to be reminded. Rishiana had ordered the forced bonding of hundreds of elves—Ellina included. The fledglings produced as a result of those unions had helped save their race. But it was ugly. This was: a daughter without a mother. A mother without a choice.

"Yes," Ellina said.

. . .

A duel was to be held on the palace grounds. Courtiers were invited to watch the southerners' prowess in battle. "So that you may become better acquainted with your new comrades," Farah told the court during their last stateroom meeting. A space was cleared on the southern lawns with chairs enough for the senators and dignitaries. Everyone else could stand.

Ellina was given a seat at the front of the ring next to Farah, though she did not take it. It was her legionnaire's training that prevented her from enjoying such a spectacle; she did not like to see others wield weapons when she bore none. If she was to watch, she would not stand in the most vulnerable position, and she certainly would not *sit*. She found a spot deep in the crowd.

Ellina had assumed Farah's chosen duelers would be conjurors, but these two elves were not. They were young, white-haired, male. Both taut with lean muscle. Both long-faced. It occurred to Ellina that they might be brothers. They stepped into the makeshift fighting ring and stripped away their shirts, not to protect the fabric from sweat—elves rarely did sweat—but to make it easier to spot the winner. The victor would be the first to draw blood.

Farah lifted a slender hand. A trumpet sounded.

The duel began.

In the north, legionnaires fought with a particular slyness, relying on tricks and feints and quick maneuvers. These southern elves, by contrast, were blunt. One dueler—the younger of the two—wielded a shortsword, while his brother bore a belt of throwing knives. As they moved about the ring, slashing and parrying, there were no ruses or coy moves, no snake games. Rather, the southerners fought with a kind of grim openness. They were like ships plowing through high seas, dependent on strength alone. That was fitting. The southerners were not known for their wits.

Raffan appeared at Ellina's side. He settled into a legion stance, his expression steady, his chin tipped down. For a time he simply watched the match in silence, and Ellina thought that he would not speak. Then he did. "I heard you visited the crypts."

A breeze buffeted the courtyard, swirling robes and braids. The crowd ducked as a throwing knife went wide, missing its target and zipping dangerously overhead.

Raffan continued, "I wonder what you had hoped to find there."

Ellina mimicked Raffan's stance, hands behind her back, eyes steady on the duel. She had visited the crypts twice more since that first time, hoping to provoke another guard into revealing information as she had provoked the first. With Ermese missing and likely dead, speaking to the guards directly was her best chance at uncovering what Farah might be hiding. The guards, however, seemed to have tightened their ranks. They gave away nothing.

"I only wanted to visit my mother," Ellina replied, feeding him the same lie she had fed the others. Raffan was silent again, though this silence was different. It was expectant. It asked a question, which Ellina answered. "Farah closed the crypts, anyway. I was not able to enter."

The knife-wielding dueler threw another blade, which his brother deflected. Their green glass weapons hissed and whirred.

Raffan said, "Your mother is not buried in the crypts. As you know."

"Actually," Ellina answered coolly, "I did not know that."

"Really? No one told you?"

Raffan's voice was nothing like this fight. It was sly. It held a trick. But Ellina, who had come to trust in her own ability to outmaneuver anyone, reassured herself that he could not trick *her*. She faced him squarely. "I assure you, I was unaware of it."

"The guards tell me otherwise."

Ellina went still.

"You lied."

"I did not—"

"Mean to? Ellina. These *mistakes*." Raffan's eyes were hard. His mouth was angry. He looked almost…torn. "Have I not made myself clear? Farah is watching you."

Ellina sharpened at his words. "Are you disloyal to her?"

"Of course not."

"Yet you warn me anyway."

"Only because you do not listen."

"I do not listen because I do not *understand you*," Ellina hissed in a surge of her own frustration. "What would Farah think if she heard you deliver that warning? What does it gain you?"

"It gains me your safety."

"You do not care for my safety."

He held her gaze. "I did, once."

Ellina shut her mouth.

"The resistance stands no chance," Raffan said quietly. The sun angled into his face, accentuating the line of his brow, the plane of his nose. "Farah knows that those elves plan to rise against her. She knows how they gain confidence. They are even learning to strategize in the human way. It makes no difference." His voice was blunt. "Farah cannot be beaten. If there is land to conquer, she will conquer it. If there is a war to win, she will win it. It does not matter how strong the resistance grows. She will crush it—and anyone who dares stand against her."

Raffan's eyes were back on the fight. The knife-wielder had discarded most of his knives. He had only one left. He could throw it, and risk missing, and surely lose. Or he could keep it and attempt to fight his brother hand-to-hand. But a knife was no match against a sword.

The knife-wielder balanced on the balls of his feet at the edge of the ring, watching his brother. Out of options. Cornered.

Like Ellina was.

"Consider this my last warning," Raffan said. "If you are so determined to act against your own best interests, I cannot help you." He stalked away.

Ellina stared hard at the spot where the crowd had swallowed him, hard enough that her eyes began to water. Back in the ring, the knife-wielder cocked his arm. He took his chance—risky, potentially ruinous—and threw his final knife. The sword-bearer dodged the blade, which sped past his neck, barely missing.

Or so it seemed. The sword-bearer blinked. He brought a hand to his skin.

He drew it away, bloody.

. . .

Ellina had not quite forgotten Raffan's warning when she met Farah in her parlor the following afternoon, but rather set it alongside all his other warnings, to be taken out and examined at a later, more convenient time. She entered the queen's chambers from the south end, winding through a reception room, a reading room, an atrium. These chambers had played host to each queen of centuries past, but in Ellina's mind they belonged only to her mother, then and still.

One memory seemed to stand out above the rest. Ellina could still recall the night Queen Rishiana had called her three daughters into these chambers to announce that Miria would take the throne. It might have been the queen's right to decide when her daughter was ready, but Miria was clearly *not* ready. It was not only that she was young, though that was part of it. Miria was just…different. It was her laugh, which was too wild, and her smile, which was too free, and her pastimes, which were, frankly, too human. Miria was more willful than most elves, more spirited. Quick to yell, quick to joke, eager to break the rules. She struggled with social expectations. She hated to hide herself. The throne was not meant for her. Perhaps it would never be meant for her. And so, rather than accept her fate, Miria—with Ellina's help—had chosen to escape.

Together, they contrived a plan that would make it appear as if Miria had died while on a diplomatic voyage to the south, when really she was escaping into the mainlands, into a little city named Irek. There, Miria had found the life she always wanted. She fell in love. She was happy.

Ellina wished the story ended there. She did not like to think of what came next: how her sister was discovered by the southern elves, and ambushed in her home, and killed. Ellina shoved those thoughts away.

But this was like discarding a dagger only to pick up a throwing knife. Because there was Venick, in the everpool of Ellina's mind, and there was her reading room, cold with his absence, and there was Irek, and the history he and her sister had shared.

Ellina's steps were unsteady. Her lungs blazed. She felt a flash of something ugly, an emotion she had never allowed herself to feel before, because to feel it was wrong, and beneath her.

The feeling was jealousy, and Ellina was a fool.

How dare she feel jealous of her sister, whom she had loved, and was dead. Ellina had only ever wanted Miria's happiness. Venick had made Miria happy. And anyway, that was all years ago. A distant history.

Yet the feeling remained.

Ellina moved deeper into her mother's old rooms. She wondered if she would be feeling this way if Rishiana was still alive. She thought of Dourin and Venick together on their journey. She thought of the elves who refused to meet her gaze in the hallway. It occurred to Ellina that jealousy felt startlingly close to abandonment.

But this was unfair. If she felt abandoned, it was of her own doing. Dourin had not wanted to leave her behind. Venick would not have, either, had he known the truth. Yet Ellina insisted that she stay.

As she turned a final corner, Farah's voice sounded from out of sight. She was speaking to someone within the parlor, her tone clipped. Ellina slowed her pace, moving to her toes. She heard her sister's voice lift with a question.

"My comrades grow restless," came the reply. Youvan.

"You and your fellow southerners will have everything I promised," Ellina could hear Farah say. "In return, I want your cooperation."

"You want our *servitude*."

"Is something about our alliance not meeting your expectations?" Farah's tone had gone silken. Ellina knew that voice. It was how her sister sounded when she was laying a trap. "Am I not still your queen?"

"The south has no queen."

"I have been patient, Youvan. I have allowed you many liberties. Do not make me regret—" Farah cut off, and Ellina froze, listening as the silence shifted to footsteps coming her way.

Farah appeared in the doorway. "Sister."

"You asked to see me?" Ellina prompted.

"Yes." Farah turned her head. "Youvan. That is all for now. You are dismissed."

The conjuror did not argue. His face was blank as he swept by, his shadow sticking to the walls behind him. He did not spare the sisters another glance.

Farah motioned Ellina into the parlor. "I have a task for you." She began rummaging through a wooden cabinet, opening and closing the little drawers at random. "It seems that your human is more resourceful than previously thought."

This old argument. "He is not mine."

"You know what I mean."

Farah pulled a blank piece of parchment from one of the drawers, along with an ink bottle and quill. "It will come as no surprise to you that the human has involved himself with the resistance. We always expected humans to rise against us, and *that* human..." She trailed off as if to say *well, you know he was always trouble.* "What is surprising is that the elves have named him their commander."

Ellina blinked. "The resistance has named Venick their commander?"

"Yes."

"That is—are you certain?"

"My source is good."

Ellina's blood seemed to slow. She felt oddly breathless. Dourin had said nothing of this in his messages. Though, perhaps she should not be so surprised. Ellina knew how Venick could be, had seen his effect on others. Elves tried to resist his charm, only to succumb to the pull of it, like flowers towards the sun. Venick had a way of breaking down barriers, not all at once but slowly, brick by brick, as he had with Kaji and the palace servants. With Dourin.

With her.

Farah set her supplies onto a nearby pedestal table, the ink and parchment both. "I have given your suggestion more thought, and I believe that you are right. I cannot expect to conquer the mainlands if the humans retain any advantage over me, and right now they do have an advantage: their battleships." Farah tapped the paper. "If the humans have not yet realized this advantage, they will soon enough. And then what will they do?"

There was only one answer. "They will take to the sea."

"Indeed. But we are not ready to face a seafaring attack. And so, your task: divert their attention. I do not want your human—"

"He is *not mine.*"

"—getting any ideas about ambushing us here. I want you to send him a letter. You will propose a treaty. Peace between our countries."

Ellina huffed a laugh. "You must be joking."

"No."

"He is not a fool," Ellina said, though this brought a jolt of pain. How many times had she called Venick exactly that? "He will never believe such a letter."

"You have influenced him well before."

"That was different. He does not trust you. He certainly does not trust me. He will see through the lie." Just as he had seen through all of Ellina's lies. All but the last.

Farah's tone was icy. "Are you refusing to do it?"

"No."

"Good."

She pulled out the chair, motioning for Ellina to sit. Farah dictated while Ellina scribbled. When the letter was finished, Ellina blew lightly on the ink until dry, then rolled the parchment tightly and sealed the roll with wax.

It stung a little, handing that message to Farah. Knowing that Venick would read it and hate Ellina even more than he already did. Knowing—hoping, dreading—that he might be prompted to write back.

"I noticed you have befriended one of the palace servants," Farah said. "A fledgling named Livila?"

Ellina stiffened. "I would hardly call us friends. She is my maid."

"Nevertheless. I have heard that the servants are…discontented with many of my recent changes. I want you to question Livila. Ask her for the gossip among her fellows. How do those elves view their new queen? Do they fear me? Are they loyal? I want her to give names of potential rebels, too."

"She does not know anything."

Farah must have heard the defensiveness in Ellina's tone. She lifted a brow.

"If you want information," Ellina continued, "there are elves better suited to give it."

"Oh?"

"Yes." The moment seemed to appear before her, like sunlight on stone. "What about the servant from the kitchens? Ermese. He seemed to have more to tell."

Farah gave her a strange look. "Ermese no longer works in the kitchens."

"Oh." Ellina pretended to misunderstand. "Of course. He was blinded."

"No." Farah was still giving her that look. "He was a spy. I thought you would have gathered that from the interrogation. Traitors such as him cannot be allowed to wander free."

"So he is dead?"

"Not dead."

Ellina's pulse jumped. She waited.

"We did not want to hold him in the city," Farah explained. "That would have been too public. He is being kept in a private room beneath the palace, under the library. To your point, that servant has given us as much information as he can. He is no more use to us. We will not be questioning him further."

TWENTY-ONE

Venick crumpled the letter in one hand.

He was in the city's library, in a chair that had once belonged to his father. Outside, the day was clean. The view from the window showed the ocean, with its waves and warships dotting the horizon. Closer inland, fishing boats crowded for a slice of the shore.

The library's hearth—a wide, marble confection—was unlit. It was too hot for a fire, too bright a day to justify burning wood. Venick itched to light one anyway. He wanted flames. He wanted somewhere where he could watch Ellina's letter burn.

Lira took the letter from his hand and smoothed it over the table. She had been the one to invite him here, which Venick had taken as a good sign until she'd handed over the letter and said, "Explain."

He couldn't accuse her of intercepting his messages, because the letter hadn't technically been addressed to him. Written on the envelope in thin, looped cursive were the words, *To the Commander of Irek's Men.* Really, that described his mother better than it described him.

Yet the message was clearly not meant for Lira.

"It's written in code," his mother had said.

"That's not code, Mother. It's elvish."

"I do not speak elvish."

Venick stifled a sigh. "I know."

And so he'd been forced to translate while Lira grew cold, darkening to hear her son speak the language of the elves. *You killed your father for them, and now you've become one of them.*

"The letter is a lie," Venick said now, leaning back in his seat. "The Dark Queen doesn't want a treaty—it's a distraction." But a distraction from what?

There was only one answer.

Venick said, "She's planning an attack."

Lira was stony. "I thought elves couldn't lie in elvish."

"Only when they speak it."

"How do you know? How do you know so much about them?"

"Mother."

Lira turned her face away. She wore her hair in a single plait, her dress woven in the classic lowlander style. She spoke without looking at him. "You will write the elven princess back. Accept her peace offering. If what you say is true, your reply will buy us time. Meanwhile, the council and I will convene to discuss our next move."

It was the best Venick could have hoped for. Given their recent history, he wouldn't have been surprised if his mother had dismissed his concerns outright. And writing Ellina back was the right political move. Venick could tally the reasons.

But he felt a wash of resentment. He didn't want to write Ellina back.

He didn't want to imagine her reading his letter, or wonder if she would be as affected by the sight of his handwriting as he'd been by the sight of hers. He wanted to cut whatever ties still existed between them. To rinse himself clean of her.

Sometimes, Venick could almost understand the choice Ellina had made. Even now he could recall the grim purpose in her face whenever she spoke of duty to family and country. Like a yearning. Ellina had once saved Venick's life in honor of her eldest sister's memory. Had, more than once, risked her own life to do it. And she'd held hard to her laws, putting herself in danger in order not to break them, convinced that honor to her country was worth dying for.

Venick had hated that. But it had also somehow warmed him. Venick knew the impulse. He too risked himself when he shouldn't. He too felt how the heart sometimes chooses its path against all reason.

He thought of his walk into Irek that morning, and how the townspeople had eyed him, clearly distrustful, but under orders to do Venick and the elves no harm. He thought of the highland woman in their camp whose name he didn't know because she refused to tell him. He thought of her burned hands, and what his mother would say if she discovered he was hiding a highland fugitive when he was supposed to be proving his loyalty to the lowlands.

Venick saw that there were no good options.

He saw that even when he won, he lost.

"Alright," he said. "I'll write the letter."

. . .

The healer's hut was located on the west edge of the city. It was a single-roomed shop that had once been situated at ground-level and now…

wasn't. The hut was halfway sunk into the marsh, having been built—for reasons Venick couldn't fathom—in an area known for quicksand, and without the use of stilts.

Maybe the original builder hadn't known about the quicksand. Maybe they'd been afraid of heights, or couldn't afford better. Whatever the reason, the sight of the shop brought to mind a dead fish: a steaming pile of old bones and sagging flesh all stacked together and flopped in the sand.

It took Venick most of the walk there to get his mind off Ellina and the letter that was, at this very moment, winging its way back to her. Even then, by the time the hut came into view he wasn't exactly clearheaded. His hand ached from squeezing it. His heart felt small and tight.

Venick found a man-high stick and stepped off the gravel path. He made his way through the marsh towards the healer's hut, probing the earth as he went, testing each step before trusting it with his weight. He'd done this often as a boy, and even more often as a soldier. The healer—a middle-aged woman named Isha—was no physician, but she was skilled in herbcraft and offered things every soldier desired: remedies for pain or pleasure, tonics to boost strength or to ease nerves, and perhaps most importantly, discretion.

When Venick pushed through the narrow door and entered the stuffy little shop, however, it wasn't Isha behind the counter, but an elderly man Venick had never met.

"I get that unhappy look all the time," the man told Venick cheerfully. "If you're looking for Isha, she's gone. The constellations told her to pack her things and head north, so that's where she went."

Venick stared. Where Isha had been grimy, this man was impeccably clean. He wore *white* of all colors, which seemed impractical given the nature of his profession and the condition of his surroundings. And yet, the man was spotless. His grey hair was combed neatly back, his robes tied in a careful knot, his nails filed short and smooth. "She smoked too much jekkis, if you ask me," the man continued. "Leaving because of the *stars*. What nonsense." He pressed his hands flat against the counter. "My name's Erol. You're here for a salve, I presume. Something to ease stiff muscles?"

Venick followed Erol's gaze to where he'd been unconsciously rubbing his hand.

"Not for me," Venick replied. "But yes, a salve. Whatever is best to treat burn wounds."

Erol peered over his glasses. "Cooking accident?"

"Something like that."

"Interesting story from the firepit the other day. Did you hear? Four highlander prisoners went in, but only two bodies were found in the rubble." A pause. "I seem to recall that it's against our laws to aid a foreign enemy."

"You're not aiding a foreign enemy. You're aiding me."

"As I said."

Venick held back a sigh. "I'll pay you double."

"It's not about the money, lad."

"Something more than money, then."

"Oh?"

Venick pulled Traegar's book from his pocket. He fingered the binding, then held out the volume. "A trade. You're free to borrow this for as long as I'm in town. Copy whatever you want, take notes. That, in exchange for the salve."

Venick was fully prepared to explain what this book was and why it was worth borrowing, but Erol's eyes had gone suddenly wide. He cradled the book between his palms. "How did you come upon *this*?"

"You know it?"

"Know it? Hell. I *wrote* it. Or," he gave a smile, "half of it. But Traegar didn't mention that, did he?"

Venick blinked. "I don't understand."

"Well, that would be like him, taking all the credit. And it wouldn't have been hard for him to—"

"No, I mean, how do you know Traegar?"

Erol's smile twitched. "I spent some time in the elflands, in my youth."

"But the border…"

"Did not always exist, as I'm sure you know. There was a time when humans lived among the elves. Our conjurors even helped build their cities."

"Yes, but…" Venick's mind was spinning. He stared at this strange man, with his spotless white clothes and neat hair and wrinkled hands. "That was, what? A century ago? You would have to be ancient to have lived…" He realized what he was saying and closed his mouth. "I didn't mean—"

"Oh, enough." Erol waved a hand. "I *am* old. But things didn't happen as cleanly as the history books would have you believe." Another smile. "Do they ever? The border took some years to—how should I say?—*sink in*. Humans and elves still mingled after it was drawn, at least for a time. And Rishi was not always so strict about her laws."

"You knew Queen Rishiana too?" He didn't know what made him add, "Ellina's mother?"

Erol's smile faltered. "That was all long ago." He turned away, moving to examine the bottles on a nearby shelf, running his finger along their tops. Venick remembered Ellina once doing something similar to avoid meeting his eye.

He pulled a jar from the shelf. "You can have the salve." He slid it across the counter. "And you can keep the book. Gods know I don't need it."

"You don't want payment?"

"It would have been a good trade under different circumstances." Erol shrugged in a way that seemed to avoid the moment. "I'll consider that payment enough."

Venick knew better than to press his luck. And anyway, he recognized a cue to leave when he saw one. But… "If you were friends with Traegar, does that mean you were friends with Dourin too?"

"Aye, I knew Dourin."

"But he's here." Venick felt a flutter of excitement. "He's back at camp. We've—well, he's as infuriating as ever, but if you know Dourin, that should come as no surprise. I'm sure he'd be glad to see you."

Erol hesitated. There was uncertainty in his face, and discomfort, and also…remorse. Venick didn't understand it. As he waited for the man's answer, Venick realized that some furtive part of him was hoping that *this* might be enough to cement his place back in the city. Erol—established lowlander, respected healer, former friend of elves—could be the link the alliance needed. He knew that elves could be trusted. He could speak on Venick's behalf.

"Well?" Venick prompted. "Do you want to see him?"

"No," the healer finally replied. "I don't."

• • •

Venick found the highland woman sitting on a dry slab of tree bark at the edge of camp. He unstoppered the bottle and handed her the salve. "For your burns." She took the small glass jar gingerly from his palm, brought it to her nose, and sniffed.

Venick crouched beside her. "I'd like to know your name." When she gave no reply, he continued. "I want to help get you home, but I can't do that if I don't know anything about you. Who are you? What city are you from?"

The highlander's gaze flicked to him, then away. Nervous, Venick had once thought, except they'd done this enough times now for Venick to notice that her eyes were too narrow to be nervous, her shoulders too rigid.

Not just nervous, he'd decided. Angry. Defiant.

Well, she had every right to be. She'd been imprisoned, beaten, burned. She'd watched her friends die at the hands of his people. And now here was Venick, asking for her secrets.

It wouldn't be wise for her to share them. This woman wasn't naive. She was a refugee in a foreign land, weaponless, defenseless. She knew better than to give away information that might put her fellow highlanders at risk. And Venick—despite having saved her life—was by no means a friend. As far as she knew, he was planning on taking her hostage himself. Maybe sending his army north to her homeland, finishing what his people had started.

"Alright," Venick said. Then again, "Alright. You don't have to answer. But I want you to know that you're safe here. We're not going to hurt you."

He started to move away, but paused when his gaze fell, as if for the first time, to her black eye. Puffy skin, discolored, a mottled bruise forming up across her nose. Something about it nudged his mind, unsettling his thoughts in a way that he didn't understand...until he remembered.

She was hurt, Rahven had said about Ellina. *It was her wrists. They were bruised.*

She fought in the stateroom battle, Venick had replied. *Many elves were hurt.*

Except, bruised wrists were an odd injury for battle. In fact, Venick could think of only one reason someone might suffer an injury like that…

A hot summer day in the southern forests. Ellina's slender wrists outheld, a coarse rope, the knot used to bind them. Venick's own hands restrained, blood roaring, knees pressed into the dirt.

The memory punctured, it went deeper. Venick's fury. The tight clench of helplessness. How he'd been forced to watch as Ellina's comrades turned her around and ripped open her shirt and tied her hands to a tree. A whip was set in Raffan's grip. The lashes were red, and wept down her back.

She was not allowed to leave the palace, Rahven had said. *We were supposed to report to Farah if she attempted to escape.*

Escape. Like she was a prisoner.

As this last thought occurred to him, Venick recognized its danger. He squinted up into the cloudless sky and told himself to stop. He needed to bring himself back to *this* moment, to the here and now, before his mind began playing its favorite twisted game, inventing scenarios in which Ellina was not a traitor, and he was not betrayed. Venick had renounced her, he reminded himself. He didn't trust her. Remember the balcony. Remember how she had looked standing beside that conjuror, with their black uniforms and black hair and pale skin. A unified front.

Or *were* they? Venick couldn't help it, he couldn't stop himself from thinking what he was thinking. He saw the highland woman, who refused to answer his questions for fear of retaliation. How she glanced up at him, anxious and angry. He thought of Ellina on the balcony, and how she'd looked at the conjuror in just that same way.

What if Ellina had been afraid too?

What if *she* couldn't answer his questions plainly because she was afraid of the *conjuror's* retaliation?

Venick ran both hands through his hair. Gripped and held tight. He'd never known anyone who could lie like Ellina, but that was just the problem—she was a liar. He didn't trust her to tell him the truth. He didn't trust himself to see her truths clearly. He could only guess at what he didn't know, but guessing about Ellina had served him badly in the past.

The highland woman was staring at him. Venick saw himself as she must see him: pale, seemingly ill. She must have misinterpreted his unease, or else wanted to do something to wipe that look off his face, because she spoke for the first time. "My name's Harmon."

"What?"

"You heard me."

Venick focused his attention. The ground seemed to settle again. "Harmon." He tested the name. Gave a nod. "I'm Venick."

TWENTY-TWO

Livila surprised Ellina with a knock on her bedroom door. A light tap, the rap of a half-closed fist. She held a package in her hands. "A gift," Livila said. Ellina moved to let the elf in and accepted the package. It was hard, wrapped in plain cloth. Ellina knew what it was even before she pulled away the wrapping to reveal what lay underneath.

A dagger. The scabbard was simple yet sturdy, the metal ferrule sharp enough to do damage. Ellina turned the weapon over in her hands, appreciating its weight, its size, the tight seams. A fine make.

She pulled the blade free. Simple green glass, double-edged, a sharply tapered point. Either the gifter knew Ellina's preferences, or had guessed well. The dagger was exactly the kind of weapon she would have chosen for herself. "But who...?"

"Raffan," Livila supplied.

Ellina frowned, turning the dagger over in her hands. She was puzzling through the gift when Livila spoke again. "Why do you do that?"

"Do what?"

"Make faces."

Ellina smoothed her features. "A bad habit." She returned the blade to its scabbard. "You say Raffan gave this to you?"

"Yes."

"And he told you to give it to me?"

"Yes."

"Did he leave a note?" Ellina asked. "Or a message?"

"No. Neither."

"But he must have said *something*."

"He only asked that I deliver the package to you. Nothing more."

Ellina was quiet. She squeezed the leather scabbard between her fingers. Perhaps it was another trick. Maybe this, like Raffan's words at the duel, was a test…or a caution. The gifting of a dagger *did* have a sort of worried quality, as if to remind Ellina that—dagger or no—she was still at Farah's mercy. And yet, Ellina had the sense that the gift was also a kind of apology.

"How long have you worked in the palace, Livila?"

"All my life."

"And yet I only met you recently. Why is that?"

"Servants are not meant to be seen. We are taught to stay out of sight until we are needed. We use the servants' passages to move through the palace."

Ellina knew this. She had used the passages herself, though her knowledge of that labyrinth was thin. To an outsider like Ellina, the maze was to be used with caution. Elves had been known to lose their way down there, never to resurface. Only servants knew the full extent of those tunnels. Like a language, fledglings were taught the dialect of the labyrinth, and grew up traversing its dark twists and turns.

"Can you take the passages anywhere?" Ellina asked.

"Almost anywhere, except to some of the suites, and the queen's chamber."

"But say, the towers?"

"Yes."

"And the crypts?"

"That passage is blocked," Livila said. "It caved in last summer."

Ellina had expected this, but the pang of disappointment was as sharp as if she had been wholly unprepared. "What about a private room under the palace? One hidden beneath the library?"

"Do you mean Princess Ara's old suite?" Livila nodded. "Yes."

Ellina looked at her new dagger. She wondered if it was the sight of a weapon in her hands that had her feeling this way. Like she wanted to take a risk. She met Livila's eye. "I need a favor."

• • •

Ellina trailed a hand along the smooth tunnel wall. She listened, attuned to every sound, every distant echo. She carried no candle to light her way. No torch. Nothing to guide her but her own silent counting and Livila's instructions, ringing clearly in her head.

Ten paces forward, then left.

When Ellina had laid out her request, Livila had not balked. She had not asked *why do you need to get to Ara's old suite unseen?* or *what happens if you are caught?* Instead, the young servant asked for pen and parchment to sketch the path Ellina would take, explaining as she went. *Here, you must be careful of the missing step. Here, the path is tricky, do not be fooled by the shadows. Here, watch for the trap door, it often swings open without warning.*

When Livila was finished, she tried to hand the map over.

Keep it, Ellina had said. *It will be too dark for me to read.*

You can read by candlelight.

I am not bringing a candle.

That was when Livila had balked.

I cannot risk being seen, Ellina explained. What she did not add was that she refused to be caught carrying Livila's map, which could easily be traced back to the young servant. Ellina had already mired Livila enough in her plans. She would not risk her further.

Let me come with you then, Livila had offered, uncharacteristically bold. *My father taught me the labyrinth himself, and even he does not like traversing it alone. None of the servants do. It is one of the reasons we work in pairs. And it is not so simple as counting steps. If you miss even one turn…*

I will not lose count.

Ellina moved quickly though the tunnels, one hand on the wall, her eyes open and sightless. The passages smelled like summer earth, cool and dry. Ellina imagined herself a worm in the dirt, pushing between roots.

She reached the end of the tunnel.

You will come to a flat wall, Livila had explained. *Find the slender groove in its center.*

Ellina ran her hand along the wall until her thumb found a divot. She pushed and the wall gave way, slipping sideways along a cleverly-designed track built into the stone. A secret door.

The room on the other side, though not brightly lit, seemed blinding compared to the dark. Ellina squinted, blinking, listening. She knew from scouting the corridors earlier that two well-armed guards were stationed outside this chamber's door. She had assumed there would be more guards within, but she was wrong. The room was empty.

She stepped inside.

Ara's old suite looked more like a dungeon than a highborn's chamber. There were no plush rugs or silver decanters, no shimmering sconces or bowls of freshly picked fruit. The bedframe remained, as did a chest of drawers, but both looked bare and skeletal in the cold light. More notable than what was missing, however, were the additions. Three makeshift cells had been hammered into the back wall, two of which were small and square and outfitted with metal bars, and one at the end that was made of solid stone. There were no windows on that third cell, no way of peering inside. If a prisoner was currently housed within, Ellina could not see.

But here, in one of the barred cells: the servant Ermese.

At the sound of her footsteps, he approached the bars. His face came into the light, revealing sightless eyes.

"It is me," she whispered. "Ellina."

The servant's fingers wound around the metal like pale grubs. His expression became keen. "*Cessena*. Are…are you alone?"

"I am."

"Have you come to free me?"

His voice brimmed with hope. It made her answer sound worse by contrast. "No."

Though his eyes were unseeing, he dropped his gaze. Ellina continued, "I do not have the key to your cell. But…did you see where it might be kept?"

He motioned to his face as if to say, *how could I have seen?* "I suppose I deserve my fate. I should have known better. Your sister has spies everywhere, even among our ranks."

Ellina padded closer, glancing at the closed bedroom door, worried about the guards stationed on its other side. She was reminded of how

Venick had once been held prisoner in a suite much like this one, though they had not stationed guards outside of *his* door, nor locked him behind bars within the room.

Farah was being careful with her new captive.

"Do you know why I am here?" Ellina asked.

"You want to know what I saw in the crypts."

He was quick. His sharpness surprised Ellina. From the looks of him—milky soft, blooming with youth—she would have thought him naive.

"I am sorry," he continued, his voice a scrape of a whisper. "I promised that I would never again speak of what I witnessed. I made that oath in elvish in exchange for my life. My silence is bound."

"But you did witness something? My sister has something to hide?"

Ermese gave a slow nod. Ellina's pulse quickened. "A guess, then. Elven oaths do not prevent you from confirming guesses."

"I...suppose not."

"Does Farah's secret have something to do with the war?"

Ermese nodded.

"Is it a weapon of some kind?"

Again, he nodded.

Ellina wracked her mind, trying to think of how to narrow this down, of *what* kind of weapon could possibly necessitate the use of the crypts under the cover of night. "Is it—alive?"

Ermese shook his head. *No.* "It is—" he began, but broke off, coughing.

"Hey," came a guard's voice from outside the door. There was the sound of keys clinking. "What is going on in there?"

"They gather at midnight," Ermese whispered quickly, pressing his face to the bars as if he could push right through. "When there is no moon in the sky. You must wait until then."

"Who are you talking to?" a second voice asked. A key scraped into the lock. In a bare moment, that door would swing open.

Ellina did not dare thank Ermese, nor say anything else. Quickly, she slid back into the tunnel's opening, pressing the groove in the wall to return the door to its original position. The light sliced away, throwing her back into blackness.

・・・

Ellina did not attend dinner that night. She complained of an illness, kept to her rooms. All the servants were sent away.

She stared at her hands. Long fingers. Nails kept short. The palms were calloused, the skin scarred. Capable hands. Deadly.

Useless.

What could Ellina do? She had questions, puzzles yet to be solved, but she could not simply kill her way to an answer. The dagger—that *dagger*, so tempting and solid and new—lay on the table at her side. It seemed to call to her. It opened its throat and sang her name.

It was not the first time Raffan had gifted her a dagger. There had been a time once before, in their early years, shortly after he had become her commander. Back then things had been easy between them. Tender, even. Raffan had taken a certain interest in Ellina from the start. *You have potential*, he once told her. *I will teach you how to use this well.* He set the dagger into her palm, curled her fingers around the hilt, and lingered. *I want you to carry it always, and be safe.*

Later, years later, she would throw that dagger into the bay. He would watch her do it. His eyes then, too, had been torn. The first of many hurts they would inflict on each other.

The resistance stands no chance, Raffan had said during the duel. His voice had been blunted like a cannonball, meant to do the most amount of damage to the widest range. Ellina saw the danger in his words, that he might see straight to her heart and know that this was how to most quickly wound her: with threats towards the resistance. *Farah knows that the northern elves plan to rise against her. She knows how they gain confidence. They are even learning to strategize in the human way...*

But how could Farah possibly know that? Any scout could have observed the resistance heading south and reported back on its position, but this—understanding the thoughts and moods of an army, understanding how they strategized—went beyond mere scouting.

It was not the first time Farah seemed to know more than she should. She had learned of the negotiations for an alliance sooner than seemed possible. And then there was their conversation from the parlor.

The elves have named him their commander, Farah had said.

Are you certain?

My source is good.

Ellina looked again at her fingers. They curled into fists.

She thought of Ermese in his prison. His round, sightless eyes. To become blind was to be utterly helpless. If *she* had been a prisoner, she would have rather they cut out her tongue.

I suppose I deserve my fate, Ermese had said. *Your sister has spies everywhere, even among our ranks.* His words reminded Ellina of something that Youvan had said, something similar. *Do you think we do not know that the resistance has spies among us? Or perhaps you did not consider that we might have our own spies. Our messenger-raven reports movement from your ranks...*

Raven. It was an odd bird to use for delivering messages. Currigons were more common. In fact, Ellina had never seen a raven relay a message. They were too willful to be trained and they could not fly long distances. Ravens would make terrible messenger birds.

Ellina paused. A door seemed to open deep in her mind. Like playing the tiles of a dangerous game, she switched around the cadence of those words.

Our messenger-raven.

Our messenger, Raven.

What if raven was not a bird?

What if it was a name?

. . .

She entered the kitchens. The servants were busy with the morning's breakfast preparations, the oven fired, mounds of floured dough heaped along the worktables. Ellina caught a worker by the shoulder. "I am looking for Livila."

Livila did not work in the kitchens, so Ellina was left to wait—a quiet body amidst the rush—while someone went to fetch her. The young elf emerged looking ruffled, as if she had been woken from sleep. Which, Ellina reminded herself, she probably had been. It was the middle of the night.

"*Cessena?* Is something the matter?" Livila became more alert. "Did something happen with—?"

Ellina pulled the young elf into a corner of the kitchens where they could speak more privately. "I need to ask you something. Not about the palace tunnels." She took a breath. "You said your father left the city. That Farah ordered it."

Livila rubbed her eyes. "Yes."

"I want to know why. What task did the queen assign him?"

"I do not know. He did not say."

"He must have said *something*."

"No." Livila's face pinched. "Why? Has something happened to him?"

"No, nothing like that. But—did he tell you where he was going?"

"He did not, though…he writes to me. He speaks of warm weather. Maybe he is somewhere in the south?"

Irek was to the south. Ellina's heart seemed to shrink. "What did your father do? You said he was a servant. What was his duty?"

"He was a chronicler."

A storyteller. Unassuming, good with details.

"When did you last see him?" Ellina asked. "When did Farah send him away?"

"I do not remember, exactly."

"Please, try to think."

"I know, I am. But I still do not understand…"

"Did anything significant happen on the day that he left?"

"Not that I can remember."

"Are you certain?"

"Well…"

"Yes?"

"It was at the start of autumn. The same day the human returned to the city."

Ellina sucked in a breath. "Livila." She dreaded the question. "What is your father's name?"

"Oh." The young elf blinked again. "It is Rahven."

TWENTY-THREE

Venick thumbed his frosted mug. The ale was bitter and cold, darker than he was used to drinking, but good. He brought the mug to his lips again.

Around the tavern men and women worked and drank. Here, a man tuning a lyre. There, a woman polishing a table. And there, another sweeping the floor. None of these lowlanders were employed here, save the barkeep, but this was the way it was done in Irek. The tavern was a common area, the hearth of the city, and it was everyone's duty to help keep their home.

If anything was out of place, it was the few elves mingling there, their unblemished skin at odds with the rough wooden walls, and with the humans, who were bearded and grease-stained and ruddy. The elves hung around the tavern's edges, talking softly, mostly keeping to themselves. Rahven was among them, as was Branton, both of whom had come at Venick's request. He wanted the elves to—well, if not to mingle with the humans, then at least to grow more comfortable sharing space. At present, men and elves sat at separate tables, happy to ignore each other. But no one had yet drawn a weapon. No threats had been made, no insults muttered under breaths. It was better than he'd expected. And a start.

Venick drained the last of his mug and was just pushing away from the table when Dourin stalked into the tavern, looking murderous. "Dourin?"

The elf went straight for Rahven. "Empty your pockets."

Rahven appeared startled. "What?"

"Empty your pockets. *Now.*"

"I do not—"

Dourin lashed out, gripping Rahven by the wrist, using his free hand to find a sensitive nerve in the chronicler's elbow. Rahven gave a cry, doubling over, helpless in Dourin's hold. "Do it."

Venick rushed to intervene. "Dourin. Stop."

"He is a spy."

"What?"

"He is a spy for the Dark Queen."

The entire tavern was on their feet now.

"That's impossible," Venick managed. "We asked him. Outside Evov, we asked him in elvish if he had any ties to Farah."

"And do you remember his reply?"

Rahven's hair had fallen into his face. The column of his throat bobbed.

Dourin shoved the elf to the floor and drew his sword. "Rahven, empty your damn pockets."

"Please." Rahven's eyes were bulging. "You do not understand."

"I think I understand perfectly."

Venick's mind was scrambling, searching for purchase. What had they asked Rahven that day on the mountain? How had he answered?

They said they would have me killed if I did not join Farah, Rahven had said. *They gave me a choice. Join their new regime, or die.*

And so you wish to avoid death by joining us?

Yes.

Dourin aimed a hard look at Branton. "Search him."

Branton was rough. Rahven tried to fight his way free, but he was outmatched, and soon Branton had retrieved a scrap of parchment from the elf's pocket. He gave it a glance, then passed it to Venick.

It was a coded message. Venick couldn't read the words, but that hardly mattered. There was only one reason Rahven would be carrying a message like that.

And so you wish to avoid death by joining us?

Venick understood. He saw how Rahven might have twisted his reply. The chronicler had never actually specified whether he'd taken Farah's deal. It was possible that Rahven *had* avoided death by joining Venick. He'd joined them as a spy, just like Farah wanted.

"How much does she know?" Dourin demanded. "What have you told her?"

Rahven quailed. He didn't answer, but his answer was obvious: everything.

Dourin swore.

"The Dark Queen has my daughter," Rahven pleaded. "She would have killed her if I did not obey."

"And you think your daughter will live if the Dark Queen is not defeated?" Dourin's voice burned. "Did it not occur to you that we might have been able to *help?* Innocents will die because of your treachery. You have undermined everything we have been working for."

"Please..."

"What of the poison?" Dourin went on. "We found a vial of amberwood hidden in our supplies. Was that your doing as well?"

"The queen gave it to me," Rahven said. "She told me to hold onto it, only that. She did not even tell me who it was for."

"And I suppose you were too stupid to guess."

"I would not have used it!"

"Say it in elvish."

Rahven fumbled. He could not.

"Traitor," Branton hissed.

"I had no choice," Rahven cried.

"You had a choice," Dourin said, hefting his sword. "You just chose wrong."

And he stabbed.

Rahven's mouth popped open. He wrapped a surprised hand around the hilt protruding from his chest. His eyes rolled, and he fell.

A long silence. The tavern seemed to ring with it. Venick stared at Rahven's lifeless body, stunned. He glanced around, expecting to see the humans' shock, but the men and women were looking at Dourin with a kind of steely approval. In the mainlands, the law on traitors was clear.

Dourin's lip curled as he pulled his blade free. He was still fuming, still furious, no doubt pulsing with what he'd just done. What they'd just learned. His eyes sought Venick. "The currigons," he said. "He's been using those birds to pass messages to the queen. He said they were a symbol of hope. Of course they were for *him*."

Venick remembered seeing a currigon hawk circling above the city. The gentle wings, the blood-red tail. He'd thought it odd that a wild currigon might fly so far south. He'd known that elves used currigon hawks as messenger birds, but he'd been distracted by that same tale. *When we see a currigon hawk in the sky, we know it as a symbol of hope.*

"We have to assume that Farah knows everything," Dourin went on. "About the alliance and our plans to unite the mainlands. About our strength, our tactics, the size of our armory, the skill of our fighters."

And the location of their black powder stores, Venick thought numbly.

It was one of the oldest rules of war: always stay one step ahead of your opponent. Keeping those secrets had been a precious advantage, which they'd now lost. It was a heavy blow.

And it was his fault. Venick had grown complacent. He'd been preoccupied with things he shouldn't have let preoccupy him, had failed as a leader. A spy should never have lasted so long among them. An assassin should not have.

Venick watched blood pool under the chronicler's body. He promised himself that from now on, he'd be more diligent. He promised that from now on, he'd question everything.

Starting with Dourin.

. . .

He waited until Rahven's body had been hauled away and the tavern was clear. He cornered Dourin. "How did you know?"

The elf sat at a table in the tavern's center, wiping blood from his sword—or pretending to. The blade, as far as Venick could tell, was spotless. Yet Dourin continued to work it with a rag. "I told you already," he replied. "The currigons."

"I saw them too, flying over the camp. That doesn't mean I immediately suspected treachery."

"Maybe you should have."

It was no less than Venick had thought earlier, yet he felt a rush of anger to hear it voiced. He crossed his arms, planting himself squarely in the elf's line of sight. Dourin gave a sigh and set the rag aside. "It was a hunch."

"Convenient, these hunches of yours."

"Rahven was too nosy. He was too curious about things that did not concern him."

"All the elves are curious. Are you saying we're surrounded by spies?"

"Rahven was cunning," Dourin continued. "He had something to hide."

"So do you, I think."

The accusation landed. Dourin flinched and looked away. There was a tense silence.

"Perhaps," Dourin said slowly, "we should take a walk."

"I don't want to take a walk."

"I think you might."

They left the city behind. Dourin led the way, guiding them off the road into the northern woods. The land here was marshy, the trees stunted. Their rubber leaves shifted in the afternoon breeze.

Dourin picked up speed. Venick followed, silently at first, then huffing a little, trying to keep pace. It was easy to forget how quickly elves could move when they wanted. Easy to forget how far they could travel, alone and on foot, in a few spare hours. Quick enough to scope these entire woods in an afternoon. Quick enough to find something worth returning for now.

Dourin came to a halt in an unremarkable grove. The trees here were skinny, their finger-like roots arching over scummy ponds. Somewhere nearby, a frog sang her throaty song. But this was nothing unusual.

Venick touched Lorana's necklace through the fabric of his trousers, a recent habit. "There's nothing here."

Dourin planted himself on a patch of dry earth and began stripping off his boots. His socks. Venick watched, frowning, as Dourin set them neatly aside and stood once more, coming to the edge of what appeared to be a small puddle. He stepped inside, toes first, careful not to splash. The puddle was barely wide enough to fit both of Dourin's feet.

"Is this some kind of joke?" Venick asked. "It's not very funny."

Dourin closed his eyes and inhaled. "*Do you have a message for me?*" he asked in elvish.

"No, of course I don't—"

The puddle began to ripple. It brightened, shimmering with an almost silvery light, and Venick understood everything all at once. Dourin hadn't been asking *him*. He'd been asking the puddle, which wasn't a puddle at all.

It was an everpool.

A miniature one. Venick moved closer, seeing now what he'd missed before. Unlike the surrounding marshlands which were swampy and green, this water was clear, its surface perfectly smooth, like a mirror.

You step into the water and ask it your questions, came the memory of Ellina's voice. *Sometimes it gives you answers.*

From the shallow bottom of the everpool something appeared. A ribbon, Venick thought at first, until Dourin reached into the water and pulled it out. It was a thin strip of parchment.

Dourin read the note quickly, then met Venick's eyes. "Farah is beginning to call her forces back to Evov."

"Who told you that?"

"My contact."

"You have a contact in Evov?" Dourin didn't answer. He was pulling his boots back on. "Dourin."

"Yes."

"Who?"

"I cannot say."

"Yes you can." Dourin went on ignoring him. "Let me see that message."

The parchment was dry, despite having just emerged from a puddle. The handwriting was thin, black, splotchy in places. Familiar, now that Venick thought about it. Hadn't he encountered this handwriting before? Or was it just that he wished he had?

They gather in the high city, the note read. *She plans soon to strike.*

Venick turned the parchment over, looking for the rest of the message, but that was it. Two short sentences, no explanation, no signature.

"How often do you communicate with this envoy?" Venick asked.

"We try to keep our interactions limited. It is not safe to send messages too frequently. And there are few everpools this far south. I am lucky to have found this one at all."

"Is your messenger someone in the palace? Or the city?"

Dourin was reluctant. "In the palace."

"Male or female?"

"Venick."

"Just answer the question."

"If you are worried about the reliability of this elf, do not be. I trust them completely."

"I want a name."

Dourin shook his head. "You do not need a name."

"I don't like that you've got a contact in Evov and I don't know who it is. I don't like that you didn't tell me from the start."

"I promised to keep the spy's identity anonymous. Do not make me break my promise." Venick crossed his arms, ready for more argument, but Dourin cut him off. "Do you trust me?"

The question startled Venick. Did he trust Dourin? *Yes*, he thought, and *no*, and *hell*. He couldn't help but think of how he'd put his trust in Ellina. How he'd pledged his loyalty to Lorana and his father and his country. Each time, he'd been given reason to regret it. Venick had a bad habit of sticking his faith where it didn't belong, of believing in others too blindly. Wasn't this the reason he hadn't uncovered Rahven sooner? Wasn't this why he'd been blindsided by Ellina's deception, and Lorana's before that, and his father's?

It occurred to Venick that it wasn't Dourin he didn't trust, but himself.

Dourin finished lacing his boots and straightened, looking very un-Dourin like. He held his arms awkwardly at his sides. His eyes were unsettled.

Do you trust me?

Venick released a breath. Maybe he wished Dourin had told him about his envoy from the beginning, but so what? Dourin was telling him now.

Venick touched a hand to his own chest, then set that hand on Dourin's shoulder: the elven symbol of friendship. He gave his answer in elvish. "*I trust you.*"

TWENTY-FOUR

"Rahven is believed to be dead."

Farah stood before the fireplace of her parlor, hands joined behind her back, her attention on the flames. Outside the glassless window it had begun to snow. The flurries were light, fuzzy-looking. Not fat enough to stick. They melted as soon as they touched the windowsill.

Ellina could tell that Farah was furious.

"I do not know how his position was uncovered," Farah continued. Firelight played across her armor, swirling red and gold against the metal. "He was a crucial emissary, and now he is gone."

This news was not unexpected. Venick had taught Ellina that in war, even a single advantage could mean the difference between winning and losing. If Rahven was working as a spy for the queen, how many advantages had they lost because of it? The resistance would kill him for his crimes. There was no other option.

Yet the news of Rahven's death cut deep. Ellina's mind reached not for the chronicler, but for Livila, that young elf who had no mother, and now had no father either.

Ellina knew what it was to be an orphan. To belong to no one. She knew how it felt to wake in the night, disoriented, the memory of her mother's death dancing across her skin. How it shaped and reshaped her with each new imagining, and how Ellina realized, only after her mother was gone, all the questions she wished she had asked. The things she wished she had said.

And what of Ellina's father? An elf she had never known, and never would.

"I am sending Youvan south with a few others to find out what happened." Farah said. She turned to meet Ellina's eye. "You will go with him."

The room, already dense, became oppressive. "You wish for me to leave the palace?"

"And find out what happened to Rahven. Yes."

"I—am surprised." Ellina chose her words carefully. "I thought you wanted me to remain here."

"Do you object?"

"No."

"Then it is settled." Farah returned her attention to the flames. Her spine was locked straight, her angular shoulders like twin wings. "Be prepared to leave by morning. Take with you only what you will need. You and the others will be traveling to where Rahven was seen last—to the city of Irek." An odd note had entered Farah's voice. Ellina could not see her sister's face, but she thought she knew what she would find if she could: the ghost of a smile. "It will be like one of your old legion missions, will it not?"

Ellina stiffened. Her old legion missions had often been to hunt and kill humans along the border.

"Our deal," Ellina started slowly, hating to even mention their bargain for fear of drawing attention to it, yet hating more the thought of leaving it alone. "It still stands. I will travel to Irek. I will help uncover what happened to Rahven. But no harm will come to those humans."

"Our deal," Farah said absently. "Of course."

• • •

There was no visible line separating the elflands from the mainlands. When the border had been drawn, elves simply claimed everything from the southern forest east. They said that if humans did not like it, they could fight to reclaim what they wanted.

The humans decided the border was fine where it was.

Ellina had always imagined the border to be a solid thing. A black gate, tall iron bars, pointed finials marching along the top. Or perhaps an ocean, glassy and grey.

In truth, the border was not a gate, or an ocean; it was a slab of marble, the same all the way through. And indeed, when Youvan led their small party across the border into the mainlands, none of them really knew *when* they had crossed. The land looked the same in all directions: grassy, fertile, pocketed with lakes and rivers. Gusts of wind came in sudden, violent bursts, tugging at their clothes and hair. The clouds were puffy and white and swift.

Youvan set a grueling pace. They traveled by night, fifteen elves total, three of whom were southern conjurors. Ellina did not actually know that last for certain—they looked like conjurors, with their black hair and bony fingers, though she had seen no actual magic from any of them. Conjurors or not, the southerners kept to themselves, throwing Ellina icy looks if ever she ventured too near. Their message was clear. She was not one of them.

Ellina ignored them. She refused to be intimidated. She was better than that.

And yet, their hostility seemed to touch Ellina in a way it usually did not. Perhaps it was because she was away from Kaji and Livila, the last of her allies. Perhaps it was her recent conversation with Farah, and the knowledge that Rahven was dead in part by her own hand. Perhaps it was the quiet nights with no one to talk to, and how Ellina would gaze up at the stars, and feel small.

She missed Dourin. She missed Miria. She longed for a friend.

She had no right to feel lonely, not when there was everything *else*. But loneliness found its way into her heart nonetheless. It was there—small, hard, a pebble that rattled when she moved—as they traveled from the northern elflands to the southern mainlands. It kept her company as she rode along in the conjurors' wake, until the night Irek finally came into view: a twinkling bundle of lights in the distance.

"We split up," Youvan said. "Find him."

. . .

Ellina crept through Irek's streets. Though the hour was late, the city was wide awake. Light streamed from windows and doorways, music sounded from taverns, laughter echoed between buildings. Men and women strolled arm in arm, their steps a little uneven, their faces turned to the breeze.

It had been easy sneaking up to the city. Easy, sliding past the fallen watchtower and into Irek's muddy streets. Youvan had ordered that they leave their horses out of sight, but that precaution seemed unnecessary. Ellina doubted anyone would have looked twice even if they had ridden in on horseback. The city was distracted, its attention turned inward. No one paid any mind to the fifteen black-clad newcomers smoking through the streets.

Ellina moved nimbly, darting between puddles of light, her steps careful, quick. She remembered doing this as a child, moving soundlessly from shadow to shadow, sneaking up on Miria just to hear her squeal. It was the kind of game they both had loved, each in their role: the hunter and the princess.

Ellina lingered on that thought. Here at last she was seeing the place where Miria had made her new life. Where she and Venick had come to know each other. Had they, too, walked these streets arm in arm? Had they turned their faces to the breeze? Ellina could almost see it, the image vivid enough to make her pause…and pause again, to remember that Venick was, at this very moment, somewhere in this city.

Ellina realized she was nervous.

She brushed her hands down her front, touched the dagger she now wore strapped to her belt. It had felt good to don her legion armor once again, but armor suddenly felt like not enough. Like nothing, actually. A useless defense.

She reached the mouth of an alley and halted, waiting for a band of young men to pass. They hung on each other, laughing, smelling of booze. They did not notice her.

She lifted her eyes and saw the tavern.

It seemed to burst into her vision, a spill of light and color. Through the windows Ellina could see the scene inside, filled with humans and— her heart thumped at the sight of it—*elves*. They lounged in chairs and gathered around tables, talking. To each other.

Ellina had of course known that a human-elven alliance must mean the interconnection of humans and elves. And Dourin often reported on their progress—shaky, slow, but growing strength—in his messages. Yet to *see* it, to see the results of their work, to witness the melding of their two races...

It was a gift.

And then, a better gift: *Dourin*. Ellina spotted him there inside the tavern's main room, weaving through bodies, a drink in each hand. He lifted the mugs overhead to avoid being jostled, nudging someone with an elbow to get their attention. Ellina saw that person turn, and give a tired grin, and accept the offered drink.

Venick.

Ellina ducked away, feeling caught and unbalanced and totally unprepared. Though, if she had stopped to examine her thoughts more closely—something Ellina did not want to do—she might have admitted that she expected to find Venick here. That she hoped she would. Or maybe worst of all: that she had come looking for him.

Ellina felt dizzy under the star-speckled sky. A sour taste rose to her mouth. For several long seconds she did nothing but crouch, tense, poised for flight...until she became aware of how she must look, hunched in the darkness like a thief. Rather than shame her, the image gave Ellina confidence. She was a shadow. She was a ghost.

Slowly, she looked back out of the alley.

He was sitting in a chair near the window, an arm draped over the chair's back, a map spread before him. There was color in his cheeks. A familiar glint in his eye. He looked worn, but well. Venick said something to Dourin, and though Ellina could not hear him through the tavern windows, she imagined his voice as it was in her memory: confident, maybe a little hoarse. But open, too, as he shared some opinion, some hidden thought.

Or maybe his voice would sound a different way. Maybe it would drop low, go deep, playing across her skin like music as he came closer...

Ellina's throat was dry. Her eyes pricked. She had stayed too long. It was time to go.

Venick turned his head.

He peered out through the glass. His brow furrowed. For a moment, Ellina imagined that he met her eye.

Her heart began to hammer even as she knew that it was impossible. Ellina was swathed in darkness while he was bathed in light. She could see *in*, but he should not be able to see *out*.

Yet he was standing. He was moving towards the door. There was purpose in his gait.

Ellina took a startled step back. She tripped over her own feet. Now came the shame. She *never* stumbled.

She turned and vanished into the night.

• • •

Venick didn't know what had made him look up.

Maybe it was the ale. This tavern had always served strong stuff, and Venick had long ago lost his tolerance for it.

Or maybe it was the exhaustion. The way he couldn't stop replaying the memory of Rahven's death in his head. The now ever-present paranoia of more spies among them.

Maybe it was fate. The hand of a god.

Whatever it was, Venick felt almost ill with the sudden, chilling certainty that he was being watched. He stood from his seat, peering through the window. He couldn't see anything beyond the tavern's bright reflection in the glass.

"Everything alright?" Dourin asked, brow hitched.

Let it go, Venick told himself.

Sit down, he told himself.

But.

Venick muttered something about needing air. He stepped out into the night.

. . .

Ellina slipped through the city. She had drawn up her hood, though she was tempted to lower it again, if only to better help her see. She moved away from Irek's brightly-lit center, leaving the lamplight behind. The shadows thickened. Here, there was nothing but moonlight to guide her.

It was too soon to return to Youvan's meeting point outside the city, so Ellina picked a path, following the sound of the ocean. She could hear the waves, their faint hush, soft in the background until she chose to pull them to the forefront of her awareness. Then they were a deep roar.

She reached the shore. She could not really see the ocean, which melded seamlessly into the black sky. But she could see the sand glowing white under the light of the moon. And she could smell the water, salty and strong.

She moved—more quickly now, as if pulled by an unknown force—towards the shoreline, then came to a halt. This was, she realized, a terrible idea. The shore was wide open. Utterly exposed. If Ellina wished to remain hidden, she should return to the alleys, or the nearby woods. The marshlands, even. There were many options better than this.

Footsteps behind her. The quiet slide of feet through sand.

Ellina turned.

And it was as if no time had passed. Venick stood there, his face bleached of color in the moonlight, his grey eyes pinned to hers. He was quiet, his gaze searching, mouth slightly parted. Not angry. She had thought he would be furious, but he was...

What was he?

Stunned. Confused.

He seemed to shake himself. His surprise gave way to something darker. He crossed his arms, settling into a posture of determined nonchalance. "Well. This is a surprise."

Ellina swallowed. She felt lightheaded. She wondered dizzily, almost giddily, what would happen if she fainted. Would Venick move to catch her? Step back and watch her fall? But of course she would not faint. She was the hunter in this story, not the princess, despite having just been hunted, and being a princess besides.

"What are you doing here, Ellina?"

His voice was as she remembered: deep, demanding. Behind Ellina, the waves washed, and folded back, and came again. "Nothing."

"It doesn't look like nothing."

Her stomach jangled with nerves. When she spoke, her voice was all wrong: high and breathless. "I was just passing through."

"Really."

"Yes."

"Forgive me if I don't believe you." He wore a tense smile, nothing like the one he had given Dourin in the tavern, nothing at all like the one he might have once given her. "Not that I expect the truth from you. But never mind, I think I can guess. You're dressed in your scout's uniform. And it was *you* watching me through the tavern window. So, you were sent as a spy? Now that I might believe, though…" he took a half-step back, appraising her, "if you're here as a spy, why would you reveal yourself to me?"

"I did not reveal myself. You found me."

"You *let* me find you."

His words surprised her. Ellina realized only then that what he said was true. She was a legionnaire. An elite scout. If she had not wanted Venick to find her, he would not have.

But this made no sense. Ellina had fled when she saw Venick exiting the tavern. She had not wanted to be discovered.

Had she?

Ellina recognized this feeling. It was the same way she had felt on Traegar's balcony all those months ago: like she was skating close to ruin. Venick had asked for the truth that final time and Ellina had been tempted to give it, despite the fact that they had been trapped in a city swarming with conjurors, or that Youvan had been *right there*, or that admitting the truth would have undoubtedly led to a fight, and Venick's death. Ellina could not have told Venick anything then, even if she had wanted to.

And now? What did she want now?

"It must be strange for you," Venick said. His posture was stiff. He shoved his hands into his pockets. "Coming to the place where your sister was murdered."

These words were meant to be an insult, as if he wanted to shame Ellina by the mention of Miria, but Venick's voice had cracked at the last moment, too sincere to do damage. Ellina was aware of his every movement, every taut muscle, every thought behind his face. She said, "It must be strange for you as well."

"It is." He threw her a swift look, as if waiting for her to mock him for it. "You two are so unalike," he barreled on. "But then, you both had secrets. I bet you're keeping secrets even now."

"And what if I am?"

The words were out, she could not draw them back. Ellina held her breath, waiting for Venick to hear the yearning in her voice, to see right through to her hidden heart. But he only said, "I don't care about your secrets anymore."

"That's not true."

He gave a dry laugh. "You don't want it to be true, maybe." His tone was sarcastic. He didn't believe his own words. Yet Ellina's cheeks warmed, and *that* he saw. Venick blinked. His eyes shone like ice, all sarcasm gone now as his gaze sharpened, picking her apart. Her heart scurried along. "Gods. You really don't."

He continued to stare. Ellina saw the quick rise and fall of his chest, the way his brow creased. He started to speak but stopped himself, pressed fingers into his eyes, frustrated. "What are we doing." It wasn't quite a question. "What are *you* doing? You said that you didn't care about me. That you wanted me dead." He dropped the hand. "You said it in elvish, and gods Ellina, I've tried to see a way around that. *Is* there a way around it? Is that what you're trying to tell me?"

The night swirled around them. It swaddled them thickly in its folds. Ellina felt distant here, as if they had traveled to another world, a world where their lives were their own, where there was no war and no secrets and nothing at risk. She had good reasons to hide from Venick, she knew that she did, yet Ellina could not quite remember what those reasons were. Back in Evov, keeping her secrets had seemed so vital. And yet…what if she could simply let go? What would happen, really, if she told Venick the truth?

It would be a relief to tell him. She could explain everything. She would step into his arms, bury her face into his chest and apologize, beg forgiveness. The vision was so vivid that it made her chest ache.

She licked her lips. "I think you should know," she tried, but the words were too thick. His eyes no longer looked like ice—they were dark oceans. She swallowed and tried again. "I think you should know that—"

An explosion split the air.

Ellina felt the shockwave judder along the shore, up her legs, into her bones. Her chest trembled with it. There was a surge of hot air and night became day again, bursting brightly behind her eyes. Ellina ducked, flinging up an arm. When she lowered it again, she did not believe what she was seeing.

The ocean was on fire. In the distance, a cloud of flame mushroomed into the sky. Its red belly glowed like the eye of a giant monster.

"The black powder barge," Venick murmured, face pale. His eyes jumped back to Ellina and he demanded again, darkly, "What are you doing here?"

Ellina was shaking her head. "No," she managed. Farah had promised. Their bargain... "It cannot be—"

The sky began to fall. Debris from what must have been an exploded ship rained down in huge, burning chunks, arcing over the ocean and into the city like falling stars. In the distance came peeling cries of alarm. A moment later, the city's war bells began to ring.

Venick cursed and drew his sword.

Ellina barely registered the movement. Her mind had caught, snagging. This could not be happening, Irek could not be under attack.

Venick's sword went to her neck. "Tell me your plan," he snarled. Behind him, the smoke continued to balloon towards land. "Tell me what's happening."

"I do not know." Ellina's voice sounded like it was underwater. She stared at Venick's blade, the sheen of green glass in the fire's light. She spoke in elvish. "*Venick. You must believe me. This was never supposed to happen, there was never supposed to be an attack.*"

Venick gave her a look of such open loathing that she drew back. "But there was supposed to be *something*." Ellina started to reply, but he cut her off. "I should kill you. I should kill you right now."

It had not occurred to her, before, to be afraid. Now fear struck like a needlepoint in her brain. It closed her throat, turned her thoughts to dust. She froze, and Venick saw her fear, stole it from her eyes, wrapped it up in all the awful things he believed about her. He looked different then. Terrible. He grimaced and lowered his sword. "I *am* a fool."

He darted away.

TWENTY-FIVE

Ellina raced after him.

Her mind fuzzed the way she had seen algae scum over marshland ponds. She was desperate to break through the murk. To punch her fist through that green layer. Her heart climbed as she followed Venick into Irek's streets, then promptly lost sight of him.

The city had devolved into a state of panicked confusion. Overhead, debris from the destroyed barge continued to rain down in huge, fiery chunks. Bits of wood and metal crashed through the streets, smashed into wagons and roofs. Into people, too. Ellina saw a woman with a bloody, ruined arm. A man with a deep gash in his thigh. The air smelled like a million candles burning.

Ellina pushed forward, dodging townspeople, aware of the chaos yet somehow untouched by it, or perhaps simply unable to distinguish the chaos around her from that of her own mind. She scanned the streets, searching for those broad shoulders, those grey eyes. She would find

Venick, she would explain everything. This was not what he thought. This was never supposed to happen.

A keening sheet of metal smashed into a woman beside Ellina. The woman's limbs jerked, her head snapping at an awful angle. Ellina ground to a halt.

The woman's body lay in ruins. The force of the falling debris had split her scalp in two. Gore splattered the cobblestone. Nearby, someone else saw the fallen women and screamed.

And then, a different sound. One that Ellina did not recognize, could not place. A whip, she thought at first. The sharp snap of leather.

Not a whip. Those were *ropes*, splitting as a nearby building wobbled on its support beams. Overhead, falling clumps of wood and metal were cutting through the network of ropes that looped between shops and homes. The building beside Ellina strained against its remaining tethers, heaved, and broke free.

For a moment Ellina did nothing. Then it was as if the fear that affected everyone else finally found its way to her. As the building began to fall, her heart screamed, *move*. It screamed, *now*. She rushed to dodge out of the way.

Not fast enough.

The building's shadow expanded: a black maw swinging wide. It roared, and crashed to the ground on top of her.

• • •

Venick went for the tavern.

He wasn't thinking. He wasn't thinking about all the miserable ways he'd failed, how he had been the one to show Rahven where the black powder was kept, how he'd brought destruction upon this city simply by returning to it. He wasn't thinking about how he'd allowed himself to be tricked, how the mere sight of Ellina had been enough to lure him away while the southerners set fire to the barge. She'd been the siren and he the hapless sailor, and now Venick was drowning, he was taking on water, he was being swept away by all the things he refused to think.

Around him, fire rained. The city was blurred with smoke, everything chaotic, disorienting. Venick had never been to the far west, nor had he seen the volcanic eruptions those lands were known for, but he imagined that they must look something like this: as if the world had been cleaved in two.

He put on a surge of speed. He crashed into someone, caught them by the upper arms, spun and kept going. Venick's pulse was so quick that he couldn't feel the separate beats. He thought of Dourin back at the tavern. Branton and Lin Lill and all the others. He thought of the danger they were in and how this, too, was his fault.

"What are you *doing*?" A voice to his left brought him up short. Venick spun to find his mother marching towards him. Her words threaded high. "Where are you going? The exit is *that way*."

"My friends—"

"Damn your friends. We need to evacuate!"

"I can't just leave them."

Lira strode closer. Nearby, a building lay in splintered ruins. Overhead, ropes pulled and snapped, the city's rigging all unwinding. His mother's face shone chalky white. "This is no time to be noble."

"It's not about that."

"If you think—"

"They're only here *because of me*," Venick burst, flinging out his arms. "Because I brought them south, I asked them to come into the city, and then…" He thought again of Rahven's coded messages. Ellina luring him to the shore. Their most precious weapon currently hailing from the night sky. "There isn't time. I have to go."

Lira grimaced. "Alright." And then again. "*Alright*. If we can make it to the tavern, we'll use the escape tunnel."

The escape tunnel. That single hidden passage built under every manmade city, meant to sweep dignitaries away in case of an attack. There was an entrance to the tunnel inside the tavern, but it wasn't the reminder of its location that startled Venick, nor his mother's suggestion that they reveal that human secret to the elves. It was her use of the word *we*.

"You're not coming with me," Venick said.

"Of course I am."

"It's not safe. The tunnel—there are risks."

"There are always risks."

"There's still time for you to get out by the main road if you go now."

"Would you choose my path for me?"

Venick shut his mouth. It was the start of an old human saying, to which he was supposed to reply, *Not I, but the gods*. He couldn't bring himself to speak the words. *You're all I have left*, Venick wanted to say instead. He couldn't bring himself to speak those words either. "Mother, please. Go. I'm right behind you."

At last, Lira relented. "Alright." But she had hesitated, and it was a gift, couldn't she see that it was a gift? Venick realized that he hadn't believed, before, that his mother could ever love him again. Now he knew that she did.

She gathered up her skirts and raced away, and Venick watched her go, heart in throat. She'd almost made it to the main road when a fresh trail of debris plunged from the sky, sending fiery shards into her path.

Into her.

The street was smoky. The night was dark. Venick couldn't quite see the chunk of metal impale her. He couldn't quite see her open-mouthed surprise, the tiny grimace as she lost her footing, stumbled to the ground, and went still.

But he saw enough.

. . .

Ellina's face was in the dirt. Her limbs were a weak tangle. She coughed wetly, spat, and tried to roll over.

The building lay on top of her. Everything was dark. Yet somehow—miraculously, she did not understand the miracle of it—she was unhurt.

Again, she attempted to roll over. Wood heaped over her. She tried to lever it off. Her arms shook. They gave out. She could see the fleeing townspeople in slices through broken slats, heard their shouts.

And a new awareness.

Heat coiled around her boots. It snuck through the leather of her soles, her trousers, all the way to her skin. She tasted smoke. Realized, with a sense of unreality, that the building was on fire.

With her, stuck underneath.

. . .

Venick's ears were ringing. His eyes were dry rocks. He watched his mother fall. She didn't get up.

He had the strange thought that it was snowing. White specks eddied along the air. He wasn't cold. He wasn't anything. He moved towards his mother like a sleepwalker.

Behind him, his boots left a trail.

. . .

Ellina stopped struggling. She closed her eyes, took a deep breath, and began to count.

One.

She wiggled her arms under her body.

Two.

Twisted her torso, levered one foot, the other coming around at her side…

Three.

…to find a weak spot in the wood, which she angled upwards. A crack appeared. A slip of light. She brought her leg to her chest and *pushed.* The crack widened. Ellina gripped the outer edge of the building and wormed her way free.

For a moment, she could do nothing but lay and breathe.

Her breath became ragged. The smoke was thick. She coughed and looked up.

The city was unrecognizable. Bodies littered the road. Some of them were bloody, but others, more disturbingly, appeared untouched. Firelight illuminated bloated smoke, giving the world a red, shifting glow. The streets were emptying of townspeople, everyone rushing to escape the teetering deck of falling buildings. Only a few stragglers remained.

One, actually.

Ellina's vision narrowed. Venick.

He was moving towards the body of a woman. His back was to Ellina, she could not see his face, but she saw his stiff footsteps. She saw his open hands.

Ellina knew who that woman was. Knew that she was dead.

She pushed to her feet. Her ears were ringing, her tongue coated in soot. Unthinkingly, she began moving towards Venick.

Youvan stepped into her path. "It is time for us to go."

Ellina blinked up. Thoughts were hard to hold. She felt like the smoke, pulling away from herself, glowing red. "No."

Youvan's eyes darted across her face. "No?"

"I am not coming with you."

"I will shadow-bind you," the conjuror threatened. "You cannot escape."

Ellina laughed: a wide, wild sound. His threat seemed absurd. What did Ellina care of his shadow-binding? How could that possibly matter?

Youvan must have seen her thoughts because he darkened. "Your sister will show you no mercy."

"Nor will she *you*, when she learns what you have done," Ellina snapped. "We were meant to stay hidden. *Find Rahven*, that was the mission. Irek and its citizens—they were not to be harmed. We had a deal."

"You and Farah had a deal. I have no part in your bargain."

"You report to Farah."

"We have allied with the Dark Queen. We are not her underlings." He turned his eyes on the burning city. "Maybe now she will remember that."

Ellina felt as if she had been struck in the gut. "This was meant to be a *message*?"

"When Rahven reported his discovery of the humans' black powder barge, the Dark Queen debated whether to act. She hesitated. She has not yet learned that in war you must never hesitate."

"So you made the choice for her."

"Enough. We are leaving."

"I said *no*."

Youvan did not like that. He made a grab for her arm, but Ellina's dagger was in her hand in an instant, held between them. Youvan pulled back. "You will regret that." He widened his stance, lifted his hands. Ellina did not know what conjuring Youvan intended, only that when he curled his fingers and drew his arms down, nothing happened.

Something moved across his face. A moment of frustration.

Cut off, suddenly, by movement out of the corner of his eye. Youvan spotted Venick in the distance at his mother's side. Recognized him. Glanced once at Ellina, who saw Youvan's mind. *You will pay for this.*

Youvan swept towards Venick.

Ellina did not shout. She did not panic. Youvan was a conjuror who, for some reason, could not conjure. And she had a dagger.

In war you must never hesitate.

The green glass was almost invisible in the low light. It seemed flat in her hand as she cocked her arm, aiming at Youvan's retreating back.

. . .

Venick had come to his knees. He didn't remember doing this.

Fallen debris lay on top of his mother. It obscured her face. But Venick saw the streak of blood. He saw her lifeless hands.

Her eyes. The way she used to smile at him.

The songs she would sing. The stories she would tell. About elves, yes, sometimes. But about dragons too, and knights and quests and all the other things little boys liked to dream. About bravery and friendship. About becoming the person you were meant to be.

He shuffled forward. He was afraid to touch her, afraid that it was somehow a violation, yet his hand was already moving, as if it didn't belong to him, as if this wasn't his life, wasn't his world.

He didn't want it to be. He didn't think he could bear it.

A smudge of black made him look up.

Venick didn't even have time to reach for his sword. One moment, a conjuror was sweeping towards him, that same conjuror from the balcony, his hands made to claws, something deadly in his eyes. The next, the conjuror was faltering. He stumbled to his knees. His breath seemed to shudder.

A dagger in his back. Green glass. The smooth handle, small, the curve of it.

Venick looked past the conjuror, but the streets were empty.

TWENTY-SIX

He told himself not to think.

Venick could do. There was plenty to do. Fires to be doused, roads to be cleared, bodies buried. They would need to set up an infirmary for the injured, and they'd better get a few soldiers on watch in case the enemy elves decided to return. Venick could see to these things. He could make sure they were done right. As dawn crept across the sky and townspeople slowly reemerged into ashen streets, Venick began giving orders. No one seemed to remember that he didn't command this city. If anything, people were glad for direction. They needed order, needed to fall back into the familiar hierarchy of leader and follower. Anything to make them feel less lost, less hopeless, as if their town hadn't just come apart at the seams.

Venick circled through the streets, checking for survivors, tallying the things that needed to be done. He saw buildings charred black, some missing roofs or walls, some just *missing*. He saw deep gouges in the roads and bodies—the ones that hadn't yet been collected and covered and carted to the city's cemetery—silent and pale where they'd fallen.

Venick imagined how the cemetery would look now. There would be mounds of earth shoveled loose. Bodies set into holes, roots sticking sideways, the living mingling among the dead. And there would be rituals: rosewater dripped onto brows, hawthorn crushed over hearts, prayers spoken to the gods.

Venick should be there. He should be carrying that rosewater, speaking those prayers. He should help heft the weight of those bodies. But his mother was among the dead, and he could not. He delegated those tasks to someone else.

He walked on. Venick wished, not for the first time, that he was a boy again. He wished that he could return to the days when he'd been small, and his greatest worry had been how many fish he could catch on his hook, and what kind of pie his mother was baking for dinner. He wanted to be young enough that he could tuck himself into the folds of her apron and tell her that he loved her, because he hadn't done it enough as a child, and not at all as a man.

But he was thinking again.

...

Venick returned to the city square sometime after midday. Dourin was there. He'd found Venick as the dust had begun to settle, shaken but—like most of the elves—unharmed, and had spent the morning acting as Venick's right hand.

Dourin returned to his side now. The elf's forearms and biceps were smeared with ash, though his hands were clean. Venick focused on this. It felt good to focus on something that wasn't death or destruction.

Dourin must have washed his hands. Not in a well or fountain. The water was all polluted. But the ocean, maybe.

"Venick."

Venick's eyes came up. A crowd was gathering, elves and humans drawing close. Their faces were wary yet expectant, as if they were waiting for—hell, what? A eulogy? A rousing speech? Venick bristled at the idea.

"Venick," Dourin said again. Prodding.

"I don't have anything to say to them," Venick muttered.

"Yes you do."

The onlookers waited. Venick thought about everything he'd done to gain redemption. How little any of it mattered now. The council was dead. There was no one left to pass judgment, no one left to turn him away, nothing even left to turn him away *from*.

"You were right," came a voice from the crowd. Venick looked around. He couldn't be sure who'd spoken. "Everything you said about the dark elves, everything you've been warning us about. You were right."

There was a murmur of agreement. Someone else said, "They'll infiltrate our cities."

"They want to kill us all."

"They'll be back, you mark my words."

More nods, more mutterings. Venick spotted the healer Erol in the crowd, the white canvas of his robes flecked with ash and blood. Behind him, Venick was surprised to see Harmon. She met his eye and crossed her arms. Waiting, like everyone else, to hear what he had to say.

Venick cleared his throat. "I'm going to the highlands."

The crowd shuffled, their cloaks ruffling like winter birds. This was not the speech they were expecting.

"I'm going to the highlands," Venick continued, "to ask the Elder for his support."

What? came the crowd's murmurs.

The Elder?

You can't.

"I've seen the Dark Army," Venick pressed. "I've met the queen and fought her conjurors, and I can tell you that *this*," he swept his hand around, "is the least of what they can do. You're right. They'll be back, and when they come, they'll bring the full force of their power with them. We can't win this war alone. There's no hope of it.

"In two days' time, I'll ride north to Parith to request an audience with the Elder. I'll visit our lowlander brothers along the way, recruiting as many men as I can. I ask of you what I will ask of them: join me. Fight this fight. Help me avenge those who died here tonight and protect our home from another purge."

That word seemed to light something inside the crowd. *Purge.* This attack was just like it had been all those centuries ago when elves had exterminated every last human conjuror. Always, humans had believed that elves would return to finish what they'd started. It seemed now that fate was upon them.

For a long moment, no one moved. Then Erol stepped forward. He drew his dagger and held it up into the air. *By my blade*, the motion meant. A symbol of support. "I will join you," Erol said.

The man behind him did the same. "And I."

All at once, the *shing* of swords filled the air as every soldier drew his weapon and held it to the sunlight. After a beat, the elves followed, pulling out their swords, hoisting them up in that human way. It was a sea of steel and green glass shimmering brightly over the blackened streets: a phoenix from ashes.

...

The highlander woman dogged him all the way back to camp. "You don't know what you're saying. You don't know what you're promising them."

Venick ignored her. He was stiff, he was sore. There was a burn on his forearm that had come from he didn't know where, but it had begun to ache. He flexed his fingers, trying to work some feeling back into the limb.

Harmon said, "The Elder doesn't make allies."

"I know that."

"He'll order you dead."

"I know that too."

"So you're a fool."

Venick's eyes snapped to her. Wrong, to be called a fool by this woman. Strange, to hear those words from anyone except...

"You saw what happened here," Venick bit out. "And this was just one attack by a handful of elves. What happens when they return with their full army? Do you think you're safe because the highlands are tucked away to the north?" Venick started walking again. "What happened here—it's going to happen *everywhere*."

They reached the camp. Venick found Eywen's saddlebag and rummaged through it, looking for something to dress his burn. His movements were short. Rough. His fingers found a roll of gauze and gripped tight. "Do you know why every lowland man becomes a soldier? We need the numbers. The lowlands are half the size of the plains, a quarter of the size of the highlands—and still the elflands dwarf us all." He stood. "Our people need each other."

Harmon gazed at him, then down at his forearm, huffing a sigh. "Here." She pulled the salve he'd given her—the one meant for burns—from her pocket. "Give me that." She took the gauze from his hands and wrapped her fingers around his wrist. He resisted, but she pulled harder until he allowed the limb to come away from his body. She examined the burn. "You've burned the outer layer of skin but no deep tissue. I'd suggest a compress, though something tells me you won't bother with that. Either way, this will help." She unstoppered the salve.

Venick peered at her. "Are you a healer?"

"Yes," she said simply.

She began dabbing ointment over the burn. It stung, but Venick made himself hold still. When she spoke next, it was quietly, with the air of someone who was speaking against their will. "There is another reason why you won't convince the Elder."

"Which is?"

"We know of you."

Venick frowned. "What do you mean?"

"You are Venick, son of General Atlas. You killed your father and were exiled."

Venick shook his head. "Why would you have any reason to know that?" Harmon threw him a short look, as if he'd asked the wrong question. He tried again. "I've been absolved of that crime."

"In the highlands there is no absolution for murder."

"We're not highlanders."

Harmon exhaled through her nose. "Don't say that to the Elder. He won't care that your rules are different. No—" she cut him off. "Don't make excuses. This is important. When you speak with him, you must own up to what you've done."

"I thought you just said I won't be speaking with him," Venick muttered.

"You will," Harmon said, and looked at him full-on, in a way she hadn't yet. As if she was really seeing him. Making sure he saw her. "I'm going to take you."

• • •

The day before their departure, when their soldiers were packed and ready and waiting outside their ruined city, Venick did the thing he hadn't wanted to do. He went alone. He took nothing, save the one thing.

Lorana's hut sat on the eastern edge of the city. He could imagine, from a distance, that it looked exactly as he'd left it four years ago. But when he came closer he saw the truth. The door was smashed in, hanging on broken hinges. The paint was peeling. The flowerbed, left to its own devices, spilled with weeds.

Inside it was worse. The place had been ransacked, stripped of everything but a few pieces of furniture. The air was stale and reeked of mold. A mouse scurried from her corner.

Venick's lungs blazed. He threw open a window.

The fresh air cleared his head. He found an old bucket. A broom. A crumbling bar of soap. He filled the bucket with water, worked up a lather, and began to clean.

Venick's mind was quiet. He scrubbed the floor, the walls. Weeded the little flower bed. Straightened the furniture. When he was finished, he found a small hand shovel and went back outside. The afternoon had ripened, split open like a fruit. Sunlight streamed long through the trees.

Venick pulled Lorana's necklace from his pocket. Its silver links glinted. This necklace had been the start of everything. It had saved him. Or maybe it had ruined him. He hadn't quite decided.

He dug a hole. Set the necklace inside. Covered it over again.

Venick had so long dreamed of returning to Irek. Once, it had been all he'd wanted. But what was this city, devoid of those he loved? What happened to a place, stripped of everything that made it a home?

Later, Venick would think back to this moment. He wouldn't remember his thoughts exactly, except for the last: he was never coming back here.

He set his palm flat over the freshly dug earth, stood, and said his final goodbye.

TWENTY-SEVEN

Ellina rode alone. Her horse's hooves pounded the earth, to match her beating heart. They drove into her, hammering her thoughts as a mallet hammers metal, forming and folding and bending into something new. Or, really, something old.

Grief etched deep lines into her heart.

Fury did, too.

Ellina's fury was like a living thing. It paced inside her, an animal with an appetite. Ellina imagined all the ways she might feed it. She had killed Youvan. She would ride north and kill Farah. She would set a great fire to the palace, and watch it burn, and all her anger with it.

And yet, Ellina had always had a predator's sense for when to strike and when to wait. She knew how to tamp down her animal fury, to shush and corral it into a corner of herself, to be released later, when the time was right.

The time was not right.

Irek was burning. Venick's mother was dead. Dourin—she did not know what had become of him. These things were set like roots under rock, grown full into being. Killing Youvan had not changed them. Killing Farah would not, either. Ellina could not undo the terror that had been done to that city, which was home to the human she loved and the sister she had lost. She could not bring back the lives of the men and women and elves who had died there.

But there was still more she *could* do. She thought of Evov. She thought of Farah, and the crypts, and some secret yet to be uncovered. It seemed suddenly vital that Ellina uncover it.

Outside the burning city, she had saddled her horse to ride north. The southerners eyed her warily. "Where is Youvan?" someone asked.

She felt the weight of her dagger at her hip. She had retrieved it from Youvan's body but had not yet cleaned it well. The blade was flecked with his blood.

Ellina had shrugged and said in elvish that, truly, she did not know.

Now, she spurred her mare towards Evov. Her hair came loose from its braid. It whipped behind her like wings as she flew across the shadowed earth.

The silver moon rose.

• • •

She requested an audience with Farah. The hour of Ellina's arrival was late, as was her request, but Farah made no complaints. She invited Ellina into her private chambers. They stood alone in what had once been their mother's library, and Ellina felt it again: the animal of her fury. The swift, sweet longing for Farah's death.

How would Ellina do it?

She would draw her dagger across Farah's throat. Her sister's body would become dead weight. Her blood would shine thickly against the floor.

Or maybe she would kill Farah in a different way. Ellina saw it: her hands at her sister's neck. Squeezing tight. The life draining from Farah's eyes.

"I have returned from Irek," Ellina said. A nearby lantern guttered. Outside the window, the moon had waned away. "It is as you feared. Rahven is dead."

It was no more or less than Farah had expected. She made some reply, perhaps thanking Ellina for her duty, or giving further instructions. Ellina did not know. She was not listening, and then Farah had dismissed her. Ellina was almost to the door when Farah asked, "Why have you returned alone? Where are Youvan and the others?"

Ellina thought of her journey back to Evov, flying across the grasslands, then the tundra, into the mountains. She had pushed her horse to its limit, stopping only when the animal's lathered muscles began to tremble. Even then, she had not allowed much time for rest, for either of them. The other elves were likely days behind.

Ellina did not know what Farah would do when she learned of Youvan's insubordination, or his subsequent death. Would she dismiss Ellina? Punish her? *Thank* her? Farah would not like that the southerners had attacked Irek against her orders, but the matter of Irek itself was of little concern to her—Farah had never truly cared about those humans.

The real issue, if Farah cared to find one, was their bargain. Farah had promised Irek's safety in exchange for Ellina's support, but she had failed to control the southerners and therefore failed to uphold her end of the deal. Their bargain was off, which meant Ellina no longer had any reason to show her sister loyalty.

Best, Ellina thought, that Farah not realize that yet.

Ellina gave a shrug. "The others are slow."

. . .

Kaji intercepted Ellina in the entrance hall, having learned or guessed of her return. He caught sight of her and was instantly worried. "Ellina? What happened?"

"I need you to do something for me."

Ellina told Kaji about Livila. She explained how the young servant's father was a spy for Farah, that he had been uncovered and killed. *It is my fault,* she might have added. *I was the one who discovered his secret. I told Dourin.* But Ellina did not share her guilt. Kaji would only say that it was not her fault, that Ellina had done the right thing. Of course he would think so. Kaji did not know how it felt to lose a parent so young. He would not recognize the horror of what she had done, regardless of its necessity.

"You must look after her," Ellina said. "She has no one now."

Kaji's worry grew. "If you care so much for this young servant, why are you asking *me* to look out for her?" The elder elf captured her hands. "I have been concerned, *irishi*. First you leave unannounced in the company of conjurors, and now you show back up here looking as if…" His golden eyes spoke his fears. "What are you planning?"

She did not want to lie to him. Ellina pressed her lips together and looked away, towards the colorful mosaic glittering on the wall behind them. It showed a dozen figures: a horse with three heads, an elf holding a staff, a blue lizard with a forked tongue. At this hour, the entrance hall was empty, all the palace elves in bed. Kaji should be, too. He had risked himself to come find her.

"You *are* planning something." Kaji's shoulders sagged. For once, he looked his age. "What is it?"

Ellina wondered if every question was a way of putting yourself at the mercy of another. She thought of Venick's questions on the beach, the ones she had finally been ready to answer. Ellina wondered if the way she felt—hollowed, echoing, like wind through a tunnel—was merely because of what she had witnessed in Irek. Or was there more to it than that? Perhaps it was the emptiness of lost opportunities. Of things that could not be taken back. She looked at Kaji, whom she had known since birth. She thought of the father she had lost and all of her unanswered questions about who he was and what he was like and what he wanted. She thought of Venick walking towards his mother's lifeless body, and how that, too, was her fault.

Her grief swelled. Maybe Venick could have forgiven her before, but he would never forgive her now.

"There is something I have to do," she said.

"Whatever it is, let me help you."

"You cannot."

Kaji let go of her hands. He seemed to sense how Ellina felt: like she was hurtling towards some inevitable end. "You are scaring me."

"I know. I am sorry."

She told him not to worry. She told him that she would be careful, now and always. She told him thank you for everything that he had done for her.

When she walked away, he let her go.

• • •

Ellina killed the guard at the entryway to the crypts. She used her dagger, then took his sword.

It felt wildly reckless to kill him. It was something she had long avoided, but that cavernous tunnel inside her was making the rules now. It whispered instructions into her ear. No more time for careful mouse steps. No more time for ploys and lies. You know what you must do.

She caught his sagging body and lowered it silently to the floor.

The passageway leading down to the crypts was airless and dry, the ceiling low enough that most elves would have to stoop. Ellina did too, in some places. She imagined the weight of the palace pressing down on her. A mountain of stone as old as the whole earth, hanging overhead.

She went deeper. Here in these narrow corridors, she felt woefully out of her element. Ellina had the guard's sword, but there was hardly space enough to use it. If she was caught, she would have to flee back the way she had come. The thought was unpleasant, a swig of wine when she wanted water.

Then again, if she was uncovered maybe she would not flee. Maybe she would see just how narrow these corridors were after all.

Her steps were soft as a breath. The air seemed to strain with the absence of sound.

Then: a faint murmur ahead. A shuffle, the light gust of a cloak. There was no door at the end of this tunnel, merely an opening that curved and widened into an underground room. Ellina crept to its mouth, pressing flat against the wall. Slowly, slowly, she peered sideways into the crypts beyond.

A dozen conjurors were gathered there. They formed a half-circle around a stone casket, their attention on one conjuror in particular, a long-nosed, thin-browed southerner who stood slightly apart from the rest. His hands were lifted, fingers clawed, shoulders hunched inward. He loomed over the open casket where a second elf—another conjuror, perhaps—was sitting inside.

It was difficult to see much else. The elves had lit only a single candle, which burned on a little stand at their backs. Its light was feeble. Almost useless. It was hardly even bright enough to cast shadows.

Conjurors do not need fire to see in the dark.

Ellina risked another step closer. It was an odd scene: their somber faces, their single silly candle, the elf in his casket. Ellina could not begin to fathom the meaning of it all.

The forward-standing conjuror opened and closed his raised fists. The elf sitting inside the casket moved to stand. He swung his leg over the casket's lip, used an arm to push himself upright. His neck was tense, his movements stunted. He turned his eyes towards Ellina.

But he *had* no eyes. No lips, no hair, little flesh. His face was bone-white, stretched taut. A skull.

Ellina bit back a scream. She clutched at the wall behind her, blood wailing.

The dead elf stood on unsteady feet. It was naked, its dried flesh sagging off bloodless limbs. It moved in jerky bursts and stops. Its frame hung like a shriveled oak.

Nearby, the conjuror was still moving his fingers, controlling the corpse like a puppeteer. He clawed upward and the corpse came forward. He twisted his arms and the corpse assumed a fighting stance.

Someone handed the creature a sword. Ellina thought, surely no. She thought, it cannot be. But the corpse took the sword. Another conjuror—a female—had one too. She came at the corpse, who lifted its sword heavily at its master's command, parrying the first attack, but not the second.

The female conjuror hacked off the corpse's arm at the elbow.

The creature did not even falter. Its arm lay severed on the floor, but it raised its weapon and kept coming.

The female parried, dodged, and broke through, piercing the corpse where its heart should have been. The creature stumbled, readjusted its grip, and kept coming.

Finally, the female chopped off its head. And still, the corpse kept coming.

The duel continued, but Ellina saw no more. She bolted back up the tunnel. She had thought she would not flee, as if that was what mattered. Her stomach lurched, mind racing. Necromancy. Corpse manipulation. *This* was Farah's secret. This was what the conjurors had been working on in the night. They were practicing, learning how to use corpses as weapons. And what a weapon it was. What would war become, if one side could not be killed?

The thought seemed to puncture something vital inside her. An army of undead. *This* was what the resistance was up against.

Ellina had to get to the everpool. She had to warn Dourin.

Now.

. . .

She did not waste time returning to her rooms, which were set on the opposite end of the palace. Instead, Ellina entered an empty library. She found pen and parchment, bent over a low table meant for taking tea, and scrawled her message. In a bare minute, it was done.

She folded the note and shoved it in her pocket. Her hands were shaking. Her pulse beat fast. She left the ink unstoppered on the table, the pen rolling.

Later, Ellina would understand what her haste had cost her. She had not been thinking. When she turned her head, all she could see was that corpse looking right through her.

She made for the stone gardens.

The shadows followed.

. . .

The sky was lifting. Dawn crept slowly over the world. The gardens were calm, everything impossibly quiet. The everpool waited, patient as always.

Ellina came to the pool's edge. Though the morning was chilly with early winter, Ellina felt warm. Her skin was flushed. The air hung heavy all around her, thick in her throat. She kicked out of her shoes and pulled the message from her pocket.

A hand came around her mouth, stifling her scream.

TWENTY-EIGHT

At first, Ellina could not see who held her. She strained against her assailant, her hair in her face, her breath sharp and fast. "Ellina." Raffan's voice came close at her ear. "Stop."

She did not stop. She slammed his foot with her heel, jabbed his ribs with her elbow, on the left side, where she knew an old injury still pained him. He released her with a grunt and she spun, pulling her dagger from its sheath, slashing the green glass through the air.

He disarmed her. Just as she knew his weaknesses, he knew hers. He used the trailing end of her swipe as an opening to grab her wrist, digging a thumb into the tendon there, forcing her fingers to open. The dagger dropped from her hand.

"Ellina."

She aimed a punch at his throat.

"*Stop.*"

She kicked him in the gut. She was wild, she was reckless, she was seeing white. Ellina watched Raffan dodge two more blows, but she did not really see him. She saw corpses rising from the earth. She saw an army of undead crawling out of the shadows like cockroaches.

"Enough," said Farah.

Ellina spun to find her sister standing a few paces back.

"Bring it to me," Farah said. Ellina stood dumbly, not understanding, until Raffan stooped to pick up the note Ellina had dropped. She watched, almost as if from a distance, as Raffan handed the letter to Farah. In the low light of dawn, the slip of paper looked pale and yellow. It was thin, it was nothing, no more menacing than a feather.

All the blood rose to Ellina's face as Farah unfolded the parchment. She watched her sister read the letter. "*What is this?*" Farah asked in elvish.

There was a tense, terrible silence. *No*, Ellina thought. Her mind revolted, it slipped and spun. This could not be happening. For months Ellina had plotted and planned, always careful, always one step ahead. She did not make mistakes. She was too smart for mistakes, and certainly for *this* kind of mistake. The impossibility of her situation made Ellina do the worst thing. She lied. "*I do not know,*" Ellina replied in elvish. "*It is not mine.*"

Farah's gaze dropped to the letter, then came up again. Her eyes glowed in the everpool's silvery light. "But...it is." Farah's voice sounded strange. Ellina could see the thoughts swirling behind her gaze. "This is your handwriting. It is your letter. You lied. You can lie in elvish?"

Ellina went cold. Somewhere over the distant mountains, a hawk cried her hunting call.

"I had heard the rumors," Farah continued softly. "The wildings once told of such a thing. But those elves are superstitious. Full of whim. I never truly thought..." A pause. A small shake of her head. Ellina did not understand how Farah could be so calm, not when she felt like screaming. Around them, the dawn continued to break.

Farah said, "You have dark hair."

It was over. Farah knew the truth, had the proof of it there on that scrap of paper. And Ellina was weaponless, defenseless, trapped on this palace island with nowhere to hide, nowhere to run.

She ran anyway.

She bolted, sliding past Farah and Raffan, disappearing into the garden's stony maze. She heard Farah's muffled *seize her*, followed by the sound of her sister's hollers, a call of her guards to arms. Ellina sprinted faster, crashing through turns, twisting and winding. She had no idea where she was going, no real sense of where this maze would take her. It did not matter. She had a sudden vision of Ermese trapped in his prison. Her mother, stabbed through the stomach. Ellina could not end up like them. She could *not*.

Gasps tore at her throat. It was, for several seconds, the only sound she heard.

Then: footfalls. The swift cadence of boots gaining ground behind her. Ellina risked a glance back to see Raffan closing in, her dagger in his hand. She heard the huff of his breath as he skidded to a stop, followed by the awful silence that could only mean he was taking aim, cocking his arm to throw.

She looked up at the sky. Wind-tears slipped from the corner of her eyes. The morning's stars winked their final goodbye.

The dagger pierced Ellina's back, up in the shoulder. She heard the sick pop of skin and muscle. Numbness, followed by hot pain.

She screamed, and she fell.

. . .

Ellina did not know where they were taking her. She was dizzy, blood-soaked, seeing stars. There was a guard on either side of her now. They held her up by the arms, hauling her gracelessly through the palace. Ellina tried to get her feet back under her, but the world dipped and whirled, and she could not seem to keep her footing. When she faltered, they dragged her with no more regard than a sack of grain.

Farah led the way. Her white hair bounced a little, her steps eager. Though Ellina could not see her face, she sensed her sister's contained intensity, as if she were a box full of writhing snakes. Farah paused at the top of a stairwell, spoke a quiet word to the guard stationed there, and began her descent.

Ellina knew now where they were headed. This was the way to Ara's old suite, which was no longer a suite but a prison. If Ellina had been more clear of mind, she might have been heartened by this. Farah would not be leading Ellina to the prisons if she intended to kill her. But Ellina was not clear of mind, was not even lucid enough to grasp the hopelessness of her situation, and so when they entered the chamber and came into sight of the barred cells, she began to struggle.

"Ellina." Raffan spoke from behind. He sounded tired. "Do not make it worse."

She struggled harder.

"You should hold that wound still."

She did not give a damn what he thought she should do.

The room was as Ellina remembered: two barred cells and a third made of solid stone. The candles sputtered on their wicks. Ermese's cell was empty.

The guards halted.

Ellina realized what was coming and tried once again to find her footing. She could not, and when the guards released her arms, she crumpled to the floor, the pain in her shoulder knocking the breath right out of her.

Farah's voice was smooth. "Balid. Bring me the dagger."

A conjuror stepped past Raffan and came forward. Ellina recognized him. Long nose, thin brows. Those sunken, hollowed eyes. He was the one she had seen controlling the corpse in the crypts.

Ellina felt a fresh throb of fear. Maybe Farah intended to kill her after all. Maybe she was to be made a corpse. Her body could be reanimated. She could be used as a weapon against her friends.

Farah took the dagger from Balid and crouched before Ellina, holding the bloodied weapon out for her to see. "Raffan gave this to you," she said, twirling the green glass between her fingers. "He did so at my command. Look. Do you recognize it? No? It is the same dagger my assassin used to poison your human. It is the blade that put a hole," she touched Ellina to show her, "right in his hip."

Ellina's gaze darted up. Farah was not smiling, but her voice was dipped in pleasure: a candied apple. "There is a kind of symmetry to it, do you think? That the same knife used on him has now been used on you. But do not fear. *You* will not be poisoned. Your crime deserves greater punishment than death." Farah straightened, peering down her nose. "My sister, the human-lover. When you pledged allegiance to me, I suspected there was a lie hidden somewhere in your words. But how could there be? You swore your oaths to me in elvish in a dozen different ways. I crafted the wording myself. I never considered that maybe you did not need to hide the lie. You spoke plainly in our language, and you deceived me." Farah's lip curled. "What a little snake you are."

"And *you*," Ellina choked out. "I saw what you have been hiding in the crypts."

"A new weapon. Brilliant, is it not? Just think. A band of soldiers who cannot be killed. We all know that humans have the experience, but this way," Farah spread her hands, "we even things out."

"With black magic. With *witchery*."

"Conjuring comes in many forms. And the dead do not mind. But this is a dangerous secret that you now possess, and we nearly allowed you to spread it. We cannot risk that again." Farah saw Ellina's fear and clicked her teeth. "No. As I said, I am not going to kill you yet. Bring her to her feet."

The guards gripped Ellina by the arms and hauled her upright. Hot pain burst through her, darkening her vision.

Farah slapped her face, stinging her back to life. "You will stay awake for this."

Ellina's pulse was soaring. Her breath was coming again, hard and fast.

Farah looked at the conjuror. "Balid." His name. A command.

The conjuror raised his hands. Ellina flinched and tried to pull away from the guards. Balid inhaled, his eyes fluttering briefly closed. His fingers squeezed slowly into fists.

The pressure began in her chest, then worked its way up her throat. Ellina wheezed, gagging. Balid was choking her, he was using conjuring to close her windpipe. Panic coated her tongue, her worst fear manifesting. This was drowning, come a different way. Ellina had always feared water, feared it worse than most. Her father had died by the water. Ellina had never wanted to go the same way. She writhed in her captors' grip, bucking as the sensation worsened, squeezing out her last breath...

And then it was over. The guards released her. This time, Ellina managed to keep her footing. She took several deep, shaky breaths.

She glanced at the elves around her, Balid and Farah and Raffan and the others. She did not understand. Surely that could not be all, a few seconds of terror. Where was the rest of her punishment? Ellina opened her mouth to ask.

No sound came. She tried harder. And again. Nothing.

Understanding arrowed into her. Balid had not intended to choke her. He had meant to *silence* her.

She could not speak. She truly could make no sound.

The conjuror had stolen Ellina's voice.

TWENTY-NINE

Venick leaned over a steel sword, sharpening the blade with a whetstone. Somewhere behind him, men and elves sparred, the *hiss* and *shing* of their swords drifting across the flat landscape. Venick rarely joined the sparring these days, but he liked to listen as he worked, the clang of weapons strangely comforting.

He kept at his task. All around him, red, crumbling earth reached in every direction. Venick had been this far north before, but never this far west, and so he'd been surprised by the quick and drastic change in scenery. Here the earth was more clay than dirt, the vegetation sparse, the days warm but the desert nights bitterly cold.

Or, well, *desert* wasn't exactly the right word. There was water, after all, a whole black river full of it, along which the road had been built. When they'd set off for the highlands, Venick hadn't liked the idea of traveling along that road. He'd been worried about the possibility of running into highland soldiers. What happened if they met the Elder's army before making it to Parith? Harmon, however, had been certain. "You have nothing to worry about."

"I wouldn't say *nothing*."

"If we run into soldiers, I will speak with them."

And your word's enough to stop an army? Venick had almost asked, but didn't. He wasn't stupid enough to insult their single highland ally. And Harmon had remained firm, insisting that the road was the best way, pointing out that the highlands only grew drier the farther north they went. By the time they reached Parith, the land would be nothing but dirt and dust. They'd need the water from the black river for their horses and themselves. "If I'm going to guide you, this is the way we're going," Harmon had said, and that had been the end of it.

Venick had to remind himself that he was lucky to have Harmon. If not for her, they'd likely have no chance of speaking with the Elder at all. If Venick had any misgivings, it was merely because of what had happened in Irek. It was because they were exposed out here on this flat non-desert with no high ground, nowhere to fall back in case the Dark Army decided to attack. That was all. Nothing more.

Tell yourself that.

Venick refocused on the whetstone. Slowly, the sounds of the camp receded from his awareness, his mind filling with nothing but the soft grate of stone on metal, the wind through the grass—

—and footsteps, approaching.

He looked up.

"That is not your sword," Harmon said.

Venick paused. "No."

"Yet you sharpen it anyway."

He shrugged. "It needs to be done."

She studied him. Her black eye was nearly healed now, the skin showing only the faintest green tinge. Her burned hands were better too, though Venick rarely saw them. She liked to keep her arms crossed. They were crossed now. "In the highlands, men don't touch each other's weapons," she said. "It's bad luck."

"What if you lose your weapon?"

"Who is going to lose their weapon?"

"What if it's stolen? What if you drop it in battle?"

"If you're foolish enough to drop your sword in battle, maybe you deserve your fate."

Venick squinted a little, amused. "Swords are heavy. They're easy to drop."

"I wouldn't know."

He was surprised. "You've never held a sword before?"

"My father doesn't like it. He thinks women shouldn't fight."

"And what do you think?"

Harmon uncrossed her arms. Crossed them again in the other direction. Trying to see if he was patronizing her. Considering how much to tell him. For someone who'd never been to battle, Harmon was awfully on guard.

"Well?"

"I dreamed of being a knight once," she admitted. "When I was little, women still fought in our army. The highland army doesn't just answer to the Elder. Did you know that? Their fealty is sworn to his whole family, anyone bearing the Stonehelm name. The Elder's wife was a general. Many believed that of the two of them, she was the better commander. She was certainly fiercer, but the Elder never minded. He loved her. After she died in battle, the Elder changed the rules."

"He forbid women from fighting?"

Harmon nodded. "I sometimes wonder how things would have been if his wife had never died. If women were still allowed to fight, would I have become a soldier? A *knight?*" She shrugged, but her eyes were hard, as if daring him to mock her. "I know it's silly."

"It's not silly."

Harmon shrugged again, her gaze darting to where the men sparred. Lin Lill was among them.

"You could join them," Venick said, softer now. "Lin Lill would be glad to teach you."

"I shouldn't. I'm likely to bruise. My father will see."

"Does your father control everything that you do?"

Harmon scrunched her nose. "More or less."

"Well he's not here now." Venick handed over the sword.

"It *is* heavy."

She gave a practice swing. Her form was terrible, but Venick only said, "You're a natural."

"I was trained in medicine." She gave the sword another swing, this time with a little more force. "I told my father that if I couldn't go to battle with a weapon then I would go another way. I serve our army as a healer."

Venick had a sudden vision of the first time he'd seen Harmon: bound in chains, hair in her face, her comrades set in a line behind her. Venick met her eye and knew she was remembering the same.

She lowered the sword. "I never thanked you for saving me."

"I don't deserve your thanks."

"You didn't have to do what you did that day. I owe you my life price."

"Harmon." Venick faltered. "I don't want your life price."

She handed back the sword. Her gaze was steady, the air between them somehow different. Her expression turned mischievous. "If I came home knowing how to spar, our soldiers would have kittens."

Venick laughed.

· · ·

The Elder's castle was built like a shell, all the rooms spiraling inward.

As Harmon led the way inside Venick gazed up, feeling dwarfed by the high ceilings, the huge doorways. The air here was stiff, the windows thrown open as if to tempt a breeze, or perhaps to air the halls of that musky, earthy smell. Though servants could be seen sweeping the corridors, it seemed to make little difference. The ground was dusted with soil and gritty sand, no doubt drug in by the endless stream of men and animals, pigs and dogs and the occasional small monkey, screaming in the rafters.

"You can choose three men to join you," Harmon had told Venick outside the city. Her face had reflected sandy red shadows. Overhead loomed the gates of Parith, which were mountainously tall, yet so narrow that two horses could scarcely pass through them abreast. "The rest of your army will wait for your return."

When Venick chose Dourin and Lin Lill, Harmon had shot him a look. "That's only two. And I said men."

"What does it matter if they're men?"

"The Elder likes things done a certain way. He'll be offended if custom isn't followed. Can you at least choose one man?"

"I would be happy to fill the role," said the healer Erol. "I have always wanted to see this city." He had glanced at Dourin when he'd said it, and the two of them had eyed each other with a tension Venick hadn't understood.

But Venick had been slow.

Traegar liked to experiment, Dourin had explained. *He was good with potions and remedies—and also poisons. He met another healer who shared his interests. They became work partners and close friends.*

Know it? Erol had said of Traegar's book. *Hell. I wrote it. Or half of it. But Traegar didn't mention that, did he?*

Venick blinked. *Oh.*

"Well?" Harmon prompted.

"Dourin?" The elf threw Venick a swift look. A tiny nod. "Alright," Venick agreed. Three fighters and a healer. His father would have approved. "Erol, you'll be my third."

If the land outside Parith was a dry desert, the inside was a paradise. Everywhere there was greenery: high palms and creeping vines, pungent gardens and fountains of lilies. The buildings themselves were mostly sandstone, the doorways and windows carved with an intricacy that made Venick wish for a magnifying glass. He'd never seen such a city, not in the lowlands, not in the elflands. Parith was busy, colorful and rich. Its wealth oozed out of its pores.

"What do you suppose our chances are if they decide to kill us?" Dourin asked as they'd marched up the hill towards the Elder's palace, eyeing the archers on the roofs.

"Not great," Venick admitted.

"Encouraging."

"There might be a way to escape, if it came to that."

"These walls are much higher than those in Kenath," Dourin replied. "And I do not fancy another trip through the sewers."

Venick smiled faintly, though he'd been thinking of something else. Just like Irek, Parith would have an escape tunnel—perhaps even multiple escape tunnels—built under the city. The locations of such tunnels were always kept secret, though there was usually a point of access somewhere within the palace walls. Venick explained this to Dourin.

"A secret tunnel in an uncertain location?" the elf had replied dryly. "That solves everything."

Now, Harmon walked a little ahead as she led the way through the Elder's castle. Her steps were sure. The castle guards nodded when she passed, making no move to stop them.

Venick felt a tick of apprehension at that. He could be an assassin. A spy. If nothing else, Venick and Erol were lowlanders and Dourin and Lin Lill were elves. That alone should have warranted questions, but they were not questioned. They were not searched or disarmed. They passed through the castle uncontested.

Harmon halted before a set of wide double doors. "The great hall," she said. Behind the doors, Venick could hear the midday feast underway: the muffled chatter of a hundred men, the clink of plates and goblets, the light trill of a flute. "When I give the signal, the guards will open the doors. I will step back and allow you to go first."

Dourin crossed his arms. "This is your city. You go first."

"It is a show of strength," Harmon explained. "Whoever enters a room first commands it."

"Whoever enters a room first gets *ambushed*."

"They are not my rules. If you want the Elder's support, you must first gain his respect."

"How do you know so much?" Dourin's agitation was growing. "Do you serve on the Elder's court?"

She gave a laugh. "The Elder has no court. His opinion is the only one that matters."

"Then you are a noblewoman of some kind. You have spent time with him."

"I was raised here. And the Elder's ways are no secret. Anyone could tell you what I just did."

Dourin shot Venick a look. I *don't trust it*, his eyes seemed to say. Harmon had paraded them through this city—hell, through this country—utterly unchallenged. She'd arranged a meeting with the Elder, despite his reputation for holding no court. She'd done it with ease.

Harmon watched their silent exchange. "You've trusted me this far," she said with a prick of offense. She looked at the guard. "Open them."

The doors swung at her words, sliding smoothly on oiled hinges. The room appeared before them, a wave of color and noise. The hall had been outfitted with a single long table running down its center, and ten dozen men occupied its seats. Venick felt a hand nudge his back.

No turning back now.

He entered the hall.

Venick knew the Elder at once—it could be no one else. The man sat at the head of the table, dressed in richly dyed purples and reds, his fingers and neck draped in gold. He appeared both older than Venick had expected and more haggard—until he smiled. Then his face showed an unmistakable youth. "Our lowlander friends have arrived at last," the Elder said. "Come, and be welcome."

THIRTY

They were given a seat at the hall's center. Servants came with heavy helpings of stew and ale, which were refilled before the dishes were even half empty. This attentive service—and hell, the meal itself—was not what Venick had expected, but he had sense enough not to refuse. Harmon had warned that the Elder liked things done a certain way. Perhaps this was tradition in Parith: to serve your guests first, even if you later planned to slit their throats.

Venick ate in silence, spooning the stew into his mouth without really tasting it. Slowly, the volume in the hall rose. Lin Lill and Erol sat to Venick's right, speaking quietly and eating what was offered. Dourin sat across the table. He didn't seem to care about traditions or courtesies, and left his food untouched.

Harmon had taken a seat a few places down the table. She was the only woman in the hall, aside from the servants who returned again and again with more food and drink, offering sweets and wet hand towels, their faces like smiling dolls, stitched into place. Finally, the Elder raised his hand and the plates were cleared. The chatter quieted, the room swelling with anticipation. Even the servants stopped to listen.

"The time has come," the Elder said, "to properly greet our guests." He motioned to Venick. "Rise."

Venick stood from his seat. He felt the weight of a hundred gazes.

"You have come for a purpose," the Elder said. When Venick began to speak, the man cut him off. "There is no need to explain. I know who you are and why you are here. We, too, have heard of the Dark Army. Do you think we are blind? We keep our eyes and ears open. The Dark Queen wants another purge." It was that word again, *purge*. The one that so easily rattled men, that got the hall humming—until the Elder raised yet another hand, and the men fell immediately silent. "But we are not friends, you and I. Our countries share a history of bloodshed. And you have brought with you an army that will—as far as I can tell—attack my citizens as soon as they are allowed within these gates." He steepled his hands. "You wish, no doubt, to convince me otherwise."

Venick didn't like speeches. Not hearing them, not giving them. Give him a sword and a good fight—he was no diplomat. But this, too, Harmon had warned. *You must not stutter, you must maintain eye contact. They say the Elder is like a shark hunting blood. He can smell even the slightest weakness.*

"It's true," Venick began, his voice low and clear. "Our nations have been enemies. We've fought each other for generations, but I'm asking now for a change. We cannot defeat the Dark Army alone. Stand with us and let us fight together. We need each other."

"*Need*," the Elder repeated. He'd remained gracious thus far, his expression one of pleasant interest. Now, however, his eyes seemed to shimmer. "That word is so...slippery. An alliance would benefit the lowlands, clearly. You are the weaker fighters. You have the smaller army."

"If the lowlands fall, the highlands will be next."

A rumble of outrage, like the buzz of hornets. Venick saw the way the men bristled, as if to face a threat. But the Elder was mild. "My army is the largest in the land. Even if you are right, the lowlanders will hardly swell our ranks. What need have I of a few thousand more soldiers?"

"We bring with us the northern elves," Venick said. "They have joined our resistance and share our interests. Humans have knowledge of war, but elves are the superior fighters. Their techniques are unmatched. They could teach your men their tactics."

"While that is an interesting offer, I am not yet persuaded."

The men grinned at each other. Venick saw one soldier draw a finger across his throat.

"However," the Elder continued, "you do have something else that I want." His smile was a nested doll. It seemed to hide inside itself. "The lowlands have an excellent seaport. Your ships are some of the best—a fleet worthy of an emperor. And your land is fertile. All that mountain water running through your fields. Not to mention the Golden Valley. It is quite a prize."

Venick replied carefully. "The lowlands are not mine to give."

"Yet here you are, speaking as if you own them."

"A spokesperson is not a king."

"Your mother was Spokeswoman on your council, before her death." Venick stiffened. He didn't know how the Elder knew about that. "From what I understand, you have taken command of the council in her place. Do you mean to tell me, as Spokesman, you have no power over your people? Now, you will insult me if you think I would believe that.

"A marriage," the Elder announced. "I have a daughter. I offer her hand to you in marriage. Our lands will be joined. You will have access to my army, and I will have access to the lowland's riches. A true alliance."

For a moment, Venick couldn't speak. "Your daughter wouldn't want to marry me."

"My daughter will do what is best for her people, as I thought you would. Or am I mistaken?"

"I haven't even met your daughter."

"Actually," the Elder said, "you have."

The scrape of a chair. Harmon stood from her seat.

Venick gaped. "*You?*"

"You see?" the Elder continued. "My daughter is beautiful. She is my only heir. A marriage between you will solidify this union. You get my army, and I get your land, and together we can defeat the dark elves. It is the perfect solution, I believe."

It all ticked into place. How easily Harmon had arranged this meeting. How she'd marched them through the city with little friction. How she stood there now, the only female in a hall of men.

The Elder had always wanted the lowlands. He'd attacked the Golden Valley more times than Venick could count. Had this been the man's plan all along? Had it been Harmon's?

Venick's neck was hot. He realized he was furious. He'd been tricked, utterly fooled. Harmon must have known this was what her father would offer, yet she'd allowed him to walk into this hall blind, unaware of who she was, unaware of who her father was. Venick needed the Elder's army. Gods knew that was true. Had the man's proposition come a different way, Venick might have even considered it. But it hadn't come a different way, it had come in exactly the *worst* way, and so all Venick felt was his own disgust, his utter contempt of his man and his daughter and their schemes.

Venick was sick of schemes. Gods knew he'd endured his fair share.

"Well?" the Elder prompted. "What say you?"

Venick spoke through his teeth. "My answer is no."

The man's face closed. "Then so is mine."

. . .

They were given permission to leave without interference. The Elder watched them go. "As soon as you are out of this city," he warned, "my protection ends."

Harmon did not escort them out. Instead, a steward walked their group back through the city. By the time they exited Parith's gates and reached their waiting army, the sun was making its final descent.

Venick spoke to his soldiers plainly. He explained what had happened as best he could, though he could tell from the faces of his men that they didn't understand. So what if he'd been asked to marry someone he didn't know? They needed the Elder's support.

"What does your happiness matter if we are all dead?" Branton asked, golden eyes flaring. "You should have taken the deal."

Branton wasn't the only one. Mutters seemed to follow Venick through the ranks as they readied to ride. By the time night had fallen, Venick found himself unable to look anyone in the eye.

Dourin found him at the edge of camp. The elf came quietly, his footsteps making no sound. Venick held in a sigh. "I suppose you're here to tell me what an idiot I am too?"

"No." Dourin's gaze was steady. "I am here to discuss what we should do now that you have refused."

THIRTY-ONE

The cell was small and dark. Stone walls. Damp. A door so perfectly set that when it was shut, not even a sliver of light leaked through its seams.

Ellina had watched Raffan pull that door closed. It scraped roughly against the ground. Then the latch clicked, and the bolt turned, and Ellina was thrown into darkness.

Now, she paced. Her muscles all seemed to gather in a single, tense cord. Her teeth chattered, though Ellina did not feel cold. It was the shock, she thought. Or the fear.

She had tried to call out to Raffan. As he pulled the prison door shut, Ellina had opened her mouth, thinking to reason with him, or to plead. But the words had not come. As before, when Ellina attempted to speak she could make not even the smallest of sounds. It was as if the air from her lungs could find no purchase in her throat, which had become an airless well. The sensation frightened her, worse than the dagger wound in her shoulder, or the prison, or even the reality of being discovered. To be without a voice...

She continued to pace the tiny cell. Her shoulder burned. There was a jagged, too-loose feel to it. Blood soaked through her shirt and into her hair, warm and wet. Better sense told Ellina to stop moving, to hold the wound still, but she had no interest in better sense. She needed to move, needed the sound of her feet brushing the floor, the back and forth rock of her steps, the way that movement made her feel less trapped...

Trapped. She was trapped. Weaponless, injured, silent.

Ellina had always been a strong fighter, but only in the way that all elves were strong fighters—she took to weapons easily, but her skill was nothing special. What Ellina had always been known for, what she had been best at, was her knack for deceit. She had been recruited into the legion for that skill, had earned a reputation for her wiles. It was her strongest and most valuable weapon, this ability to speak past any obstacle, to trick and deceive, to watch her opponent sense the trap and fall into it anyway. Ellina had prided herself on this ability. Even before she had learned to lie in elvish, she wore her cunning like armor. Who was she, without a voice?

She knew her fear now. It came plainly, as the sun comes over the earth. There would be no more mistaking it.

Her head spun. This time, Ellina did stop. She set a hand to the stone wall, forced herself to take deep breaths. Her back screamed as her lungs expanded, pain slicing fresh through the wound. But her pulse calmed a little. Some of the dizziness subsided.

The quiet that followed was solid enough to hold her thoughts, so Ellina began to think.

She was weaponless, but perhaps she could steal a blade from the next guard who entered this cell. She would crouch by the door—low, where they did not expect her—and wait for a prison-keeper to come. She would lunge before the guard could muster a counterattack and grab whatever she could manage: a dagger, a sword. Even a helmet could become a weapon in the right hands. She was trained for this. Ellina's wound would not stop her. Her fear would not. She would fight her way free, and then she would escape.

• • •

Yet no guards came.

Ellina sat at the back of her cell. She opened her eyes. Closed them. Nothing changed. Hours could have gone by like this, or days. She had no way of keeping time. She did not trust her body to tell her, either, through hunger or thirst. She *was* thirsty, but the feeling was distant, almost dreamlike. It felt small in comparison to everything else.

The shock had mostly worn off. This was bad. Where before Ellina had needed to move, now she focused all her energy on staying perfectly still. Her breath was a ragged wind. Her throat ached. And her shoulder…

Ellina tipped her head back against the wall. Her eyes pricked. She swallowed her misery, trying instead to count her breaths. Then she remembered that it was Raffan who had first taught Ellina the trick of counting to calm her thoughts, and she stopped.

• • •

Her condition worsened.

Ellina could not get warm. The stone walls leached heat from her body. Blood loss did, too. She wrapped her arms around herself and tried to quell her shivering. And still no one came.

The dark was disorienting. It played tricks on her mind. Sometimes, Ellina imagined that the cell door was opening. Light would flood in. A figure would appear, his broad shoulders silhouetted by torchlight, his winter eyes lit from within. Venick would enter her prison, his voice storm-heavy. *You should have told me.*

"I know," Ellina whispered to the empty cell.

How could you keep the truth from me? How could you let this happen?

"I made a mistake."

Ellina had thought Farah's secret vital. She understood now that it was not merely the secret that drove Ellina to return here, but the idea that if she uncovered that secret, she could somehow justify everything that had gone wrong…and everything she had given up. All of her lies would have been worth it.

Or maybe there was another reason. Maybe she had needed the lure of that secret to block out what had happened in Irek, to erase the image of Venick reaching for the lifeless body of his mother. One horror exchanged for another.

You always called me a fool, Venick said. His eyes softened. He came closer. *But you are the one making all the mistakes.*

"Help me undo them."

He crouched before her. He was close enough now that she could count his eyelashes. He brushed her cheek with a warm thumb. *Yes.*

He pulled her into his arms and swept her away.

• • •

Ellina woke with an unpleasant start. It took her a moment to sort through her thoughts. She had been dreaming again.

Yet it had seemed so *real*. Part of her could not quite believe that it had not been.

She pulled her knees to her chest. She tried to shake the feeling that she was losing her grip on reality. It had been days since she had eaten. She was sore all over and hot with fever. But she was not hungry anymore. She was not thirsty. Even her shoulder, which had been a source of almost constant agony, scarcely bothered her.

She was dying.

The thought offered itself up plainly, rising like the sun only to set again. It touched her, and it also did not.

She was so tired. Her heavy head sank into her hands.

She closed her eyes and tried to find her way back into Venick's arms.

THIRTY-TWO

The door swung open.

At first, Ellina thought she was imagining things again. She stayed huddled in her corner, eyes closed, willing the harsh light away. When that did not work, she turned her face. Ellina did not want to be drawn in by dreams. Though they promised escape, they always hurt afterwards. During, even. They reminded Ellina that that door was never going to open, and no one was coming.

A hand touched her forehead. There was a press of warm fingers at her pulse. "Ellina?"

She blinked her eyes open. Kaji loomed in her vision.

"Move quickly," ordered a second voice. Ellina came fully awake. Her eyes found him over Kaji's shoulder.

Raffan.

She jerked back, pressing against the cell wall, baring her teeth. *Get away from me*, she wanted to say to him. She wanted to snarl it. *Do not come any closer.* The words stuck in her chest. Ellina choked on her own silence. When Raffan stepped through the doorway into her cell, her choke became a sob.

Raffan nudged Kaji aside, coming to crouch before her. He peered into her face, then reached out a hand to grip her wrist. Ellina tried to twist away, heels scraping the stone floor. Her pulse went on and on.

"Get the supplies," Raffan told Kaji.

"I have them here, but..." Kaji hesitated. "This is worse than I thought. That wound...she needs an *eondghi*. A real one."

"And which *eondghi* shall we call?" Raffan's tone was cutting. "Farah's personal healer? Do you trust Jival to keep quiet?" He kept his hold on Ellina's wrist, even as she struggled. "It is not worth the risk."

A muscle moved in Kaji's jaw. "I wonder why you have risked coming at all."

They locked eyes. The room strained with the effort of things unsaid.

Kaji said, "Wound-fever is the least of it."

Raffan broke their gaze. "It was never supposed to be this way."

Raffan pulled Ellina off the cell wall, spinning her around with ease. Ellina continued to fight him even though it was useless, it was comical, his strength to her weakness. Her energy was already sapped, everything dizzy and dark and warping. She was a puppet in his hands.

There was a sharp tug, and the cloth of her shirt ripped at the shoulder. Raffan dug his fingers into the tear and ripped it further, exposing her back. Hot tears sprang to Ellina's eyes. It was as it always had been between them: her, bared and vulnerable, and him, ready to inflict pain. All that was missing now was the whip.

She began to struggle anew.

"Ellina, please." Kaji trapped her hands. "We are here to help you.

Let us help you."

She heard the light *pop* of a bottle being unstoppered. A cool liquid was tipped over the wound. It ate into her skin like acid. She tried to scream.

In the end, Kaji restrained her while Raffan cleaned the wound. When it was over, Ellina lay limp, her torn shirt exchanged for a fresh one, the wound tended but too deep for stitches. Raffan's hands were slick with her blood.

"You could have made that easier," he noted, but the words held no bite.

While Raffan packed up the supplies, Kaji handed over a small wrapped bundle. "Bread and cheese, and a water canteen. It should last you at least a few days. I will return with more when I can."

Ellina gripped the bundle tight. Again, she tried to speak. *Do not leave me here*, she wanted to plead. *Take me with you.*

"There are guards at the end of this hall," Kaji said. "Guards everywhere. They believe we are only here to speak with you. If they knew we had come to help..." He need not finish. Ellina knew what would happen if Farah learned of this. "I cannot break you free yet, but hold on, Ellina. Just a little longer." He set a hand to her cheek, and they were gone.

THIRTY-THREE

Venick couldn't sleep. He left the camp to walk the land. The night curled around him, but he carried no lantern. He wondered if this was why conjurors summoned their storms and shadows: so that they could feel as if they were part of the darkness. He heard the wind sough through the grass. He peered up at the stars and thought of the Elder's sparkling, beringed hands.

Venick turned the man's offer over in his mind. He wondered for the thousandth time if he'd condemned them all by refusing. He still couldn't say exactly why he *had* refused, or why he didn't turn back and accept the Elder's offer now. It was disgust, he thought again. Resentment. The doomed combination of pride and anger.

Not just that.

No, Venick thought, not just that. But the other reason he didn't like to think. It made no sense. No sense at all, that Venick had refused marriage to Harmon because of Ellina.

It was times like this, when the night was dark and Venick was alone, that he remembered her most clearly. He could still see the thick fan of her lashes, the gentle arch of her neck, those golden eyes. He hadn't always noticed these details. Or maybe he had, but he hadn't understood them…at first. Later, he'd wondered how he'd ever missed her beauty. Ellina's beauty was like a first winter star: utterly singular.

He never knew he could hate someone so much.

Venick remembered drawing his sword on her. His fury had been so fierce it had burned like fever, yet he'd known the moment he hefted the blade that he couldn't do it. Ellina deserved death. She deserved the worst the gods could give her. Venick could know that, could know it as surely as he knew his own name, but it made no difference. He couldn't be the one to end her life.

Another regret to add to his list. Gods, what was *wrong* with him? He'd thought he'd left this softheartedness behind, that he'd become the hardened warrior his father had always wanted. The kind of man who could make ruthless decisions when necessary, who could end a life because it needed ending, and who cared if it was his sword that dealt her death, or someone else's?

Venick thought of his mother. He thought of her freshly dug grave.

His grief was starting to feel like a sweet, slow song. Venick hadn't wanted to listen to it before. Now he did. He wanted to linger on the pain, to bathe in it. In a way, his grief was fitting. He deserved it. He should sink down to its bottom and never resurface.

Venick kept moving, his thoughts spiraling deeper. Maybe if he'd killed Ellina, his mother would still be alive.

Maybe if he'd killed her, he could finally let her go.

· · ·

Their army set off again the following morning. They would continue west until they reached the plains. Now that they'd lost the Elder's support, it was more important than ever that they gain an alliance with the plainspeople, the third and final region of the mainlands.

Overhead, storm clouds were rolling in. The wind smelled like rain.

"I do not like the look of those," Dourin said meaningfully.

Venick didn't either, but he tried to put the storm out of his mind. Maybe it was just a storm. Maybe he was seeing ominous signs where there were none, because the last few days had gone so poorly, and he felt primed for the worst.

Maybe that was why, when the Dark Army arrived, Venick wasn't prepared.

. . .

They appeared over a ridge in the distance, a wave so dark that at first Venick didn't know what he was seeing. Then he heard it, the roar of a thousand hooves, to mix with the thunder.

Venick called his men to arms. He felt numb, as if he'd been cut but didn't yet feel the pain. He'd wondered when this attack would come. For months he'd been wound tight, always looking over his shoulder, always watching the horizon. Venick had seen Farah's army. He'd seen its size, large enough to rival the Elder's. He knew that eventually they must face it. Venick remembered a message from Dourin's contact in Evov. *They gather in the high city. She plans soon to strike.* The attack on Irek had been a test—which they'd failed. That ambush had proven that the resistance could be easily overwhelmed. When the Dark Army returned, Venick had thought they would return in force, with confidence. And now they had.

Venick spurred Eywen through the ranks. He hollered commands, ordering his men into position. Overhead, lightning flashed. "Stay close to me," he told Dourin.

The elf, grim and silent on his white horse, nodded.

They came quickly. Some infantry, mostly cavalry. Venick watched the enemy elves wash across the red earth and looked for conjurors among their ranks, but all he saw was a field of black. At his command Venick's army surged forward, rushing to meet their enemy. Their frontlines met. Collapsed. And just like that, with no time to think or plan or prepare, no time for speeches or calls for bravery, no time even to size up their enemy, to get a true handle on what they were up against, it began.

A spray of arrows, from his soldiers or theirs, Venick couldn't tell. One moment he was spurring Eywen through open air. The next: a clash of bodies and steel and green glass. A gurgled shout, a rush of heat. Venick heaved his sword up and then down again, into armor and flesh, over and over. His shoulder was on fire. His breath came in strained lungfuls. Dirt flung into his eyes, his mouth. He spat it out, only to be sprayed with more dirt, and with blood, which seemed to fall from the sky like rain.

An elf with a spear appeared in Venick's vision. The elf flew forward, white hair streaming, arm cocked to throw. Venick unhooked his foot from the saddle's stirrup, flung himself sideways to dodge the quick slice of the spear through the air, and then—against all his training, and to the appalled cry of Dourin behind him—he leapt to the ground.

Idiot, he thought he heard Dourin snap, but the elf's voice was lost in the roar of battle. Venick brought his sword around, a wide swing that took the spear-thrower by surprise, that caught him squarely in the chest. The elf fell, but Venick was already spinning away, dodging a new opponent, narrowly missing the swing of—reeking gods, was that a *mace?* Venick came to his knees and parried. He shoved back to standing. The elf's next swing went wide, which was a blessing, a mercy, because Venick wouldn't have been ready for it, would never have dodged that attack at such close range.

It began to rain. Venick's vision blurred as he thrust his sword into the mace-wielder, withdrew with barely enough time to check if the elf was dead before moving to sidestep a speeding horse, catching its rider in the gut, cutting the elf out of the saddle. Dead? Not dead. The elf was back on her feet, pulling a throwing knife from her belt, taking aim. Venick ducked. The knife missed. Yet she was on him, a new knife in hand. A cut to Venick's brow from an earlier strike throbbed. It ran fingers of blood down his face. As Venick focused on staying out of the way of the female's knives and lightning turned the dark world bright, he found himself thinking that this elf looked like Ellina, even though she didn't, not even a little bit. Yet there was a similarity. Maybe she *fought* like Ellina: that quick arm, the viciousness.

It got Venick thinking when he had absolutely no business thinking. He was remembering Ellina in the stateroom battle, and how her poise was as beautiful as it was deadly. He was remembering how she'd looked in Irek, how he'd expected to see that same viciousness come through, and hadn't.

Her letter, which he'd read under his mother's probing gaze, asking for a truce. Her handwriting. Familiar. Hadn't he seen that handwriting somewhere before?

And then there was that dagger in Irek, appearing so suddenly in the conjuror's back. It had saved him. Venick recalled the short blade, the simple handle. That too had been familiar.

Venick was distracted. His mind was where it shouldn't be. The female drew her final knife and went for his neck.

He was almost too slow. Venick knew better than to let his thoughts wander on the battlefield, not when a split-second distraction could end in death. He flinched away from the blade just in time, bringing his own up in its place, impaling the elf on its end.

Venick pulled his sword free, stumbled back. His hands were shaking, his stomach in knots. Nauseous. Why was he nauseous? This was not his first battle, not his first time soaked in someone else's blood. But: the dead elf who did not look like Ellina. Her small hands, the long rope of her hair. Her eyes, glassy and golden and unseeing. He blinked. Drew a breath. This should not have repulsed him.

"Venick."

Dourin's voice made him turn. Around them, bodies had begun to pile. The earth was muddied with gore. And still the battle raged. Horses crashed and screamed, their white teeth flashing. Many of his men were fighting on foot now, as he was. Infantry against cavalry. Never a good position.

Venick saw more. His army had lost ground. Their ranks were disassembled, confused and broken. Overhead the storm had condensed, darker and lower than he'd ever seen. It could only be the work of southern conjurors, and if that was true, Venick knew what would happen next. The storm's shadows would spread. They'd eat the earth, and his soldiers would be thrown into blackness. They'd be left to fight blind in a battle they were already losing.

Venick grabbed a man by the shoulder, one of his own. "Quick. Gather our archers. Tell them to target the conjurors."

"We've almost used up all our arrows."

"Then gather our fastest horsemen, tell *them* to target the conjurors."

"We can't *find* the conjurors!"

Venick released the soldier. He understood. The enemy elves all looked the same, outfitted in black, their hair and faces hidden under steel helms. Even if Venick had been able to pick the conjurors out of the mass, he suspected they'd be in the safest position: the back ranks. Targeting them like this would be next to impossible.

Venick's eyes sought Dourin. The elf was on foot now too, engaged in a skirmish with a thickly-muscled southerner. The southerner came forward but Dourin was quick: a burst of green glass and he'd severed the enemy's arm at the wrist. The southerner wailed.

"Dourin."

At a look, they retreated to their own back ranks. Here, men and elves stood pale-faced, weapons drawn, waiting to enter the fray. It was a bubble of calm in the midst of the chaos.

Dourin seemed to know what Venick would say before he spoke. He cut Venick off. "You do not have to do this."

"We're being overwhelmed. We can't win. Not like this."

"A message might not make it to the Elder in time," Dourin insisted. "He might not accept your change of heart."

"I have to try."

Dourin was stony. "We will send my steed. Grey. He is fastest."

Venick called for parchment and ink. He wrote the letter with a shaking hand. He rolled it tightly, slid it into a tube, and tied it with a leather throng to Grey's mane.

Dourin touched the horse's face, and the animal was off.

• • •

In battle was the only time Venick's mind went truly quiet. He had come to love that feeling. The blessed emptiness. The break from thought.

The fighting was vicious. There were losses—heavy and quick—on both sides. But when the Elder's reinforcements arrived, the battle began to tip. The Dark Army, large but underexperienced, began to waver.

As the fighting continued, Venick reclaimed Eywen, charging to the front ranks to lead the assault. Sword-blisters had torn his hands open. His hip and foot ached from old injuries. There was blood on his face, it was in his mouth. At one point, an enemy slashed his arm. The wound burned, but it was a detached sort of pain. The kind he could put off for now. He would feel it later. After this battle was over, Venick would return to himself. His wounds would hurt then as they should.

His decision to marry Harmon was like that. Later, he would feel the scope of it. He would understand. But not now. Now, he did only what he must do. War had a certain flavor, Venick had learned, not so different from the blood in his mouth. It was thick, coppery. It pushed all thoughts from his head, so that his only focus was his sword, and the elves dying at its end.

THIRTY-FOUR

The Elder came on a red stallion.

Venick and his soldiers watched the man ride across the now quiet battlefield. The earth smoked where fires had recently burned. The sky, limned with the sun's last light, was as deep as an ocean.

The Elder approached their waiting army. He rode alone, a solitary figure against a wide landscape. No sigil banners. No guardsmen. He was armored in a full metal kit, a sword on one hip, a war hammer on the other. He looked huge atop his horse, like a god. Untouchable.

It was only after he dismounted and drew off his helm that Venick remembered how old the man truly was. The Elder's skin was loose around his jaw. His hands were a web of wrinkles.

"A decisive victory," the Elder said to Venick. There was approval in his voice, clean and sheer. "My men report that you command an army well. With the help of my soldiers, you overwhelmed the conjurors and drove the Dark Army out."

Venick peered across the battlefield, which was no longer a battlefield, but a graveyard. "They'll be back."

The Elder gave a slight smile, as if that's what he'd expected Venick to say. "We'll be ready."

...

"You and my daughter make a good match," the Elder told Venick later in the city. Their men had marched through Parith's gates, some on horseback, many on foot, their wounded borne on carts and litters at the army's head. Venick's own injuries had been tended by the Elder's personal healer in the privacy of his new rooms. After his cuts had been dressed, he'd been given fresh clothing, boots, and a steel sword that was beautifully forged, but bulkier than the green glass blades Venick was accustomed to wielding. The new sword felt clunky in his hand. When he pulled the steel from its scabbard, it dragged. Yet Venick understood that all of it—the rooms, the sword, the healer—were a gift from the Elder. Venick couldn't refuse them without offending the man. He belted the sword to his waist.

"The timing is good, too," the Elder continued. He'd invited Venick to walk the castle's battlements. The city stretched beneath them, the afternoon sun setting the red and gold rooftops afire. "It is the perfect season for an engagement banquet."

Venick glanced sideways at the mention of a banquet. "I'm not sure it's wise to put our resources into a banquet," he said carefully. "Not when we might need them on the battlefield."

"We have resources enough for both."

"But not time enough. The Dark Queen won't wait. We suffered heavy losses in our last battle, and she knows it. She'll order her army to strike again, soon, while we're recovering. She's likely already planning her next attack."

The Elder clapped Venick with a friendly hand. His eyes, though, were cool. "The war can wait a few more days. Besides, the people of Parith are curious to meet their new master, as well as their elven allies. The banquet is a wise political move. Unless there is some other reason you do not wish to celebrate your engagement to my family?"

"No," Venick replied. There was nothing else he could say.

They walked back through the castle and onto the grounds. The Elder wanted to show Venick the barracks and the armory. "So that you may see what you have won." He didn't seem to mind drawing attention to the fact that Venick's marriage to his daughter had been a bargain with human lives as the prize.

The Elder's army was as impressive as the stories said. It became quickly apparent that the men he had sent to defend Venick in yesterday's battle were only a fraction of their total number. As they walked the training grounds, they passed men sparring with blunted swords in rows of six and ten, men currying horses and sharpening blades, men waiting for the baths in long, neat lines, their shirts flung over their necks, skin gleaming with sweat. Everywhere there were soldiers, polishing swords, weaving nets, hauling cannonballs, fletching arrows. Their activities were organized, their movements collective. The Elder pointed them out. Here was where the men worked. Here was where they rested. Here they ate, and drank, and wrote their letters. Here they planned for battle, and here—if they were discovered in disloyalty or deceit—they were hanged.

Harmon was there, sitting among them. The soldiers crowded her like eager children, smiling, teasing, asking for her opinion on this injury, then that one, showing off their new wounds and the size of their scars. Despite Harmon's claim that she'd never trained as a soldier, she'd clearly spent time around these men. A lot of time, if their adoring faces were any indication.

The Elder followed Venick's gaze. "The army will be yours to command," he emphasized. "After the wedding, of course."

Venick forced himself to meet the man's eyes. "Of course."

• • •

In the days that followed, the castle became a hive of busy activity. The banquet was to be held in five nights' time. *No chance to prepare*, the Elder's staff could be heard whispering, their words jagged and fretful, like chewed nails. *No time at all.* The servants dashed frantically through the halls, opening unused rooms, washing linens, chopping wood. Wine barrels—huge, iron-bound things—were rolled up from the underground cellars, and winter wheat rations were torn open early to be ground and baked into bread. The Elder had invited dignitaries from every major highland city, and many smaller ones besides. They would come to the castle and stay through the engagement banquet. There would need to be food and drink and room enough for all.

The Elder kept Venick close. He asked questions of Venick's homeland, his journey through the elflands, his ability to speak elvish. That last, especially, caught the man's attention. "What a marvel you are," the Elder said, "that you have opened your heart to the elves, enough even to learn their language."

Those words, though they sounded like praise, filled Venick with unease.

"The old man wants to show you off," Dourin said after Venick had confided in him one evening. Most of Venick's army spent their nights in the barracks or the city's inns, but Venick had requested that Dourin be given a set of rooms within the castle near his own. "You are his new warrior son."

And yet, Venick wasn't sure that was the whole of it. He found himself studying the older man. The Elder wasn't a king—the mainlands had no king—yet the man's power couldn't have been all that different for lack of a crown. Venick saw the way he treated his subjects, how he bent others to his will with a simple word, or even a gesture. He could be as solicitous as he could be cruel. The Elder's temper was an ever-shifting breeze.

"There is someone I want you to meet," the Elder told Venick two nights before the engagement banquet.

It was a soldier. He had a patchy frizz of beard, a knot of an Adam's apple. He couldn't have been a day past sixteen. Venick wondered if he'd ever looked like this, so skinny and timid. He remembered that he'd been sixteen when he first met Lorana.

"Harold is from the town of Igor," the Elder explained with a smile. "He came all the way to Parith to serve in my army. His family must be so proud. You have a mother and sister, don't you, lad? So proud indeed." The Elder continued to smile, but the compliment, like the one he'd given Venick, felt flat. "He is one of my hardest workers," the Elder continued. "All the money he makes, he sends back home. I have heard his family has even saved enough to buy a new house. Isn't that wonderful? What a marvel he is."

Venick's eyes darted up at the Elder's choice of words. The soldier bobbed his head nervously.

The next morning, Venick learned that the young soldier had been hanged. "He was a thief," the Elder explained over breakfast. They sat in a parlor overlooking the gardens, the windows flung open to let in the day. The Elder dug his thumb into an orange, peeling back the skin as juices dripped. "He'd been stealing from my imperial coffers. My soldiers earn a stipend, but not enough to explain the expense of a new home. *That* was how his family managed to afford it."

"How did you find out?"

"He confessed." The Elder noted Venick's surprise and smiled. "The guilty ones always do."

It was in this way that Venick came to learn how the Elder used compliments to ask questions, lapping on praise to test his men's loyalty. Rather than force a confession, the Elder liked to draw it out, sometimes over the course of days or weeks. He dug his thumb into his men like he dug into that orange, watching them twist with guilt and discomfort until they split open under the strain. The Elder's daughter, it seemed, was the only one who held his true affection. To Harmon, the man was nothing but kind.

"Harmon my dear, shouldn't we set a date for the wedding?"

It was the afternoon before the engagement banquet. They strolled the gardens, Harmon and her father side by side, Venick a little behind. Harmon glanced at Venick over her shoulder.

The Elder said, "Our banquet guests will be anxious to know a date."

"Perhaps springtime," she suggested, looking at Venick for clues. What did he desire?

Venick should have given a nod. He should have asked to be married as soon as possible. The sooner they were wed, the sooner he would have command of the Elder's men. Yet Venick found that he couldn't speak.

"Or we could wait for summer," Harmon continued. "The highlands are beautiful in the summer. The weather is mild, and the skies are clear."

"The start of summer," the Elder agreed. "So it will be."

. . .

When Venick returned to his chamber that night, he was surprised to find Harmon there inside, waiting for him. He froze in the doorway. "How did you get in here?"

"This is my father's castle," she replied, as if that explained everything. Which, in a way, it did.

Venick stayed where he was.

"Relax," she said, pushing off the wall. "I came to talk."

Since returning to the castle, Harmon had traded her plain homespun clothing for the colorful, extravagant dresses favored by highland women. The one she wore now was floral, stitched with vibrant purples and pinks. It didn't suit her.

She crossed her arms. "You've been angry with me."

Venick was silent. He couldn't deny it.

"If it is any consolation," she said, "I didn't know what my father would offer you that day in the great hall. I certainly would not have guessed *marriage*."

"He didn't tell you?"

"I am not so much in his confidence as you might think."

Venick closed the door slowly behind him, letting that information settle. "I thought you knew. I thought this was what you wanted." He met her eye. "*Is* this what you want?"

"I always knew my marriage would be arranged," Harmon said simply. "I suppose I even knew it would be to a soldier, though perhaps not one from the lowlands. Though, why not? My father has had his eye on the Golden Valley since before I was born. And you're a commander of elves and men both, leader of the lowlands. You'll be like the son he never had."

Though she kept her voice light, Venick didn't think he imagined the resentment there.

"Harmon." He shook his head. "Your father adores you."

"He adores the idea of me." She shrugged. "He doesn't really know me."

Her dreams of knighthood. Her father's decree. Harmon had told Venick the story of how the Elder forbade women from fighting after his wife—Harmon's mother—was killed in battle. Historically, the Elder's army had belonged to the entire Stonehelm family, but since Harmon had never learned how to fight, she could hardly be expected to command those men. That duty would fall to Venick.

Venick corrected his earlier thought. Harmon wasn't just resentful. She was *jealous*.

"Even after we're married," Venick said, "those men will belong to you more than they do me. You must know that."

She flashed a tight smile. "I could have been a soldier, maybe, if I'd started training when I was young."

"Who says you have to be a soldier? Commanders lead without actually fighting all the time."

"Not in the highlands."

"I've seen how the men act around you. You really think they wouldn't go to battle for you if you asked it?"

She shrugged. "I don't know. Maybe. But I didn't come to talk about any of that. I came to tell you to be careful."

"I have been—"

"No, Venick, you haven't. You accepted my father's offer, yes, but only after you turned him down. He won't soon forget that…or forgive it. Any further resistance, any hint of opposition from you—he'll sense it. And if he thinks he can't mold you into the son he wants you to be, he'll find another."

"You're not saying…"

"I am saying," Harmon interrupted with a significant look. "My father has been keeping you close. He's been showing you what you've won. This isn't generosity, Venick. It's a test. A game. He wants to see how you play."

THIRTY-FIVE

The engagement banquet was a massive affair. Highlanders came from every stretch of the region, arriving in twos and threes throughout the week, most of them flushed and excited, all of them boasting about the lengths they'd taken to make it to the capital on time. Appointments were cancelled, harvests postponed. Some had even ridden their horses to death in order not to miss the event. With so little advanced notice, it could be said that the guests had no other choice. The Elder would be deeply unhappy if his favorite lords and ladies were not in attendance at his daughter's engagement celebration, especially if the price of such attendance was the lives of a mere few horses.

On the night of the banquet, Venick and Harmon arrived to the great hall last, as planned. They stood outside its closed doors, listening to the scrape and chatter of the guests within as they waited for a herald to announce their arrival. Venick stared at the door's handles, which were carved in the same intricate detail as everything else in Parith.

Upon entering the city, Venick had been enchanted by the beauty of that intricacy. Now, it made him dizzy.

"Be sure to greet my father first," Harmon told him. She was dressed in red velvet, her hair loose down her back. Thin golden chains draped over her shoulders, bringing out the burnished tones of her skin. She looked beautiful, Venick realized. Somehow, that made everything worse. "He expects your eyes to find him first, even if you cannot speak to him right away."

The herald's muffled voice lifted within the hall. Harmon slid her hand into the crook of Venick's arm. He thought, from her next words, that she could feel how he stiffened. "It is expected," she said, meaning their interlocked arms.

"I know." Venick tried to relax. "Sorry."

"You are nervous."

No, he wasn't. He was sick. He was drowning in the sudden certainty that he was making a terrible mistake. He felt like he was on the receiving end of bad news, except the news kept coming, and coming.

"It'll be hectic at first," Harmon said. "Just stay close to me."

The doors opened.

There was a flash of light and color and sound. Venick felt Harmon tug him forward. A rush of the crowd's excitement, a hundred faces pushing in. They were touching him, reaching to stroke his hair, his vest, his arms. Harmon had warned him about this custom, explaining that it was good luck to place your hand upon a newly engaged couple, especially a wealthy one, as it was believed to channel wealth into your own family. Yet Venick was not prepared for this—*fanfare*. The adoring gazes of men and women he'd never met, the way their faces shone like stars, eager for his words, his nods, his smile, which felt frozen on his lips.

He remembered Harmon's warning and lifted his eyes to search for the Elder, who stood at the far end of the hall. Like his daughter, the man was strung with thin golden chains, but while on Harmon the effect was demure, on the Elder it was striking, like a crown to be worn against the skin. The man caught Venick's searching gaze and gave a nod.

For a time—minutes? Hours?—Venick and Harmon merely stood in the hall's center, accepting the well wishes of these strangers until at last the tide calmed and the guests returned to their seats. A flutist struck up a cheerful tune. Food was brought out on great silver plates, wine was poured, and the feast began.

Venick and Harmon were seated at the end of the long table, the Elder at its other end. This too was tradition, meant to signify the new distance between Harmon and her father. At last, a custom Venick could be glad for. The Elder saw too much, and Venick didn't think he could fake happiness well enough right now.

When the feast was over, the tables were cleared, and men and women took to the dance floor. Venick, who knew only the boisterous dancing from Irek, was unprepared for this coupled type. It seemed choreographed, partners switching partners, the entire dance floor unfolding like a kaleidoscope.

Dourin appeared at Venick's side at the edge of the dancefloor. Some of the elves wore human clothes, sashes and tunics likely purchased for this event, but many, like Dourin, simply wore their armor. Venick didn't think the elves meant to intimidate, yet he couldn't help but notice how they appeared—that cold, marble-cut beauty set against the banquet's garish colors. Dourin's cool elven mask was firmly in place.

"Don't look so cheerful," Venick commented dryly.

Dourin merely shook his head. "It is the noise. What *is* that?"

"Music," Venick replied, and a true smile tugged at his mouth, the first true smile of the night. "Don't tell me you've never heard music."

"Of course I have heard music."

"It is meant to be enjoyed."

Dourin's eyes jumped to Venick so quickly that for a moment Venick thought he had said something wrong. "Yes," the elf said. "Let us enjoy it."

...

Later that evening, a moment came between the dancing and gift giving when the Elder was occupied, and Harmon was occupied, and no one else was demanding Venick's attention. He took his opportunity. He slipped out onto one of the many grand patios that spread like wings around the great hall. Inside, the banquet whirled along, but out here there was no music, no dancing or revelry. Venick was alone. It was a relief to be alone.

It didn't last. Footsteps sounded from behind.

"Hiding?" Harmon asked lightly.

"I just wanted some air."

"We shouldn't be long. Someone will notice." Yet she came to stand beside him.

Venick couldn't quite hold her gaze. He leaned against the rough stone railing and peered out over the city, then up into the night sky. The stars, like the banquet, seemed to spin.

"Tell me what it's like," Harmon said.

"What what's like?"

"War."

He looked at her then. She was steady. There was a solidness about Harmon that would have made her an excellent soldier. It was, Venick realized, the same quality that would make her a skilled healer. Nothing seemed to faze Harmon, not her father's schemes, or a march through the highlands...or Venick, dodging their engagement party.

He offered an ironic smile. "You're a healer for your army. You know what war is like."

"Then tell me what peace is like."

She wanted to get him talking—the topic didn't matter. She wanted to ask him questions so that he could give their answers. She wanted to know him, because they'd been pledged to each other. She would spend her life with him and bear his children and watch his wrinkles deepen. Venick didn't know if Harmon had a lover, someone else she'd rather marry. He didn't know if this was simply her way: that steady sureness, like a sun across the sky.

"My father often spoke of peace between our nations," Venick replied, "but I'm not sure the mainlands have ever truly wanted peace. Men yearn for glory. There is no glory without war."

"But you want peace," Harmon said. "Even if your people don't. It's the reason you forged an alliance with the elves." Venick gave a nod, though with the uncomfortable awareness that that hadn't been his *entire* reason. "It is why you agreed to marry me." It was bold of her to speak so plainly, but Venick was coming to learn that Harmon was like her father in this. She didn't flinch away from the truth of things. "I like the idea of peace. If we'd had peace, my mother would still be alive." She moved closer. He could smell her flowered perfume. "The fighting between our people...it's senseless. I'd like to see the war's end. I'd like it if no more children had to lose their parents."

Her stare was star-bright. Venick saw it and amended his earlier thought. Harmon didn't just want to ask questions. She didn't just want his answers. He knew what she wanted.

He could have stopped her then. But he didn't.

She said, "I'd like to see the mainlands united."

And she kissed him.

Her mouth was soft. Dry. And the kiss was…quiet. Their lips made no noise as they moved against each other. Odd, Venick thought. Kissing should make some sort of noise. Or their breathing should. Her hand on his face should. His hands, snaking across her waist, into her hair, which was long. It held a slight wave. He could feel the gentle curls, the thickness. Harmon's hair wasn't straight, not pulled back tightly into a braid like…

Venick stopped the direction of those thoughts. He held his breath against the folds of his own anger.

Harmon pulled back. "Venick?"

"Come here," he said, and brought their lips to meet again. This time, he didn't think about how the kiss was different. He didn't try to compare. Yet not thinking about these things was no better, because as soon as he became aware of what he was trying to avoid that awareness grew larger than the thoughts themselves, and Venick slipped. He couldn't help it. His mind darted to Ellina, and he remembered everything at once: every hollow of her skin, every ridge, every scar, the way she smiled into his lips, her laugh and her hands and her eyes, on him.

Venick had pulled away from Harmon again. He didn't remember doing this. He only knew that they were no longer touching, and that Harmon was looking at him with the same wariness as she had when she'd been a prisoner. "Is everything—?"

A scream pierced the air.

It was followed by another scream, and another. Then: hollers. The sound of swords being drawn, the great crash of a table being overturned somewhere in the great hall. Venick was already moving towards the commotion. He glanced back at Harmon. "Go," she told him.

Inside, it was chaos. Humans and elves darted in every direction, the women lifting their skirts to flee, men and elves drawing their swords. Venick drew his own sword, ready to face the enemy, to sink his blade into this new threat…except there didn't seem to *be* any threat. Venick scanned the hall, looking for the cause of the panic, but he couldn't find it. There were no enemy elves in sight. No conjurors.

Venick grabbed Branton by the arm as the elf rushed past. "What happened?"

"A southern assassin. He came out of nowhere." Branton's face was unmasked. He looked shaken. "He went for the Elder, but Dourin… Dourin stopped him."

Venick's stomach dropped. "Where's the Elder?"

"Safe."

"The assassin?"

"He escaped."

"And Dourin?"

Branton hesitated. His eyes flicked towards the other end of the hall. A crowd was gathering there. Venick started in that direction.

"There could be more southerners," Branton called after him. "We need to prepare. We should close the city's gates, alert our soldiers."

"Take care of it."

Venick moved quickly. He felt that old jump in his chest, the mix of dread and nerves. He pushed through the crowd. Someone—Venick didn't see who—ordered everyone to back away. "Make room!" said the unseen voice. People did. A space appeared, and Venick saw.

"Dourin." Venick didn't understand. His mind wouldn't allow him to understand. Dourin lay on his back, pale-faced and quiet. Blood leaked from under his armor. It was in his hair, on his hands. His whole left side was a mess of red.

Venick was at the elf's side, he was on his knees. He fumbled to undo the armor's buckles. "Never mind that," Dourin said, attempting to push Venick's hands away, but the motion was weak. Its weakness frightened Venick. He tasted his own panic. It rose to his tongue like bile.

"Harmon!" Venick hollered over his shoulder.

"She cannot help me. If you just—"

"Harmon!"

"Shut *up*," Dourin wheezed, closing his eyes as if deeply annoyed. As if he wasn't dying. "And listen to me. Venick. Ellina is a spy."

Venick's hands stilled. He gazed down at Dourin, not understanding the sudden, random shift in conversation. "I know," Venick replied. "I know she was a legion spy…"

"No." Dourin's face shone with sweat. His limbs looked all wrong, set at rigid angles. "That is not what I meant. I mean she is a spy. For us. For the resistance."

At first, Dourin's words didn't register. He was delirious with blood loss, Venick thought. He was delusional. Then Venick's heart seemed to flip, and the earth tilted, everything going sideways. "No."

"Yes."

"Dourin." Venick had to swallow back sudden nausea. "You were there on the balcony. You heard her admit everything. She spoke in elvish."

"She lied."

Venick was pulling away. Blood loss, he thought again. Delirium. Yet his heart seemed to have vanished from his chest, and he knew. He knew before he saw Dourin's small smile, or before every moment Venick had ever spent with Ellina crashed over him like a violent wave. Dourin said, "She can lie in elvish."

Venick was on his feet. "That's impossible."

"Not for her. She is a conjuror. A northern one. This is her power."

"She's not a conjuror. She can't be."

"She has been sending information through the everpools. That is how I knew about the ambush in Abith. That is how I knew Rahven was a spy. Because she discovered that information in Evov, and she told me." Dourin drew a long breath. His eyelids drooped. "She did not want you to know. She said that you would go back for her if you knew. That you would never allow her to risk herself in such a way."

"Of course I wouldn't allow it." Venick's voice broke. The world was unraveling. He felt it: the moment it all came apart. "You kept this from me," he said, and found that—despite the fact that Dourin was bleeding out beneath him—he was furious with the elf. "Why?"

"I promised her that I would not tell you."

"You promised her in elvish?"

"No. I *can* keep a promise, you know, without the bonds of elvish to hold me to my word. I promised Ellina that I would keep her secret for as long as I lived." Dourin's smile dimmed. "Well. As you can see, I am soon to be relieved of that burden."

Venick's anger evaporated. "Dourin. No."

"I might have told you anyway," Dourin went on weakly. "I have not heard from her in weeks. And you know Ellina. I fear…"

He didn't need to finish. *Weeks.* Venick's mind lurched from thought to thought. Ellina might have been captured. She might be hurt, in trouble.

He didn't allow himself to think the worst thought.

Harmon appeared. "I've just spoken to my father. What—?" Her eyes fell to Dourin, and Venick was wretchedly grateful that she didn't flinch, or balk, or even bother to finish her question. "He needs to be taken to the infirmary."

"Please," Venick said. *Help him. Save him.*

Harmon nodded once, grimly, and got to work.

• • •

Venick saddled Eywen as quickly as possible. His movements were short. Too rough. Eywen flattened her ears and gave an anxious whuff. She could sense his panic. Venick knew that if he didn't relax, she'd pull away. She'd never let him ride her. Yet his hands continued to shake. His pulse rode high. He couldn't get ahold of himself.

Harmon appeared in the stable's entryway.

Again, Venick begged her. "Help me."

She came to his side and picked up the task where he'd left off, reaching under Eywen's belly for the saddle's buckle, pulling it through the loop, cinching the saddle tight. Eywen calmed under her sure hands. When Harmon finished, she stepped back. "Your friend's condition is stable for now, but his wounds are severe. And we have not caught the attacker. Given that, I wonder what is so important that you must leave *now*." She pinned him with an expectant look.

So Venick tried to explain. He tried to describe what was going on and why, that he'd been right about Ellina all along, she hadn't switched sides, hadn't betrayed them, that she'd trapped herself on an island with the Dark Queen and lied to him about it because that's what she *did*, and now Dourin hadn't heard from her in weeks…but Venick's words, like his hands, wouldn't stay steady. He skipped over details, rushed through others. He knew he wasn't making sense. Nothing was making sense.

"I'm sorry," was all he kept saying. "I have to go."

"But why?"

"I'm sorry."

He took the reins and hurried Eywen into the night.

"This is unwise," Branton told him a short time later. The elf had intercepted Venick at the city's gates. He'd heard of Venick's leaving and demanded an explanation, but Venick's account to Branton had been no better than his account to Harmon. Unlike Harmon, however, Branton seemed less willing to simply let him go. The elf planted his feet. "Have you lost all sense? You are leaving now? And for what? To chase a memory."

"Ellina's not dead."

"We just secured the highlander alliance. The Elder was attacked by a would-be assassin, the enemy is loose in the streets, and Dourin might not survive the night. We need you here."

"I'll be back."

Branton didn't believe him. "What does the Elder say?"

"I haven't told him."

"You have not..." The elf's face went slack with disbelief. "Venick, *think*. You will ruin everything. All that we have worked to gain."

"I won't."

"We need the Elder's soldiers. And this city needs its leaders." But Venick was done listening. He pulled himself up onto Eywen, urged the horse forward. Branton grabbed Eywen's halter and Venick felt a rush of wild fury. He had to fight the urge to kick the elf in the face. "What are we supposed to tell the Elder?" Branton asked.

"Tell him whatever you want."

"That is suicide."

"I don't care."

"No," Branton said, releasing Eywen's halter. "I can see that you do not."

THIRTY-SIX

Venick peered through the night at the palace. He saw its sharp spires. The thick parapets. He saw the way the mountains seemed like fingers interlocked, a handhold to hoist the castle up between them.

He reined himself in. During his windswept journey across the elflands he'd given himself over to his impulses. He'd cursed the bitter winds, the too-short days. He'd pushed Eywen as hard as he dared, resting little, sleeping even less. Venick had been driven by fear and fury and something less easily named, a feeling that seemed to sink its claws into his bones and howl. He was edgy, nervous, sleep deprived, and possibly insane.

When he reached Evov, however, Venick was nothing but careful.

He left Eywen at the edge of the city. He had nothing to tether her there, nothing even to tether her *to*. This high in the mountains, the rock was sheer on all sides. The path—a narrow back passage—bore no life. No trees or shrubs. "Stay," Venick told Eywen, and prayed that she would. Then—without thinking too hard on what would happen if she didn't—he turned his back on her.

Venick entered the sleeping city.

He moved carefully, keeping to Evov's edges, slipping through the shadows that pooled between buildings. The streets were quiet, the windows dark. The road was crusted with a thin sheet of ice that creaked and crunched with every step, and though Venick grimaced at the sound, it seemed that for once the gods were on his side. The streets stayed empty. The windows stayed dark. No one saw him.

He crested a ridge and again the palace came into view.

Venick thought he would have remembered the queen's palace in detail, but the sight hit him fresh: those clawing towers and razor edges, the pinprick lights floating high in the black sky. A deep ravine separated the fortress from the rest of the city, connected only by a single bridge that currently played host to a literal *swarm* of black-clad guards. For a brief moment Venick imagined facing those guards, drawing his weapon, cutting them down one by one. The vision filled him, a cup to the brim.

Spilling away. Venick might be a fool, but he knew this much—he'd never be able to fight them all. If he intended to enter the palace, he'd need to find another way in.

But where? The palace was a stronghold. It had been built for the very purpose of keeping outsiders out, and stood like a sentry, as it had for a thousand-thousand years: silent and cold and colorless.

Or...mostly colorless. It occurred to Venick—oddly, in a way that seemed both unimportant and yet also vitally significant—that there was a room inside the palace that hadn't been built with dark stone, but brightly colored glass. The entrance hall. Venick had been a prisoner the first time he'd set foot in that hall, and though at the time he'd been focused on his impending death, he'd still been distracted by the huge, glittering mosaic that covered the entire back wall of the entrance hall. He remembered a few of its figures: a three-headed horse. A blue lizard.

That mosaic was strange. He'd thought so then, and he thought so again now. Elves didn't make art, so what did they know about glass craft? What were they doing, adorning the queen's hall with that beautiful, intricate mosaic?

Unless they hadn't.

Venick blinked. He drew that thought back, pulled it in close. Wait. Wait.

What if they hadn't?

It was well known that humans had once roamed Evov. This was before the purge, before the border, when humans and elves had lived peacefully side by side. In those days, humans had conjurors among their own ranks, men and women who could bend the elements and shape the earth. *Our conjurors even helped build their cities*, Erol had told Venick in Irek. But if humans had helped build elven cities, who was to say they hadn't built this palace, too? And if that was true...

All manmade palaces have a secret escape. Venick had said this to Dourin in Parith, though the memory seemed to speak in his father's voice. *If ever there's an attack or a siege, it's a way for dignitaries to quickly get out.*

Or for someone else to get in.

Venick turned away from the bridge and angled north. He stepped off the path and began his descent into the ravine.

· · ·

The moon rose. Its soft light glinted off the water below. Venick concentrated on his hands. On the wet, frozen earth crunching under his fingers. He forced himself to move carefully down the cliffside, to test each foothold before trusting it with his weight. If he slipped, he'd fall far. His body would shatter on the rocks below.

The pace was agony. Venick felt the hard tick of every second passing, the pressing weight of every moment that had passed already. He was terrified that he was too late. How long had it been since he'd last seen Ellina? Months. He hated himself for it. He could hardly stand his own thoughts: that she was hurt, in pain. That she needed him and he hadn't been there. It was all Venick could do not to rush, to simply let go and let gravity speed his decent. Maybe if he did, the fall wouldn't kill him. Maybe he'd hit the water and somehow not break his legs.

Maybe you're an idiot.

Venick refocused, traversing the rocky cliffs as carefully as ever, hand over hand.

He reached the water. Waves battered the cliffside. He was close enough now to feel their wet spray. There was no shore, just rocks and ledges. He'd have to jump. He wasn't bothered by the prospect of freezing water, and when he dove in, he barely felt it. He began to swim, pushing himself to move faster, faster.

He emerged soaked, trembling, on the other side. He gazed up at the palace. It stretched higher than the stars.

He began to climb.

• • •

The mouth of the tunnel, when Venick found it, was nothing. Child-sized. He would have missed it if he hadn't known what he'd been looking for.

There had been a path here in the mountainside once, which was his first clue. It was crumbling and grown over, nearly shapeless in the dark, but it caught his attention. Elves would have had no reason to build a path here, not unless they'd planned on docking boats in the water below, and clearly, they weren't.

So. Some other reason.

He found the tunnel half by accident, a stupid stroke of luck. His foot had slipped and he threw out an arm, his hand catching not rock as he'd imagined, but loose roots. Air and dust. His arm had gone clean through the rockface. Blinking, he'd pushed the roots aside to reveal a hole. More digging then, scrambling with fingers and elbows to create an opening wide enough to squeeze through.

Using up all your luck, Venick.

He hoped not. He'd need more, much more, if he was going to sneak past the guards, and somehow find Ellina, and get them both out alive.

The tunnel was pitch black inside, the ceiling low. Venick had to get on his hands and knees to climb through. He felt his way along, his sword thumping bruises into his hip, until eventually the tunnel opened and widened and allowed him to stand.

He picked up pace, one hand on the wall for balance, more useless blinking into the dark. His heart had turned molten. It cracked at the corners, seeping under his ribs.

Soon, the tunnel changed again, sloping upwards. Venick could hear noises. The clatter of metal. the sizzle of oil. Up ahead, light seemed to leak from the ceiling. A trapdoor. As Venick came closer, he could smell baking bread. That metallic clattering was the clattering of pots.

He was beneath the kitchens.

Which was not where he'd expected this tunnel to lead. Most escape routes were connected to a more practical location. Not necessarily the dignitary's chambers—that came with too many of its own risks—but somewhere *private*, at least.

The kitchens, he thought again in disbelief. Hell and damn. His luck really had run out.

Venick set his hand to the trapdoor overhead, which was not in fact a door but a slab of stone. He pushed it up just enough to glimpse the room, and the two dozen or so elves preparing the morning meal.

His heart sank. He'd never be able to sneak past them all. He could possibly fight his way through—most of these servants appeared unarmed—but he hated the thought of killing innocents, let alone doing it *quietly*, or how many guards would come swarming once the blood started to flow…

So don't fight.

Sure, don't fight. So he was supposed to just push up into the kitchens and—what? Beg for help? That was more likely to end in disaster than fighting would…except at that moment, Venick realized he knew some of these elves. Not well, not even by name, but from when he'd been a prisoner in this palace and Ellina had ordered servants to bring him food and linens and soap. Some of the elves, curious about a human in their city, had stayed to talk. They'd swapped stories. The elves had seemed kind.

Which shouldn't change anything. That realization should change *nothing*. He shouldn't feel bolstered just because these elves had once been *nice*…

Venick realized what he was planning and smothered a laugh. Reeking gods, he really was insane.

He pushed up through the floor and stepped out into full view. The elves saw him, and froze.

"Please," Venick said to the now quiet kitchen. "Help me."

There was a sudden flurry of movement as the elves sprang into action, some rushing to close the doors, others corralling him into a back corner of the kitchen to keep him out of view.

"How did you get in here?"

"Are you mad?"

"You are going to be caught!"

"Please," Venick said again, speaking over the tumble of angry whispers. "I'm here for Ellina."

"*Cessena* is..." one of the elves started to say, then trailed off, looking grim. Venick's nerves twisted. He wanted to grab the elf by the arms and demand that she finish that sentence. *The princess is what?*

He forced himself to speak calmly. "Will you take me to her?"

They looked at each other.

"Is she in her rooms?" Venick tried.

"Not in her rooms," another servant replied. "In a cell. Under the palace. Deeper even than these kitchens."

"Tell me how to get there."

"There is no need," said a third elf, a young female with wide, watery eyes. "I will take you."

・・・

They used the servant's passages. The young servant carried a lantern. The light seemed to drain her of color. "I do not have a key to her cell," she said.

"Don't worry about that. Just get me there."

The elf threw him a glance. Her expression was unreadable. "I have not seen her since she was taken. No one has been allowed to visit. But we have heard..." And again, that grimness. Again, something they weren't telling him. "I wish I could have done more for her."

Venick struggled to keep his voice down. "Is she hurt?"

"I do not think it hurts."

"You don't think *what* hurts?"

The elf came to a halt. They had reached the end of the tunnel and were now standing before what appeared to be a plain wall. The servant lifted a hand and pressed her thumb into a slit in the stone.

The wall gave way. Venick had only a moment to take in the room on the other side—an old bedchamber-turned-dungeon, two empty cellblocks, a third solid cell at the end—before his eyes landed on the single elf inside the room, the one who must have heard them coming, because he was standing perfectly still, waiting, on the other side.

Raffan.

Venick's vision went white. He didn't hesitate. His sword was in his hand, his feet were taking him forward. Raffan sidestepped the first swing and said, "Wait." Venick brought his sword up again, arcing high, coming down. His molten heart was spilling in earnest now. His blood burned through him. "Wait," Raffan snarled again, but Venick wasn't listening. He wasn't himself. If he was himself, he would have noticed how Raffan didn't reach for his own weapon, how he made no attempt to fight back. Venick would have noticed Raffan's expression, which was so hard as to appear almost stricken. Venick had held himself in tightly all the way here, had been restrained and contained, but now here was an enemy, someone he could rip into and make pay.

Raffan snarled, "Do you want to save her or not?"

That stopped him.

Venick drew his sword back mid-swing. Raffan was breathing heavily, his white hair sticking to his face. He said, "If you kill me, she dies."

Venick didn't lower his weapon. His shoulders trembled with restrained effort as they stood, glaring at each other. "What are you talking about?"

"I am going to reach into my pocket and pull out a key," Raffan replied.

Venick ground his teeth, but didn't move to stop Raffan as the elf slowly reached into his jacket. Venick kept his sword lifted between them. He was thinking, *trick*. He was thinking, *enemy*.

Raffan produced a key. He tossed it to the ground at Venick's feet.

Venick stared. "I don't understand."

The elf spoke deliberately. "I just remembered, I left a candle burning in my suite, and the window is open. The winds are strong tonight. That candle might tip."

Venick lowered his weapon a fraction. "A fire might kill innocent elves."

"Then let us hope enough palace guards rush to douse it before anyone is harmed."

Venick still didn't understand. He wanted to press the elf. *Why* and *Since when?* and *I thought you wanted us both dead*. But Raffan didn't give him the chance. With a final haunted look, the elf swept away.

Venick watched the door Raffan had disappeared through. He was gripping his sword as if he planned to squeeze the pommel to dust. For several moments he did nothing, half expecting a swarm of guards to come bursting back through that door.

He went for the key.

"At the end," the servant said, her voice shaky and small. She had pressed herself against a wall during their fight and looked as if she had no intention of peeling herself away. "The stone door."

Venick set the key into the lock. Turned, and felt the smooth click of a bolt come undone.

And she was there. Curled up on the stone floor, seemingly asleep. Her back was to him, her hair a tangled mess. She was so thin that for a moment Venick couldn't believe it was truly her. Yet he recognized the curve of her spine and the slope of her neck and the rise of her hip, and he knew that it was.

"Ellina."

He was on his knees at her side. He kept saying her name. He brought a hand to her shoulder, the words spilling out of him now, hardly even aware of what he was saying. "Ellina? Ellina, please, wake up."

She did. Her eyes came open. She blinked, and saw him.

She jerked away. Venick let his hand fall. He'd frightened her—or he believed that he must have. Her eyes were wide, scanning his face like she couldn't believe what she was seeing. Like she didn't trust that he was real. The sight made him swallow hard.

"Ellina." His voice was nothing but a hoarse whisper. "It's me. I'm here. I'm getting you out."

She said nothing. She was still searching his face as if she didn't know him, her chest rising and falling heavily.

"Ellina? Are you—?" He couldn't stand the way she was looking at him. His voice turned desperate. "Please. Say something."

"She cannot speak."

Venick spun. He'd almost forgotten the servant. "What do you mean, she can't speak?"

"The conjurors," the young elf replied. And there it was, finally, the truth they'd all been avoiding. "They stole her voice."

THIRTY-SEVEN

Venick blinked at the servant. He looked at Ellina, the grim set to her jaw, her eyes suddenly anywhere but him. "They *what?*"

"It is the power of the conjuror," the servant explained in that quiet, quivering voice. "They can turn another blind, or deaf, or mute."

It was as if all the air had been sucked from the room. Venick's head spun. *No.*

He pulled back.

No.

Not possible.

That's not possible.

His thoughts continued to spiral. He couldn't believe it. He was cracking under the weight of his own disbelief. "Ellina." Her name on his lips, the way she still wouldn't look at him. His anguish, not slow, but sudden and sharp, a knife to part his skin. "Ellina. Is this true?"

She glanced up at him, and Venick wished back the question. He couldn't bear to see the answer in her hollowed eyes. He couldn't bear to see the way her expression revealed all the missing pieces of her, as if she'd been flayed open by the same knife that flayed *him*. Venick's heart twisted. He took a shallow breath. Still not enough air. "We don't have much time." He turned to the servant. "Get us out of here."

They retraced their steps, keeping to the castle's deepest, darkest passages. The servant led the way, Ellina next, Venick close at her shoulder. He kept glancing over at her. He couldn't stop doing it. She was so pale. Like a ghost. Like she was no longer fully part of this world. Venick was seized with a sudden urge to grab hold of her, as if she might float away. *Stay with me*, he wanted to say, even though she was right beside him. *Please Ellina, just stay with me.*

When they emerged back into the light of the kitchens, the servants were all gathered, somber and silent. No one was working.

"Here," said the young elf. She exchanged her lantern for a lightly wrapped bundle, which she passed to Venick. "Take this."

"We'll have to swim back," Venick said. "Any food will be ruined by the water."

"It is not food. It is…something to help." The servant took Ellina's hands in hers. She kissed them both. She spoke to Ellina in elvish, soft words meant only for them. Then she let go.

Ellina peered uncertainly at Venick. Her eyes were still wary, her expression still full of disbelief. She had been locked in that cell for who knows how long, in the dark, without the ability to speak, or even anyone to speak *to*. And now here was Venick, appearing out of nowhere, working with the palace elves—gods, with *Raffan*—to set her free. No wonder she didn't believe it. He hardly believed it himself.

"This trapdoor connects to a secret tunnel," Venick told her, motioning to the hole in the kitchen floor. "The tunnel leads to the bay." He tried not to imagine that bay. He tried not to think of Eywen, and whether the horse would be where he'd left her. He didn't consider the conjurors, or the guards, or what would happen when they discovered Ellina's empty cell. Venick was gripped with a determination so severe it felt like fury. He would get Ellina out of here. Whatever needed to be done, he would do it. "We just have to make it to the other side. I'll go first," he added, but Ellina was already dropping down into the hidden passage. Venick tucked the gifted bundle into his belt and hurried after her, pausing just before he was out of sight. "*Gai shila,*" he said to the room of elves. *Thank you.*

The young elf placed a hand over her heart. "*Vani am lana.*" Keep her safe.

. . .

The moonlit bay, when they emerged on the other side of the tunnel, was quiet.

Which wasn't true, of course. The waves churned and splashed against the rock. The wind whipped their clothes, whining across the water. Overhead, seabirds cried into the night. But there were no soldiers waiting to ambush them. No guards or conjurors. Nothing…except, perhaps, the distant holler of some alarm, and the faint smell of smoke.

"We'll do this together," Venick told Ellina. She stood at his shoulder, staring out across the dark water. It was difficult to make out her expression in the low light. He couldn't guess what she was thinking. "It's just like I taught you. The principles are the same. You have to remember to stay calm. Can you do that?"

She opened her mouth and Venick's heart lurched, thinking that surely she would speak, surely the elves had been wrong, that there'd been some kind of mistake. But then she closed her mouth again. She wrapped her bare arms around herself.

"Ellina." He touched her shoulder, and she flinched. He dropped his hand. "You can do this."

She gave a stiff nod.

They moved closer to the water, creeping down the rocky path towards the mountain's base. They were low enough now that the rocks were spotted with moss. Water sprayed their feet.

Venick watched the waves carefully. In, then out, and again. He waited until he had a feel for their rhythm. "On my count." He considered taking her hand. "One." He thought of how she'd flinched away from him. How she couldn't seem to hold his gaze. "Two." The lump in his throat was worse now. It changed his voice. "*Three.*"

The timing was good. They jumped, landing on a downward crest, riding the wave out away from the rocky crags. Venick started swimming through the open bay, keeping his eyes on Ellina all the while. She was kicking hard, churning the water. She seemed to favor her left side. "Use both your arms," Venick instructed, "like this. Good, Ellina. Keep going."

She was immediately exhausted. Venick watched her face whiten with effort. Her teeth began to chatter. She kept her eyes firmly on the opposite shore, fighting to stay afloat, but her mouth dipped under the water. Her nose.

In the end, Venick pulled her. He wrapped one arm across her chest, swam for the both of them. He found a small shoreline on the other side of the bay and hauled her into the gritty sand. For a time they simply lay there, breathing.

Ellina came to her feet first. Dawn was coming. The world was soft and grey.

She stared up at the steep cliff.

"There might be a better path, if we look…"

Ellina dropped her eyes to his. They both knew that there was no path. Even if there was, they couldn't afford to waste time searching. Up, straight up, was the only way.

Cold, drenched, they began to climb.

• • •

Eywen was standing where Venick had left her. As they came down the path and Venick spotted her golden coat, he let out a breathless laugh, feeling stupid and grateful. Another gods' given stroke of luck.

He glanced at Ellina. It frightened him, how weak she seemed. A human wouldn't have made it up that cliffside in her condition. Most elves wouldn't have, either. The climb had drained what little was left of her strength, leaving her face pinched, her eyes hazy, like she was fighting sleep.

Or death.

Venick shoved that thought away. "Can you mount Eywen on your own?"

She could, though her movements were labored. She pulled herself up onto the horse with none of her usual grace. Once Venick was sure she was steady, he mounted Eywen behind her. "Just hold on," he murmured, and spurred the mare forward.

• • •

They rode until the city disappeared behind them. Twice, Venick thought he heard the sound of elves in pursuit and pulled Eywen off the path, but never did anyone appear. If Ellina's escape had been noticed, the elves hadn't yet caught their trail. The mountains remained empty.

Ellina continued to weaken. As they descended into the foothills, Venick saw how she curled into herself, as if in pain. He kept asking what was wrong. She kept waving him off. Finally, he couldn't bare it any longer. He dragged Eywen to a halt and dismounted, waiting for Ellina to follow. She did, slowly, too slowly, relying heavily on her left arm. Not her right.

She had done this in the water, seemingly favoring her left side. She'd done it again as they'd climbed the cliffs, her face thinning in pain that he'd mistaken for determination, though he'd asked her then too what was wrong and she hadn't answered, not with words or hand motions or anything else. But it was obvious to him now.

"You're hurt." He should have noticed it sooner. How stiffly she was moving, how reluctant she was to use her right arm. "Where?" She shook her head again as if to say *it's nothing*. "It's not nothing. Ellina." He wouldn't force her. He was afraid of what would happen if he did. "Please."

She held his gaze. Slowly, with shaking fingers, she undid the draw at the collar of her shirt. Venick made a noise, ready to stop her, but then she was spinning around, pulling the shirt over her head and holding the fabric to herself.

Venick inhaled sharply, and swore.

Her back was a maze of scars. He'd seen them before, but it was somehow worse seeing them now. Knowing the scars were there and having thought he remembered. There was a web of crisscrossed lines where she'd been whipped, the marks on the top the reddest where she'd taken a beating for him last summer. Beneath the scars, he could see each rib clearly.

But there, up in her shoulder…it looked like a knife wound. Perfectly punctured, like the blade had gone in and out again without any drag. It was old, clotted over, scaly around the edges. Partially healed, maybe a month old, but still swollen and red. He'd seen wounds like that before. Had a scar in his own hip, as proof.

Venick felt like he was swimming through time. He knew that he wasn't processing this, that he hadn't fully accepted the depth of what had happened. He saw Ellina, the skeleton of her frame, the way she began to tremble, and he knew in that moment that he would never, ever forgive himself.

He flipped open Eywen's saddlebag and rummaged inside for a fresh shirt, kicking himself for not having come better prepared. He hadn't anticipated this. He'd had no idea. But: the bundle.

Inside were a few items. A salve sealed in a glass jar, sticks of witch-root, another ointment of some kind. Venick unstoppered the bottle and sniffed, recognizing the scent of yarrow mixed with *lhaivsa*. He wasn't a healer, and a few late nights reading Traegar's book hadn't made him an expert, but he was grateful for what little knowledge he did possess. *Something to help.*

He used his knife to cut one of his spare shirts into strips. "I'm going to wrap your wound. It will hold for now, until we can get to a healer."

He worked quickly, rinsing the puffy skin with water from his canteen, applying both ointments, then wrapping the makeshift bandage around her frame and over her shoulder, tucking the edges into itself. He made sure that his movements were precise, his touches light and quick. He didn't linger.

When he was finished, Ellina pulled her shirt back over her head. She fussed with the sleeves, avoiding his eye. Venick watched her sudden self-consciousness, wondering what had affected her.

Can't you guess?

That tightness still hadn't left his throat. He tried to swallow around it.

Keep staring, why don't you?

He forced his gaze away.

Ellina approached Eywen and gripped the pommel with one hand. This time, Venick didn't hesitate. He moved to help. He lifted her up onto the mare's back, his hands at her waist. He remembered his hands going to Harmon's waist and felt instantly ashamed.

He should tell her.

Later, said a voice in his head.

Coward, said another.

Venick mounted Eywen behind Ellina. He took up the reins and spurred them on.

. . .

They rode. Melted ice slushed mud around Eywen's hooves. The sun wavered as it touched the horizon.

The pain and exhaustion was wearing on Ellina. She held her pain close, cupping it to herself like a fragile bird, careful to keep it hidden, but Venick knew better. He knew how Ellina was gritting her teeth when he couldn't see. He knew how she'd be counting the horse's hoofbeats to help steady her thoughts, how she'd dig her nails into her own palms until the skin broke, one pain to distract from the other. Venick knew how pride tended to be Ellina's undoing. He knew her.

Not well enough.

No, Venick thought, not well enough. If he'd really known her, he'd have understood her schemes, seen her game. He would have insisted on her integrity from the first, as Dourin had.

Dourin.

Again, Venick had the thought: he should tell her.

Later, said that same voice.

Selfish, said the other.

The thought made him miserable.

All of his thoughts did.

. . .

Night was coming, and with it, a new set of problems. Soon, temperatures would plummet, but Venick hadn't thought to bring a tent. Two bedrolls, sure, but nothing more. He'd left in too much of a hurry.

He slowed his horse.

"It's getting dark," he told Ellina. "We need to find shelter. Do you know of any place?"

She blinked around blearily. He wasn't even sure she'd heard him.

"Ellina?"

She focused her attention. Around them, the tundra was tufted with coarse brown grass. The mountains shone orange with the last of the day's sun. After a moment, Ellina shook her head.

Venick rode a little farther. Eventually he dismounted, pulling Ellina down after him. Venick left her with Eywen while he scouted, returning a short time later. "There's a little cave nearby. It's small." He cleared his throat. "But it'll keep off the worst of the chill."

The cave was indeed small. It was bear-sized with a low opening so that they'd have to get on their hands and knees to crawl inside. "I'm sorry," Venick said, though he wasn't sure what he was apologizing for.

Ellina took one of the bedrolls and disappeared into the cave.

Venick didn't immediately follow. He curried Eywen, refilled their canteens in a nearby stream. He gathered firewood, which he wouldn't light yet, not while they were still so close to Evov, but would be grateful for later. He pulled Eywen towards the cave's mouth, hoping the horse's body might block the worst of the wind. Then he simply toyed with his hands, having run out of things to do.

Quit stalling.

He could sleep out here. He could lean against Eywen for warmth.

You'll freeze.

He could build a fire after all. Just a small one. No one would see.

Don't be an idiot.

With a heavy sigh, he grabbed his bedroll and ducked into the cave.

Ellina was curled up with her back to him. He strained to hear her breathing, some sign that she was still alive. He couldn't, and felt a spike of fear. He reached out a hand, touched her pulse.

She startled, and Venick felt a wave of relief—and embarrassment.

"Sorry," he muttered again.

She craned her neck to look at him.

"I thought…" he mumbled, trailing off. Ellina eased back into her bedroll. She pulled the material tightly around her chin, eyeing him in a way that made Venick realize he was staring again. He looked away.

• • •

Venick didn't know how long he lay awake. He felt terribly split, as if half of him was from *before*, and half was from *after*, as if a great chasm had opened in his life. His thoughts were scattered, hunted and haunted. His eyes grew heavy, but he couldn't stop straining to listen for Ellina's breathing, or for movement outside the cave, Farah's conjurors come to reclaim their stolen prisoner. He hung like that, somewhere between sleep and wakefulness—until he slipped, and was fully inside his dreams.

He dreamed that he was back in Irek. There was a holler, the boom of a cannon. Overhead, storm clouds gathered and spread, reaching towards the earth. Venick drew his sword. He slashed at the cloud, which wasn't a cloud at all, but the cloak of a conjuror. The elf materialized, coming for him. Venick lifted his sword again.

Somewhere behind him, someone was calling out. But Venick couldn't look, not while he was occupied with his own fight. Yet that voice continued to cry, tugging at his awareness. It broke, and shuttered...

He woke. He was disoriented when the crying seemed to continue, someone muttering, thrashing in their sleep...

He was there in a breath. He wrapped his arms around Ellina, pinning her arms to her sides to stop the thrashing. In the dim light of dawn, he could see her terror-stricken face. A nightmare. "Ellina. Wake up. Wake up." Once he started speaking, he didn't stop. "It's just a dream. I've got you. Ellina, wake up."

She did wake, yet continued to fight him. Venick gripped tighter. "It was just a dream, Ellina, it's not real."

She stilled. Her chest heaved. Her eyes were wide and full of tears.

Slowly, Venick began to untangle their bodies, but froze when Ellina turned and bowed her head into his chest. Her shoulders trembled. Venick wrapped his arms around her. He pulled her close, murmured into her hair that it was alright, that he had her. This time, he didn't let go.

THIRTY-EIGHT

Ellina was not sure how they escaped. It seemed impossible, but they did.

She had imagined this. Venick, storming north for her. Venick, fighting his way through the palace, bursting into her cell, gathering her up in his arms. He had done those things and more, but it was nothing like she had imagined.

At Venick's suggestion, they began traveling by night and sleeping by day, finding hovels or hillsides to bed down in, each in their own bedrolls. Never again was it like that first night, and Ellina was grateful. She burned to think of her silent tears; she was alive, she had nothing to cry for. Yet sometimes she would see the sunrise, or a pair of speckled doves, and her throat would close. She did not understand the reaction. She hardly understood anything about herself anymore.

Venick must not either. That would explain why he seemed unable to stop looking at her, as if she was something wholly new, some unfathomable creature. Ellina felt his eyes on her even when he tried not to let her catch him at it. She caught him anyway, and then he would avert his gaze, his cheeks staining red. His shame was something she was coming to recognize, even if she did not understand it. He had nothing to be ashamed of.

She, on the other hand.

Ellina touched her tender shoulder. The wound was clotted and rough. Swollen. Her skin no longer felt as if it belonged to her. She recoiled the hand.

She remembered showing the wound to Venick: the slow rotation, the pull of the fabric up and off her skin. The wind had been stronger then. It rippled goosebumps across her tight flesh.

Venick had sucked in a breath. Though Ellina had not actually seen Venick's face in that moment, she could imagine his horror at the sight of the gaping flesh…and his disgust. She remembered the way he had paused. His hesitation had melted over her skin.

He had not wanted to touch her. Her wounds must have repulsed him.

They repulsed *her*. Ellina felt wretched inside. Rotten. She could not stop thinking about how this was all her fault. If only she had been a little stronger, a little braver, a little more clever, things might have gone another way. She would never have been caught, her voice never stolen. She would not have become *this*, this tired, silent husk of a creature.

It was not the first time Venick had seen her back, but it was the first time she regretted him seeing. She thought of the knotty scars, the pink skin, flesh mottled from a dozen prior whippings. Her scars were a map of her mistakes, the dagger wound the crowned king of them all. She would not have wanted anyone to see them all laid out like that. But especially not Venick.

• • •

They rode together on the blind mare. Often, Ellina slept. She tried not to—Venick had done enough already, and if *he* had to stay awake, then so should she—but she was sore and muddy-headed, and there was really no resisting the gentle sway of a horse.

Or so Ellina told herself. When her limbs grew heavy and her eyes began to droop, she liked to pretend it was the horse rocking her to sleep rather than certain, other things.

Like him, fitted along her spine. Strong arms on either side. How he was warm when she was still achingly cold.

Or the smell of him, comforting and somehow nostalgic, like old summer earth.

The way it felt to sink back into his chest, and rest her head against his shoulder, and close her eyes.

He didn't seem to mind her sleeping against him, but nor did he appear to welcome it. Whenever Venick felt her body growing heavy, he would stay still, his arms stiff, his breath tickling her hair. Ellina sensed him struggling, and felt—or *imagined* that she felt, it seemed quite possible that her untrustworthy mind had invented this entirely—the way he warred with himself. As if he thought he should pull away but did not. And Ellina, who was hardly clearheaded enough to decide whether it was wrong that she slept against him, and too tired to resist even if she could, did not pull away either.

• • •

He had something he wanted to tell her. As they rode across the nighttime tundra and she drowsed against him, she would sometimes feel his ribs expand at her back, as if readying to speak. He had done this several times over these past days, but each time he would stop himself, his motions turning jerky and stunted, as if held by an invisible rope. "You need…I should tell you…"

Once, Ellina had twisted in the saddle to look at him. She regretted it. She did not like what she saw in his face, or how his expression seemed to lift the lid off something deep and dark within her own heart. From then on, whenever he struggled for words, she simply waited in silence, eyes forward, unwilling—unable—to push him to continue.

Though, she was not sure she *would* have pushed him, even if she had still had a voice. She was suspicious of whatever it was that he wanted to tell her. If the halting way he spoke had not alerted her to its danger, then the way he would always sigh afterwards, frustrated, suggested its difficulty.

A secret.

Ellina was wary of secrets. They had cost her much. As she listened to Venick struggle with what he could not say, she felt it, like the pause right before a whipping: the promise of pain.

. . .

Her strength was slow to return. She was feverish in random bouts, often dizzy, rarely hungry. Some days she woke feeling better, only to later sink back into that tired, achy daze. Still, as the tundra passed underfoot and the mountains shrank behind them, she swam out of the fog. Her mind was clearer, Ellina thought, than it had been in a long time.

She began to look at Venick. To really look at him, straight on, as he used to look at her. It felt almost defiant to do this. They had been hiding from each other, him speaking softly and only when necessary, she responding as she only could—with a silence that took up far too much space.

She knew that he felt guilty. She knew that something was wrong. She just did not know what.

It was infuriating not to know, and to have no way to ask. On her stronger days, she wanted to scream at him. *Look at me. I am here. What secrets are you keeping now?* Maybe it was her stronger days that tired her out and kept the fevers returning. She always felt weaker after. As if she really had spent the day screaming.

He sensed her shifting moods and continued to avoid her. He kept busy: steering Eywen by night, making camp by day, hunting and bathing and cooking in between. Items seemed to fling themselves into his hands: buckles that needed polishing, clothing that needed mending, his sword and his dagger and his boots and hers. Even Eywen was in on the scheme, nudging Venick's shoulder for attention, nibbling his hair. It was the whole world together, conspiring to keep his eyes off Ellina.

It had been five days since their escape from Evov. The tundra—never exactly welcoming—had grown hostile with early winter. Shallow-rooted plants had long since flowered, their husks now hunched and brittle underfoot. The land, soft and boggy in the summer, was frozen over, and though it had scarcely snowed, white lichen stuck to everything, giving the world an icy, unfriendly feel. As Ellina scanned the barren land, she began to understand the scope of what Venick had done. That was twice now that he had come north for her. Twice he had risked his life to do it.

It made his growing awkwardness all the stranger. He no longer seemed at all like the person who had stormed into the palace and broken into her cell and dared anyone to stop him. Before, Ellina had wondered if she was imagining his angst, but that seemed foolish now. He wore his anxiety around his neck like a great flashing cloak. She imagined nothing.

She continued to try to make him hold her gaze. He refused, and began sleeping with the campfire set between them.

He had given up attempting to tell her whatever it was he was not telling her.

When they rode the blind mare, she no longer rested against him.

. . .

"You should let me check your wound."

Ellina looked up from what she was doing, which was kicking dirt over their small campfire. Dusk was upon them. Its golden light struck Venick's back, throwing his face into shadow.

"I know you haven't wanted me to." He cleared his throat. "I understand why. But I think I should."

It was startling to hear his voice. He had been using it less and less these past days. And he was right—she did not want him seeing. She was tempted to refuse, as she had the last time he had asked, and the time before that. The wound was not infected. It was nearly a month old and healing fine. There was no reason for him to see it.

And yet, something in Venick's face gave her pause. *I understand why.* Venick thought modesty was the reason she did not want him looking, but he was wrong. It was vanity over her marred skin. Stubbornness. Things that should have shamed her.

Or maybe it was more than that. Maybe it *was* a kind of modesty. She hated to feel exposed when there was still that ugly secret sitting between them. She already felt too vulnerable under his gaze, for how little he met her eye.

He sighed. "Please."

She turned away from him before she could change her mind, pulling her shirt over her head. She stared out across the rocky land, shivering when he began to unwrap the bandage from around her shoulder with light fingers. Peeling back layers.

"It's looking better." He sounded pleased, his breath warm on her neck. Ellina suppressed another shiver. "The swelling has gone down. I'll get the ointment. This won't take long."

He was quick, dabbing the strong-smelling paste over the injury, re-dressing it with fresh strips of linen. This time when he finished, his touch lingered. He rubbed a thumb over the cloth to smooth it.

Ellina stayed very still. He withdrew his hand. She expected him to move away, and was surprised when he instead helped her back into her shirt. His palm brushed her torso, her hip. Her blood turned to wine.

She was suddenly angry. Who was she, to melt simply because he had touched her? Things had changed between them. It was not like that anymore. Maybe it never had been like that.

His secrets seemed to breathe.

Venick's hands fell away, and she was cold once more.

...

"I buried Lorana's necklace."

Ellina opened her eyes. Dawn was edging into the sky. They were tucked in their bedrolls, readying once again to sleep through the day. She turned to look at him.

"She lived in a little hut on the edge of Irek. I wanted to see it. And when I was there...it felt right." A pause. "I—did I do the right thing? I didn't think I'd ever see you again. I don't know if you would rather me have given the necklace back..."

Ellina remembered the first time she had seen that necklace hanging from Venick's neck. The hot rush of anger, followed by a soldier's detached calculation. She felt as if she held that chain now, gripping hard, its links stamping her palm.

Was this his secret? Was this the thing that seemed to bind him so tightly? Maybe. His expression had a haunted quality as he waited now, watching for her answer. Then his expression changed. "At the time, I told myself that I was burying that necklace for Lorana. It wasn't true. I buried it because of you." His words were blunt. "I thought burying the necklace would help me forget you. Like I could finally say goodbye. I never wore it again, not after the everpool, but I always had it with me. It was like—if I could let it go, I could let you go, too. And what if I had? You'd be—you'd probably be—" He smothered himself to silence. His eyes were wide, and too shiny. "I've been so *angry* with you. I hate that you lied to me. I hate myself, for not seeing it sooner. I wish you'd told me the truth, that you could have trusted me that much. And it's true, I probably wouldn't have agreed to any of it, I probably would have come for you ages ago, but wouldn't that have been—wouldn't it be better than *this*?"

For all she had wanted him to look at her, Ellina suddenly could not hold his gaze. She sank back into her bedroll. Her heart shriveled like a snail in the heat.

In the distance, a morning dove sang her high, trilling tune. The sun wheeled into the sky.

THIRTY-NINE

They rode into Parith on horseback.

Venick wasn't sure how they made it back. Wasn't sure what kind of reception they'd be walking into, now that they had. He half-expected the gates to stay closed shut, for the city to lock them out, call them traitors and defectors and bar them for good, or worse.

But when they arrived the gates opened slowly, a yawning dragon's mouth. And the dragon's treasure. Parith's buildings sparkled in the late daylight, the city at the height of its beauty. Venick stole a glance at Ellina, watching her take in the dazzling windows, the swirls of fabric, everyone draped in jewels and perfume. Sunlight glinted off red rooftops and blown glass lanterns, turning the road to living rainbows. It was like a hallucination, so bright that it hurt to look.

He should tell her now, Venick thought. He should explain everything so that she might have some sense of what she was walking into. He shouldn't have waited this long. He shouldn't have waited at all.

Ellina lowered her gaze. On the tundra, she'd looked weak to him, but here surrounded by luxury and wealth, it was worse. She was so thin. She still wore the same ragged clothes she'd been wearing in that prison. The absence of armor on her was almost obscene.

Venick dismounted Eywen and Ellina followed, refusing his help. She gripped the pommel, swung a foot over the saddle and landed on unsteady feet. He tried again to search her face, but she sensed what he was after and kept her eyes averted.

Their progress to the castle was slow. The sun was warm, but Ellina huddled into herself as if chilled. By the time they wound up the path and approached the wide double doors, it seemed as if the entire city was aware of their arrival.

A crowd had gathered in the castle's courtyard. Venick spotted Lin Lill pushing forward, her boots clicking across shining tiles. Her eyes came to Ellina and she jerked to a halt. Behind her Branton, Artis and Erol followed, and behind them, Harmon.

"So it's true." Harmon spoke with her father's voice, that cool displeasure. Etiquette required that she offer a new guest food and drink and a place to rest, but Harmon clearly had no intention. She crossed her arms. "You've brought the Dark Queen's sister home to our city."

"Harmon." Venick cleared his throat. "This is Ellina."

"I know who she is."

Venick fumbled for what to say. "I think we need to talk."

"You think?"

More fumbling. "Dourin. Is he—?"

"He's alive," Harmon said. But she was grim.

Ellina's gaze snapped up. She turned accusing eyes on Venick.

"He was hurt," Venick explained. "An attack." She continued to glare. "I would have told you. I know I should have…" Venick looked back to Harmon. "Please. Take us to him."

"Oh certainly. I live to serve."

"Harmon."

Harmon looked like she might refuse. She was furious for all her own reasons. Venick could only guess what kind of rumors had been circulating about his sudden disappearance and subsequent reappearance with a stolen princess in tow—a princess with whom he shared a history.

He watched Harmon consider all of this. She pressed her lips together. But at last, she gave a nod.

. . .

Dourin lay on a narrow cot in the castle's infirmary. The air was closed and smelled of medicine. The light in here was muted, but even still, the elf looked grey. His cheekbones were stark ridges. The skin was stretched too taut. Even as they entered, his eyes remained closed.

"His recovery has been slow," Harmon explained. "Slower than I'd like. Abdomen wounds are dangerous, and this one was especially deep. Too deep to stitch. We've been packing it from the inside with gauze, and there hasn't been infection, but…" She let the thought trail.

"Is he unconscious?"

"Asleep. I've been giving him a sleeping draft, though he fights me about it every time. But he needs rest. The draft is his best hope at getting it."

Ellina moved soundlessly to Dourin's side. She knelt at his bedside, rested a pale hand over his. Her golden eyes returned to Venick, imploring.

"There must be something more you can do for him," Venick said to Harmon.

"There isn't."

"He should be getting the best treatment, the best care."

"And you think he isn't? He saved my father's life. This city owes him everything."

"You said his recovery has been slow."

"Because the wound was severe. Look around, Venick. Do you think this room is always so empty? There were other patients in here before. My father sent them to the infirmary in the city. The castle's entire medical staff has been dedicated to—*what*, princess?"

Ellina was shaking her head. Harmon crossed her arms. "I'm telling you both, this is the best we can do, and *why are you still shaking your head?*"

Ellina motioned at Venick's feet. He looked down, not understanding. "My boots?" Ellina's exasperation was clear. *No, you idiot.* She made the motion again, and this time it clicked. Not his boots. His injury. After Ellina had rescued Venick from a bear trap, she'd wrapped the mangled mess of his foot with leaves. That plant had been a miracle. It had helped his injury heal faster than seemed possible. Let him keep his foot.

"*Isphanel*," Venick said.

Harmon's brow furrowed. "The plant?"

He was surprised she knew of it. "Its leaves have healing powers."

"How do you know that?"

"Because I've seen it." Then, to Ellina. "I'll find it. Just—" *Tell me where to look* died on his lips.

"That plant doesn't usually grow this far north," Harmon said.

"I'll ride south."

"It's past season."

"There hasn't been a frost yet."

Harmon set her hands to her hips, but Ellina was nodding, and Venick had eyes only for her. "It's only midafternoon," he said. "If I leave now, I can cover good ground before dark."

Ellina came to her feet, a new glint in her eye. Venick knew that look. She intended to come with him.

"Ellina." He held out a hand to stop her. "You need rest too."

She ignored him. She touched Dourin's cheek once, gently, before striding from the room. Venick started to follow, but Harmon stepped into his path. "We need to talk."

"Later."

"Not later. Now. My father is furious, Venick." Harmon puffed out her cheeks. "What have you been thinking? First you run off like a man possessed, and now you show back up here with that elf—"

"*That elf* risked her life for our cause," Venick snapped. "She's been spying for the resistance."

"And you didn't see fit to explain that before?"

"I didn't know."

"The Elder won't believe that."

Venick glanced at Dourin sleeping in his cot. He thought of the way Ellina's jaw had set when he'd suggested that she stay behind to rest, that old determination, so at odds with the tired bruises under her eyes, the poverty of her frame. He felt something inside him begin to slip, some emotion that he'd kept bundled tightly all across the tundra come loose. He rubbed his face. "I can't worry about that right now."

"It's all you should be worried about."

"Did you see her?" He flung out a hand. His voice reverberated around the chamber. "Did you see what they did to her?"

"She's alive, isn't she?"

"Harmon. They stole her voice."

Harmon opened her mouth. Closed it. Gave a half shake of her head. "What?"

"You noticed, I am sure, that she wasn't speaking. They took her voice. The conjurors. As punishment. Ellina was a spy for us. She was caught, but they didn't just want to imprison her." Venick pressed the heel of his palms into his eyes. "They wanted to disable her. A punishment befitting the crime. They stole her ability to speak."

It was his fault. He should have known. Should have seen. Every moment he and Ellina had ever spent together rushed through him, all the opportunities he'd had to guess the truth. There had been times when he almost had. But then he'd think of how cold Ellina had become, how she'd called for his death in elvish, had threatened to kill him herself, and it had seemed absurd. Absurd, to think that she'd ever truly felt anything for him. Absurd, that she might still secretly be working for his cause.

Venick had thought her selfish. Coldhearted. He'd blamed her for the death of his mother. Her remorse, that day on Traegar's balcony. Her stricken expression on Irek's beach. She'd tried to tell him then, but he hadn't listened. He'd convinced himself that her choices made sense. In a way, they *had* made sense.

Of course the elven princess didn't love him. Of course he was nothing to her. She was as bright as a burning star, and he was a human. An outlaw. No one.

Venick dropped his hands. "I can't marry you."

Harmon wasn't surprised. Likely, she'd known from the moment Venick went racing away that it would come to this. Yet she gave a long sigh. "This is foolish."

"I don't care."

"My father will kill you."

"I'd like to think otherwise." When Harmon started to argue, Venick cut her off. "You don't want to marry me."

"I *want* this constant warring to end. I want our nations to be allied, for no more daughters to ever have to lose their mothers. And my father—"

"Do you always do exactly as he says?"

She was silent.

"He's one man," Venick said.

"One man with a giant army and a lot of power."

"The highland army belongs to both of you. You said so yourself."

Harmon gave a dry laugh. "Technically, it belongs to the Stonehelm family, yes. But that doesn't change anything. I am no commander." She sighed again. "My father will want to see you."

But Venick was already halfway out the door. "Your father can wait."

FORTY

The land around Parith was hilly, which made for good cover, though it was difficult to see far. Ellina strode ahead, her shoulders set, eyes trained on the land. Venick followed at a distance. He didn't try to close the gap. He wondered if he'd ever be able to close the gap between them.

Ellina halted, and Venick's heart lurched. He rushed to her side. "Did you find something?" he asked, despite there being no greenery here, no greenery anywhere, nothing but dry, chest-high tufts of brush and shiny, twisting cacti. Venick paused, and it was then that he noticed her expression. He faltered. "Ellina."

Her eyes were glistening. Her fists showed their veins.

"He won't die," Venick said softly. He stepped carefully closer. "Dourin is strong. He'll survive this."

A tear fell over her cheekbone. She impatiently brushed it away.

Venick's stomach was hollow. His heart was a dry rock. He'd never felt so useless. He wanted to reach out, to pull Ellina into his arms, let her cry against his shoulder while he murmured reassurances. He wanted so desperately to be that for her. A comfort.

It was an impossible thought. Venick wasn't a comfort to her. He was the opposite of comfort. He thought again of everything he still hadn't told her. His secret had become a living thing between them, a dragon with smiling teeth. It eyed him, sardonic, a reminder of everything he'd done, all the ways he'd been wrong, all the ways he'd wronged *her*.

And her voice, her voice. Venick's despair dropped deeper.

There were things she wanted to say. His pulse still thudded every time she opened her mouth to speak, a reflex she couldn't seem to quit. She probably wanted to rage at him, and he wanted to let her, because he deserved it. Reeking gods, did he ever deserve it.

"I'm engaged to Harmon," Venick said. Ellina flinched a look at him. He swallowed his shame and barreled on. "It was political. The Elder wanted to solidify the union between our nations. He seemed to think marriage was the best way to do it. I refused. Then we were ambushed by the Dark Army. We were losing that battle, we needed reinforcements. The Elder's army—it seemed like our only hope. So I agreed.

"I shouldn't have." His voice was raw, scraping its lowest register. "I would never have done it if I'd known the truth about you. I can't forgive myself for not knowing. Ellina, please look at me."

She did. Her golden eyes showed their molten cores.

"I've told Harmon we should break off the engagement."

Ellina's expression didn't change. She was shutting down, closing up, turning to stone. She looked away to peer across the landscape. The wind lifted her hair.

"I don't expect your forgiveness," Venick said. "But I wanted you to understand."

He couldn't be sure if she did. She gave a single, short nod before moving away again. Venick waited until she'd put that silence and space back between them. He followed at a distance behind her.

FORTY-ONE

They returned to the city shortly after nightfall, emptyhanded.

Ellina would have continued searching. She would have searched all night if it meant giving Dourin a better chance at survival. But when the sun was just a slice above the horizon, Venick caught up to her. "We should turn back." She had crossed her arms, *no*. "Yes, Ellina." Venick's expression was emptied out. He looked dead on his feet. "We won't be able to find the *isphanel* in the dark. And it's not safe to be out here at night. We'll look again tomorrow, I promise we will, but right now we need to go back."

She had agreed then, only because she was not sure she was strong enough to continue. Ellina had never resented her own body as she did then. Then again, her body had never turned on her in such a way. She had always taken her seemingly endless strength for granted. She would not do that again.

They moved through the city together. A night market was emerging, stalls springing forth like mushrooms in a forest, splotches of color between shadows. There was a candlemaker, a baker, a cobbler. Torches were lit along the road and humans mingled around them, swigging from flasks, wiping their beards, talking business. They nodded when they saw Venick, but then their eyes would shift to Ellina and their expressions closed. Their greetings went dead on their lips.

Ellina knew enough now to understand their hostility. The Elder was the ruler of this country. Venick had been promised to his daughter. So what was Venick doing, riding into their city with the Dark Queen's sister between his arms? What was he doing, wandering the land with her at dusk? Ellina did not know what stories were being told about her, but she saw well enough the suspicion in the humans' eyes. She saw them see her black hair.

They hated her. They did not care what Ellina had risked. Ellina was not even sure they knew about her role as a spy. All they knew was that she had been an ally of the Dark Queen, and now she was here, meddling.

Ellina wanted to scream. She sometimes felt full of such intense frustration that she wanted to cut off her own hands. But then the frustration would warp into sadness, bleeding her dry. She felt infected. Diseased. She half agreed with the humans' estimation of her: that she was a parasite, a witch. She deserved to be burned at the stake.

She risked a glance at Venick. It was difficult to look at him. Looking at him was like looking at her own, ruined heart. *Engaged.* He was engaged to that highland woman. Venick had said that he wanted to break off his engagement, not that he actually had. Ellina had not missed that distinction.

The two of them looked good together. Even Ellina could see that. Harmon was about Ellina's height, but the similarities ended there. Harmon was soft and womanly, with long wavy hair and pretty tanned skin. And Venick…well, he had changed since last summer. He looked less like an outlaw and more like a human commander. It was in the way he walked, the way he spoke. Harmon's marriage to him might have been political, but surely she did not think it was a hardship.

Ellina looked down at her own skin. Pale, like a grub. Ellina was not human. Lately, she had not really felt elven either.

Her throat closed. She did not know what she was doing here, did not truly understand why Venick had risked so much to come for her. It would cause him trouble. It was causing him trouble already. He should have left her in that prison.

When they returned to the castle, Venick asked a soldier named Lin Lill to share her room with Ellina. Lin Lill was gracious, but Ellina could not stand the charity…or the sneaking suspicion that Lin Lill was also meant to keep an eye on her. Ellina went to the infirmary instead.

Dourin's eyes remained closed, his chest rising and falling softly. His arms were arranged like a cadaver's, folded neatly across his chest. Ellina knew someone must have set his hands like that. The real Dourin slept like a sea-battered ship, tossing and turning, his arms flung wide.

She knelt beside the bed, listening to his breathing. When her knees could take no more of it, she crawled into the cot, curling up at his side like they used to when they were younger.

Ellina did not believe in gods, but she prayed hard that night. She prayed to every god she could think of, promising to do anything, to give up anything, if only they would let Dourin live.

. . .

She did not sleep. Each time Ellina felt herself starting to doze she would startle awake, gripped with the chilling conviction that if she fell asleep Dourin would die. Who would watch over him, if not her?

The hours slithered by. She drifted in a strange daze.

She did not hear Venick enter, did not sense his presence until he set a hand to her shoulder. "Ellina."

She sprang to her feet. Her vision tunneled; she had stood too quickly. The hand on her shoulder tightened as she swayed. "Ellina? Hey."

Her sight returned. Venick's forehead was pinched. "Have you been here all night?" She waved a dismissive hand, which he caught. "The palace physician is outside. She has been waiting to come in." His palms were calloused, the skin warm. Or maybe it was her skin that was cold. She felt as if she had been cold for a long time. Venick peered at Dourin and said, "His color is looking better."

Ellina was skeptical. Dourin's color did not look any better to her.

"Come on." Venick still held her hand. The thought occurred—ugly, unwanted—that he might have held Harmon's hand like this. He saw her expression and let go. "Let's find you something to eat."

She allowed him to guide her through the castle. It was the first time she had taken a true look at this place. The colors were dizzying, so different from home. Light seemed to ooze from the castle's pores, ricocheting off gilded hung shields and framed ochre paintings. And the smells: cinnamon and straw, perfume and bread and horse and wood. Ellina wondered how the humans could stand it. She felt as if she was drowning in sensation.

Venick guided her up a flight of stairs into a wide, low-ceilinged parlor. She realized that this must be his bedroom suite. "I figured you didn't want to eat in the great hall." He gave a sheepish shrug. "The Elder's staff leaves meals for me by the tableful. I don't know how they expect me to eat it all." This was true. There was a buffet piled with dishes:

meats and cheeses, bread and pies, stew, eggs, porridge, and something that looked like cake but smelled suspiciously fishy.

Ellina's stomach turned. She had no appetite for any of it. Instead, she motioned for parchment and ink.

Venick disappeared briefly into another room, returning shortly with the supplies. Ellina sat at a table for writing letters and began scribbling. She thrust the finished page into his hand. Venick stared at the words for a long time.

"The southerners can control the dead." It came out flat, but Ellina could sense his fear. How would they defeat soldiers who could not die? "You learned this in Evov?" Ellina nodded. Venick dragged a hand down his face, then began asking questions. How does the conjuring work? How long does it last? How many conjurors have this power? What, exactly, are we up against?

"Can they control more than one corpse at once?" A frightening thought, but Ellina did not think so. She made the elven hand motion for uncertainty, then rubbed her eyes. They had been talking for what might have been hours. Her mouth tasted like ash. She had not slept since the night before last.

"We'll need to call a meeting." Venick had propped himself against the nearest wall, jacket unbuttoned, arms crossed. His hair was ruffled from running his hands through it, his eyes sharply focused. The sight of him like that, disheveled and determined, did something to her. "The Elder will want to bring the generals in. I'll ask our elven commanders to come too. We'll need to begin preparing. This changes everything." He sighed. "I don't think the mainlands will ever be able to repay their debt to you."

Ellina turned her face to the window. The late morning sun was bright. The windows had been dressed in silver and white curtains shot through with random bursts of red. It reminded Ellina of blood on armor.

Venick would call a war meeting the following afternoon, he told her. He said he wanted her there. Ellina nodded, though she was not sure how she felt about attending that meeting when she could not speak. She imagined how it would be, the wary eyes of the humans, the Elder's daughter at Venick's side, Ellina forced to bear it all in silence. She was a spy, not a war general. She would rather advise from the shadows.

She thought of Miria. Her sister would have fit in well in this world. She *had* fit in well. Ellina remembered how Miria had seemed to shine with the prospect of her new life. Yet Miria had worried, too. On the day of her escape, she had taken Ellina's hands, and Ellina had seen the thought in her sister's eyes: what will become of you? Miria had pulled Ellina in close and whispered, *Be happy.*

Ellina had not been happy. She still was not.

Her exhaustion was catching up to her. She blinked blearily out the window and remembered the stateroom battle. She thought of Venick's heartbroken face across the hall.

The pen was still in front of her. The parchment was. There was more she should tell him. She should explain her lies, what she had said that day and why. She had claimed not to care about Venick, had all but called for his death. Later on Traegar's balcony, she had threatened to kill him herself. She should explain her reasons. But reason felt suddenly distant. She thought it again: she was so tired.

"I've kept you too long," she heard Venick say. His voice was murky. "You need sleep."

She thought she might have nodded. Sleep. The craving for it seemed to crack into her and spread, runnels in a riverbed.

She felt him tug her upright. There was a dizzying shift that meant she was being lifted, her legs swept out from under her. Then: a soft bed. Covers pulled to her chin. A warm hand on her cheek, and a prayer for soft dreams.

FORTY-TWO

She woke to darkness.

Ellina sat up. The sheets shifted around her torso. The room was empty, the curtains stiff. It must be past midnight or no— near dawn. The sky showed the faintest color. She realized with an uncomfortable jolt that she had misplaced him from his bed.

She stood, smoothing the covers as if to erase her presence. She had not showered since her escape, except for quick washes in freezing streams. Her cheeks burned as she arranged pillows, feeling all at once the ugly tangle of her hair, the dirt caked beneath her nails. She was filthy. She could not understand why he had allowed her to sleep here.

Ellina set her feet into worn slippers, glancing over her shoulder as if expecting to find Venick watching her. She poked her head around corners, listened at the door. She did not find him, but she did find the bathing room, its polished surfaces, the tub gleaming bronze. Ellina stared at that tub and considered, for a shimmering half-second, a bath.

But not yet. There were more important things.

She crept out of the castle. Overnight, temperatures had plummeted. She shivered in her thin clothes, her breath smoking the air. The sky had lightened. Everything was swathed in shades of blue.

She made for the city's gates. As Ellina moved down the quiet path, her foot crunched into something. A puddle, she saw, crusted over with ice.

She pulled back, horrified.

Isphanel was a miraculous little plant with one important power: it could quicken the healing process, enabling a body to regrow bone and reknit muscle at speed, and in doing so the plant could save lives. Ellina knew that while *isphanel* could grow this far north in the right conditions, it would not survive a frost.

She stared at the cracked ice puddle. Time seemed to warp. Winter was reaching the highlands at last, and the first frost had arrived. If there was any *isphanel* to be found, she needed to find it now.

It was this thought that drove Ellina out of the city and across windy hillsides, deeper and deeper into the highlands. She moved on foot, ignoring her lightheadedness, the empty hunger. The land was scattered with bushes, and each time she came upon a new clump of growth her heart seemed to leap between her ribs. She searched the shadows under yucca and foxtail where *isphanel* liked to grow, tearing plants up with random, careless haste, her fingers clumsy in their fervor. She wondered how she must look, and gave herself the answer: like a human.

Not a human, a little voice reminded her.

Human, another insisted.

Ellina pushed the thoughts away and kept going, her anxiety climbing. The sky was brighter now. Soon, morning would arrive.

When she finally found it—a good-sized cluster of *isphanel* crusted into the frozen ground, Ellina came to her knees. Tears stung her vision. She began chipping away at the ice, prying the leaves from the earth. She cradled them against her chest. Over the horizon, the sun was finally showing its face. Ellina lifted her chin to feel its warmth. She pressed her lips together, held her breath to stop herself from coming apart. It was several long seconds before she could move again.

When she opened her eyes, something snagged at her memory. Ellina blinked through her tears, gazing towards the sun. There was something about its bright rays—and her, soaking them in—that seemed to tug at the back of her mind.

Ellina came to her feet. Her knees were wet, her slippers soaked through. In the distance, Parith was as still as a painting. Ellina nearly abandoned whatever half-thoughts had made her pause, eager to get back to the castle and to Dourin…until she remembered.

She remembered descending through the servant's tunnels into the palace kitchens with Youvan. The way he had flinched away from the torch in her hand. Later, he had complained of the heat. He had ordered that every kitchen fire be doused. Yet it was winter.

She remembered traveling to Irek, and how Youvan had insisted they move only at night rather than during the day, despite there being no obvious threat, no real reason to do so.

Ellina remembered stories about the purge. Human conjurors had been rounded up by elves, beheaded and burned. But why would elves take the time to behead *and* burn the conjurors?

The sun was higher now. Ellina could feel its golden light. She was crushing the plant in her fists.

An idea dawned inside her. It lit up the shadows of her mind. Ellina suddenly knew how they would defeat the conjurors and their army of living dead, because she knew their weakness.

It was daylight. It was fire.

It was the reason they summoned storms—to block the daylight. It was the reason they always attacked at night, or in the shadows. Ellina had seen Youvan conjure during the day only once, that afternoon on the palace bridge. She remembered how he lifted his hands but at first, nothing had happened.

Again in Irek he had attempted to conjure. Fires had burned nearby. There had been a moment of frustration, plain on his face. Youvan's conjuring was rendered useless.

The palace conjurors met in the crypts only on moonless nights. Ellina remembered their single, tiny candle. They had wanted as little light as possible. To practice their new horrors, they had needed their full strength.

Conjurors were stronger in the forest where the trees covered the sun. They grew weak whenever there was too much light, or too much fire. The trick to defeating an enemy was to know their weakness and exploit it, but the conjurors had seemed to have no weakness. Their power, if anything, was only growing stronger. If the conjurors had a failing, they had not been able to find it.

Not until now.

・・・

Ellina went to the infirmary first. She was brought up short to find Harmon there. The woman gave her a level look. "I've been waiting for you."

Ellina moved past the highlander. She warmed the leaves with her hands, brushing away the ice, then used a nearby knife to scrape off their waxy skins until they were fleshy and wet. She peeled back Dourin's bandages, held her breath against the smell. She packed the leaves into his wound. She did her best to cover it entirely.

"You are full of surprises," Harmon remarked. "A fighter, a spy. Are you a healer too?"

All soldiers knew the basics. It was a matter of survival. Ellina shrugged.

"I've been told you were quite the little liar." Something in the woman's voice made Ellina look up. Harmon looked—what? Approving? Ellina thought maybe so, until Harmon spoke again. "Your presence here complicates things."

Ellina stepped away from the bed. Her hands were slick with Dourin's blood.

"I am not your enemy. And I think you and I want the same thing." A pause. "I've spoken to Venick."

Ellina's fists went tight.

"We've been speaking quite a bit, actually. He's explained a few things. I'll admit, I've been angry with him. But I understand better now." Ellina did not know what this woman understood. She felt as if *she* did not understand. Harmon continued. "Venick has a mind for strategy. Have you seen him at it? I suppose you have. He has come up with a plan. I'll admit, it's a good one. I don't think you'll like all of it—particularly the part about Venick and I remaining engaged. It's for the best, though. Highlanders are more likely to fight alongside lowlanders if they believe us betrothed, and now more than ever it is vital to show a face of unity. But I think you'll like the second part of the plan. I'll tell you about it, if you stop looking at me like you want to stab me in the throat."

Ellina released a breath through her nose. She cleared her face, calling upon every old elven trick she had ever known. She made her expression perfect, and Harmon smiled. "Better."

FORTY-THREE

The Elder welcomed Venick into the great hall with grace.

They sat in cushioned chairs by the window. A servant appeared to serve tea, but left at the Elder's insistence that they could serve themselves. The Elder poured the steaming liquid into delicate floral cups. He smiled. He told Venick to help himself to the sugar.

He was determined, Venick thought, to make this more difficult.

"Did you know that slaves built this castle?" the Elder asked, leaning back in his seat. "This was during my great-grandfather's reign. My grandfather killed his father and set the slaves free." He seemed amused by this story: his ancestors bathed in blood. "Who do you think was in the right?"

It was the kind of question the Elder loved. "I think neither man was right."

"Come now. In war, you must choose a side. I am asking, which side would you have chosen? Would you act selfishly to further your own interests, as my slave-owning great-grandfather did? Or would you sacrifice your honor for the greater good, as my grandfather chose?"

The Elder must know why Venick had come. By now, rumors of Ellina's reappearance were on everyone's lips, as was Venick's role in her escape. And it was no secret that the royal princess and lowland commander shared a history. Those stories reached farther and wider than Venick liked to think.

I cannot marry your daughter, Venick imagined himself telling the Elder. *I seem to recall you saying that once before*, the man might reply.

It would shame the Elder. If Venick broke off the engagement, the Elder would retaliate by withdrawing his support. He would shut Parith's gates, imprison Venick's army in his city. He would hurt Ellina. He might even kill Venick. The Elder was like his great-grandfather in the story, serving his own desires no matter the cost. There was no limit to what he might do.

"I know why you have asked to see me today," said the Elder. There was no humor in him now. He was taut as a strung bow. "But like my ancestors, you have been given a choice. You can marry my daughter and remain in my good graces. Or you can refuse, and earn yourself my wrath. I require your answer now. Which will it be?"

Venick had once thought that the Elder was like a king, but he saw now that the man was more like a child, forever expecting the world to go his way.

This was not about to go his way.

"You're wrong," Venick said. "I didn't come to end my engagement."

The man's white brows arched. "Oh?"

"I came to inform you that your army has left the city."

The Elder paused, then barked a laugh. "What is this? A joke?"

"Not a joke. As we speak, your men are marching west. If you don't believe me, you're welcome to go look for yourself."

The man became stone. "That's impossible. My army answers to me, and I haven't ordered them anywhere."

"Actually," Venick said, "they answer to the Stonehelm name."

He saw the moment the Elder understood. "Harmon wouldn't."

"She already has."

"She cannot command an army."

"She can, actually. She's rather good at it. Giving orders is kind of her thing."

The Elder came to his feet.

"Harmon has taken control of the highland army," Venick said, standing as well. "As of now, they believe she is acting with your blessing."

"No."

"As soon as we are done here, I intend to join Harmon in the west. We will recruit the plainspeople to our purpose, then prepare to do battle with the Dark Army. Our men and elves will fight together. It will be as it always should have been.

"But it seems *you* now have a choice," Venick continued. "You can allow us to continue what we've started. Your army will be returned to you at the war's end, more or less how we found it. You can even take credit, once we've won. The glory will be yours. Your honor will remain intact.

"Or you can try to call your forces back. You'll lose the respect of your men in doing so, not only because you're turning them away from battle, but because they'll realize that your own daughter wished to undercut you, and succeeded."

The Elder shook with fury.

"If you do attempt to call your men back, and Harmon attempts to keep them, they may be forced to choose a side. I am not sure they will choose yours. The gamble, of course, is up to you. Will you risk it?" Venick tipped his head, feeling a smile curve his lip. It was the same sly smile that the Elder had worn earlier, the one that said that he'd reached the end of the game, and knew he held a winning hand. "I require your answer now. Which will it be?"

FORTY-FOUR

Ellina was hidden high in the great hall's scaffolding, watching the scene below.

She was more armed than she had been in ages: a shortsword on her hip, daggers at her wrists and thighs, and a bow—nocked, drawn—in her fist. She rested her knuckle lightly against her cheek and shut one eye, though she could aim just as well with both eyes open. She heard the Elder give his answer and loosened the bow's tension.

Ellina had bathed in Harmon's rooms, which felt like an overstepping of bounds, but the woman had insisted that Ellina could not continue to traipse around looking like a winter-starved wolf. Ellina recognized the peace offering, even if this was a backwards way of doing it. "I'll be gone with my army by the time you're finished," Harmon had sniffed, eyeing Ellina's tangled hair. "I'm trusting you to keep Venick out of trouble until we reunite on the western plains."

Hot water poured into a copper tub. Harmon's oils were overly scented and made Ellina's nose itch, but the bath was delicious. She scrubbed every inch of herself, taking special care around her shoulder. The wound was nothing now but a thick, raised ridge of cartilage. Ellina told herself she was lucky. The dagger could have struck something vital. She could have lost the arm. She should be grateful that a scar would be the only lasting damage.

When she emerged from the tub, she carefully avoided the mirror.

After she had donned the armor and weapons Harmon had left for her, Ellina crept into position. She listened to Venick explain the terms of his plan, her silent arrow trained on the Elder's heart. She felt the man's fury like the heat of the sun, even as he agreed.

...

Ellina was waiting for Venick in the hall outside of his chambers when he returned. He stopped short at the sight of her. "You're supposed to be with Harmon."

Yes, that had been the plan. Ellina was to leave the city with Harmon and their armies while Venick dealt with the Elder alone, undefended and—she looked him over—unarmored. The fool.

"I know, I know." Venick waved her off. "I'm a fool. So, what? You chose to stay behind in case things took a turn for the worse?" He rubbed his forehead. "Where were you then? Hiding in the rafters?" Ellina smiled, and Venick looked horrified. "That was supposed to be a joke."

Ellina tapped the knife strapped to her thigh beneath her trousers, an absentminded motion that seemed, nonetheless, to explain everything. It was good to be back in armor, even if it was human and heavy and slightly ill-fitting. It was good to feel the flat side of blades imprinting her skin, the hard curve of a bow at her spine. She was still too tired, still too weak. She would be useless in a fight in her current condition and would need to rest if she wished to recover. Yet these things, more than anything, gave her strength.

"You could have at least warned me," Venick said, attempting to move past her into his chambers. She planted her feet, indignant. *He could have warned her.*

"Alright," he said. "I get it. I shouldn't have met with the Elder alone. I should have told you my plan from the start. But I would remind you that the last time I saw you, you could barely keep your eyes open. You were asleep before I even got you into bed."

Ellina blushed. His words were too pointed.

"Come on." He softened her discomfort with a smile. "I'll tell you everything now."

They entered his rooms. Venick took a seat on a low settee, wide enough for two. After a moment's hesitation, Ellina chose the seat across from him, a wooden armchair carved with the faces of gods. Venick was still smiling, but in a way that nonetheless made it clear he had seen her choice and understood it.

"Harmon plans to lead the highland army as far as the western plains. About three quarters of our men and elves have gone with her. The rest are waiting for me." He pulled his hair from its leather tie, swept it back up again. Ellina was momentarily distracted by deft fingers. "Dourin will stay here until he recovers, I've already made arrangements. A group of soldiers will remain to guard him, just in case."

In case the Elder gets any ideas about retaliation, he meant. Ellina did not like it, but Dourin could not very well be moved in his condition.

"The plan," Venick continued, "is to use Igor as our base. From there, we'll continue to unite the mainlands in preparation to face the

Dark Army. I can only hope that by the time your sister strikes again, we'll be ready."

Ellina ran her finger along the carved arm of the chair, tracing the shape of a lamb. Farah would be furious that her prized prisoner had managed to escape. She would be angry over thwarted punishments, all the torments she had planned. There was a reason, after all, that Farah allowed Ellina to live.

Most importantly, however, Farah would understand the danger of Ellina's freedom. Voiceless or not, Ellina still carried valuable knowledge—knowledge that Farah would not want to give time to spread. Farah would send her army back to the mainlands soon, while she still had the advantage. If Ellina was right, Venick had less time than he thought.

She told him—through a mixture of scribbled notes and hand motions—about how she had gone hunting for the *isphanel* again that morning and found it. When she told him what she had realized while searching for the plant, the trick to defeating the conjurors, a smile split Venick's face. "Ellina. You're brilliant." But just as quickly as the joy had come it was gone again, both of them sinking into silence.

"I've already asked too much of you," Venick said. "I know I can't hold you to any promises. And I shouldn't expect—" He cut off, studying his interlaced fingers. "Will you come west with us? You don't have to say yes. You could stay here with Dourin, wait for his recovery. You should be recovering yourself." He kept his eyes on his hands. "But I need to be honest with you. There's been too much lying between us. And the truth is that I want you there."

Ellina could not be sure of his words. She did not know if he wanted her there for her military capacity, or for some other reason. Things between them had been different since her escape. They were changed as surely as her voice was changed, the ease between them dried to dust.

Her thoughts went to Harmon. Ellina did not know what to make of that woman, who was confident and stubborn and so wholly human. Harmon had said that she and Venick would remain engaged…and that Ellina's presence complicated things. The thought dug into some vulnerable place. That rotten, oozing emotion. Ellina wondered how much, exactly, Venick had told Harmon about her. She wondered what *he* thought about her presence there. Did Venick agree that Ellina was a complication?

Even if Ellina had still had a voice, she would not have been brave enough to ask. But it did not matter. Venick had asked that she come, and her answer was the same.

Yes.

· · ·

They left that evening. Now that they had the Elder's forced cooperation, it felt dangerous to stay, as if any delay would be to dangle meat in the dog's face. Ellina took Dourin's horse, Venick riding his blind mare. They met their battalion outside the city, then set their course.

The days that followed reminded Ellina, in some ways, of the tundra. A true chill had descended, winter bedding into the mainlands at last. The sky was a blanket of grey. Sometimes, at night or in early morning, it would snow. Ellina had a new collection of human clothes, including a pair of black riding boots with a clever slot for her knives, a thick winter fox coat, and thin yet surprisingly warm leather gloves. The items had been delivered by castle servants at Venick's orders. "You'll need more than armor for a winter campaign," he had told her, smiling in a way that said he would not have put it past her to pack only armor. Later, when he had seen her dressed in her new colorful cotton, he stopped short. "You look almost—" he had started, then stopped, though Ellina could guess what he had meant to say. *Human.*

Their battalion was a scattered mix of men and elves. It was a strange arrangement, stranger still for her, whose place among these soldiers was uncertain. Who was Ellina? A princess, a soldier, a spy? Traitor? Target? Ellina could hear them whisper about her, particularly the humans, who underestimated the sharpness of elven hearing. Some of the whispers were charitable. *Poor thing, a prisoner and a victim, have you seen those scars?* Others, less so. *I heard she and the commander have a history. I heard she's here to win him back. He wouldn't want her of course, who would?* And then there was the worst rumor of all: that she was still loyal to Farah, that she was faking her voicelessness so that she could not be made to answer questions in elvish. Whenever Ellina heard those whispers, she would turn her horse around, gallop off in whatever direction. Sometimes Venick would come after her. He never said anything, never tried to comfort, though he could surely see her angry, unshed tears. Ellina was grateful. Comfort was not what she needed in those moments. She was not sure what she needed, but it was not that.

Venick, for his part, was like an eagle in the sky, so obviously in his place. Ellina had never seen him more at home than when he was sitting atop his great blind buckskin, giving orders. Nor, she mused, had she ever seen her brethren so eager to follow orders. They adored Venick, practically falling over themselves to gain his favor. Honestly, it was a little unfair. She knew what it was to have the loyalty of her subjects, but never their hearts. He had clearly earned both, and he had done it so *easily*.

Three days into their journey, Venick pulled his horse alongside Ellina's. He rarely did this. They still avoided each other as they had on the tundra, their conversations weighed with uncertainty—and with the suspicious eyes of the soldiers. As Venick approached her now, Ellina tried to hide her surprise.

"I was blinded once," he said. "In the southern forests, before I came north. A conjuror blinded me. I killed him, and the conjuring was reversed." He toyed with Eywen's reins. "I can't be sure what it means, but I wonder, your voice…"

Ellina was startled. She had not considered this. Was it possible that if you killed a conjuror, you undid their conjuring as well? If Ellina killed Balid, would her voice be returned?

"Even if it's not possible," Venick continued softly, "it changes nothing. What you've done, what you sacrificed—you're the strongest warrior I've ever known, Ellina. Your silence can't take that from you."

It was Ellina's turn to toy with her reins. Trust Venick to cut right through to the heart of her. But he was wrong. Silence had changed things, it had changed her, she was different now, could he not see that she was different? When Farah had silenced her, she had stolen more than Ellina's voice—she had stolen the essence of who she was.

But of course, Ellina could say none of this. She sighed and looked to the sky.

• • •

Venick began seeking her out more often. At first, it was to ask for small favors. Will you help scout for water? Will you start the fire? Will you check this horse? She is limping. Then, it was to discuss military strategy. What if we land here? What do you think of this formation? What will your sister do next, do you think? Sometimes, Ellina would write her answers on paper. Sometimes, she would reply with elven hand motions. Most often, however, Venick could simply draw the answer from her eyes.

When there were no more chores to finish and no more strategy to plan, Venick began seeking her out for no reason at all.

It was early afternoon six days into their journey. They were watering their horses by a stream, Venick at her shoulder. She felt the weight of his eyes and turned to find him staring. "You have a leaf in your hair."

The air seemed to shimmer. Ellina waited for him to reach over and pluck it out. Her chest seemed to bloom with the possibility.

He kept his hands by his side. "Ellina? Did you hear me?"

She fumbled to find the leaf and pull it free.

A soldier pulled Venick into conversation. Ellina kept her eyes on the leaf. She folded it in half, listened to the tiny dry *crunch*. In half again. Again, until the leaf crumbled to nothing.

...

They traveled on. Most of the humans continued to survey Ellina with apprehension. The elves were deferential, but that was almost worse. It served to highlight their differences, to set Ellina apart. In their down hours, Ellina would see the elves playing cards, a game they had learned from the humans. Once, she tried to join. The elves shot to their feet, all deep bows and murmured *cessenas*. When she lingered, they grew uncomfortable. Ellina tried to motion at the cards, but these elves were not Venick and could not simply read the thoughts in her face. Nor, she realized, would they ever have guessed that the elven princess was asking them to teach her cards. Self-conscious and embarrassed, Ellina made a hand motion, a little jerk of the wrists that meant nothing, and strode away.

・・・

The days were strange, they were a network of ropes, twisting and pulling against each other. Ellina was tangled, she was struggling. She felt lost in their web.

Venick had been busy lately, dragged here and there to deal with the needs of his men. He had not sought her out in a while. Ellina tried to go about her evenings as usual. She found things to do that kept her busy…and kept her eyes from wandering back to him.

She told herself that she was being foolish. Ellina could not expect Venick to spend all his time with her. Yet it was difficult to be alone so much. Ellina had only her thoughts, but her thoughts were a mess. In the Elder's grand hall with a bow in her hand, Ellina had felt a spark of her old self, but as quickly as that spark had come it was gone again, leaving her cold. Ellina had come to realize that Venick's presence, for all it confused, helped a little too. When he was there she did not feel quite so hollow. She could see herself through his eyes, and it grounded her. *The strongest warrior I've ever known.*

Ellina should be able to know herself without Venick around. She thought about this one evening as she walked the camp's perimeter, having put herself on watch duty. She could not always rely on him. When they reached Igor and their war efforts began in earnest, she would likely see Venick less and less. And when Harmon reappeared? Well, Ellina would not soon forget that woman's words. Ellina's presence *did* complicate things. Maybe Venick would realize that it was better for him to keep his distance. Maybe he would decide it was safer to leave Ellina behind altogether.

The thought lit her with fear. She froze, knotting her fists. What would she do then? She might not belong here, but she did not belong anywhere else either. If he sent her away, she would have nowhere to go.

"Ellina."

His voice made her jump. He approached from a distance, his hair catching the wind, his cheeks bitten red with cold. She was breathing hard, fears crowding up her throat. *You would not leave me behind, would you? You would not have asked me to come if you planned to leave me.*

"Ellina?" He saw her expression and was instantly alarmed. He sped up, jogging to close the distance between them. "Hey, it's okay, you're okay."

She did not feel okay. She felt like she was suffocating.

"Come here." He pulled her into his arms. He had not done this since the tundra, and Ellina was momentarily shocked by the contact, the solid warmth. She leaned into him to hide her face, heart pounding.

"Shh," he whispered, stroking her hair. "I've got you. Just breathe."

She tried. Her lungs would not open. She had a flashback of the prison, of Balid's slim, curling fingers. She felt as if she was choking, like she was being silenced all over again.

"Hey." Venick pulled back so that he could meet her eye. "I think you're panicking a little. Try to take a breath. Here, with me."

She followed his lead, breathing in with him, then out, and again until she had calmed.

"Better?" Venick asked, peering at her with an uncertain smile. Ellina tried to smile back, but embarrassment made her waver. She did not know what had happened. She had never been someone who panicked, particularly for no obvious reason.

"You know," Venick said gently, brushing back an errant piece of her hair, "it's okay to be afraid. You don't have to hide. Not from me."

His words only made her want to hide more. She could not quite look at him.

"I get scared too," he went on. "And for you…it's hard for me to imagine what it's been like for you. What you suffered. I can't even—" He shook his head, pulling his hand away. She watched his throat move as he swallowed. "I would take it all back if I could. I'd give anything to go back to…" He made a face. "Well, I don't know. To the forest, maybe? Or to when it was you and me in Evov? Before the whole getting stabbed in the leg thing, obviously."

She huffed, but his attempt at humor had worked, and he knew it.

Venick glanced back toward camp where his duties no doubt waited for him. Ellina expected him to bid her farewell and tried to hide her disappointment, and so she was surprised when he said, "You're on watch, right? Can I walk with you?"

She did not care that she might not always be able to lean on him. She did not care that things between them were tangled, or that he was promised to someone else. She wanted to lean on him now.

She nodded, and he smiled.

• • •

Venick woke her from sleep with a nudge.

Ellina startled awake. She sat up quickly, her thoughts going to the worst: the conjurors, an attack. But she caught Venick's expression in the glow of a nearby lantern, and something in his face stilled her. His eyes were full of wonder. "Come look."

She slid from her bedroll. They were a day away from Igor, the farthest west Ellina had ever been. The air smelled of woodsmoke and frost, the stars pinpricks in a velvet sky. Venick pointed, and Ellina saw.

Wild horses. They streaked through the night in a closely-knit group, silent in a way that should not have been possible, not for how near they were, or for how many. The camp split their herd in two, a rock in the center of a river, and the horses swept by on either side. They were small. Elegant. Thinner than the war beasts favored by their soldiers, and much less colorful. These horses were a black wind in a moonless night.

And just as quickly they were gone. What must have been a hundred wild horses had flown by in a matter of moments. None of the camp's soldiers had even stirred.

Beautiful, Ellina wanted to say.

Thank you, she wanted to say, because she was suddenly moved. She turned to Venick, wishing now more than ever for a voice, but found in the end that words were not needed. Venick had been watching her. His gaze touched hers, and Ellina thought he must understand how she felt, because he smiled.

Ellina would come to cherish this moment. Later, when she set out to face her sister, she would think back to a cold winter night in the middle of war, when the sight of wild horses had been enough to remind her that there was beauty still left in this world, and that silence did not come at the cost of strength.

Ellina closed her eyes. Maybe Venick had been right, she thought. Maybe identity was not about the parts of you that were missing. She considered it again: who *was* she? A princess, a soldier, a spy. Scarred by her past, yes, and forever sentenced to bear those marks. Silent and lost and uncertain, Ellina was all of those things. But this, too: she was strong. She was brave. And she was alive. She had fought hard to live.

Elves did not like to talk about death. It was why they did not openly mourn each other—they would rather pretend an elf never existed than acknowledge that one day it will all come to an end. Ellina had thought her life over, but she was not dead, she was not ruined, only changed.

There was courage, she decided, in admitting that. There was wisdom, too, in knowing the difference.

She opened her eyes, and stepped back into the world.

Acknowledgements

My second novel is out and I can hardly believe it.

When I finished Elvish, I didn't really understand what I'd written. I was ecstatic to be published, of course I was, but the whole experience felt out of my reach, in the way of someone who stands too closely to a painting so that they grasp the details but never the full picture.

Or maybe that's the wrong analogy. Maybe publishing Elvish was akin to dreaming. I did it, my mind made it, but I hardly felt responsible. I woke up blinking, surprised by what I'd created, just like everyone else.

Writing Elder was not like that. I knew what I was doing, knew what I wanted and where I was going, and it made everything so much harder. I had expectations for myself. I felt the expectations of others. I was happy to publish Elvish, but it's one thing to stumble upon a dollar and pick it up and marvel at your luck. It's another to bleed for it.

I bled for this book. I fought hard to write it, and then to write it better. And now it's finished, and I've earned it, and I'm so damn proud.

As usual, I have many people to thank. To my beta readers. You guys are my legion, and I'm so grateful for you. To my editor Suzanne, who did a little less tearing this time (thank heavens), but challenged me to be better all the same. To Cappy, for instilling confidence when I needed it most. To Mom, for her meticulous notes and endless encouragement. To Dad, who is my role model ever and always. To Nathaniel, who has been the most delightful ally and can line edit better than the best of them. To Damon and the team, once again, for their fantastic design work.

To all my readers. Your support means everything. I couldn't do this without you.

And finally, to my husband. Oh Monster. What can I say? I'll never understand what I did to deserve you. I'm so lucky, stupid lucky, bursting at the seams with it. I told you once that I'd put writing books above all else, above my own health, our dogs, money, everything. "Above me?" you asked. No babe, never, not ever anything above you. I hope you know that. I think you do.

Stay Up to Date

For more information on upcoming books releases, visit my website sgprince.com or follow me on Instagram (@s.g.prince) or Twitter (@SarahGPrince).

Printed in Poland
by Amazon Fulfillment
Poland Sp. z o.o., Wrocław

23776376R00222